THIEVING FOREST

Martha Conway

Noontime Books
San Francisco, CA

Noontime Books
San Francisco, CA
info@noontimebooks.com

Publisher's Note: This is a work of fiction. Names, characters, places, and incidents are a product of the author's imagination. Locales and public names are sometimes used for atmospheric purposes. Any resemblance to actual people, living or dead, or to businesses, companies, events, institutions, or locales is completely coincidental.

Cover Design by Kit Foster
Cover Image, *Cottonwood,* by John Steins (www.johnsteins.com)
Map by Creative Map Solutions© 2014
Book Layout ©2014 BookDesignTemplates.com

Ordering Information:
Quantity sales. Special discounts are available on quantity purchases by corporations, associations, and others. For details, contact the "Special Sales Department" at the address above.

Publisher's Cataloging-in-Publication Data

Conway, Martha.
Thieving forest / Martha Conway.
pages cm
ISBN 978-0-9916185-0-7

1. Women pioneers--Ohio--Fiction. 2. Potawatomi
Indians--Ohio--Fiction. 3. Indian captivities--Ohio--
Fiction. 4. Frontier and pioneer life--Ohio--Fiction.
5. Ohio--Fiction. 6. Adventure stories. I. Title.

PS3603.O565T45 2014   813'.6
QBI14-600068

Printed in the United States of America

For my sisters

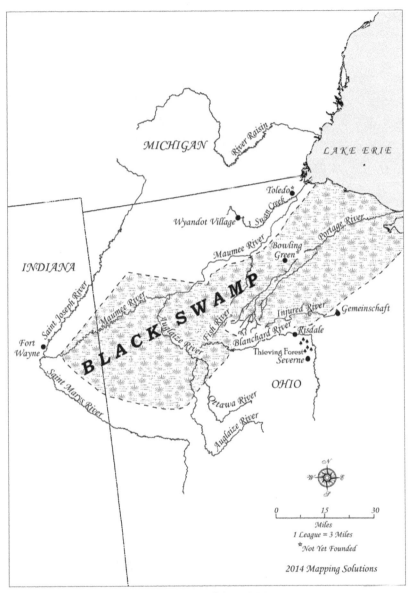

MICHIGAN

River Raisin

LAKE ERIE

Toledo

Swan Creek

Wyandot Village

Maumee River

Bowling Green

Portage River

INDIANA

Saint Joseph River

BLACK SWAMP

Maumee River

Auglaize River

Fish River

Injured River

Gemeinschaft

Risdale

Blanchard River

Thieving Forest
Severne

Fort
Wayne

Saint Mary's River

Ottawa River

OHIO

Auglaize River

0   15   30
          Miles
1 League = 3 Miles
* Not Yet Founded

2014 Mapping Solutions

Northwest Ohio, 1806

Severne

One

O n the day the Potawatomis come, Susanna Quiner is in her cabin splitting open peapods with the blade of her mother's silver nail scissors.

"A peapod with just one pea in it is very lucky," she says glumly, pulling one open into the shape of a canoe.

"Only if you don't like peas," her sister Beatrice says.

Susanna looks into the pod. "Well, this one has two."

She exhales and does nothing more for a moment, wishing she was done with this task. The door to their cabin is open and a warm breeze wafts into the room. It is the first of June and unseasonably humid. It's been raining for weeks, although it isn't raining now, and outside the flat Ohio landscape is like a warm wet sea. From where she sits at the end of the table, Susanna can see the first few trees of Thieving Forest standing like sentinels or spies, marking the end of their settlement. Her sister Penelope, at the other end of the table, is crushing salt with a rolling pin.

Despite the break in the rain no one wants to go outside, and all five of them are in the cabin, five sisters, ranging in age from seventeen (Susanna) to twenty-three (Penelope). Aurelia is lying next to the hearth near Beatrice, who is warming bread for a chilblain on her heel. Naomi is playing her violin while she minds the store on the other side of the cabin, although there are no customers and haven't been any since their parents fell ill. That was the same day it started to rain.

When Susanna looks down at the peapods again she sees the new black lace on her cuff. Her parents died almost two weeks ago and only one day apart, Ellen first and then Sirus, as unexpected as two suns setting in the same evening. Susanna, who is superstitious, has put a piece of rowan wood in the pocket of her black dress to guard against ghosts, although she misses her mother, and would almost chance the frightening encounter in order to see her again. She's lonely for her. She's lonely for both of them. Part of her feels gone as well, like there's a room in her home that she can't go into anymore, a locked door. She thinks of her mother's freckled hands cutting bread.

Her sisters probably feel this way, too, although today their grief is taking on the form of irritation. Penelope looks at Susanna, frowns, and puts down her rolling pin. The crushed salt is scattered on a dark cloth before her, still mostly in chunks.

"Susanna, what have you got on your hands?" she asks.

"Mama's gloves. Her old ones." Susanna likes to think she has the nicest hands of all of her sisters and wants to keep it that way. Also, the gloves still carry the faint scent of their mother.

"Goodness," Penelope says. And Beatrice adds, "Susanna, that's absurd."

The two oldest sisters look at each other with shared opinion. When they rule in unison they are nearly impossible to overcome, but they are rarely in unison. Beatrice goes back to the bread she is toasting and Penelope hits the salt again with her rolling pin. Her hands, Susanna notices, are chapped and red.

"She likes to keep her hands nice," Aurelia says from the hearth.

"Well good luck to her," Beatrice says.

"Mama told me I should rub bear oil on them," Susanna informs them. "She said that would keep them smooth."

Aurelia tucks their mother's blue pieced bed quilt under her feet. She is just getting over a fever and has pulled her straw tick over so she can lie near the fire.

"There's not enough bear in the world," she says.

Aurelia has strawberry-blond hair and a heart-shaped face, and Susanna thinks of her as the prettiest one. Beatrice is the smartest. Penelope is the best storyteller, and Naomi is the musical one. Ellen Foxworthy Quiner gave her daughters strong names as if arming them for a difficult life: Penelope, Beatrice, Naomi, Aurelia, Susanna, and Lilith. Or, as their father Sirus used to say, Please Be Neat And Seldom Late. They all have their mother's small nose and small face and small full mouth, but they are best known for their red hair and rude manners. Susanna's hair is the darkest shade of red—in winter almost brown—and she has equally dark eyebrows with hardly an arch to them, giving her a serious expression. But her sisters are not fooled by this, for they know her to be superstitious and fanciful and not good at chores, not even the simplest ones like shelling peas. Lilith, the youngest at fifteen, was adopted by their Aunt Ogg and never left Philadelphia. Only Penelope has been married, but her husband died almost eight months ago. Their parents are buried near him in the little plot set out as a graveyard, although the settlement as yet has no church. Graveyards are needed before churches.

Susanna wonders if Lilith in Philadelphia even knows yet; the letter to her was written only last week and mail is slow between Ohio and anyplace else. She looks at the black lace on her cuff again. It's not shock, exactly, what she feels, but a stubborn kind of disbelief.

How can Ellen and Sirus be gone? Especially considering they only had Swamp Fever, and almost everyone in this corner of Ohio gets Swamp Fever every year. Some call it Marsh Fever and some call it Fever and Ague or even just The Ague, but it usually plays out the same: a week of shaking and low fever that eventually passes. The farmers claim that it comes from decomposing plants in the Great Black Swamp, ten miles away, and although it's uncomfortable while it lasts, it isn't an illness that generally kills you. Only sometimes another strain shows up, this one affecting the brain. That's what Sirus and Ellen had the misfortune to contract. Susanna was shocked one morning to hear her mother call out to her own mother, a woman twenty years dead who never left Scotland.

"*Màthair,*" Ellen said, looking at the corner of her blue pieced bed quilt. "I've missed you! Where have you been?" That's when Susanna understood she would die.

It was raining on the day of their burial, and so muddy that all of them had to pull their boots out of their last step every few feet. Afterward, back in the cabin, Naomi would play only Bach on her violin. This is the first time I've eaten an apple without my mother being alive, Susanna found herself thinking. This is the first time I've darned a stocking. This is the first time I've opened the ledger. Even Beatrice was seen crying in odd places although she tried to hide it. Susanna felt at any moment she might see Sirus's head poke out from the narrow doorway between their store and their living quarters—"What shall we give for three untanned martens?" He had an opinion but wanted to hear your ideas. His thatch of thinning white hair was like a nest on his head. At last Penelope said, "We can't keep on like this. We have to make a decision. Should we stay here or move back to Philadelphia?" But even now, ten days later, they can't agree on a plan.

The peapods are getting more and more tiresome to open even using her mother's good scissors. The scissors' fingerholes loop up into the shape of bird heads—swans or egrets. Through the open doorway that divides their home from the store Susanna can hear Naomi on her violin: Bach again, "Sleepers Awake." No one has come into the store all week because of the rain, and now that the rain has finally stopped the farmers are all out frantically putting in their corn, late already. The Quiners are getting low on meat, and their shipment of broadcloth from Cincinnati is three weeks late. They've been alone in the cabin for days, but Susanna doesn't mind. In the absence of her parents, their sudden and what will now be constant silence, she's comforted by her sisters' voices. Even their quarreling, familiar as it is, is almost consoling.

"We can't stay here," Penelope announces abruptly. She has said these exact words again and again over the last ten days. "We have five mouths to feed and no man to hunt for us. Every winter will be a worry."

"Well I can't move my chickens to Philadelphia," Aurelia says from the hearth. "They'll die." Even when ill, she has only two interests: her hens and Cade Spendlove. And between those two, Susanna suspects that the hens come first.

"How can we support ourselves here?" Penelope asks.

"Sirus made a good choice of land," Beatrice counters. "Three rivers and a road mean people passing through, and that means customers." She has made this point before. They live in a prime location for trade, and where's the competition? In Philadelphia there are already too many dry goods stores.

"It would be different if we could get married," Naomi says from the doorway to the store, her violin resting on her hip. Penelope smacks the rolling pin on the table as if at a particularly stubborn chunk of salt.

"It's not my fault!" she says, her voice rising.

"No one said it was," Susanna puts in quickly.

"But you're all thinking it. It was probably Thomas's fault." Thomas Forbes, her late husband.

"Don't speak ill of the dead," Beatrice tells her. She takes the bread off her toasting fork and looks at her heel. Susanna cannot see anything there, but Beatrice claims a chilblain is forming. Besides being the smartest Beatrice is also the most sensitive, often fancying little aches or pains on some part of her body.

"It's ridiculous to think that just because I didn't have a baby none of my sisters can have a baby," Penelope goes on. "Ignorant farmers, they don't know beans from bird eggs."

"But there's also Aunt Ogg," Aurelia says wickedly. "She couldn't have any babies, that's why she adopted Lilith. And Aunt Carsen, too." After ten years of childlessness, their Aunt Carsen died giving birth to a dead baby boy.

"And who told them about Aunt Ogg and Aunt Carsen, that's what I'd like to know. Anyway, I did everything right. I married him and did everything right. When we get back to Philadelphia we can leave that rumor behind. They only say it because they don't like us."

"Well I'm not moving back," Beatrice says, turning from the fire at last. Wisps of her red hair, the brightest red of them all, stick out all around her face. "And I told that to Amos Spendlove yesterday."

"You what?" Penelope stops breaking up the salt and holds the rolling pin by one end like a club. "How could you tell him that?"

"We've been here ten years. This is our home."

"Philadelphia is our home. We can open a store there."

"With what money?" Beatrice asks. "Or do you think you're going to buy it with an armload of pelts?" Their store takes payment mostly in goods.

"With Amos Spendlove's money," Penelope announces. She looks around pointedly at each of them. "He made an offer on the store two days ago. A cash offer. And I accepted."

Everyone stops what they are doing and stares at her. Susanna feels a flutter of excitement. "A cash offer? How much?" she asks. She hates Ohio and wants to leave, but Penelope and Beatrice barely count her opinion. In the doorway to the store, Naomi drops her violin to her side.

"He's coming over today with the money," Penelope tells them. "Although maybe now he thinks the deal is off, because of you." She glares at Beatrice.

"No. I won't go," Aurelia tells her, sitting up. "You had no right."

"I'm the oldest. I have every right. Susanna, what are you doing with those scissors? Go take the slop out to Saul."

"But I fed Saul yesterday!" This isn't true, Naomi fed Saul yesterday, but Naomi never remembers anything except the fingering on any song she's ever learned how to play.

"Penelope, you can't..." Beatrice begins, her voice tight. "You just cannot..."

"Go on, Princess," Penelope says to Susanna.

"How will we even *get* ourselves to Philadelphia?" Aurelia asks. "No. I'm not going. My hens will all die."

And so they begin again. Susanna stands and looks for the slop bucket. Familiar though their voices might be, maybe she's had enough for one day.

⚬

Out in the yard the sun is already beating down although it is barely midmorning. Susanna puts down the bucket for a moment and feels for the sliver of rowan wood in her pocket. Then she feels in her other pocket for the turkey hen bone that her father once gave her. The bone is her good luck talisman. Sirus found it in a field of wild rye after a herd of buffalo ran through it, crushing the stalks into carpet. Susanna still remembers the sound of their hooves like a waterfall moving closer and then away. Afterwards, Sirus walked into the rye to see what they'd trampled. It was the last buffalo they ever saw.

Susanna picks up the bucket again with her two gloved hands so she won't get blisters and turns her back to the settlement's few clustered buildings: Amos Spendlove's iron goods shop, the public stable, the wheelwright, and their own cabin and store, all connected by a raised pine walk. On the other side of the walk are bare lots, empty spaces for a courthouse and a jail someday when there are resources to pay for them and people to put there. Once a Wyandot village stood in this spot but that village is long gone, and the Wyandots sold the land ten years ago to the settlers for horses. Every so often they come back to hunt or to meet with other tribes; with all the rivers and streams here the area is easy to reach by canoe. A few tribes are meeting now. Susanna has seen them. Last week a group of Kickapoo men with pounded muskrat pelts came to their store, followed by a Kickapoo woman selling baskets. A few days later some Wyandot men looked in, wanting salt.

Frogs croak in competing choruses and pockets of newly hatched insects are buzzing about in the air, but there is not one person in sight. All the farmers are out desperately planting before the next rain, and the settlement feels deserted and lonely. After she pours out Saul's slops Susanna straightens two of the pen's fence boards, one of which needs to be replaced. Some people believe that pigs can see the wind coming but Saul rouses himself only for food. A sour old beast if ever there was one. Susanna knows that she ought to tell Penelope about the loose board but Penelope will probably just tell her to make a new one herself and then not like how she did it. She wishes they could leave for Philadelphia right now. A room with an even floor and long glass windows and a proper brick fireplace: this is what she pictures when she pictures what she wants. A place where they can buy cut wood and the milk is delivered.

After a while the heat makes her turn back. The heft of Thieving Forest is to her left but there are a few stands of maple trees between here and their cabin, and she makes her way toward their shade. She doesn't want to be just the younger sister who never does anything as well as the others. What if I just never go back, she wonders. What if I saddle Frank or Bess right now—Frank is gentler—and ride to Risdale, and find some way to get to a coach stop, and go east by myself?

She imagines writing her sisters: while you were quarreling I made my decision. Maybe they would see the sense of her actions and follow. That would be something, to have her sisters follow her lead for a change. Just as Susanna reaches the last of the maple trees Black Peter, Aurelia's rooster, makes three sharp crows. He is standing in the doorway of the henhouse. Something tugs at her memory but before she has time to think what it is all the frogs abruptly stop calling out. Later she couldn't say if it was this or something else that made her look toward the forest, but that's when she sees the Indians.

At first she can't tell who they are—Shawnee, Wyandot, Potawatomi, Kickapoo? Six of them—no seven, she counts. Maybe a few customers for the store at last. She watches as they step out from behind the trees like long-legged spiders, walking carefully over the bracken in their ankle-high moccasins and looking at the ground as if hunting small game. They wear straight sewn skins decorated with paint and beadwork, and a few have painted their hair and faces, too.

Potawatomi.

One of them steps neatly over the low wattle fence into Beatrice's bean garden where he makes a complicated signal to the others. They are not going around front to the store. Susanna's heart begins beating hard and high up in her chest. She steps behind the widest tree and looks down at her hands. Ellen's gloves are dirty but still white. She tugs them off and stuffs them into her pocket. Then she takes off her bleached sunbonnet and drops it into the long grass beside her. She wants to scream, but who would hear her? Her throat feels suddenly very dry, too dry to reach above a whisper.

Another sharp crow makes her look toward the henhouse again and that's when she sees Aurelia, astonishingly enough, standing there with a bucket of feed. When did she leave the cabin?

"Au-*re*-lia!" Susanna hisses.

But Aurelia doesn't hear. There is a good fifty yards between the maple trees and the henhouse with long yellow grass in between. Susanna can see Aurelia talking to her hens. Her face, pale from her recent illness, looks even paler out in the sun. She hasn't noticed the Potawatomi. The hens bob toward her as if offering kisses but really they are just greedy for their feed.

Suddenly as if on a signal the Potawatomi all let out a shout and run into the cabin. Aurelia jerks her head around at the noise, and Susanna steps out from behind her tree. Now is her chance. She waves both her arms at Aurelia, *Come here!* There are two other maple trees on either side of her, both wide enough to hide behind.

But Aurelia doesn't move, and Susanna realizes that the shrieking she hears is coming not from the Potawatomi but from Aurelia's hens. She shouts her sister's name. Aurelia looks over at Susanna with a wild, frightened expression but still doesn't move. Susanna doesn't know what to do—should she rush to the henhouse and grab her? But before she can take a step three Potawatomi come out of the cabin, one holding Beatrice by the arm and one holding Naomi and the last one carrying their mother's blue pieced bed quilt. Susanna steps back behind the tree, beckoning to Aurelia—there is still a chance if she runs now.

At last Aurelia steps forward but instead of running to Susanna she picks up Black Peter, who immediately flaps his wings and makes such a noise as Susanna has never before heard. What is Aurelia doing? Is she in shock? Two Potawatomi run to the henhouse, both holding up axes, one with half of his face painted red. The other one, smaller but with a thick white scar running down the side of his face, begins to cut off the heads of any chicken he can grab, felling them neatly with one blow each. Black Peter, released from Aurelia's arms, half flies and half jumps back to the henhouse door.

"Stop!" Aurelia screams at the man with the scar.

The Potawatomi with half his face painted red looks at her and then he says something to the man slaughtering the chickens, who puts down his axe and begins to tie the ones he's already killed together by their feet.

That's strange. Did the Potawatomi just spare Aurelia's hens? But even stranger is this: he suddenly turns and looks right at the maple tree where Susanna is hiding, and in that first moment she swears that he sees her. He stares directly at her. She draws back, suddenly aware of her red hair and white neck and each glistening black button marching down the front of her dress. She pulls her head down and looks at her boots. She waits, her heart rocking in her chest. She hears Black Peter crow hoarsely again.

And now she remembers. A rooster crowing in a doorway means visitors are coming. An old Scottish superstition.

The saying fixes itself in her mind like a stone while she waits for the Potawatomi to come drag her away, and when no one comes she makes herself look again. The area by the henhouse is deserted. Aurelia is now on the other side of their cabin next to Beatrice and Penelope and Naomi, and the Potawatomi are roping up bags of loot.

Susanna grasps the tree trunk in front of her with her bare hands, feeling for any small holds in the rutted bark. Her mouth is so dry that it hurts. She can't see her sisters' faces but wisps of their red hair, each one a different shade, lift in the wind. Their black mourning collars and dark dresses bleed into the color of the trees, and only Beatrice has a cap on her head. One Potawatomi wrenches Naomi's violin out of her hands and ties it up to the bundle of dead chickens. Then he pushes her with the handle of a spade—their father's spade—and drives her and the others into the bracken and trees and the vines of small, unopened roses that mark the edge of Thieving Forest.

Two

Thieving Forest is an ancient forest crowded with decrepit elms and maples and oak, too many of them fallen for a comfortable crossing, a place settlers generally go around rather than through. It got its name after a band of Sauk Indians tried to hide some stolen horses there. Severne sits on its southern edge like a fly on the rim of a saucer. On the other side of the forest lies the Great Black Swamp—a dark wooded bog nearly the size of Connecticut—and beyond that is Lake Erie. Rumors circulate about the unholy creatures that make their home in the Black Swamp: swine wolves, frogs with fins and teeth. Naomi has even heard that there are bands of backward men living among its stunted trees, and that there is no end to it, and no sunlight within, and no food.

They are heading north toward the Black Swamp now, half running among the elm trees on paths that seem to vanish underfoot, reappear, and vanish again. A second group of Potawatomi joins them near two gray boulders, and one of the men gives each of the four sisters a pair of moccasins since they were taken in their stocking feet. After that they can run faster. Although no one speaks, Naomi feels as though a din of conversation is thrumming around her, the voices so relentless that they degrade into meaningless noise. She can see her violin tied to the bundle of dead chickens on the back of a small but broad-shouldered man.

Aurelia weeps to see them. Naomi hears Penelope say in a low, scared voice: "Hush, Aury, don't vex them. They're only chickens." But that only makes Aurelia weep more.

When they cross a small clearing one Potawatomi stays in the rear to sweep up the trampled grass with a long staff. On the other side Naomi takes hold of a sapling to steady herself. A man with a thick, white scar down the right side of his face scolds her. "Do not breaking branch! I will knock on head!" he says in English. She pulls her hand away.

Her head is spinning with noise. Usually in any situation Naomi can conjure up her music—this is her gift. She has famous recall, and even if she can't put her hands on her instrument she practices a piece in her head while performing some tedious task, like making soap or mending. Out of all the Quiners, she is the quietest. She was always her father's favorite. Now she can't hear anything except chaotic noises playing—what? Not music. Nothing like music.

"*Ke-nup,*" the scarred Indian says. Hurry. "Or I will knock on head." He isn't in charge, though. The one in charge is the one with half of his face painted red. They call him Koman. Koman's black dog, running next to him, wears a string of deerskin around his neck, a red feather dangling from that like a flower. A promise. Naomi knows she should not let such fanciful thoughts in but instead concentrate on keeping pace. And she would if only the noise in her head would stop and she could remember her music.

When at last they stop to rest Penelope finds herself looking around for landmarks, something familiar, but she has never been so deep in the forest before.

"How are you, Naomi, all right?" she asks. "Beatrice, all right? Aurelia, listen to me now, you must stand up straight. Give no sign that you've been ill."

"What about Susanna, what happened to her?" Beatrice asks in a low voice.

Aurelia glances back at the Potawatomi, who are talking among themselves near a trio of oak trees. "I saw her," she whispers. "She was hiding behind a maple tree near the henhouse."

"She'll get the men, then. They'll come after us," Penelope says. She looks at her sisters' faces. Beatrice's skin is tight with fright, Naomi appears to be in shock, and Aurelia's forehead is flushed and sweaty. Penelope is the most worried about her.

"I saw a man in the forest," Aurelia says. "When we first went in. A white man watching from behind a tree."

"Nonsense," Penelope tells her. "Any white man would have done something."

"I couldn't see his face but he wore English trousers."

"One of the Indians. I've seen plenty of them wearing trousers. You have, too. Now stand up straight. Your face is very red."

"Does that dog seem strange to you?" Beatrice asks.

The leader, Koman, is walking over to them with his dog by his side. He gives them each a shelled walnut.

"Where are you taking us?" Penelope asks, but he doesn't give her an answer. When he turns around, Penelope gives her walnut to Aurelia.

"You must keep up your strength," she says. Even to her ears it sounds like a scolding. But she doesn't mean to scold. She's frightened. As the oldest, it's her job to protect the others, but how can she? She looks at her hand, which is shaking, and she clenches it, trying to stop. She tries to drink some water from the stream but the stream is so shallow that she scoops up equal parts mud and water, and in her haste swallows a mouthful of grit. For a long time afterwards she works out tiny pebbles along her gum with her tongue.

"Beatrice is right about that animal," Aurelia says, catching up with Penelope on the trail a little while later. "It's not a dog. It has a snout like a pig but the body of a wolf."

Penelope can guess where this is heading. "There's no such thing as a swine wolf," she says. "Those are just swamp stories. It's just a dog."

"It isn't! Look at it!"

The scarred Potawatomi turns to stare at them.

"It's not a dog!" Aurelia says again. She stumbles over a root that is protruding up from the ground like a knuckle and she puts her hands out in front of her.

"Aurelia, for pity's sake, pay attention," Penelope says.

—❈—

Beatrice discovers in her pocket a bit of corncake leftover from breakfast. She touches it every so often, hoping it will help her feel better. Then she stops, thinking of Susanna and her little good luck charms. She considers good luck charms ungodly and foolish. Her chilblain is hurting but there is nothing she can do about that. The warm bread she used as a compress this morning didn't work. Nothing ever does.

She tries to remember what she knows about the Potawatomi. They are good hunters but they haven't brought in many pelts lately. The fur trade is declining, some say. She looks up, trying to locate the sun through the tree canopy. Where are they going? The men seem to have a plan. One man gave her water from his skin pouch, which carried with it a faint taste of animal fat. Another helped Naomi when she tripped over a root. They do not seem cruel, except for the one with the white scar down his face.

Where are they taking them? Probably she should pray but to pray is to hope, and she is afraid to do that.

Penelope comes up behind her. "We're going north. That means we're going toward Risdale."

"Will they ransom us there, do you think?" Beatrice asks.

"Maybe. Or maybe they've hidden their canoes along the river there. Maybe they want to make us their wives."

Beatrice shudders. She puts her hand in her pocket and feels the corncake, and again thinks of Susanna. Susanna has always been lucky, and she was lucky today. Whereas I am constantly plagued...but that is an un-Christian thought. To make up for it, she gives Penelope some of her corncake.

"Here," she says.

"What is it?"

"Don't let them see you."

Penelope coughs, then puts her hand to her mouth. Beatrice watches her swallow. It irks her that Penelope is older and thinks of herself in charge. It is irrational but she has always felt this way, ever since she can remember.

"I'm worried about Aurelia," Penelope says. "If you get a chance, give her some too. How is your heel?"

They are all wearing the deerskin moccasins that the Potawatomi gave out to them. As soft as they are—much softer than boots—her chilblain rubs like fire against the leather when she walks, and it throbs when she rests.

"I hardly feel it," she lies.

⋘

Toward midday they come to a spot where three rivulets empty into a fast-moving stream. Here they are given water and parched corn and are told to wait. Three Potawatomi station themselves north, east, and south on the lookout. Another Potawatomi signals with his hands for the women to lie on the ground. Like swine, Aurelia thinks. Like Saul, their pig. Even my birds have their pallets but we are treated like swine. She can't bear to see the carcasses of her hens carried on the back of that man, each one of which has a name. Her head feels open and strange, almost bright, as though pierced at the top by a ray of sunlight. What will become of Black Peter and the others? she wonders. In general she is not a lover of animals, only her birds. Koman's dog especially makes her nervous. He is not a dog, no matter what Penelope says. That creature is not a dog. She shivers, but also feels hot.

Beatrice is wondering aloud why they aren't in Risdale already. "It doesn't take this long to get there. Certainly not at the pace we've been going."

"We seemed to double back at one point," Penelope says.

"I thought so, too!" Naomi says. "I recognized the same stream with yellowish water. We passed over it twice."

But Beatrice is skeptical. "All the streams have yellowish water. They all look alike."

Koman walks over to them. Although his face is painted like a warrior his voice is gentle. "We wait here," he tells the women. "Do not worry." His eyes look at each of them, taking them in, a kind of regard Aurelia has never seen from a man except maybe her father. Even Cade Spendlove, her beau, is shy about looking at her, as if he fills up quickly at only a glance. But it's just a trick, she thinks. A show of concern.

Her face hurts from the effort of staying awake. She closes her eyes and listens to Penelope asking questions. Koman does not know much English or he does not want to answer. He says again, "Do not worry." He says, "Soon you will be..." but Aurelia can't hear the rest. Free? Dead? Beneath her eyelids she sees blood-red swirls and points of yellow light.

"Aurelia! How do you feel?" Penelope suddenly asks. Aurelia opens her eyes. Koman has gone back to his men. How long has she slept? Her body feels white and boundless.

Penelope kisses her on the forehead. "You're burning up."

The men are making a small fire and Aurelia can smell meat cooking. It smells delicious. Then she realizes it is one of her chickens.

"Aurelia, don't," Penelope says as she begins to cry.

"I can't help it."

One man notices that she's crying and he brings her a pouch of water. The water is warm and she takes a long drink. The scarred Potawatomi also notices. When the man leaves with his water pouch, the scarred Potawatomi crouches down in front of her with his face very close to hers. She can smell his rotting teeth. He puts the palm of his hand on her cheek and she keeps her face very still. She is not sure what he will do if she pulls away.

" *Yaknogeh*," he says. "Ill."

"No," Penelope tells him. "Not *yaknogeh*. Strong."

They all know a smattering of Indian languages from trading with so many Indians at the store. But the scarred Potawatomi takes no notice of Penelope. With one hand he grasps Aurelia's head, his thumb on her jaw. With his other hand he presses two fingers above and below Aurelia's eye, stretching the skin to see her pupil.

She is frightened, but she says, "I am warm from all the running." She tries to think if she knows the Potawatomi word for running. From the corner of her eye she sees Penelope nod: good.

After a moment he takes his hand away and stands up. When he goes back to the others she closes her eyes again. Her weariness is like a veil pulling her down. She drifts into sleep and dreams that her arms are dry sticks without leaves, and although they are light she can't move them no matter how much she tries.

Some time later she wakes to Koman and the scarred man shouting at each other in Potawatomi. She hears the word *cmo-kamanuk* repeated. White men. Koman takes up his hatchet and goes off, saying something over his shoulder. His animal, the swine wolf, stays behind.

The afternoon lengthens and still Koman does not return. Penelope tries to work out what they are doing here but can think of no explanation—if the plan is to ransom them for money, they should be in Risdale already. If the plan is to take them home and make them into wives or servants, they should be in their canoes. If the plan is to kill them they would have done so long ago. They would not be giving them water and walnuts and moccasins. She thinks of her knitting in the sack with the tea and candlesticks and everything else taken from their home. She could knit stockings for Koman perhaps, to show her worth. Or Aurelia could. Aurelia is a fast knitter.

"They want us to make a shelter," Beatrice says coming up to her.

"How do you know?"

"One of them speaks a little French. Look, they have Naomi at it already."

Penelope picks up a couple of long twigs and makes her apron into a nest to carry them. Two younger men—the ones carrying the sacks with the Quiners' goods—are cutting limbs off a tree. When they have three good ones, they pound them into the ground. Then they show the Quiners how to push and weave the twigs around them. Despite the men's stony expressions, Penelope tries to talk to them. She points to one of their sacks.

"My knitting?" she asks. "Do you have my knitting bag in there?"

They do not understand. "*Mik-chay-wee-win*," one says. Work.

When the shelter is done the four sisters are told to go inside. It is tall enough for them to stand up in, but narrow and cramped and dim. The men roll a fat log against the opening to serve as a makeshift door, which only partially blocks it. Naomi feels like she's being buried standing up. Sweat runs under her collar and turns cold. There is hardly room to turn.

"Do you see anything, Aury?" she asks. Aurelia is in the middle with the widest view. When she leans forward Naomi sees a tiny leaf stuck in her strawberry-blond hair from sleeping on the ground. In spite of her sore legs Naomi wishes she were outside again running along the path. In here she feels like an animal.

Aurelia says, "Koman's swine wolf has taken up a place in front of the shelter. He's standing guard."

"The dog is just a dog," Penelope tells her again.

A moment later Aurelia says, "The one with the scar, he's coming over here. And he's holding up his hatchet!"

"What? Let me look." Penelope puts her face to the opening.

The man is shouting in Potawatomi as he walks. Naomi sees Koman's dog rise. He lays flat his ears and makes a low rattling noise. Is he snarling? The man stops and says something to him, a command. The dog doesn't move. The man steps closer and the dog crouches as if to strike, but with a quick sweep the man hits the dog alongside his snout with the blunt end of his hatchet. Naomi can't see where the dog lands, or if he's all right.

"What's happening?" Aurelia asks. She is standing back now, not looking.

"Koman's dog...the man hit him," Naomi says.

"Why?"

"I think the dog...I don't know. He wouldn't move out of the way. I think he was protecting us," Naomi says. She wants that to be true. They need some protection.

"You!" the scarred Potawatomi shouts. "*Yaknogeh!*" He pulls away the log and then kick-rolls it over in the direction of the dog. The women are standing in front of him now, fully exposed, their dresses in tatters from their forced run among the trees, dirt in their hair.

"Wait," Penelope tells him. "Wait! Listen to me! Do you have my knitting bag? She can knit for you! A pair of stockings?" She pulls her skirt up a fraction to show him her stockings. Like her dress, they are torn and dirty.

"She can make stockings for you!" Penelope says. "She is a very fast knitter!"

He reaches in to grab Aurelia by the hair. Penelope holds on to Aurelia's arm and keeps pleading with him. He waves his hatchet so close that Naomi is afraid for a moment he will cut off Aurelia's arm and Penelope's hand with it. Beatrice must think so too, for she says, "Penelope! Watch yourself!"

"It's all right," Aurelia says in a tattered voice. The Potawatomi pulls her out with a hard jerk and Aurelia falls outside on her knees, the dirt shooting up in a cloud and then resettling around her. He drags her to her feet. Then he pushes her toward the trees with two hands, forcing her to take one step and then another. Penelope calls out, "Fight him!" But Aurelia only says, "I am so tired." And she does look tired. Tired and ill. *Yaknogeh.*

"What should we do?" Beatrice asks. "He'll kill her!"

Naomi makes a move to get out of the shelter but the two young men who supervised their work now step in front of them, making escape impossible. So she can only watch as the scarred Potawatomi pushes Aurelia into the trees. She thinks she sees the leaf in Aurelia's hair loosen and fall in a slow arc behind her. It disappears in the sunlight before it hits the ground. She is squeezing Penelope's hand hard on one side and Beatrice is squeezing her forearm on the other. If the two Potawatomi who are guarding the shelter suddenly sprouted wings and flew across the water she could not feel any more bewildered. Her old world with all its rules is surely gone.

"He'll take us one by one," Beatrice says.

The birds outside are momentarily quiet. Although Naomi still can't hear her music and does not even try to, she can hear, in the cramped space, the even beat of her sisters' breath, and this seems both beautiful and sad, a kind of music in the way that a whisper can be a kind of song. The sun is going down and the light seems to fall farther and farther away from them. She closes her eyes. The fresh green wood of the shelter smells strange. How much time passes she can't tell.

"He's back," Beatrice says finally. "He's alone."

Naomi waits. Penelope's hand tightens in hers.

"He's wiping blood off his hatchet," Beatrice says. "He's walking this way."

Three

Later Susanna cannot remember how she got herself to
Spendlove's cabin, she only remembers that her legs felt
like lead and that her heart was beating so hard that it
hurt. She knows she pounded on the ironworks door with its
horseshoe nailed crookedly above the lintel with one nail missing
and flecks of rust on the outside edge. She must have stared at it,
she remembers it so well. Then she sat down on the bench outside.
This is where Betsey T. and her son Mop find her—how much
later?—when they come by with a bucket of milk for Spendlove,
who does not own a cow.

Even sitting Susanna feels like her body is being pulled down
to the ground by invisible ropes. She tries to tell Betsey T. and
Mop what happened, pressing her two hands against her stomach.
Why, she thinks, and the word is like a bird that won't stay still.
She can't think what to do. Amos Spendlove comes out from
around back, where he'd been working he says, and she has to
start the story all over again. She can't remember what she has
already said. Afterward, she stands up and vomits into the grass.

Betsey T. gives her water to drink. Amos Spendlove is drinking whiskey from a tin cup, which he calls tea. That isn't unusual.
His hands are shaking and that isn't unusual either. He's a mean
drunk whom her father Sirus never trusted, but he is the only
man not out in the fields.

"We have to get them," Susanna says. She means the men, but Betsey T. misunderstands.

"We'll find your sisters, honey, don't worry. Do you need to be sick again?"

She is called Betsey T. to distinguish her from Betsey Mowatt, wife of John Mowatt, another settler. Betsey T.'s husband died two springs ago when a lightning storm hit while he was hunting and a heavy tree limb fell on his back. Susanna decided long ago that Betsey T. was a foolish, empty-headed woman but she's the only woman besides the Quiners who live in town. Her son Mop is foolish to the point of dim-witted but he has a rare talent for trapping and fishing, which means that he and his mother can live a tolerable life out here without farming. Besides the Quiners and the Spendloves, they are the only ones who don't farm.

"The men," Susanna corrects her. "We have to call them in."

She stops and swallows. Her stomach feels watery but she wills herself not to be sick again. Somehow she must be to blame for all this. If only she hadn't—what? She remembers thinking she'd had enough of their quarreling for one day, but it's ridiculous to think that that meant anything, could *do* anything. She takes her turkey hen bone out of her pocket and makes a fist around it. She feels inadequate and foolish, as foolish as Betsey T., and the thought comes to her that really she is no better than a child, that up to now her deepest wishes have been childish wishes: to leave home; to have someone else do her work. If only I could go back to the world of an hour ago, she thinks. But that wish is childish too, and painful because impossible.

"Where did you say you were at during all this?" Spendlove asks her. He is standing before her with his back to the forest, scowling. His shoulder-length hair holds a good deal of oil from the roots to the ends.

"Between the pig's pen and the henhouse," Susanna says. "Behind a maple tree."

"And how is it they didn't see you?"

She doesn't know. She can't tell him. Mop, who left to check on the Quiners' cabin, comes back to report on what has been stolen: all the candles, all the food, Sirus's tools, and their horses and wagon, which they keep in their own small barn rather than the public stable. Susanna presses her left thigh with her fingertip, testing for feeling. Her shock is wearing off and the seeds of her later, full-blown emotions are beginning to emerge: grief, horror, and the fear of being alone. What little breeze there'd been earlier is gone, and the air feels warm and thick. If she leans forward she can see her own cabin and she wants to be able to see it.

Why is nothing happening? "You go raise the cry," she tells Spendlove. "We've delayed too long already."

But Spendlove makes no move. "The men are racing as it is to get their grain in. When they come back we'll get together a proper search."

"But the Potawatomi will be long gone by then!"

"They're long gone now."

That stops her a moment. "Where's Cade? He'll go."

At the river with his brother, Spendlove tells her. "They'll be back by nightfall."

"Nightfall! But Aurelia is sick, he'll want to find her!"

"How sick?" Betsey T. asks.

"Getting over a fever. But still weak."

"The Indians won't keep her then," Spendlove says.

"What do you mean?"

"If they see she's sick they'll kill her and go on their way."

Susanna stares at him. How can he say such a thing? His eyes are watery and his pupils dart around like black flies. An uncouth man who eats his food with a knife.

"Or drop her at the nearest village," Mop says hopefully. "That would be Risdale."

"Maybe the Potawatomi hope to get a ransom there," Betsey T. suggests.

"Didn't I see you talking to some Potawatomi yesterday?" Mop asks Spendlove. "Over out by Stilgoe Creek?"

Spendlove spits into the grass.

"You spoke to some Potawatomi?" Susanna is surprised. She thought Spendlove hated Indians. "What did you say?"

"When the men come in we'll organize a good search," Spendlove tells her. "Meanwhile we can send a runner to the river, maybe Mop."

"The river? But they went into the forest!"

"They stole your horses and wagon. That means they're going by road."

"I saw them," Susanna insists. "They went into the trees."

But Spendlove just spits again. "You don't know what you saw. You're in shock."

Susanna's face flushes with anger. "And you're drunk."

"Susanna!" Betsey T. scolds.

"This is tea," Spendlove tells her. He throws the word out like a punch.

Susanna leans forward and looks at her cabin again. Spendlove won't help her. He is even more useless than she is. She turns to look down the other side of the settlement. "Old Adam knows the way through the forest." She is thinking aloud.

"You wait on the men," Spendlove says. "This is not advice, this is the rule for the situation."

But she's waited too long already. "If no one will go now," she says, "then I'll go myself."

For a moment no one says anything. Mop and Betsey T. look at her with identical expressions: heads cocked and mouths half open as if trying and failing to parse her words. Spendlove spits again and bends over to cough. Then he takes another pull from his cup.

"You go into the forest," he scoffs.

Amos Spendlove's two sons, Seth and Cade, are on their way back from a partially successful trip to the ferry landing when they hear the news about the Quiner sisters. Successful in that they were able to sell the Quiners' horses and wagon at a good price, but the iron Amos ordered had been either sold off to someone closer on the line or lost overboard in a thunderstorm so violent that it kept the barge from being able to land for a full day. This according to the bargeman, a thick Scot with a weblike beard. He claimed it was a miracle the whole vessel didn't overturn and he himself drowned.

"Work like his, you'd think he'd take it upon himself to learn how to swim," Cade says.

Seth is under their wagon with his coat off. They are only a couple of miles from Severne but had to stop because one of the tree axles is tangled with switch grass. Seth is lying on his back trying to clear it. "Almost a matter of pride with these rivermen that they don't know a stroke."

Although Cade is the younger brother, he is taller and broader than Seth. He has his father's blue eyes and fair hair. Even in a town of large farmers, Cade stands out. Seth, however, people sometimes forget about until they need a tool mended or the mechanism of a turning wheel explained. Unlike his brother, Seth has dark eyes and very dark, very straight hair, which even the recent rain and humidity could add no curl to. Is he part Italian, the settlers wonder? Or even Hebrew? It is known that the two brothers come from two different wives. As brothers they are close, and notwithstanding their difference in size it is Seth who feels protective of Cade.

The sound of cicadas rises and falls. The sun is out finally, and the scent of moist, green, newly sprouted life hangs in the air. Seth untwists the last rubbery length of grass from the shaft and cuts it with his knife. Then he stretches out on the grass next to Cade, who is eating plums and saving the pits in his pocket.

They say if you can see enough blue sky to make a woman's apron then the clouds will soon clear off, and Seth can see enough for an apron, a cap, and the sleeve of a dress. He closes his eyes, tilts his head toward the sun, and inhales as if breathing it in. In his pocket is a ring. A small ring, but pretty with a tiny cream-colored pearl surrounded by even tinier seed pearls. His father told him last night that the Quiners are staying in Severne, which is why they want to sell their team and wagon—they need capital for supplies. At first Seth was surprised, but then he recognized an opportunity. The bargeman had with him but two rings to sell, and the one in Seth's pocket now was easily the nicest.

He plucks a long piece of grass and ties his dark hair back into a ponytail. He is not Italian, as most people think, nor Hebrew, but Indian. Amos's mother was full Potawatomi, though you would never guess it from Amos's fair skin and fair hair. Amos lived with his mother's people until he was ten, and can speak Potawatomi as well as he can English. Seth can speak it too but Cade doesn't have any talent for it. Sometimes Seth thinks that all of Amos's Indian blood was passed on to him, the eldest son, leaving none for Cade. At least that's what it looks like. The brothers have two different mothers to be sure, but their mothers were both blond and Bavarian—cousins, in fact, who had come to Virginia together. When the second one, Cade's mother, died some six or seven years ago, Amos took up the boys and moved to Severne and never bothered to marry again.

Seth hears a sound in the distance: horse's hooves. There is enough blue sky now for a full dress and maybe a parasol cover. They left Severne last night at moonrise to get to the ferry landing by morning, and Seth is tired. At the river he and Cade tethered the two wagons together—the Quiners and their own—and each brother slept in one for safekeeping while they waited for the barge. A couple of hours' rest at most. What Seth wants now is just a moment to close his eyes.

Cade says, "It's Mop."

Seth turns his head. The horse's reins are flopping up and down in waves and the rider keeps such a loose seat that he seems to be holding on with his ankles. But Mop's dark curly hair, parted in the middle to make two shelves that hang to his shoulders, is recognizable at almost any distance. After Mop slows his horse up by the wagon he reaches for his water pouch and tips it back to drink. His collar hangs on by a button.

Neither brother stands. Not for Mop. Seth closes his eyes again. He can feel the ring in his pocket pressing on his thigh but makes no adjustment.

Mop takes a breath and says dramatically, "The Quiner sisters have been taken."

"Taken?" Seth asks. "You mean sick?" Mop's first words often make no sense. Probably he is here to see if he can earn a few coins in some way and this is his awkward preamble.

"Taken. By Indians. Run out of their home. I thought they usually set fire too, but the store is still standing."

Now Seth opens his eyes. Taken by Indians? Sunlight seems to shift away from his body and settle somewhere else, and for a moment he can do nothing but wait for something to connect this minute to the last one. He stares at Mop, who is still talking: Indians, no fire, a group from the forest. His lips flop apart like the reins on his horse.

Cade is the one who recovers first. "What do you mean? All the Quiners? Every one?"

"All except Miss Susanna. She hid somewheres."

"What about Aurelia?" Cade's voice sounds as though it is coming from a tube. Aurelia is his sweetheart.

"Taken, like I said, all but Susanna."

That's when Cade springs to action: he re-hangs the tar bucket that Seth had removed to get underneath the wagon, throws his coat into the wagon box, and catches hold of Clyde and Ginny, their horses. But Seth still can't make sense of it. They've never had any trouble with natives. They trade with them, buy their pelts, compare trap lines. What changed? An insect with wings like hinged wood flies into Seth's face and he slaps it away instinctively. The movement serves as a gate opening, letting him breathe. He jumps up to help Cade.

Mop is still talking. "And Susanna not right in the head after what she saw, that's what my ma thinks. Shock. She began quarreling with your pa. Seems the Indians stole the Quiners' wagon, too, and their horses, so your pa says they'll be on this road here. But Susanna, she says she saw them go into the forest on foot."

Now Cade and Seth both stop to look at Mop. Cade says, "What do you mean, the Quiners' wagon?"

"I went around to their place and saw it was gone. Your pa says they stole it."

Cade and Seth don't look at each other. One thing they both got from Amos: the ability to suddenly stand very still.

"Amos said the Indians stole the wagon," Seth says. He is speaking to Cade. The two hundred dollars he got for the wagon and team is still in his pocket, next to the ring. What is Amos about? He told his sons to sell the wagon, said that Penelope Quiner commissioned it.

A lie.

"It's her pride," Mop is saying. "The Quiner pride. Amos said he would round up the farmers soon as they're in from planting. She tells him, My sisters are more important than grain! To which your pa says, Not if your livestock goin' to starve over winter. Says Susanna, But if we don't start now the Indians will be long gone. And here I say, They're long gone now."

"Which Indians did you say they were?" Seth asks.

"She said Potawatomi. But like I say, she's a fair way in shock."

Seth looks over at Cade, whose face has a white, hard sheen to it.

"Susanna says if your pa won't help her she'll go into Thieving Forest herself." Mop snorts. "With her bonnet and gloves just so."

Seth says, "Mop."

"Well but she scoffed at me when I offered to help," Mop says. "Instead she's fetching Old Adam. I came out here to look for clues but my ma says if I see anything I'm to ride back double quick."

So Amos sent the fool out for advance work. There are no Indians on this road. Seth pulls Ginny's reins back over her neck and pushes his fingers into her mouth to check the bit.

"I'm going to kill him," Cade says. He climbs up to the wagon seat and takes the reins although usually Seth is the one who drives.

Mop says, "So you didn't see anything? Should I keep riding down to the ferry?"

"You do what you like," Cade tells him, and without waiting to see what Mop will do he jerks the reins to get the horses going.

"Listen, Cade," Seth says jumping up next to him. "Could be he just sees an opportunity to keep the money." That is certainly possible.

But Cade says, "Even at the time it seemed fishy. Why sell their wagon? They have to get to the river to get supplies."

"They needed the capital."

"You don't believe that."

"I don't know what to believe," Seth says. He holds on to the seat plank beneath him with one hand. He can feel neither the ring nor the money through the fabric of his trousers, but at the same time his pocket seems to be the center of a dark world that an hour ago didn't exist. Cade jerks the reins again to urge the horses faster. The wagon lurches crazily to the right and then straightens. Seth moves his hand along the seat to get a better grip. He is sitting on his hat.

"That axle will surely break if you keep on." He has to raise his voice to be heard.

"We'll drop the horses at Dunn's stable," Cade says. "The forest is too overgrown for a wagon. We'll have to go on foot."

The wagon lurches again and rights itself.

"Don't you give him one cent of that money," Cade says.

Four

By the time Old Adam finds the narrow opening where Susanna last saw her sisters—the backs of their dresses—it is well past noon. She follows him into the trees where a horde of insects rushes out to meet them, hitting hard against her netting as they look for a place to land. Old Adam's dog snaps at them once or twice in irritation but Old Adam makes a gesture, silence, and the dog immediately stops. Like all Indian dogs, he is well trained and obedient.

Susanna has known Old Adam for so long that she does not think of him as an Indian, but he is an Indian—a Miami, or Twightwee as they call themselves. His wife Mary, who is Shawnee, calls him a Pkiwileni. The settlers call Old Adam a Christian Indian, and that also is true: he was saved by missionaries after most of his village was killed off by the smallpox, and later they saved his wife Mary, too. The newspapers that come up from Cincinnati are filled with accounts of thieving Indians and lying Indians and bands of Indians who roam around attacking settlers, but Sirus always told anyone who would listen that plenty of natives, like Old Adam, live peacefully side-by-side with white men, either adopting their ways or keeping their own. Sirus in particular liked the Potawatomi who came into the store. He used to say that they were stubborn but fair, and so great fun to bargain with.

Susanna pulls her gloves a little higher on her wrists. None of what has happened makes any sense. What she is doing now, she suspects, makes no sense. But she has to do something, and she likes Old Adam, she trusts him. He used to hunt with Sirus and afterward he told the girls, when they were young, fanciful stories about the wily animals they could not bring down. He is small and thin with badly pocked skin, and he suffers from rheumatism like so many natives. Too much sleeping outdoors, according to the settlers. From behind, his arms seem to jut out at odd angles, or maybe his elbows are just unnaturally prominent. He lives with his wife Mary on the other side of the settlement, where they raise hogs. After Susanna went there and told them her story, Mary fetched her a cup of rye whiskey. Susanna took a sip and handed the cup back. A peppery feeling remained in her mouth.

"Usually the Potawatomi take for revenge," Mary had said, looking at Old Adam. "Or to replace someone in their tribe who has died. But no battles since a long time."

"No battles, no," Old Adam agreed.

"So want money?" Mary asked.

Old Adam said, "For that they go to Risdale."

Susanna adjusts the netting that Mary gave her and steps over a fallen branch in the middle of the path. Risdale is on the other side of Thieving Forest, over two leagues away. It would take a young man almost four hours to walk that distance, and that is if he had a cleared track. This path will only get worse. She imagines her sisters running down it in their stocking feet. Back in the cabin their boots are still lined up near the door and their shawls are still hanging on the peg, one over the other. There are things she wishes she could give them: boots, netting, even her turkey hen bone. They need luck more than she does. She takes off one glove to feel the bone in her pocket.

But when they get to the first crossing stream, Old Adam suddenly stops and holds up his hand. Susanna draws in a sharp breath when she sees why: fifteen or twenty spiders are walking in single file along the water. Wolf spiders. They are brown with darker brown markings and huge, the size of young sparrows. She has never before seen spiders so big. She steps back, and then takes another step back. A curious hissing sound is coming from somewhere among them, and quite a few carry egg sacs beneath them using one curved, hairy leg. Has she ever seen spiders in a pack before? They are reputed to hunt and live alone.

"Where are they going?" she whispers, as if they might hear her.

Old Adam lifts his shoulders. "A safer place, perhaps. For eggs."

When the spiders have all passed Susanna crosses the little stream behind Old Adam, careful to use the same stones he uses as footstones because she does not want to wet her feet in the muck. On the other side of the stream the canopy above them thickens and the air begins to smell like wet moss, a smell Susanna particularly detests since it is her job every spring to fill the chinks in their cabin with clumps of it. Last spring she used Naomi's violin bow to push the moss in until Naomi noticed and screamed. Where is Naomi now? Somewhere ahead with no water, no netting, no boots. A swarm of insects hovers around her head and she swats at them with both hands. She is both afraid that she won't find them and afraid that she will—that she'll come upon their bodies in the bracken. She purses her lips and forces that picture out of her mind. Concentrate on walking, she tells herself. That's what Penelope would say.

When Old Adam stops to examine a broken tree branch, Susanna takes a moment to adjust the grain sack on her back, which Mary helped her to tie on. In it is anything she could think of that the Potawatomi might accept in trade for her sisters, since there was almost no money in the store. Their silver dinner knives, her mother's silver hand mirror, her gold wedding ring, and the red buttons from Ellen's wedding dress that are shaped like cherries. On an impulse Susanna also took Ellen's fancy nail scissors with their loopy bird-head design. But she didn't think about food, and now she's hungry.

A branch cracks and she looks up into the trees. Sirus claimed that there were panthers still living in Thieving Forest. They jump silently from tree to tree before falling on their prey. Old Adam takes his hand from the broken branch and rubs his fingers on his breeches.

"People here lately," he says.

"Potawatomi?"

"Could be."

Susanna tries to see down the path. Another branch cracks above them. "What about panthers?" she asks.

"Haven't seen any prints." He is wearing an old leather shoe around his neck as a pouch, and he takes from it a few dried berries. He gives her a couple and then helps her over an old nursing log in the path. "But if you sense danger, stop, stand still. Close your eyes."

"Why should I close my eyes?"

"The bright pupil gives you away."

The path narrows and Susanna finds herself staring at Old Adam's back, his sloping shoulders, his thin legs like rubbed sticks in their leather breeches. All at once he seems very slight. She feels in her pocket for her turkey hen bone again. As they walk deeper into the forest the trees grow darker and ropes of stiff, dead vines rise up around their trunks. She thinks of her Aunt Ogg's house in Philadelphia, where her younger sister Lilith lives, with two brick ovens in the kitchen and an iron railing outside painted green. There would be a boy bringing in a bundle of cut wood for the kitchen and another for the fireplace in the parlor. Old Adam's dog trots around a burnt-out tree trunk with a single crooked branch pointing up like a finger back at God.

"In forest you must lose fear," Old Adam says over his shoulder. "See with all your senses. Only way to be safe."

She will get to Risdale and ransom her sisters. And then, she promises herself, she will never set foot in a forest again.

-⁂-

Four hours later Susanna is hot, scraped, and sore, and whatever ignorance or pride started her off on this journey is by now long gone. Trouble comes to those who bring it upon themselves, her mother used to say, and she would certainly say that now if she were here. When at last they stop at a muddy stream to rest, Old Adam brings out a few strips of dried venison from his pouch and Susanna finds a flat rock next to the water to sit on. She leans over to fill Sirus's wooden canteen, but the stream is so choked with debris that getting clear water is difficult. Old Adam's dog stands in the middle where the water runs cleanest, taking a long drink. He turns to face Susanna, staring at her as though he has something to say but no means to say it. Water drips from his muzzle.

"How much further?" Susanna asks Old Adam. Behind him the sunlight makes bright handprints where it can along the bank. He looks up at the treetops.

"Turn west in little while. After that, soon there." Not really an answer. "Must watch for *kineepikwa*," he says. The snake.

Susanna pulls her skirt closer to her body, and then, still not feeling completely secure, she stands.

"Rested now?" Old Adam asks.

She made the mistake of taking off her boots to bathe her sore feet; putting them on again is difficult and now her feet feel worse than before. Old Adam helps her to retie the grain sack to her back, but after only a few paces it falls into an uncomfortable position that she can't put right. She wishes she had Old Adam's long moccasins. She wishes she had a split skirt. Why on earth didn't they leave for Philadelphia immediately, when the question first arose? Her gloves will have to be soaked in new milk to get all the stains out.

Old Adam says, "In Swamp would take longer. See that?" He points to a line of rocks off the path. "Limestone. Unusual in woods."

"I would never go into the Swamp."

Everywhere she looks all she can see are thick trees and thin trees and trickles of yellowish water. Isn't there a fairy story about a forest that never ends? A girl looking for her brother, who has been turned into a swan? However, this forest is not some magical place, it's only an overgrown maze with ingenious ways of stabbing her legs. Get to Risdale, pay the ransom, go home. But as she quickens her pace something hits her like a bout of vertigo, and instead of her body moving forward everything else seems to be falling away. The tree canopy closes up completely, sealing them in, and a bag of cold air seems to enshroud her. Old Adam slows but Susanna carries on past him anxious to get to the end, wherever that is. As the path turns a warbler calls out not for joy but in warning, and all at once Susanna stops dead.

A panther is standing not ten yards away from her.

It is a long skinny beast, one rib sticking out when it draws breath, and although she is close enough to see the mud on its fur it hasn't yet noticed her. It is intent on something on the ground. She wants to turn and run but she remembers Old Adam's advice and instead closes her eyes. Her mouth is very dry but she is afraid even to swallow. When she hears a noise she opens her eyes again. The panther has lifted its head and is staring right at her.

"Sees you," Old Adam says behind her in a low voice.

The animal's eyes do not leave her own, and yet she senses it is distracted. The noise comes again, perhaps a trapped animal, whatever the panther has just been sniffing. Susanna stands very still and tries to think what to do. She cannot hear a whisper from Old Adam until suddenly his knife hums through the air and clips the panther on its shoulder. The animal jerks once and then shifts its weight to leap away from them. In a moment it is gone.

"Why didn't you kill it?" Susanna asks him. She can hear it crashing through the undergrowth.

Old Adam plucks his knife from the nest of ferns where it landed. "Did not wish it dead."

She swallows, trying to get moisture back into her mouth. A breeze circles them like a ghost and brings with it a strange heavy scent. A sour, heavy scent.

Blood.

She pulls away from Old Adam with the worst sort of dread and Spendlove's words in her head: *If they see she's sick they'll kill her.* And there, just off the path, behind a pitted log, she finds what she is afraid she will find: her sister Aurelia lying there in the dirt and bracken.

Susanna drops to her knees. Aurelia's eyes are closed. Her beautiful strawberry-blond hair is full of dried mud, and there is mud on her cheek, too, and mud on her collar. She is wearing Indian moccasins on her feet. Old Adam says something but Susanna doesn't hear what he says. Aurelia's left hand is raised, covering part of her forehead, and Susanna touches it. Her hand is cold, but it does not feel dead. It does not feel like dead flesh. But that isn't mud on her cheek, Susanna realizes. It's blood.

As gently as she can she pulls Aurelia's hand away to look at her forehead, and then her stomach clenches and rises. She's been scalped—partially scalped. Insects are already nesting inside the unclosed wound. Old Adam is crouching beside her and he puts his hand in front of Aurelia's mouth, testing for breath. The dog barks and Old Adam says something and then he stands and says something else and then suddenly—Susanna is not sure how this happened—two other figures arrive, one of them making a noise in his throat, a man with fair hair: Cade Spendlove. But she doesn't wonder how he came here, she has no wonder left in her. As she turns her head a shifting of the light makes her look past the trees to a spot not too distant, a glimpse of cleared land. Risdale? But the trees won't end, she understands this now. They will never get out of the forest. Seth Spendlove is looking down at her, his hand on her arm.

"How will we carry her?" she asks.

Five

They get Aurelia to the tavern in Risdale and set her down in the little room off the barroom where soldiers passing through eat their meals. A man named Jonas Footbound owns the tavern with his wife Liza. Liza has the men lay Aurelia on a flat board lifted off the floor by six bricks. This will help the flow of blood, she says. She takes up a clean, blue-checked cloth and begins to wash Aurelia's face.

"Will she live?" Susanna asks.

Liza rinses the cloth, dark with blood. Around here she acts as midwife or doctor since there is no one fitting either description for miles. A competent-looking woman, tall and muscular and big boned with a surprisingly small nose for her wide face. Her voice is rough from years of pipe smoking.

"There's them who've come to me worse," she says.

Eager Tavern, their place is called. Some men are at the bar when Susanna comes in but when they hear the news about her sisters they rally together to help in the chase. By the time they ride out the sun is barely above the tree line, but they are well armed with rifles and tallow jacklights. Seth Spendlove rides with them but Cade stays back to see to Aurelia. He helps Jonas transform the back room into a sick room, and together they remove the long trestle table and bring in a spindly legged oak stand and a basin of water, a straw tick for Susanna to sleep on, and two cane-bottomed chairs. The room is small and square with rough walls, easily warmed by the small fireplace. Susanna can smell mint on the windowsills to drive off mice, something her mother also did. When Liza finishes washing and bandaging Aurelia's wound, she lights a candle made out of a twisted rag floating in lard in a small tin saucer. For a moment she holds the saucer near Aurelia's face.

"Let's see if we can't get a bite of food inside her," Liza says.

How can they feed her? She looks barely alive. Susanna's heart feels tightly knotted. Anybody who didn't know her might think she'd been struck dumb by the events of the day, but she is worried that if she opens her mouth she will start crying and never stop.

Her other sisters aren't in Risdale. No one has seen them. And here is Aurelia halfway to Paradise, as her Aunt Ogg used to say. But Jonas brings in a bowl of broth—he is the cook here—and Liza puts the tiniest spoonful into Aurelia's open mouth and by the greatest of miracles Aurelia swallows.

"Why don't you go get a bite for yourself?" Liza says to Susanna without looking up. "You're done in, I can tell."

When Susanna hesitates, Cade says, "I'll stay here with her."

The tavern's main room is now empty. Its main feature is a long wooden counter along one end that has recently been polished with tree oil, or maybe she's been in Thieving Forest for so long that she can't get the smell of trees out of her nose.

"My wife is good with the injured," Jonas tells her. "Soft hands, though you'd not guess by looking." Susanna figures he means because Liza is so large and rough looking, her cap turned any which way, her skirt unkempt, her voice abrupt. Jonas is large himself but much more careful in his dress. He wears trim, clean trousers and a blue waistcoat, and his boots look freshly buffed. A small deer comes into the room and stands by his side. Their pet,

Jonas explains. He puts his hand between the deer's smoke-colored ears.

"Name's Becky. Found her out stuck in a mudhole starving and motherless. 'Twas Liza who saved her. Fed her by hand every two hours around the clock for three weeks."

They have no children, he tells her, only Becky. "You can see she never got to her natural height. Comes from losing your mother too soon."

He goes into the kitchen and brings out a wooden plate of food and sets it before Susanna, who is sitting on a chair near the window with a planed tree stump serving as her table. Roasted turkey with gravy and boiled carrots and new greens, and a smaller dish of apples and cream. While she eats Susanna thinks of Ellen, who grew up in Scotland where her father leased land near Loch Shiel. Six months a year they ate, Ellen used to say, and six months they didn't. When Old Adam and Mary lost four of their pigs to a disease of the stomach, Ellen sent over half a barrel of cornmeal. She believed in working hard and watching out for your neighbors as well as yourself. "It might be your trouble next," she reminded her daughters.

"Where's Old Adam?" Susanna asked. "He must be hungry."

"Well I don't know—off with the men? Don't worry, I'll make a plate for him when he comes back," Jonas tells her.

He begins lighting candles at the other end of the counter. The daylight is gone. Susanna tries to picture her sisters sleeping outside on the dirt: an almost impossible vision. Penelope will be complaining bitterly about the hard ground, and Beatrice's hipbones will hurt. She can hear Liza begin to sing to Aurelia in a husky voice in the other room. The tune is familiar, but what is the song? It is low and sweet and calls up something down in her that has been crouching in wait for a while. She closes her mouth but it is too late, her tears are coming. She truly believed that she would find her sisters in Risdale, either already ransomed by the townspeople or awaiting ransom. But they are gone and she is left behind.

Jonas shuts the heavy tavern door and locks it. Then he comes to where Susanna is sitting. She tries to stop crying but every time she breathes out a new wave of grief rushes in. Jonas pats her arm and then, after a moment, awkwardly, he pats the side of her head.

"We'll do our best for your sister," he promises.

But the next morning Aurelia wakes shaking with fever. Liza bathes her wound again using water boiled with herbs and then strained and cooled. She wears the same apron, the same frown as last night. Susanna isn't sure if she is worried or if those are just the natural lines of her face.

"We'll keep her cool," Liza says. "Keep feeding her. Best we can do."

Cade dampens the fire but does not put it out. He spent the night wrapped in a blanket sleeping on the barroom floor. Susanna takes Aurelia's hand in her own. Aurelia searches Susanna's face as though she has just asked a question and is now waiting for the reply.

Susanna doesn't know what her sister wants, but she says, "Aurelia, I'm so glad you're awake! Are you hungry?"

No answer. No sign she understands.

Susanna tries to explain what has happened to her, the Potawatomi, the forest. Maybe she's confused or doesn't remember. "Old Adam and I found you. We're in Risdale now. In the tavern.

Eager Tavern. Sirus told us that the owner has a pet deer and we didn't believe him but it's true, her name is Becky."

But of course Aurelia would not be interested in any animals, only her birds.

"Your hens are fine," Susanna tells her. "Mop is tending them. I showed him the feed bucket before I left. I told him about the mash."

A slight frown. Susanna touches Aurelia's cheek. Her skin is burning up. There is a knock on the door and Cade comes in with some broth.

"Are you hungry? Why don't you drink some of this, Aury?"

Aurelia is struggling to get out a word. *Not.*

Susanna bends closer.

"*Not. Mop.*"

Her voice is slurred and strangely low. It is unsettling to hear her struggle. Susanna always thought it was fitting that in Sirus's mnemonic—Please Be Neat And Seldom Late—Aurelia became a conjunction, since she usually talks in one long sentence peppered with ands and ors and howevers. A conversation with Aurelia might find you with your mouth closed for ten minutes on end. Susanna knows more about Dominico chickens than she has ever cared to. And isn't it silly, she always thought, to waste feed on penned-in birds here in Ohio, where there are so many wild ones easily caught?

Susanna touches the spoon to Aurelia's lip. "Take another sip, Aury. Just a little one."

Cade says, "Anything?"

Susanna has forgotten about Cade. She shakes her head.

"Want me to try?" he asks.

She gives him her chair. Unlike Susanna, Cade doesn't try to convince Aurelia, he just goes about tipping her head back, opening her mouth gently, and tilting a small spoonful of broth between her lips. Then he massages her neck until she swallows. It takes a long time to get half a mugful in her. Finally he puts the broth back on the little oak stand.

"I think she's asleep."

"Probably good for her," Susanna says. But every time Aurelia closes her eyes she is afraid they will never open again.

Cade pinches the bridge of his nose with his thumb and forefinger. Then he stands. It is still morning, and outside a low fog clings to the trees. "Why don't I go see if there's any news," he says. One of his trouser legs is unbuttoned at the knee and his hair needs combing. He picks up his hat but then just stands there, turning it over in his hands.

"One thing," he says finally. "About your team and wagon?"

"I already know. They were stolen." Susanna looks down at Aurelia.

"Well yes, I mean, that is, I wondered...could maybe one of your sisters, say Penelope, could she have decided to sell them?"

"That would be foolish. We were thinking of leaving, you know, going back to Philadelphia. We'd need our wagon."

Cade looks at her, still turning his hat.

"As soon as I get the others back..." she begins, and at the same time Cade says, "My father..."

They both stop. Susanna thinks of all the things she'd like to say about his father. A drunkard who wouldn't fetch the farmers and who needlessly delayed her.

"I blame him for this," she says angrily.

Cade looks surprised. Susanna knows it is unfair of her to say this to him. In truth she blames herself.

He opens his mouth and closes it again. Then he puts his hat on his head. "Well, if I find out anything..."

As he is closing the door behind him, Susanna calls out, "Cade, what about Old Adam? Where is he, do you know?" But Cade doesn't know.

Cade finds his brother walking along the stream bank ahead of a horse he borrowed off a Risdale farmer. Seth's dark hair is out of its customary ponytail and he leads the horse loosely by the reins. She's a young mare but well trained, not grabbing her mouth around every full branch she passes. Seth is looking down at the water as if for someone drowned.

Cade says, "You been back?" He means to their home.

Seth shakes his head and wipes his forehead with the back of his hand. It is humid, worse than yesterday even. The clouds are one long paintbrush stroke across the sky.

"What should we do?"

"Keep looking," Seth says. "Ransom them if we can."

"I tried to tell Susanna but I couldn't."

"What would you say? We don't know anything."

They walk not looking at each other. Seth's horse blows air out from her nostrils and stretches her neck.

"What are you looking for here?" Cade asks.

He isn't sure. Signs that people have been here, have traveled this way. Mud clings to his boots, and the horse's legs are splattered up past her forelocks. "Maybe they got hold of some canoes."

"Is it deep enough for a boat?" Cade looks at the water, which is as flat as tar.

"It was deeper a ways back."

Frogs are everywhere in evidence, most of them the same color as the mud. They rise up in unharmonious noise like they are mocking Seth's thoughts. Like Cade, he doesn't know what to say to Susanna. He wants to give her the money for her wagon and team, but how would he explain it? And if he says nothing, how can he give her the money? Back in Severne Aurelia is considered the prettiest Quiner, but Seth has always favored Susanna. He had a standing hope that she would be the one to come into the shop to get any little thing Sirus might need: new iron nails, a dent in their kettle pounded out. Before he moved to Severne Seth had seen only one red-headed woman in his life. She was thin and tall and ancient, thirty at least, and unmarried. She carried a small bucket in lieu of a purse. Miss Anders. They said she was a poet. To Seth she looked like a bird in winter, all beak and wing bone. He thought all red-headed women must be ugly until he got to Severne and saw five of them, all of them pretty, and all, according to the farmers, bad mannered and not worth the effort it might take to claim one as wife. Barren, too, they said later, or at least not able to give birth to a son. And the Quiners for their part looked down on the farmers. They might look down on Seth, too, the son of an ironmonger, but Seth hopes not so much. Susanna herself greeted them on the day the Spendloves arrived in Severne. She was only ten or eleven and came around as bold as a boy to see the new folks. She looked Seth straight in the eye, and then she looked at Cade, and then she looked back at Seth. Most people when they meet them look at Cade and stop there. He is the handsome one. Seth is the one no one could figure out where he got his looks. But Susanna looked at Seth more than she looked at Cade. That first summer they even played together sometimes around one of the brooks that fed into the Blanchard. By the next summer they were too old.

Seth halts his horse. He kneels by the stream and splashes water up onto his face and neck. There are no signs of any natives:

no canoe marks, no prints. Cade is right, this water is too shallow. He feels the ring in his pocket, which now feels insubstantial. He should go back to Severne and confront Amos. Or he should take a new route, ride more slowly, look more carefully. Or he should ride as fast as possible to Fort Wayne with ransom money in hopes of finding the women there. If the Potawatomi want ransom and they didn't stop in Risdale then that's where they would go. Fort Wayne to the west or Cincinnati down south. But the Potawatomi are northern people, most comfortable in forests, which means Fort Wayne.

He glances at Cade, whose blond hair is plastered to his neck in the heat. "How is Aurelia?"

"She can't hardly speak," Cade tells him. A muscle moves in his cheek. Seth can see how worried he is, how he carries it on his skin. A man who keeps all his big feelings to himself.

"Used to be I'd hear her talking even before I rounded the cabin," Cade says. "Now her whole face looks different. Not young exactly. Soft, but not young."

They walk along the water. Seth waits for Cade to say more. He doesn't know if talking helps or not. He fingers the ring in his pocket again and thinks, maybe I'll just carry it forever, come across it whenever I change my handkerchief: oh that, I should do something about that. Then he thinks: All right. I'll go to Fort Wayne.

"You should rub some soap up on your skin," Cade says. "Change your shirt and collar. You look a mess."

"You do too, brother," Seth tells him. "You do too."

The next day Jonas comes in with news from the men: they have found signs of a small campfire near the Blanchard River, and there are marks that might have been made from canoes scraping down the bank. Now they are following the river on horseback, and four men came back to town to fetch skiffs.

Later Liza has Jonas move Aurelia onto a straw tick with a folded quilt on top of it. The new bedding smells like vinegar, a smell that, strangely, comforts Susanna. Ellen used to wash their hair and clothes in vinegar to stave off a fever.

"How is she doing?" Susanna asks. Liza is trying to feed Aurelia some applesauce.

"Doesn't want to swallow." Liza puts a drop the size of a fingernail in Aurelia's mouth and, like Cade, massages her throat. At last Aurelia swallows. "Such a pretty," Liza says.

"I think she's the prettiest of us all, though some people say Naomi."

"You're all of you pretty. My cousin had dark red hair like yours. Always liked it. You see it brown, then she goes into the sun and you see it red. She married a *coureur de bois*, a French backwoodsman, they moved up north. Docia. Wonder about her still."

Sunlight slants in through the open window. There is not a whisper of wind. It is late afternoon, her mother's favorite time of day. Out of all of them, Aurelia looks most like Ellen: the same color hair, the same mouth. In a way this is like watching her mother die all over again.

"If only I started sooner," Susanna says. "If I had followed them as soon as they left..."

"Then they would have taken you, too. They use scouts, you know, to see what's behind them as well as what's in front."

"I just can't understand it. Why would they do this to her? The Potawatomi have always been friendly to us. To my father. They often came to our store."

"Nothing to do with that. It's just what they do if they find themselves with someone ill. So they don't carry disease back to their people."

A log from the fire shifts and falls, and Liza gets up to attend to it. Above the fireplace hangs a map hand-drawn by Jonas. It is very neat, with small upward arrows indicating trees and looping lines for streams. There is Severne, there is Thieving Forest, and there is Risdale. And at the very top in block letters: The Great Black Swamp.

Liza leans the poker back against the water cask. She sits on the chair next to Aurelia and picks up the bowl of applesauce again, but Aurelia has fallen asleep. She is asleep more than awake now. She slept for almost six hours after breakfast.

Susanna says, "I want to ask you something."

Liza gets out her pipe and lights a twig off the fire. "All right." She touches the glowing end to her pipe bowl and takes a long pull.

"The Indians, the Potawatomi..." She is looking for the right words. "Could they have taken Aurelia...taken her honor?"

"Acted like a husband?" Liza asks. "Except by force?" Susanna nods. To her surprise, Liza seems to get angry. She waves her pipe stem in front of her as if scratching the air. "You know who does that? White men. That's who. Not Indians. That's not their way."

"But in the stories..."

"I know about those stories. White men tell them to keep us afraid. Listen now. I've lived around forest Indians all my life. Before Jonas and I moved down here we ran a trading post near

Canada where we were the only white people excepting a little cripple Welshman who lived with a Mascouten wife. Only houses I've seen made of stone were made by the French before they left. Never been to a city, don't know anything about that life, but I know Indian life. Kidnap women, they do that, always have, women from other tribes, even men from other tribes. They do it to replace someone who has died or for revenge or for the ransom. But not to satisfy themselves. It's not their way. Not forest Indians, no."

"I just thought..."

"They harmed your sister, they did, but not in that way." Liza looks at her sternly. "Nor none of your other sisters I'd wager. So you chase that notion right out."

Susanna doesn't know what to say. She believes Liza and feels a little ashamed of herself. Sirus always told them not to listen to the lies white men spread about Indians, but her fear got the better of her. Liza gets up to knock her pipe against the hearth, and then she washes her hands in the basin and feels Aurelia's forehead over the bandage. Susanna watches her, relieved but still uneasy. Why then did the Potawatomi take them? Not for revenge, not for ransom, not to satisfy themselves. Aurelia's hair is spread out like the wings of a red moth, and Liza strokes the top of her head. When she speaks again her voice is a little softer.

"Stories are lies made up to make us feel something," she says. "I don't hold with them unless they have music, and then I mostly give over to the music."

The Risdale men find the company of Indians in canoes, but they are Sauk Indians, two brothers and their uncle, and they are traveling with their women. They have not seen anyone else on the water, they say, all this past week.

That day a good number of the men return to their fields. After this disappointment their energy seems to flag. There are no other signs to follow. Old Adam is not among those who have returned, Susanna notices.

"Has he gone back to Severne, then?" she asks.

No one knows.

Aurelia's fever seems a little abated, which is good, but she sleeps more and more. In the afternoon, Susanna decides to give her a sponge bath. Her arms feel heavy, like sleeping snakes. After washing her, Susanna trims her fingernails.

"I knew there was a reason I brought these," she says, getting out Ellen's nail scissors. Aurelia is breathing deeply and her pale eyelashes do not so much as flutter. But Susanna keeps talking. "The bird heads are pretty, don't you think? When I was little I was glad there were two of them, so they wouldn't be lonely. I used to pretend they talked to each other."

Aurelia's nails are hard and brittle, and Susanna takes her time. Through the door she can hear Becky's hooves clicking on the wood floor as she follows Jonas. Since Becky won't use stairs Jonas built a little ramp for her against the kitchen door so she can get out to the yard. Sometimes she sleeps there, in the sun. As Susanna finishes Aurelia's pinkie nail and turns to take her other hand, she notices that her sister's eyes are open.

"Aurelia! You're awake!"

It is the first time in almost three days that Aurelia has woken up on her own. A good sign. Susanna squeezes her sister's hand and a little sob escapes her, like a hiccough.

"Hi, Princess," Aurelia says slowly. Her voice is thick and unnatural, as if a heavy coin is lying on her tongue.

"How do you feel?"

Aurelia swallows with difficulty. She looks confused. "Where are my birds?"

"They're fine, don't worry about them. Mop is taking care of them."

A pause. "I want you to. It's past their feeding."

"We're not home right now, Aury. We're in Risdale. Remember? At the Eager Tavern. Liza Footbound is helping me take care of you. Well, I'm helping *her*."

Aurelia frowns. Her eyes are like little caves with light way in the back of them.

"You were taken by some Potawatomi. Outside by the henhouse. But now we're in Risdale. You're all right now."

Something shifts in Aurelia's expression. "In Risdale?"

"At the Eager Tavern. Aury, I've been given strict orders to feed you. Can you open your mouth? It's applesauce. I've been eating it all morning. It's good you woke up when you did or there'd be nothing left."

Aurelia allows herself to take a little. "Why are we in Risdale?"

"You were taken into Thieving Forest. By some Potawatomi. Do you remember that?"

Aurelia looks up at the ceiling. Her lips are very dry.

"There was a man there. Behind a tree."

Susanna wipes Aurelia's lips with a wet cloth. "I know, Aury. A Potawatomi."

"A white man," Aurelia says.

She is confused, delusional. Susanna spoons up more applesauce. "Another bite. Just a little one. Please."

Aurelia inhales as if gathering strength and opens her mouth. Susanna gives her the tiniest amount, but even so for a moment she thinks that Aurelia is going to let it spill out. From the other

room there is the sound of a hearth being scraped, and then Jonas
begins singing:

As Dinah was walking the garden one day,
She saw her dear papa and thus did he say,
"Go dress yourself, Dinah, in gorgeous array,
And choose you a husband both gallant and gay."
"Oh no, dearest Papa, I've not made up my mind
To marry just yet I don't feel so inclined
To you my large fortune I'll gladly give o'er
If you'll let me stay single a year or two more."

Liza comes in on the chorus, her voice as low as a man's:

Sing tura-la-lura-la-lura-la-lie
Sing tura-la-lura-la-lura-la-lie...

Aurelia seems to be listening. She closes her eyes and her
breathing changes. But she isn't asleep. After a minute she says
with her eyes closed, "I remember something else." A pause. "The
one with the half-red face. Koman. He had an animal with him."

Susanna tries to follow. "One of the Indians?"

"Like a dog. But it was..." Another pause. "One of those swamp
creatures. A swine wolf."

A breeze flutters the window curtain as slight as a caterpillar
walking a leaf. Susanna has heard about swine wolves of course.
She has always wanted to see one. Penelope and Beatrice claimed
they didn't exist.

"Don't worry," she tells Aurelia. "You're safe here."

"Its shackles were up but its eyes..." Aurelia turns her head and looks at Susanna as if seeing her face will help her form the words. "Its eyes were kind."

"The swine wolf?"

"The eyes of a friend, or, what do you call it..."

"Aury—"

"For protection."

"Aury, you can tell me all this later when you're better. Here, take another bite."

"It tried to protect us."

"One more taste. Please, Aury. For me."

"I can't." Aurelia presses her lips closed. Susanna reluctantly puts the spoon back.

"I'm cold," Aurelia tells her. "Will you lie down with me?"

"How can you be cold," Susanna says lightly, trying to tease. "It's sweltering out." But she stretches out on the little straw tick next to Aurelia, careful not to jostle her, and takes her hand. Aurelia's hair smells of blood and dry leaves and something else, something flowery—maybe Liza has brushed it with scented water?

"I'm glad you're here, Princess," Aurelia says. Susanna squeezes her hand. Jonas and Liza have stopped singing but she can still make out sounds from the next room: a murmur of voices, the clang of tinware. In contrast their little room feels still and cozy.

"You're all right now," Susanna says. Her eyes begin to close. In spite of the heat she is drifting to sleep. Some time later she hears a commotion in the tavern, excited voices in the outer room and then a lower one asking a question. Her fingers, still holding Aurelia's hand, feel stiff. Aurelia lies very still. For a moment Susanna doesn't move. A bird is singing outside the window. It stops and starts, stops and starts.

"Susanna!" Liza comes into the room wiping her hands on her apron. "There's news! Two of the brethren over at the Christian mission have ransomed a white woman with red hair."

Still Susanna doesn't move. A tear rolls out of her eye and down over her jaw.

"What is it?" Liza asks. She quickly goes to Aurelia and puts a hand on her forehead.

"She's passed," Susanna says.

Six

Seth is preparing to camp when Cade catches up with him. At this twilit hour the ground is humming with insects, and the clearing, surrounded on three sides by forest, smells heavily of moist decay, as if even air were a thing that could rot. To the west a grove of dying beech trees stands between him and the rest of Ohio. He is following an old buffalo trail, the only way out. At some point he will start coming across soldiers and that means that the string of forts between the Maumee and Fort Wayne has begun.

When he hears hoof beats he stops building his campfire and listens. Sounds like a white man riding, although if someone asked him he would not be able to say why. Sure enough, even at a distance, he makes out his brother's fair head. As he comes closer, Seth sees that Cade's face is like the mask of tragedy, his jaw so clenched it seems bound with cloth. He understands even before Cade's horse has fully halted: Aurelia is dead.

From the beginning it seemed unlikely to Seth that anyone could survive such an attack. He lets Cade tell him, though, and then he says what he can say, knowing that nothing will bring comfort so close to the fact. A good woman, gone before her time, a loss—but Cade is hardly listening. His anger and despair hold most of his attention.

"Couldn't stay in Risdale." He rubs his chin up but it has no effect on his expression. He tells Seth the news: a white woman has been ransomed by the Moravian missionaries, and Susanna is fixing to go to their village, called Gemeinschaft, tomorrow. Every settler in the area knows about Gemeinschaft, where a dozen or so white men and women live alongside fifty or sixty converted Indians. It's a safe haven for the Christian Indians to practice their faith away from liquor and marauding tribes and ill-natured Europeans, a place where they can grow their own food and start little businesses—weaving, carpentry, textiles. There are several of these Moravian villages in Pennsylvania and New York, but this is the first one in Ohio.

"Old Adam found out," Cade tells him. "He came across a couple of the brethren out prospecting the woods. Guess they're thinking of clearing more land."

Seth pulls flint and charcloth from his tinderbox. There is no use pretending that they will do anything else but camp here before they return, for there is no moon to light their way. Besides, the horses are tired. Cade waters them at the stream while Seth gets the fire lit. They boil coffee and eat the cornbread Jonas sent with Cade. Insects rise in a dense, cloudy mass and find little hollows in the land over which they swarm as if trapped there. Seth watches them, staying close to the fire's smoke, which keeps them at bay.

What Seth doesn't say is this: he is still relieved that Susanna, out of all of them, was spared. How can he help it? But the feeling sits uneasily on him. He loves his brother and feels his loss. Although they sit side by side with their boot tips nearly touching, Seth feels his brother's thoughts pulling him away. They will separate. They will go their own ways. Only a week ago the future Seth saw was the two of them in Severne each married to a Quiner. Amos gone or dead, somehow no longer a problem. But Amos has always had so many tricks. Uprooting them from Virginia, as it turned out, was the least of them. But that was when they were too young to venture forth elsewhere on their own.

Seth gives Cade the last of the cornbread even though he could eat it himself and still want more. He will see Susanna through this, he vows to himself. He can't make up for what Amos did, whatever that was exactly, but he will see Susanna through to the end even though she has not asked for help and it does not even appear to cross her mind to seek it from him.

"I'll go to Kentucky, then," Cade says once the fire is banked and they are lying on the damp ground looking up at the stars. "Nothing for me here."

It is one of the things he sometimes talks about. Joining a militia. He has the weight and look of a soldier, that's certainly true.

"You would fight Indians?" Seth asks.

"More like the English, the bastards. But Indians too if need be. I'm not one of them. Not like you."

"Cade, that's ridiculous."

"What? You're the one got it all, just look at you. Besides, one quarter, what's that? Easy enough to throw that away."

"Amos will want you to work the forge with him."

Cade rolls over in his blanket. He is sleeping in his boots and they stick out from the bottom. A rafter of turkeys, gabbling aimlessly, crosses a corner of the clearing. Cade picks up his musket and, hardly raising himself, lets off a shot without aim. The turkeys scatter, gabbling louder.

"Amos be damned," he says.

In the small back room in Eager Tavern, a few hours after Aurelia died, Susanna helps Liza prepare her sister for burial. Her stomach feels loose and watery and she now understands the phrase *sick with grief,* because that is how she feels exactly: her own body is both hot and cold and also somehow strange to her. Her hands are not her hands. They move with a will of their own.

She finds herself thinking about something that happened to her years ago, when she was eight years old. They had been living in Severne only a couple of years then. It was a fine day in early summer, and her mother decided they should eat supper outdoors. A preacher was visiting the settlement with his wife and young son, and every evening they ate with another family. Tonight it was the Quiners' turn. Ellen made her famous turtle soup, and Sirus and Beatrice carried their large oak table outside. Susanna found dry flat stones to hold down the tablecloth, for there was a wind. When they could see the reverend and his family walking over—three distinct dots, one in a black hat—Ellen told Susanna to go wash up but to find Aurelia first.

Susanna went to the henhouse, the obvious place to begin, but Aurelia wasn't there. As she turned to go she heard a noise, a kind of crackle, nothing unusual, just a hen turning about, but for some reason she looked closer and saw that next to the hen there was an egg waggling on the straw. It had a big crack all the way around it. A chick was hatching.

Susanna had never before seen a chick coming out of its shell and since she thought it would be the work of a moment she stayed to watch. But it wasn't the work of a moment. It was long and arduous: the widening crack, the first glimpse of the beak pecking out, and then a claw coming up like a long forked splinter of wood. How could such a weak creature possibly break through that shell? The longer she watched the more impossible the task looked, and Susanna found herself more and more engrossed. In the middle of it, one of her sisters came into the henhouse behind her—no doubt sent by Ellen—and exhaled impatiently. But still

Susanna didn't take her eyes off the egg. She said over her shoulder, "A chick is trying to come out and I want to watch. Don't tell." So together, silently, they watched as the chick worked and rested, chipping off more and more shell until it could finally unfold itself out onto the straw: a skinny, goopy, putty-colored baby bird with scraps of eggshell still stuck to its body.

Susanna felt as victorious as if she had done it herself. She turned around to smile at her sister since together they had witnessed this wonderful thing. But there was no one behind her. She was alone. The exhale she'd heard was only the wind. And right then she realized that she had thought, or felt, that it was Lilith behind her, Lilith her younger sister who still lived in Philadelphia. She'd had the feeling of Lilith without thinking about it, so absorbed was she in the chick's struggle. But Lilith never came to Severne. Maybe Susanna imagined her because back in Philadelphia Lilith had been her particular partner, cutting out old newspapers into houses and drawing in chairs and fireplaces and people. They played together behind the house, although now Susanna can't remember what they played, only Lilith's laugh like a hiccough.

As she got older Susanna forgot to miss Lilith, but now, as she helps Liza prepare Aurelia's body in the little room where Aurelia died, she finds herself hoping that Lilith will suddenly step through the low doorway with a heavy longing that she puts down to grief.

Together Liza and Susanna undress Aurelia and cover her with a sheet. Then, delicately, as though Aurelia might care, Susanna uncovers only that part of the body she is washing. As the light crosses the room Aurelia's skin seems white then gold then a dull yellow. Susanna helps Liza sew Aurelia into a new blue dress, because why should she be in mourning now? Her brushed-over hair nearly covers the bandage on her forehead.

They bury her the next day in a thick pine box, and Jonas takes it upon himself to say a few words in lieu of a preacher: "And thus we give an end to her trouble and her life." Susanna has to unclench her fist to throw in the dirt. She doesn't feel alone, not completely, not yet, but she can sense it coming, like the wind.

That night Liza sits with her in the little back room for a long time, both of them in nightdresses, and Liza wearing a very odd muslin nightcap set back on her head.

Susanna holds a piece of paper on her lap, intending to write to Lilith. Instead she looks outside. A spreading bitternut tree grows right up against the tavern wall, and through the open window she can smell the tangy scent of its branches. Its roots are probably somewhere beneath her, right under the floorboards.

"Some weather rising," Liza says, looking out at the moon. Even sitting, her feet are firmly planted on the floor as if at any moment she might be called on to get up quickly. Susanna is glad of Liza's company, maybe just the sound of another woman's voice. She is used to her sisters all talking at once. Now it feels like she is sitting at a table with too many place settings. Both Liza and Jonas have told her that it isn't her fault that Aurelia died but Susanna knows differently. She should have started sooner. She should never have stopped to rest, not even once. She stares at the blank sheet of paper. Now that it is before her, it feels too soon to describe Aurelia's death in words.

"I wish...," she says, and then stops. There are a hundred things she wishes.

Liza waits. She looks at Susanna and takes a pull from her pipe. After a moment she blows out the smoke in a long stream. Susanna watches it rise and spread.

"I don't know. I keep thinking. The last time I spoke to Aurelia I said nothing important, nothing at all. I wish I had told her something real. Talked about something important."

Liza pulls her pipe from her mouth and rests it on her knee. "That it? Well you don't need to fret about that. Anything you might have said, she knew it when she woke up and saw you tending her."

"But I didn't know it was the last time. That I wouldn't get another chance. All I talked about was applesauce. I didn't say anything that really mattered."

"She knew what mattered when she saw you there with her. Words aren't any more telling than that."

Susanna hopes this is true. Outside the wind stirs up the branches of the bitternut tree. The leaves look like birds hanging on.

"I want to put something to you," Liza says after a moment. "Jonas and I been talking. If you want, after you fetch your sister from that missionary village, you could come back here. You both could. We could use more hands."

Susanna says, "You must be sorely in need of company if you value mine."

Liza smiles, a rare occurrence. "It's fine company."

"Then you haven't been listening to what people say."

"You've given yourself no airs around me."

The wind rises sharply and then suddenly drops as if changing its mind. Tomorrow she will go to Gemeinschaft, where her sister, she doesn't know which one, has been ransomed. And then what? Come back here? Return to Severne? She thinks about Old Adam,

whom she still hasn't seen. Clearly he has abandoned her. Gone
back to see to his pigs.

Liza gets up and knocks her pipe ashes out. "It's late. Try to
sleep, now. You need have no worries tonight."

But she does have worries, countless worries. How will she pay
the missionaries back for her sister's ransom? The goods in her
grain sack seem pitiful now: buttons, nail scissors, a ring. Her sisters are well beyond their worth, prideful as they are, and stubborn, and forever telling her that whatever she is doing is wrong.
Where are they now? Sleeping outside without even a blanket no
doubt, and probably convinced that she, Susanna, could do nothing to help.

But she is mistaken about one thing at least: Old Adam has not
yet gone back to his pigs. When she steps out early next morning
to fetch water he is waiting on the dewy grass, crouching rather
than sitting, his rheumatoid knees jutting out, elbows on thighs.
From his mouth hangs a long clay pipe not unlike Liza's, but when
he sees Susanna he takes out the pipe and stands. He is gripping
something in his other hand: the moccasins Aurelia was wearing
when they found her. He holds them out to her.

"I told Jonas to give those to you," Susanna says. "If he saw
you."

"He gave. Last night. But they are yours."

"I don't want them."

His face searches hers. "You might like. Good leather. Soft.
Try," he says. The sun is behind him, the sky faintly pink. A single bird makes its claim to the day. She bends down to unlace her

boots. He is right, the moccasins are surprisingly soft. Her feet feel warmer already.

"You can remember when you look at them."

"Remember?"

"Aurelia," he says. "To speak the name is to make live again."

His voice is so gentle it brings tears to her eyes. She thinks of Aurelia standing by her henhouse.

"Now," Old Adam says. He feels inside his shoe-pouch and pulls out a narrow piece of cloth with a bit of fur on one end. At first Susanna cannot make out what it is, but then she recognizes it as a collar, a linen dress collar, only it has a small deer tail sewn onto it. The tail is reddish brown and about the length of a child's hand. It serves to hook up the two ends of the collar like a brooch.

She strokes the tiny hairs. "Is it your wife's?"

"She made it. I give to you."

Susanna admires the cleverness of the collar's design, the mix of European and Indian. "It's lovely," she says. Then she asks him to wait while she goes into the tavern.

"I want to give you something, too," she tells him, coming back out with her grain sack.

She pulls out her mother's wedding ring but Old Adam shakes his head. Too valuable, he tells her, she might need it. He was the one, she will find out later, who went back to the cold trail in the forest and came upon the Moravian missionaries. They told him that a woman with red hair had been ransomed and taken back to their village. Susanna pulls out all the objects in her grain sack and lays them side by side on the ground. Old Adam knocks his pipe ashes behind him and squats to look. He puts Sirus's axe back inside the sack, and then the dinner knives tied together with twine, and the nail scissors with their avian fingerholes. Susanna has already given Liza Footbound her mother's hand mirror, small enough compensation for all her kindnesses.

Old Adam picks up one of the cherry buttons and rubs his thumb over the front.

"Thank you," he says, his fingers closing over it.

"Take all three."

"One is enough."

Susanna puts the other two buttons back into the little square of cloth that serves as their bag and winds a strand of cotton thread around it.

"Before she died, my sister...Aurelia...she told me she had seen a creature, one of those Black Swamp creatures, half wolf and half swine." She pauses and looks at him, but Old Adam says nothing. "Could that be true?"

"Have never seen one," he tells her.

"She also said that a white man watched them being taken away."

Old Adam looks away past her, toward the uneven roof of the tavern. His expression does not change. At last he says, "Hard to know what is true and what is illness speaking. Maybe animal, maybe no animal. Maybe man, maybe no man."

Susanna says, "That doesn't help me."

Old Adam smiles. He looks at her like a father might. "You need to know?"

"I think so. I don't know. Maybe not."

"Jonas Footbound goes with you to Gemeinschaft. He is good man. Your father was good man too." He touches her on the shoulder. "When in the wild, remember, lose fear and suspicion. See with all senses."

"We're not going through the forest," Susanna tells him.

The sun begins to spread itself more brightly over the horizon, and as if on its command dozens of birds begin chattering all at once. Old Adam's hand is still on her shoulder. She feels it like a blessing. "Be well, Susanna Quiner," he says. "Stay harmless."

Gemeinschaft

Seven

Susanna doesn't know when Liza found the time to make the heavy split skirt for her to wear on the ride, but it is a practical gift made out of strongly woven linen with a pocket for her turkey hen bone. After Jonas helps her mount she touches the bone through the fabric. It is a cloudy morning, some rain later probably, maybe even a storm.

"I think we can beat it," Jonas says as they start off.

Moments later, to Susanna's surprise, Seth Spendlove comes riding up hard. He asks to accompany them, says he has some business with the brethren. His coat is stained and his boots are so muddy at the bottom they seem to be made from two different grains of leather.

Also in their party are Barbarus Tulp, a Risdale farmer who wants to buy flaxseed from the brethren, and Tulp's grown daughter, Ada. Ada wears cracked spectacles and has bread-crumbs scattered all over her collar. She keeps exclaiming over the view, which is, like all of Ohio, a view of trees sliced through with muddy streams. Susanna finds Ada affected and unkempt and a better horsewoman than she is. It is hard to forgive her for any of that.

Susanna is not good with horses. The horse that Jonas found for her, an ornery mare called Step, has three white socks, which is very unlucky. Step keeps brushing along the trees next to the track as though hoping to crush Susanna's leg against one of them. Although Susanna tries to rein the mare over, Step's mouth is so tough that the bit means nothing to her.

"They don't know the first way about making a living," Tulp is saying as they ride. "Plant corn, but when the time comes to harvest, where are they but off hunting? Then they overhunt so they have to go to another tribe's territory for fresh meat, and war is what happens next."

"Savages," Ada Tulp says, looking back at Susanna with an ugly expression, as if Susanna, being a woman, would naturally agree. Ada swirls her reins around to avoid a puddle. Susanna tries to follow but Step plunges right into the water and mud shoots up the inside of Susanna's split skirt and onto her leg. She makes up her mind then and there never to use the word "savages" again.

By the time they stop for a quick meal the wind has met up with them and the horses are getting nervous, twitching their tails and refusing water. While Ada tries to soothe her own horse Susanna ignores Step and sits down on a mossy log a good ways away to eat her biscuit and cheese. According to Jonas there is only one more stream to ford before the small stretch of woods that marks the border of Gemeinschaft. Very soon now she will meet up with her sister. They will make a plan and leave. If it is Penelope or Beatrice they probably already have a plan. Susanna touches her turkey hen bone again through the pocket of her skirt. She is worried and anxious and hopeful. She tries not to wonder where the others might be. If they are alive.

"Excuse me, Miss Susanna?"

She turns her head. Seth Spendlove is standing there with his hat in his hand. Sometimes she forgets that he is from Virginia where their manners are so old-fashioned and fussy.

"For pity's sake call me Susanna," she says, thinking about how they used to play together in one of the little streams near her cabin.

"I just wanted to say, I'm sorry about your sister. Aurelia."

Without warning the muscles in her face seem to weaken. For a moment she can't look into his eyes.

"Also, I believe, well...this belongs to you."

To her great surprise he holds out a faded black purse. Two hundred dollars, he tells her. To pay off a debt. "One of your sisters asked my father to sell something or other for her."

"What could have possibly been worth so much?" But Seth has already put his hand in his pocket as though afraid that she would try to give it back. As if she would! Two hundred dollars! This is money enough to pay back the brethren for the ransom of her sister, and part of her does not want to question the whys of this gift too closely although clearly it is a mistake. The black leather of the purse has weathered to green, and Susanna pulls the drawstring to close it. With the sun at this angle it is hard to read Seth's expression. For a moment he looks like he is about to say something more.

"Thank you," she says, pushing the purse into her pocket alongside her turkey bone. Seth turns his head to check the sky behind them. She has always liked his profile, she doesn't know why.

"How has your ride been?" he asks.

"My horse is a rascal. She wishes me off her back and is plotting at every step."

Seth smiles. "The old ones can be the worst. They know all the tricks."

She puts her hand on her pocket, feeling the heft of the purse, and smiles back. Down at the other side of the clearing Jonas is signaling, Let's be off. The sky has become a deep purple and the wind is blowing down in long sweeps. Now the horses are even more skittish. They pass through a small grove of buckeye and Susanna has to concentrate hard to get Step to cooperate. Fortunately Seth is nearby to help, but once or twice she catches Ada smirking.

When they get to the stream Step jerks her head up in two quick hits, nearly pulling the reins from Susanna's hands. Susanna stares at the water. It is wider and faster than any of the other streams they've crossed. The trees on the other side, mostly pin oak, seem very far away. Winsome Stream, Jonas calls it. To Susanna it looks more like a river.

"Pretty full," Tulp remarks.

Seth reins in his horse. "It's been a wet season."

"Fording might be a problem."

Ada slaps at a mosquito. "Papa, they found a hole in my netting."

The sun is almost at the horizon. There is not light enough to search for a better crossing; they need to go over now or camp for the night. Susanna watches sticks and clumps of leaves being borne away by the current, but the water itself does not seem terribly deep.

"Do you want to see a trick?" she asks Ada while they wait for the men to make their plan. Although she does not care for Ada she wants to impress her, perhaps to make up for her inadequate riding. Susanna pushes up the sleeve of her blouse. After a few seconds a mosquito lands on her arm and tries to sink in its pointer. It tries again. Then again.

"I can't be bit," Susanna tells her.

"You've never had a mosquito bite?"

"I've never had Swamp Fever, either."

"You're lucky," Ada says, pushing her cracked spectacles up higher.

That's what Beatrice always says: you're the lucky one. She doesn't get chilblains or sore throats, she never gets Swamp Fever, and even her skin rarely bruises. Susanna rolls down her sleeve feeling a little bad now, as if her good luck has been taken from her sisters' store of it. But that's foolish, she tells herself.

The men decide to cross a few yards downstream where the bank slopes more gently. Jonas goes first. His horse prances a little when she gets to the opposite bank, still excited, and she throws her head up in the air.

"It's all right," Jonas shouts to them, pulling the reins to his chest. "Just move the horses through fast."

Tulp and Ada cross next without incident. Then Seth moves his horse next to Susanna's saying they'll cross together and does she want him to hold Step's reins? But she shakes her head, determined to do as well as Ada. The air is slightly cooler here and blueflies skirt over the water. Step maneuvers down into the stream and lifts her head. Susanna sees Jonas on the other side watching her. And then suddenly, she doesn't know how, she is falling off the horse.

"Susanna!" Seth shouts.

She falls on her backside as Step, relieved of her human burden at last, dashes through the water and up the bank, where Jonas grabs her by the reins. Meanwhile Susanna struggles to stand. The water is not very deep but the current moves fast and she has trouble keeping her balance. She falls again and this time the cold water seems to seep right through to her bones. As she struggles for footing she notices two things floating away: Seth's purse with the two hundred dollars, and her turkey hen bone, each one caught in a different eddy. Susanna stops and feels part of her skirt paste itself wetly against her leg. What with the pace of the current and her heavy clothing she can only reach one, she knows this instinctively. She has to make a choice. She takes a step against the current and then another and once more falls into the water but even falling she is near enough to close her fingers around the purse. The drawstring holds and she can feel the thick wad of bills inside. She stands up and holds it for a moment against her stomach as she watches her turkey hen bone carried farther and farther downstream. It rotates around a gray rock in the water and disappears.

"Susanna!"

Seth is wading toward her holding the reins of his horse with one hand. For a moment she stays very still as if waiting for him. There are hundreds of such bones, she tells herself, trying not to cry, although not one more that Sirus would give her.

"Susanna, are you all right?"

Her wet clothes stick to her skin in patches and she can feel the wind on her scalp. She looks at Step standing meekly now next to Jonas's horse, her reins dripping.

"I'm not getting back on that horse," Susanna says.

⁂

After this, disheartened and cold, she half-expects to find that a mistake has been made, that there was never a woman ransomed by the Moravians, or that it was not a white woman with red hair, or not one with the last name Quiner. She rides the rest of the way on the back of Seth's horse, her wet arms around his dry middle. The storm is still gathering behind them but soon enough they come up to one of the brethren walking along where the track opens up to the village. He turns when he hears them and waits, introducing himself as Brother Graves when they get to him. Although it is still early in the evening he is holding a torch made out of a dry linden branch. When he hears their business, he raises it slightly to look closer at Susanna.

"Your sister Beatrice," he says, "will be most happy to see you."

His eyes are as dark as his hair, and his voice, warm and gentle, sounds like it might just be Saint Peter's voice at the gate. Susanna feels Seth squeeze her forearm gently. She feels a rush of relief followed by guilt over the other two, Penelope and Naomi, where are they? She will find out soon enough. She lets herself lean into Seth's back a moment before Jonas helps her dismount, and she goes with Brother Graves while the others take their horses to the stables, the rain still behind them but barely.

Beatrice.

Brother Graves takes her to the Birthing Hut, where they care for the ill or dying or pregnant, he explains, although Beatrice is none of those things. Recuperating, is what Brother Graves says. She is at the chapel at the moment but will be back as soon as service is over. Inside, he introduces her to a Shawnee woman named Sister Johanna. She is not a nun, but a convert. He calls Beatrice Sister Beatrice, and when he turns to leave Susanna he calls her Sister Susanna, saying good night. The Birthing Hut is small, only one room, with rough walls and a stone fireplace. Sister Johanna gives her a dry shift to put on and a cup of warm liquid that tastes like grass mixed with dirt. As Susanna is sipping it she hears the rain begin.

The door opens. A woman in a heavy brown cape walks in.

"Beet!"

Beatrice stares at her, her face pale. Her bright red hair seems even redder. "Susanna?" They embrace, clinging to each other, and Susanna breathes in Beatrice's hair. It smells like wet leaves. Her cape is damp but Susanna doesn't want to let go. The rain begins pounding on the roof with a fury as Sister Johanna says good night and goes out into the storm, drawing her hood up. Beatrice turns to hang her cape on the peg. Droplets like tears streak across the single glass window.

"Are you all right?" Susanna asks. She stands back to look. No bandages. Nothing in a sling. "Where are Penelope and Naomi? Tell me everything, start from the beginning."

"Susanna." Beatrice drops down on the bed. "I'm sorry. I don't know how to say this. They're gone."

"Gone? What do you mean?"

"They were killed. Aurelia, too."

Susanna feels something white flutter near the edge of her mind, neither thought nor emotion. She takes a step back. "I found Aurelia alive. She lived for three days..." She will tell Beatrice all about that but right now she needs to hear about Penelope and Naomi. "Is it possible, could they have lived, too?"

"I can't talk about it," Beatrice says. She has a pierced look on her face. "Please don't make me say more. They're gone. They were killed. The Potawatomi killed them."

Susanna sits down on the bed next to Beatrice. She and Beet are the only ones left? Can that really be true? All the others, gone? The fire sputters as a couple of raindrops fall down the chimney. Her worst fears have come true, and she struggles to bring up a picture of Naomi in her mind. Naomi playing her violin beneath the short, dead branch of the apple tree near their barn.

"I'll dampen the fire. We can both sleep in the bed," Beatrice tells her. "We're lucky that no one is ill, we can have this place to ourselves."

Susanna thinks of her turkey hen bone floating down the stream. She doesn't feel lucky. She feels wet and exhausted and a hundred other feelings that circle around failure and loss. She's too tired even to cry. She looks at her sister, hoping for some words of comfort. But there's a deadness in Beatrice's eyes, like she has nothing to give.

"Tomorrow we'll talk more," Beatrice says.

Eight

Ever since she arrived in Gemeinschaft Beatrice has attended both the morning and the evening service, and often the one at midday, too. Her nights are uneasy but she awakens to the chapel bell ringing out in clear tones: *no, no, no,* as if it can banish the night with its ringing. As she dresses she looks forward to sitting on the hard bench with the other women, singing hymns, listening to Brother Graves preach, and then the testimony of the natives who have been saved. At the chapel she is able to think about something other than Penelope and Naomi. There are buns and coffee, prayers and a blessing. The Moravians like to bring up Christ's suffering in physical detail: the blood he spilled, the points in the skull where thorns pierced his skin. *When comforts flee,* they pray, *abide with me.*

Beatrice sees the bloody wounds in Christ's hands. She feels the mockery he endured, she can see the expression on his face when he is given his cross. These pictures take the place of those other pictures: the back of Naomi's dress as the Potawatomi leads her away. Her red hair coming out of its braid.

Yesterday at the evening service a Delaware with thick lips and pockmarked cheeks stood to give testimony. Last winter, before he came here, his wife froze to death and his infant son starved. Only the blood of Jesus could have saved them, he said. Then he said, I saved myself, but I wish it them.

Beatrice's blood seemed to stop in her veins when she heard that. A few minutes later her hip sent out its old pain. She shifted on the bench but it didn't make a difference. It never made a difference. She closed her eyes. *When comforts flee, abide with me* she prayed, and prayed again, and again. And then, just as the young girls were coming around with the honeyed buns and the coffee, the pain disappeared. For the first time in her life she made it disappear.

She thinks about this the next morning when she wakes up to the chapel bell and makes the decision to stay with Susanna instead of going to the morning service, a decision she later regrets. She touches her hip gently with her fingertips. She feels nothing, no pain.

The fire in the Birthing Hut's little fireplace is down to embers and someone—probably Sister Johanna—has put a new dress and apron and cap over the little chair near the bed. She must have come very early. The memory of Naomi's messy braid floats into her mind and she pushes it away. There are things she cannot think about. That she cannot tell Susanna. This she knows for sure. *When comforts flee, abide with me.* Naomi disappears.

The new clothes are for Susanna, and Susanna makes a face at how ugly they are.

"Better than that split skirt," Beatrice points out, which is still damp and smells like a river. Susanna looks just the same. She slept late and had to be told to help tidy the room. As they make their way to the Bell House for breakfast, Beatrice can feel Susanna staring at the people they pass without any sense it might be rude. Beatrice knows Gemeinschaft is a strange sight at first. All the women, both native and white, wear the same gray linen dress and white cap that Susanna and Beatrice are wearing. White men walk along the path arm in arm with native men, chatting socia-

bly. Many of the natives wear European clothing, and some of the
white men wear leather tunics and braid their hair. Beatrice still
finds it strange to see a white man with a long blond plait. But
they do it to affirm their unity with each other, she explains.

"Moravians believe we are all one family." She opens the door
to the Bell House, where women are finding seats at the long tables. There is a strong smell of soap and wood and, fainter, the
scent of hot ashes from innumerable fires. The fireplaces on either
end of the room are huge, and native women bend over them, la-
dling up oatmeal from six or seven large copper pots. "The name
Gemeinschaft means community. We work together, we eat together. We sleep side by side. There is no distinction between
races."

Susanna looks skeptical but after the grace is said she tucks
into the hearty breakfast: oatmeal and honey and dried berries
and thick slices of bread with butter and even one small pork chop
each. They are sitting on a narrow bench in front of a long oak
table covered with a simple brown cloth. If Beatrice looks to her
left or right she sees a row of identical white bonnets like buttons
down the row. Young native girls serve them from large baskets,
and one carries a coffeepot wrapped in cloth.

"Where are the men?" Susanna asks.

"They eat breakfast earlier. We don't share any meals together. We only see them at chapel or walking about, but we are not
allowed to converse with them."

Susanna scrapes more butter over her bread. "How old-
fashioned!"

Beatrice tells her no, on the contrary, the Moravians are very
forward thinking. "They don't carry weapons. They don't drink
alcohol or swear to any oaths, even to the government." But as she

hears herself talk their habits begin to seem more and more archaic. She cannot explain it right.

"The food is very good," Susanna says. It is the only compliment she gives.

"The Moravians believe feeding the body is just as important as feeding the soul." Beatrice feels sure that Susanna will like that at least, as someone who has always been, in her opinion, greedy about food. She tells Susanna how much work they all do, good work, not only preaching the gospel but farming and scutching flax and tanning hides, weaving, cooking, washing clothes for so many.

"*Ohne Fleiss kein Press*, as the brethren say. No reward without toil."

But she has gone too far. Susanna makes a face and says, "We must talk about how to get home."

Why can't Susanna see what she sees? This is a new kind of society where whites and natives live in harmony. The natives are settled and happy, industrious, friendly, with no face painting and no battle scars.

"We're safe here. And you should rest after your fall."

"What do you mean, safe?" Susanna asks. She looks at Beatrice more closely and closes her mouth, as though deciding not to say anything more. But after a minute she can't help herself.

"Don't you think it's funny to see a man wearing two blond braids?"

Beatrice says, "Of course not. It's perfectly fine." But she feels herself blush.

That afternoon Susanna meets Sister Consolation, one of Gemein-schaft's founding missionaries. A woman of high principle, Be-atrice whispers to Susanna as they see her approach, and Susanna can see that in the way Consolation holds her head up over her very straight spine. She is tall and fair, Danish perhaps, with a patrician nose, high cheekbones, and the teeth and skin of some-one who has always had enough to eat. They stand in the path while native women with baskets move around them, on their way to the cookhouse or washhouse or the fields.

"You must be Sister Susanna," Consolation says, putting her hand on Susanna's shoulder.

The touch feels forced, as though Consolation understands that people do this to show compassion but has not yet mastered the technique. Although she wears the same gray linen dress as every other woman here, her dress is...what? Better tailored? Per-haps she just stands well.

"How are you faring, my dear?" Consolation asks. Susanna's linen dress scratches her arms and the cap feels too tight, but it turns out that Consolation is referring to her fall from the horse. She tells Susanna that the Indians here at Gemeinschaft are very good at what she calls the healing arts. She calls the Indians "our natives."

"You must try the sweat hut," she says. "It is quite cleansing."

Beatrice says, "Thank you, Sister Consolation. In fact, Sister Johanna is meeting us there now. Thank you."

Susanna looks at her sister in surprise. She sounds like a pup-py. This is a new Beatrice: subservient, a little in awe. No sign of the know-it-all. Susanna has to admit that Consolation is a formi-dable woman: beautiful, taller than either of them, and she does not smile even in greeting. She is wearing a dark shawl, and when she turns away Susanna can see small shards of mirrors sewn into the cloth, the largest the size of a deer hoof. There are a dozen or more of them glittering in the sunlight. Why has Consolation sewn them onto her shawl? Like the Amish, the Moravians do not believe in vain ornaments.

"They serve as a reminder," Beatrice tells her as they start down one of the many paths crisscrossing the wooded village.

"A reminder of what?"

"We must put our vanity behind us," Beatrice says, and gives Susanna a significant look.

As they walk down the winding dirt paths, all of them shaded by heavy overhanging trees, Beatrice points out various buildings: the kitchens, the washing huts, and the two-story dormitory where the single men sleep, called a choir. All the structures are made from the same rough lumber and have bark roofs the color of barn owls. The sweat huts sit in a clearing near the flax fields: two low domed structures covered in skins. As they get closer Susanna can smell boiling roots and tree bark. Two men are tending a huge kettle over an outside fire and Sister Johanna is standing nearby with three small iron kettles at her feet.

She gives Susanna one of the kettles and smiles. Her manner seems to say, You will enjoy this and I will too. She has a wide mouth and round cheekbones and her teeth are very white. Susanna likes her. She is as good-looking as Sister Consolation but in an opposite way—dark where Consolation is fair, and expressive where Consolation is frozenly refined.

The men ladle the boiling root water into their kettles. Then they shout, *"Pimook!"* Go to sweat! Two other men are heating rocks the size of turnips, which they carry in hide slings into the sweat huts. When everything is ready, Johanna leads the way into the women's hut. The doorway is low, a covering of deerskin, and inside Susanna looks around. Under the pungent skin walls a complicated structure of willow branches makes up the frame.

Benches circle the walls and the hot stones are in the middle. Although there is room for six or seven women to sit, at the moment they are the only ones there.

"Women partake of the sweating much less than men," Johanna is saying.

"Why is that?" Beatrice asks.

"Men have more ailments." Johanna smiles. "Or so they think."

She tips water from her kettle onto the mound of hot rocks. Immediately a spray of steam shoots up and fills the little room. Some of the steam escapes through a hole in the roof.

"Oh," Susanna says, her face suddenly flushed. "That feels good." A moment later: "You know who would like this? Naomi."

Beatrice frowns, looks down at the ground, and touches her hip. Susanna immediately feels bad for bringing up a painful memory and she casts around for a new subject.

"Your English is very good," she says to Johanna.

"I've lived with the brethren for most of my life," Johanna tells her. "First in Pennsylvania, and now here." She tells Susanna about the natives who live in the village, mostly Delaware but a fair number of Shawnee like herself, and also some Huron and Chippewa. Any native who wants to adopt this life can live here.

"We clothe them, we give them food, we teach English to their children, but they must give up their weapons and finery. We value what is simple and plain."

"Yes, I can see that," Susanna says. Personally she thinks that the buildings are plain to the point of ugliness, and the dresses unbecoming. Johanna pours more water over the hot rocks. Susanna can feel her hair stick to her forehead. But she doesn't mind heat, it is mud she dislikes.

"You know, Beet," she says, "Seth Spendlove traveled with me here. I wonder if he might escort us back to Severne."

"Seth Spendlove—here?"

"Maybe he can hire some horses from the brethren, a cart." Susanna looks down at the steaming rocks. If Seth can hire a cart they could ride in it following the Blanchard River, which meets up with the track to Severne. But if that's not possible, they can walk. The journey would take only, what, a day and a half? Two days? Two days, that's not so bad. But just as this plan is solidifying in her mind she becomes aware that Beatrice is proposing a different plan altogether, a plan with the words *brethren* and *Christians* and *Indians* and *work*. Above all, the word *work* seems to hang in the air.

"They live in simplicity, they deny themselves many conveniences, but in this way they achieve a state of communal feeling," Beatrice is saying. "A new kind of family. You consider yourselves one family, isn't that true, Sister Johanna?"

"Yes, we call each other brother and sister."

Susanna is slow to catch up. "You want to stay here longer?"

"We can do good work here."

"But our store..." Susanna still feels behind.

"We'll sell it to Amos Spendlove. He's always wanted it." Beatrice's voice rises in a familiar way—she's just had a good idea! "And now you tell me Seth is here—so easy, we just send along a letter with him! Think of it, Susanna, we can work here together running the brethren's store, seeing to trade and supplies, ordering whatever is needed from Cincinnati. You always liked that."

"You're wrong. I never cared for ordering. And besides, we're not missionaries."

"Well of course right now I'm just a ghost, like you, but in time..."

"A ghost?"

"A guest. In time we will feel more comfortable, we'll accustom ourselves to their ways. In fact, I can already..."

Susanna has caught up at last. "You *want* this life! You want to be part of this...this *experiment!*" For what else is it? Educating Indians, teaching their children English and stories from the Bible. No white settler outside this little enclave believes it will last. The farmers laughed, in fact, some of them, when they first heard the idea. Of course, Susanna reminds herself, the farmers are fools. She is conscious that Johanna is looking at her.

"If Penelope were here..." she begins.

"Penelope!" Beatrice's face is very red. "Penelope! There's no Penelope, Susanna, there's only us."

Of course: only us. But what can Susanna say to that? In all likelihood Beatrice would not have chosen Susanna out of all their sisters as a companion, but here they are.

"What happened, Beet?" She can't help asking. She feels certain there is something that Beatrice is not telling her. "Please tell me what happened."

Beatrice stiffens. "I already told you. They were killed. They weren't saved, and I was. Don't you see, I can't just return to Severne. I have to give something back."

"You have to give back your life?"

"No. I don't know. All I know is that I can't just go home."

Noises come from outside the hut, and then a man calls in to them.

"They are here to change the rocks," Johanna says. "Do you wish to stay longer?"

Susanna stands up, more than ready to go. She is confused and concerned and solicitous all at once. Also annoyed. She feels sure that Beatrice is protecting her from something, but she doesn't need protecting. Beatrice suddenly looks at Susanna's feet.

"Why are you wearing those moccasins?" she asks sharply.

"They're comfortable. And I think of Aurelia when I wear them."

"Susanna, that's morbid. When we get back to the Birthing Hut you must take them off. Surely we can find you new boots."

"I don't want new boots."

"How can you wear them knowing what happened?"

Susanna looks down. She can imagine one of the brethren thinking that she is, like them, adopting Indian ways on principle. But she isn't principled. She doesn't want to be equal with anyone. She just likes how the moccasins feel.

Nine

Brother Graves says, "Mr. Spendlove, if you are done there, I was hoping I might talk to you about the iron trade. We've had quite a time of it lately with some merchants from Detroit."

Seth is crossing the barn floor on his way outside. The smell of dry hay, tied into bales and stacked on either side, surrounds him. There are a few pieces of farming machinery in the corner near a long trestle table, where just a few minutes ago Seth was seated mending an iron jacklight for Brother Lyle, who likes to go eel fishing at night. The horses, stabled underneath—the barn is partially dug out of the ground and the horses are in the lower level—have just been fed, and Seth can hear the smacking of their huge lips. Through a chute in the floor he sees a bay mare with her nose in a feed bucket.

"Shall we walk together to the chapel?" Brother Graves asks. Although he isn't actually smiling, he looks, to Seth, as though he might as well be, so gentle are the lines of his face. "The midday service begins shortly. Perhaps you would like to attend with me."

Although this is not really what Seth has in mind on such a beautiful, fresh morning, it occurs to him that chapel is the one place where he might see Susanna, since both women and men are allowed to attend any service. He has not seen her since he helped her off his horse two weeks ago, and has had no way to communi-

cate with her. In Gemeinschaft single men and women are not allowed to meet or even exchange letters.

"I'd be glad to," he says.

They walk out together through the wide barn doors and into
the daylight. A copper-colored horse blanket is hanging on a
fence post to dry, and the flies are very interested in that. Seth
walks beside Brother Graves while he talks about the cost of iron
goods, the labor involved in making them. In Seth's opinion, could
the brethren import raw materials and begin to forge their own?

Seth is glad to offer his advice. He has been here for a fortnight, and even to himself he has to admit that he is dawdling with
no set purpose. He has done virtually nothing to earn his keep except help out in the stable or mend bits of equipment.

As they pass a rosemary bush Brother Graves pulls off some
needles and holds them up to his nose. An unlikely sensualist,
Seth thinks.

"The country here is beautiful," Brother Graves says. "As the
years go on I find myself more and more unwilling to leave, even
just to buy supplies."

"Some think the land too flat."

"But the trees give it depth, don't you agree?"

Seth can smell a pervasive scent of cut green wood and he
watches a thin plume of smoke rise above the trees. Although he
too likes this country, he would not choose Gemeinschaft as a
place to live. Ohio, yes, but not this place. Something about it sits
uneasily with him. Perhaps it is all the mission Indians dressed
like Europeans and carrying around Bibles, their little daughters
wearing white aprons. Or is he just being closed-minded? Back in
Severne most of the farmers distrust Christian Indians, even Old
Adam who has lived among them for years. Equally so they distrust the missionaries. Well, they do not have complicated opin-

ions, those farmers. Whites should be whites. Indians should move elsewhere. Small wonder that Amos hid his Potawatomi blood from them.

At a pause in their conversation Seth says, "I have been meaning to ask you about Susanna Quiner. Is she well? And her sister? I would like to offer them my services back to Severne but I don't know how I might approach them."

Brother Graves assures him that they are both well. They are working hard and going to services. He does not say where they are working. He rubs the bit of rosemary between his fingers again and then lets it drop on the path. "Do they wish to leave?" he asks.

That gives Seth pause. "I assumed..." He stops. He does not want to insult his host.

"And you—you wish to leave us also? We could use someone with your talents in our little community. Our door, as you know, is open to everyone. But I would in particular like to welcome you in."

They are in need of more blacksmiths. Seth understood this after only a few days. Brother Lyle, who performs that job now, has not been well trained. "Thank you. But I'm not sure I'm enough of—a good enough—Christian." He is trying to imply that he rarely goes to church.

But Brother Graves says lightly, "Your heritage means nothing to us. Your heart is what matters. If you allow me to be blunt, your bloodline makes you even more interesting to me. I know your story would attract others if they knew it. I would like to know your story myself."

Seth stops walking and looks at Brother Graves in surprise. He knows about me? He's guessed? Above them the sky darkens as a fat crepuscular cloud drifts over the sun. Of course, as a missionary Brother Graves would have seen Indians from all different tribes, mixed and otherwise. Still, Seth feels caught and exposed.

Brother Graves smiles. He offers Seth his arm. "Come, here we are." The chapel is just ahead of them now. Brother Graves says hello to a group of Delaware men waiting by the steps, addressing each one by name, and then opens the heavy door to let Seth walk in first.

"An Ottawa will be giving his testimony today," he says as they go inside. "I think you will find his story compelling."

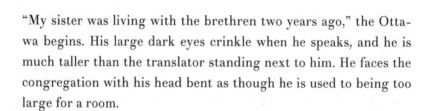

"My sister was living with the brethren two years ago," the Ottawa begins. His large dark eyes crinkle when he speaks, and he is much taller than the translator standing next to him. He faces the congregation with his head bent as though he is used to being too large for a room.

"She wished very much to be in the church, but her husband, not. So she went back with him to his people in the north. Last spring when she fell ill she begged her husband and his mother to send a message to the brethren to pray for her. This was promised but not done. I was present at her death, and the broken promise pressed itself upon my heart. After much thinking I resolved to make myself free of every thing and to come to the brethren myself. I gave to my mother all my silver ornaments and I released my weapons at the gate. When she was dying my sister told me that the blood of Jesus Christ would save her. As she was saved, so do I wish also to be saved in his blood."

Seth shifts restlessly on the bench, still uneasy from his conversation with Brother Graves. Susanna is not here, she is not sitting with the women on the other side of the chapel. He finds himself looking around for anyone with Potawatomi blood while the Ottawa continues talking about his guilt over the broken promise, even though it was not his own. This, at least, is something Seth understands—the feeling, rational or not, of being responsible for something someone else has done. For what his father has done. The chapel darkens as the sky changes itself into a mass of storm clouds, and a short while later the rain begins. Seth looks around at the native men with no axes or knives tucked into their belts. Giving up their weapons is a potent symbol.

"I met with no happiness," the Ottawa is saying, "only unrest, until I came to this place."

After the service most of the congregation stay in the little chapel waiting for the storm to pass, but Seth goes out to stand on the narrow front porch to watch it. The tree branches shake with the wind, and then the wind shifts and a spray of hard rain hits him full on the face. As he turns, he notices a few women sheltering beneath a nearby oak. One woman wearing a hooded cape is picking up an object from the ground. A few strands of dark red hair escape from her hood.

He runs out holding his hat, his coat flapping open. By the time he gets to the oak tree his shirt is drenched. He says, smiling, "The last time I saw you, you were the one soaking wet." He has to raise his voice to be heard over the rain.

Susanna turns around with a look of surprise. "Seth! I thought you'd left."

Her face is pale but alive with thought and feeling, not cloaked like so many other women here. She holds an acorn in her hand. "My Aunt Ogg always kept one on her mantelpiece in Philadelphia, she said it protected the house against lightning. I've been debating whether to take this to the Sisters' Choir or hope the wretched building is struck. Have you seen it? Awful place. We sleep on the floor on blankets."

The rain suddenly comes down much stronger, emptying itself in a rush. They both look up. For a moment the sound is deafening. A swift cool wind blows against them and moves the tree branches as if pointing the way out.

"There, that will finish it," Seth says when the sound dies.

"Do you think?"

"In a moment."

Sure enough, the rain lightens and then stops altogether. Susanna and Seth step out from under the dripping tree. The other two women peer up at the oyster-colored sky and stay put.

As they walk down the path together, Susanna tells him that she'd been living in the Birthing Hut with Beatrice but they had to move out a few days ago when a woman went into labor. Now she sleeps with twenty other unmarried women in one room. During the day she works at the brethren's store, mostly taking inventory. It is very dull, she tells him. She looks at him from time to time with a frank expression. There is something of a bird about her, he thinks, maybe her liveliness. The coarse missionary dress doesn't suit her, it is too confining and dull. Blown leaves litter the path in front of them and a fresh scent rises from the earth. Usually there would be pairs of Indian women along here gathering up the green nuts they use for tea, but the storm has driven everyone to shelter. They are alone. He wants to touch her.

"My father was not a churchgoer," Susanna is saying. "He used to say that ever since Reverend Luther nailed his 95 theses to the church door we need not be dependent on anyone to act as a liaison between ourselves and God. I don't know if he ever spoke to you on the subject. He could be quite...what is the word..."

"Persuasive?"

"Lengthy." She smiles. A lock of hair has fallen over her face. He has the urge to tuck it back behind her ear. "I'm like him, talking so much. But it is so good to see someone from home!"

His heart twists but he tries not to give her words any more weight than they ostensibly have. "What are your plans for going back?" he asks.

Her pleased expression fades and she looks away. "The trouble is," she begins, and stops.

He says, "Because I would be happy to accompany you and your sister when you decide to leave. It would be my pleasure."

"Our plans are a little uncertain," she says. She still doesn't look at him. "It is very kind of you to offer, but we may, or at least Beatrice, she wants to stay for a while."

"Stay *here?*"

"She thinks our sisters have been...Penelope and Naomi...she saw them...well, I don't know what she saw. But they are dead."

"Susanna." He stops walking and turns to her. Without thinking he takes her two hands in his own. "I am so very sorry."

She doesn't pull away. Her eyes are wet. "And now it's only the two of us, Beatrice and myself, and in thinking of our future..."

"Sister Susanna! Brother Spendlove!"

He turns to see a tall, fair woman walking quickly up the path toward them. He doesn't recognize her. How does she know his name?

"Sister Consolation," Susanna says. A stubborn look crosses her face.

"I am surprised," Consolation says when she reaches them. "I am deeply surprised. Brother Spendlove, here you see is a crossing path, which you may take. I'm sure you know that we do not permit unmarried women and men to walk together."

He feels his face grow warm. He bows. "My apologies."

Consolation lifts her dark shawl slightly and resettles it. A dismissive gesture, she does not want apologies. She takes Susanna by the arm and turns her away.

There is nothing he can do but obey. But a moment later when he looks back he notices the mirrors sewn into Consolation's shawl. He wonders about that. Gemeinschaft has its own stories and you have to learn how to read them: white men sleep in the same buildings as natives because we are all one family. Ottawas forsake their weapons because only Christ's blood will protect them. But shards of mirror on a shawl? Seth cannot read the story behind that. He is disappointed that he's let this chance slip away from him, although he does not know exactly what he wanted, unless it was just to see her and try to take her home.

❦

The next day Consolation stops Susanna as she is walking to the store with Beatrice.

"Today I would like your help, my dear, someplace else," Consolation tells her. She smiles without pleasure, as if proud of her ability to be nice to people she does not particularly like. To Beatrice she says, "Will you cut me six yards of new linen? I'll come by for it later today."

Above them a thin layer of clouds drifts across the sky like a web. Susanna follows her with some curiosity. Where are they going? She wants to ask but something in Consolation's manner stops her. She is walking a step or two ahead of Susanna as if that's her rightful place; forgetting, Susanna thinks, that in this settlement we are equals. When the sun pierces through the cloud cover, the mirrors on Consolation's shawl throw out quick shafts of light like spears.

"You are looking at my shawl," Consolation says. "Perhaps you wonder why I took such trouble over it?"

"The mirrors are very pretty," Susanna says.

"Well of course I did not sew them on for the looks of it. Quite the opposite." She smiles a hard, satisfied smile. Susanna can see that Consolation is the type of woman who enjoys leading you into the warm, lovely room of her words and then, once there, dousing you with cold water.

"One day a poor Miami wanted a mirror that I had with me. We had just arrived here, myself and my late husband Jeriah and Brother Graves and a handful of Delaware Indians from our old settlement in Pennsylvania. We were negotiating something, I don't remember what, and the man saw the mirror in one of our wagons. The mirror had been made by my grandfather, but I realize now I should not have brought it with me. The desire for such objects should be resisted."

Consolation would not give the Miami the mirror but offered him instead a bag of seed corn, much more useful. To her horror he turned the bag upside down in disgust and spilled the seed on the ground. Later that night he came back and tried to steal the mirror but it broke.

"These pieces are remnants," Consolation says, resettling the shawl on her shoulders. "A lesson in vanity. And a reminder that we can never truly see ourselves if we look from the outside."

Again that hard, self-satisfied tone. Susanna has the urge to remind Consolation that she is not her pupil. She is tired of lessons, and in fact sympathizes with the Miami, who just wanted something beautiful to hold.

"Nor can anyone else truly see another just by looking at his face," she says.

"True, my dear, true. Our actions tell our character much more potently than our looks. Self-will, vanity, a disrespect for our elders and the rules they live by—these speak of a limited person, I fear." She gives Susanna a meaningful look.

Susanna's face flushes with annoyance. She spent five minutes talking with an unmarried man, a friend of hers from home. That means she's self-willed and vain and disrespectful? Anyway, why should she take moral counsel from a woman who clearly has had every advantage in life? A beautiful, tall, wealthy woman—there is obviously wealth in her past—who wishes, as if these advantages are not enough, to be thought of as morally superior as well.

"We can also be limited by a lack of empathy for those undergoing hardship," Susanna replies. She is thinking about her own losses but Consolation says, "Ah, the natives, it is true, we feel for them, hard though it might be to understand why they cling to their difficult ways. And now here we are, my dear. The tannery."

They've come to the end of the path, where a small cabin stands by itself. The tannery? To Susanna it looks more like a potting shed than anything else. It is surrounded by dry, partially denuded elderberry bushes and has but one tiny window and a sloping door. No one else is around. They are at the very limits of the Gemeinschaft land, half forsaken and overgrown.

"But I don't know anything about tanning hides," Susanna says. She feels that nothing will induce her to go into that dark, dismal shed. "I'm better with figures."

"Oh, the girl inside will show you. Unless you want to help prepare the lower fields instead? Some native women are out there now. You can bring water to them, if you don't want to hoe."

Bring water to Indians? Or *hoe?* Susanna looks miserably at Consolation, who meets her gaze without wavering.

"We must put our vanity behind us, my dear," Consolation says. She smiles her hard smile. "It only gets in our way."

※

Inside the tannery a native girl stands at a long trestle table with her back to the door. She is looking at a lumpy hide folded unevenly in thirds. On one side of the table are two large mud-colored barrels and a narrow cask of water, and on the other side is a mangle. A couple of stools have been pushed out of the way.

"Two Seneca scraped off the flesh on this one," the girl says in English without turning around. She pushes it aside. "They did a most miserable job."

The smell of rotting meat is terrible. Susanna puts her hand over her nose and breathes through her mouth. "I've been told to help you," she says through her fingers.

The girl whirls around. She looks familiar. For a moment they stare at each other.

"What happened to the other girl?" she asks Susanna. She is young, maybe twelve or thirteen, and stands firmly with her two legs spread like a warrior. Now Susanna recognizes her: it is the girl who came to the Birthing Hut with the woman in labor, when she and Beatrice had to move out. The pregnant woman was Delaware, and Consolation called this girl her daughter. But anyone could see they were not from the same tribe. They'd arrived in Gemeinschaft only a few hours before the woman's labor began, although Consolation said they'd lived here for many years on and off. She called the young girl Miriam.

Susanna holds out her hand. "My name is Susanna."

But the girl says nothing and does not take her hand. Susanna tries again.

"*Ndeluwensi* Susanna," she says in Delaware. In English she says, "What is your real name? Not Miriam, I shouldn't think."

But the girl just makes a sound with her tongue indicating that she does not deem the question worth answering. With two hands she lifts the heavy lid off of one of the barrels that stands by the table, by far the largest barrel that Susanna has ever seen. Floating inside is a length of deerskin. Also something else, a misshapen ball of—what?

"What is that?" Susanna asks. The girl does not answer. "*Keku hech?*" Susanna repeats.

The girl looks down into the barrel. "Horse brain," she says in English.

Susanna takes a step back. "How long does it stay there?"

"Until the next horse dies."

Squinting her eyes half closed—she does not want to look into the water again—Susanna helps the girl lift the wet deerskin from the barrel. Together they carry it two steps to the mangle, where they thread it through again and again trying to wring out as much water as possible. It is heavy, wet work. In no time the front of Susanna's dress is soaked and water drips onto her moccasins. When they have wrung out as much water as they can, they lift the skin onto the table, stretch it taut, and nail it down. Then for the rest of the day they take turns pushing and stretching the skin with a heavy canoe paddle, working its surface in long strokes as it dries.

At every step the girl Miriam explains what they need to do with such a heavy tone of distaste it is as if she believes Susanna has brought on all of her troubles, whatever they are. She has a wide, young face and pale skin. Her dark eyes have the look of someone constantly reassessing everything around her. She is strong for someone so young, but Susanna is strong too from all the years working at their store, unloading goods, pushing barrels, and lugging furs from the counter to the shelves.

Miriam says, "I suppose it was Sister Consolation who directed you here." She looks into Susanna's eyes. "I do not like Sister Consolation." A challenge.

Susanna says, "Nor do I."

That surprises the girl. She looks like she might say something else but then closes her lips tightly. There is something about her that reminds Susanna of her younger sister Lilith, the stubbornness perhaps, and she decides on this basis, a whim, that she will make this girl her friend. She has never tried to make a friend before, having no need in Severne. Her sisters were her companions. But here it is different. Beatrice will only speak of the brethren and their work, and has recently taken it upon herself to learn more of their doctrine, which she repeats to Susanna with none of the storytelling skills of Penelope. Although Susanna can sometimes induce Sister Johanna to talk about her past or her people or the news of the village, the conversation inevitably leads back to missionary work, and the same is true with just about every other woman Susanna has tried to converse with, most of whom speak limited English anyway. The few white women are mostly married. Sister Louisa, a single white woman about Susanna's age, is so conscious of trying to be humble that she cannot form a sentence without six or seven qualifiers ("It is my small and perhaps erroneous opinion and if I am wrong please do me the honor to correct me..."), and her strong overbite tends to make her spit when she speaks. The only other white woman near her age, Sister Pauline, is busy embroidering a crazy patchwork of Bible quotations onto her blanket, none of them straight across but jutting up and down as she suddenly runs out of room, and she answers any question put to her with something from scripture.

Susanna is lonely, she knows she is lonely, and she also knows it is wicked to be lonely considering the fate of her other sisters. She is the lucky one. But she wishes she had someone to talk to who didn't only want to talk about opening Indian hearts and how Jesus most gruesomely died for us all.

When the chapel bell rings, the girl says, "They are calling the afternoon service. You may go if you like."

"I don't care for the services," Susanna says. "But if you want to go..."

"I am not a Christian," Miriam tells her proudly.

"All right." Susanna gives her the paddle. Miriam says, "Anyway, they make me go to the children's service."

"The children's service! But you look as old as my sister Lilith, and she is nearly sixteen!" The girl is not more than thirteen, Susanna guesses, but the comment clearly pleases her. Susanna takes the dipper from a nail above the water cask and takes a drink. Then she fills the dipper again and hands it to Miriam. While Miriam is drinking, Susanna takes up the canoe paddle even though it is not her turn. She does not like to work but she likes to impress people. That's one way to make friends, she thinks.

They pound the skin until Susanna's arms begin to ache and then a long time after that, too. But she keeps working as hard as the girl, and every time she gets herself a drink of water she gets her one, too. The skin begins to look as pitted and worn as an old man's face, still far from the smooth buttery touch Susanna knows from the tanned hides coming into her father's store. They keep at it, and Susanna finds herself comparing her work to the girl's. She tries a different technique with the paddle, pushing her weight into it. She stands the way the girl stands with one leg in front of the other like a man pushing a cow into a pen.

"Are you not a Moravian?" the girl asks finally. "One of the missionaries?"

"No."

"Then why are you here?"

Susanna leans her weight into the paddle. "My sister is here."

The girl nods as if this is something she can understand: following your family. Even to a place like this where everything—the buildings, the services, the clothes—is made to be as stark and useful as possible. There is no beauty anywhere. Susanna wonders what Naomi would have thought of Gemeinschaft. The brethren do not believe in music outside of chapel; even humming is discouraged.

When at last the dinner bell sounds, the girl takes off her apron and hangs it on a nail. She strokes the edge of the pounded skin with her forefinger to check for stray hairs. Then she turns to look at Susanna.

"My name is Meera," she says.

Ten

Later, when Susanna tries to count up the days she and Meera worked together at the tannery, the time seems impossibly short. Two weeks? Three? It seemed like several months at least. She can easily recall the smell of wet animal skin, the humid heat, the low bark ceiling—she remembers all of these things, but not the exact sequence of days. She remembers the shape of the rock they used to prop the door open, and the flies that perpetually hovered over the barrels. Also the way the dirt on the floor ribboned in the corners after it was swept, like rippled fabric.

While they work, they talk. Meera is fascinated that Susanna once lived in Philadelphia. She has never been to Philadelphia, nor any English town, as she calls it. Was it very crowded?

Oh yes, Susanna tells her, there might be two or three dozen buildings between here and the Bell House. In truth she does not remember very much, she was so young when they left.

"Every woman owns at least three dresses. There is a henhouse in every yard."

"And your sister who lives there still. She is not married? Your aunt must be rich."

"No. Her husband owned a glove shop. They adopted Lilith because they had no children of their own. Now that my uncle has died, my Aunt Ogg and Lilith run the shop together."

She does not tell Meera about her other sisters. In her stories she mentions only the three of them: Beatrice, Susanna, and Lilith. Be Seldom Late. She reasons to herself that, being a native, Meera would not like to hear about what happened to the others. In truth, however, that story isn't one she knows how to tell. She doesn't want to tell it.

"So your sister Lilith is a servant to your aunt?" Meera asks.

"Oh no! My aunt loves her. They are family."

This makes Meera fall silent. For a while she strikes the skin with the paddle particularly hard. Meera, like Lilith, was also adopted. As Susanna suspected, the woman in the Birthing Hut is no blood relation. Meera was given to her as a very small child when Meera's tribe fell in battle to the woman's tribe. Nushemakw, the woman's name is. All this Susanna learns slowly, by degrees.

Meera was given to Nushemakw to replace Nushemakw's baby, who'd recently died. Since that time Nushemakw has given birth five more times—four sons and a daughter. None of the babies lived. If they had lived Nushemakw would have given Meera to another woman, or worse, left Meera behind somewhere to starve. This is what Nushemakw often threatens, Meera tells Susanna, when Meera displeases her. They come to Gemeinschaft every year for a few months pretending to convert but really, Meera says, for the food.

But when Nushemakw became pregnant again last hunting season she had a vision: her baby would live if it were born in Gemeinschaft. And indeed the infant—a small, yellowish, wrinkly boy—is somehow yet living.

"Now will she stay here for good?" Susanna asks.

Meera shakes her head. "She is from the Turtle tribe, content with neither land nor sea, always moving from one to the other.

Consolation told me that I can stay without Nushemakw if I wish. I am old enough now. But I must accept Jesus Christ as the Great Spirit." She lifts her shoulders as if to say: impossible.

"What will you do?"

Meera puts down the paddle and goes over to the cask for a drink. Her hands, Susanna notices, are small and pretty. She likes Meera. She is tough, like a Quiner woman. She works hard and she doesn't feel sorry for herself. At the same time she won't let someone else tell her what she should do with her life. It occurs to Susanna that they are in the same situation: living with the missionaries, dependent on them, but not believing in their cause.

"I have my own plans," Meera says, hanging the dipper back on its nail. But she does not elaborate.

Beatrice, standing in the doorway of the small Gemeinschaft general store, is watching a group of native women settling themselves beneath a drooping willow tree. One of the women unrolls a horse blanket to sit on while the others take reddish-brown roots from their baskets and begin to cut them into pieces. Their faces are dappled in shadow and light, and the trees around them spread curtains of fresh, green leaves.

Gemeinschaft is beautiful, Beatrice thinks, like a forest village in a fairytale. Not everyone can see its beauty, however. Susanna, for instance. She complains almost daily about how ugly and *useful* everything is. She says the word "useful" with a tone that implies there is nothing worse. A breeze makes its way into the store and Beatrice leans back on her heels. She has not had a chilblain for over a month. *When comforts flee, abide with me,* she chants to herself automatically.

"They harvest the roots from the stream behind the Birthing Hut."

Beatrice turns to see Brother Graves approaching from the other direction and she feels herself blush. How long has she been standing in the doorway, doing nothing?

"After they dry them out, the women will pound them and then bake them into bread. Some years this is their principal food. When the hunting is bad." He is smiling and has his hands clasped behind his coat like a scholar. Beatrice moves to let him inside.

"Have you ever tasted the bread?" she asks.

"I have tasted it, yes. Surprisingly filling. Not meat of course, but surprisingly filling."

He takes from the pocket of his coat a handful of fresh quills and places them on the smooth wooden counter.

"Brother Edwards and I did a bit of hunting this morning," he explains. "I came out rather well." He spreads the quills slightly with his fingers, picks out two of the best ones, and lays them aside. "I thought I would donate them to the store. What do you think, can you cut them into nibs? Or perhaps you can do the soaking and I will cut."

"Oh, I've cut many a quill for my father," Beatrice tells him. Back in Severne they kept a small knife wickedly sharp for just this purpose, never using it to cut anything else. That was the secret, Sirus always said. He had many secrets but none that he would not share in a moment, asked or otherwise.

Brother Graves sits down on the closed lid of the pounded-metal woodbox, and while Beatrice sets out a pan to soak the quills he tells her the news. They've decided to clear another plot of land for a weaving house, they've hit upon a new method for jarring honey, and a group of Menemoni arrived yesterday with two infected dogs, which had to be shot. Very unfortunate, he says, but they could not risk the dogs infecting the cattle. His eyes are soft and sympathetic. She thinks of riding behind him on his horse, when he took her away from her Potawatomi captors. She hung on to his jacket at first, before she gave in and put her arms around him. She rested her head against his back. In all her life she'd never been so tired. Part of her wanted to fall off the horse and be trampled, but she hung on.

"I also met with Seth Spendlove recently," he tells her. "He asked me to enquire if you would like him to accompany you back to Severne. As your escort."

He looks at Beatrice steadily, and she allows herself to stare for a moment into his gray-blue eyes. For some reason his eyes make her think of a deer looking down into water. "At the moment we have no wish to depart. That is, if we are not an imposition?"

"You are welcome here as long as you like. I am glad to hear that you'd like to stay."

She smiles at him, she cannot help it, and Brother Graves smiles back. His dark hair is flecked with gray. She notices fine lines where his jaw meets his ear. He lost his wife in a fire, Sister Johanna told her, in the previous settlement in Pennsylvania. One of the reasons he came here was to make a fresh start.

"You are very helpful to us," he says. "Very useful. And we like seeing you at our services."

She notices he has switched from I to we. Of course, that is proper.

"I hope I am useful," she tells him. "I like hard work. I wish I could do more."

"That is gratifying. That is certainly gratifying." He looks at his boots and says nothing more for a moment. Then he begins, "If you are in earnest, I might suggest...it is up to you, of course. But a group of Chippewa are coming next week to parley. Sister

Consolation suggested it might be beneficial if a few white women were on hand to serve them. A gesture of good will."

Beatrice waits. Is this all? He looks at her.

"Of course," he says, "with your recent troubles I would understand if..."

She feels a flush wash over her. So that's it. Her recent troubles. And yet she can't help but feel as though she's been made worthier by his petition. Someone useful: isn't that what she wants to be? Beatrice looks out the open door to the native women under the willow tree. As Brother Graves predicted, they are now laying the cut roots on a blanket to dry. A light seems to be spreading behind her eyes; not one of her headaches, but a warm, feathery feeling. She makes herself think of Naomi. She sees the back of her dress, her untidy braid, but from a distance. To redeem others, Brother Graves likes to say in his sermons, is to be redeemed.

"I would be honored to help," she tells him. "What you do here is more important, I should think, than the single events in a family."

A week later Seth Spendlove finds himself standing with broomcorn up to his knees under a cluster of beech trees just off the path near the tannery. Hiding, really, though he calls it waiting. The sun shines hotly through a break in the canopy and the air is filled with the low, constant thrum of insects. As they swarm closer, drawn to his heat, a passage of Milton's comes into his mind:

> What dost thou in this world? the wilderness
> For thee is fittest place...

What words follow he cannot immediately recall. In Virginia, briefly, Amos let him go to school. He memorized all that he could, knowing it would be temporary. Seth scratches his neck and tugs on his shirt collar. Everything feels tight today. All the food here has plumped him out. The honey and hominy he ate this morning, and last night the squirrel stew and biscuits. Can it be that he has even grown a quarter of an inch? Surely he is past that, but the village seems to live by rules of its own, as if enchanted. All of his clothes feel uncomfortably small.

Twice in the past few weeks he has packed his things and arranged for his horse to be brought to him early so he could set out for Severne at daybreak, and twice he has changed his mind. He continues to carry out favors for the brethren that keep him from feeling he is living on their charity. Last week, with Brother Graves, he met with traders from Detroit and bargained a very good deal for a nearly new anvil. Brother Lyle was pleased when it was delivered, and even more pleased when Seth showed him a new forging technique. He has been Seth's most constant companion. It is he who mentioned that Sister Susanna is now working at the tannery.

Seth keeps his eyes on the little shed, pulling back slightly as two Menemoni brethren come down the path with four sheep at their heels, mangy little creatures that resemble long gray rats more than anything else. At any moment the bell calling the sisters to their dinner should ring. He moves his hand to check his pocket watch and receives for his effort a long scratch on his arm from a dangling branch.

At last the bell sounds. He feels foolish standing there among the bracken. Also something like despair. He cannot see his way round to getting what he wants but he will try anyway. Now it comes back:

> What dost thou in this world? the wilderness
> For thee is fittest place; I found thee there,
> And thither will return thee...

But that is the wrong sentiment entirely. What he wants is to take Susanna back to Severne, which is even less like a wilderness than Gemeinschaft, notwithstanding its smaller population.

Finally he sees Susanna leaving the tannery with a stocky native girl. A band of her dark red hair peeks out from beneath her bleached cap and glitters in the sun. Seth steps onto the path.

"Susanna, excuse me, may I have a word?" He hopes she will not remind him that they have already been reprimanded for talking together. But she seems pleased to see him.

The native girl looks at Susanna and Susanna says, "It's all right, I'll catch you up."

Seth leads her to a fallen log back behind some dark spreading ferns, and they sit there under the shadow of the beech trees, hidden from the path. He tries to think where to begin. More as a delay than anything else, he says, "You are working at the tannery now?"

"Yes, with Meera, the girl there. Her English is very good. She has lived here off and on since she was four..." She trails off and looks at him, waiting. His heart gives a little twist.

"Susanna," he says. He clears his throat. He thinks maybe it will be easier if he doesn't look at her but he can't bring himself to look away. "Do you remember the money I gave you?"

Her expression changes. "I'm afraid I don't have it—all of it—anymore. I gave it to Brother Graves to pay for...to repay what he gave for Beatrice."

"No, it's not that. I don't want it back. I'm afraid I was not entirely honest with you about it. The money came from the sale of your horses and wagon."

She tilts her head like a bird catching sight of something, not sure what. "But those weren't sold. The Indians took those. The Potawatomi."

"My father instructed me to sell your wagon down at the river that morning. The morning your sisters were taken. That's where I was."

She says, "I don't understand."

"Amos told me that Penelope asked him to sell them. I should have told you right away."

"But Amos told me that the Potawatomi stole them. Why would he say that?"

"I don't know. I wish I did. When I go back, when I see him—Susanna—" He looks down at her hands, which are clenched. He doesn't believe he can give her any kind of promise, knowing his father. Amos will only lie, and then lie some more. There is a rustling noise behind them. One of the brethren, measuring out a new plot? They are always working, these Moravians, always planning and making improvements.

"Susanna, come back with me to Severne," he says in a low, quick voice, afraid that another chance will slip away. "Marry me."

It is not how he planned to say it. He goes on before she can answer: "You needn't work at the tannery here. Let's go back to Severne. I can make us a life." Now he stops abruptly as if the words are coins and those are all he has in his hand. He has forgotten about the ring in his pocket.

"Go back to Severne," Susanna repeats. "And do what? Forge iron?"

"Or tend your father's store. Together, of course. And with Beatrice, too, if she chooses."

A suspicious look crosses her face. "And you would change its name to Spendlove's Store?"

"Of course not," he says quickly.

A rook sounds noisily above them with a mean, well-timed laugh. Susanna keeps looking at Seth's face as if his countenance might answer a question she could not yet form. She says, "But I don't want to return to Severne. I want to go to Philadelphia. I want to live in a city."

Now it is Seth who is surprised. "You want to leave Ohio?"

"Perhaps I am speaking too plainly."

"No, no."

"But if you want to know my true thoughts..."

"Of course," Seth says. "I just didn't realize...perhaps I might...I never thought of anything but Severne, but perhaps..." He stops. After a moment he says, "Susanna, let me think on it. It seems wrong to be hasty on so important a matter."

The sun has moved so that it is no longer shining through the canopy, and the greenery in consequence has darkened. A breeze lingers in the branches above them.

"Yes," Susanna agrees. She stands up, increasing the space between them. "Let us both think."

⁂

"You never came to dinner," Meera says when she returns to the tannery later. "Were you with that man all this time?"

"No. I was just late. And then I decided it was better not to go at all than to be seen coming late. I didn't want to invite any questions."

"What questions?"

"You know how Consolation is."

Susanna continues to pound the skin before her, a fisher, the only animal she knew of that ate porcupine. Its fur never fetched as much as beaver in their store but the skin is a lovely reddish brown color, rather like her own hair in winter.

"Here," Meera says. She hands Susanna a biscuit. Then she sits on a stool and begins plucking the guard hairs off another hide. "At the table all the talk was of the Chippewa chief and his counselors. They arrived a few hours ago, twenty men on twenty horses. Everyone is curious."

"I heard they were coming. My sister and I will be serving them food."

Meera looks up. "That is an honor," she says. Susanna shrugs. Meera says, "What did the man want to talk to you about?"

It takes Susanna a moment to understand that Meera has gone back to the subject of Seth. She puts down her paddle and gets a drink from the dipper. Is the room hotter than usual? She wipes her forehead with the end of her apron and notices that the cloth is not very clean.

"A marriage proposal." She pauses, but Meera just looks at her without changing her expression. "He asked me to marry him."

"I know what a marriage proposal is," Meera says. "What will you do?"

Susanna goes back to the table and begins pounding the fisher skin again.

"Beatrice will not go back to Severne. At least not yet."

"That is her choice."

"Well, it seems wrong to leave her."

At that Meera laughs, and Susanna looks up sharply. "I see no humor in this."

"It is not Beatrice who is holding you back, it is the man from Severne. If you wanted to be his wife you would go."

Is this true, Susanna wonders? When she thinks of Seth alone, without his father, she feels—she doesn't know what. But when she thinks of his father and the horses and wagon, she becomes confused. Aurelia told her that a white man watched them being taken away. But surely she would have recognized Amos Spendlove.

Seth is a good man, Susanna reminds herself, he's not like his father. He doesn't drink and he doesn't lie. But something doesn't sit right. It occurs to her that in all his talk Seth did not mention love. Something pulses in her neck and she puts her hand in her pocket to feel for her turkey hen bone before remembering it is gone. She picks up the paddle again. There are many reasons for marriage, she reminds herself, not just love.

"I ought to talk to my sister," she says.

"You say she does not want to leave."

"Maybe I can change her mind."

For a while they work in silence.

"You must make your own plans," Meera says finally. "Just as I do."

Susanna is late that afternoon returning to the Sisters' Choir, and as she approaches the bark building she sees Beatrice waiting for her in the doorway wearing a scolding expression. In the large downstairs room, all the young women in their missionary dresses are sitting on benches or straight-back chairs knitting or mending and talking in different languages. They are all native except Sister Pauline, who is busily embroidering a new quotation on her blanket and does not look up. She has loops of cotton thread set out before her which she dyes herself, eight different shades of brown.

Susanna and Beatrice go up the narrow stairs to the sleeping room. Even here it is crowded with women lying on blankets on the floor, resting after all their hard work in the fields or kitchens or scutching houses. Susanna splashes water on her face from a basin in the corner. The tepid water smells like minerals and she thinks of her mother, who sometimes put crushed mint leaves in the water to take away the creek smell.

"Your dress is all right but you'll need a clean apron," Beatrice says. She hands her a towel impatiently. All of her sisters are impatient. It is one of their shared traits, like red hair.

Susanna is no exception. When she left Severne she told herself it was because she wanted to do something for her sisters and not just wait for others to do it for her, but maybe, she thinks now, that wasn't really true. Maybe her motives weren't so pure. The truth is, she doesn't want to be alone, and that desire has been behind everything. It's propelled her to where she is now, and she really shouldn't call it anything but what it is, selfish. She decided some weeks ago that she would stay in Gemeinschaft with the hope that something would change—either that Beatrice would come to her senses and leave Gemeinschaft with her, or that she would find some way to live here, too. Both seem equally unlikely. Maybe staying here is her penance for her rash actions. Only she doesn't believe in penance. That's Beatrice's realm.

Beatrice combs out Susanna's hair for her and pins it up. Then she finds a clean cap for her to wear. But a clean apron is more problematic.

"This one has animal blood on both sides," Beatrice complains.

"They all do. I work at a tannery. Beet, did Penelope ask Amos Spendlove to sell Frank and Bess and the wagon?"

"I don't think so. Why would she? Here, you can borrow this one. No, turn it around." She makes a little click with her tongue. "Not much better," she says.

"Seth Spendlove told me today that his father instructed him to sell the horses and wagon down the Blanchard."

"Seth Spendlove is still here?" Beatrice begins to adjust her own cap.

"He asked me to marry him."

"What?" Beatrice lets her hands drop and turns to look at Susanna. Her face is bright red with surprise.

"He wants me to go back to Severne with him."

"What did you answer?"

"What would you have me answer?"

"Susanna, this is your decision."

But Susanna thinks she saw a shift in Beatrice's expression. On impulse she says, "Come back to Severne with me, Beet. Let us both go back. We can run Sirus's store the way you always wanted." Just like that, she is ready to let go of Philadelphia.

But Beatrice doesn't hesitate. "No, I cannot." She touches her nape quickly, feeling for any loose hairs. "We must fly. Consolation and Johanna are waiting for us at the Bell House with the food. We can talk about this later."

Fortunately Johanna is waiting not only with baskets of food, but also with two new aprons, freshly sewn, for them to wear.

"Sister Benigna," Consolation says to Beatrice, "you take the cheese. Sister Susanna, the dried berries and nuts. I'll take this one." When she turns the mirrors on her dark shawl glitter back at them.

"*Benigna?*" Susanna whispers to Beatrice as they follow her. "Why does she call you that?"

"I'll tell you later."

"Tell me now."

Beatrice glances at her. She slows her pace and says in a low voice, "I was going to talk to you about it tonight. I've petitioned to stay here permanently. And my petition was granted."

"What?" Susanna stops walking. "You did that? Without telling me?" She looks at Beatrice's face, which is flushed but also holds a stubborn expression. "Why would you do that?"

"I want to stay here. I told you. Hush now, let's go in. We'll talk about it later."

Johanna is waiting for them, holding open the heavy door to the Meeting House. Inside, the benches that are normally set out in rows in the center of the room have been stacked against the walls, and all the men, white and native, are sitting in a circle on blankets on the floor. It is hot in the room. The fireplace is large enough to roast a horse, and one man is sitting on a stool in front of it, feeding it bark and sticks to keep the flames high.

As soon as Brother Graves sees them he stands up and comes over. He says, "In a little while Pemitschischen, the Chippewa chief, will begin his speech. After he finishes I will say a few words. Then you can begin to distribute the rolls and the meat."

Susanna looks at the visiting Chippewa in the circle, who seem very colorful in their traditional dress, whereas the mission Indians are all dressed like white men. The room is noisy with talk, and it smells strongly of men's bodies mixed with tobacco and smoke from the fire. When Susanna opens her mouth she can feel the smoke on her tongue like a taste.

Consolation and Johanna go off to fill the water pitchers from the large cask near the fireplace, and Susanna takes the opportunity to turn to Beatrice again.

"I thought you wanted to run our store," she says. "You argued so hard for that."

"I believe in the worth of the brethren's mission," Beatrice says in a low voice. Her fervent voice. "There is good work being done here. Just look around you! I want to help."

"But what about me?" Susanna can hear that she sounds like a child. She feels like a child.

"Susanna, people grow up, they marry, they leave home. We can't always be all together. Even if...if none of what happened had happened, we still might not be together. You wanted to go to Philadelphia, and I wanted to stay in Severne. Remember? You might have left, I might have stayed."

Strangely, that never occurred to Susanna. She thought they would all go or stay together. The barren sisters, the sisters who give themselves airs. She doesn't want to live by herself.

Consolation and Johanna return with full pitchers just as a thin, tall Chippewa stands up. Susanna guesses that this is the chief, Pemitschischen. He is wearing many ropes of necklaces and his tunic is embroidered with a beautiful pattern of green leaves edged in blue thread. The young man next to him also stands, and the smoky room becomes quiet.

When Pemitschischen begins to speak, the young man translates his words into English.

"Grandfather," he begins, looking at Brother Graves. "The Chippewa, Tawa, Potawatomi, and Wyandot have charged me to come to you and in their name bring you this message of peace. This string"—he lifts a white string of wampum—"is proof of the agreement among these four nations, and our promise of goodwill to you." He passes the wampum down the line to Brother Graves, who accepts it with a bow of his head.

"Grandfather, you perhaps have heard evil rumors which have caused you and those like you pain and uneasiness. Tonight let me wash your eyes so you can see the truth of what I am saying. Let me make clear your heart so that with your heart you may understand we offer not war but peace, not discord but friendship. We of the four nations stand by your new nation and call your president our king. To this we give you another string as a promise."

He talks for a few minutes, and in spite of her argument with Beatrice Susanna finds herself drawn to his words and to the gentle cadence of his speech, although she does not know what rumors he is talking about. When Pemitschischen finishes, she looks over at Beatrice. Her eyes are shining.

Brother Graves stands to give his own brief thanks to the visiting Chippewa for coming, and then he nods to Consolation. These are only the short speeches before the meal. After they eat the real parley will begin.

"As you serve them," Consolation tells Susanna and Beatrice, "do not look at any man directly. Cast your eyes only upon the food. Now wait until I have served the chief."

She picks up a basket and goes first to Pemitschischen, who selects a piece of dried venison from it. Afterward, Johanna presents to him her basket of rolls, which he waves aside. Susanna and Beatrice start at the other end of the circle.

It is hard not to look at Pemitschischen as she walks around. Even sitting, he is a powerful presence. When she comes to him, he selects two nuts from her basket and for a moment holds them in the open palm of his hand. Then he says to her, in English, "Stay."

Susanna looks at him in surprise. From the corner of her eye she can see Consolation stop and look over.

"You walk in shoes of Potawatomi," Pemitschischen says. "Why is this?"

She has forgotten about Aurelia's moccasins. She looks at Consolation, who stares back at her, for once without a suggestion. Then Susanna looks at Brother Graves. He nods.

"They were my sister's," she answers.

"She lived with Potawatomi?"

"They—she was taken by them. She died by their hand."

Pemitschischen looks at the rough wall behind her as if something small there has caught his attention. Consolation makes a noise and when Susanna looks over she motions with two fingers to the floor. Susanna looks down. Pemitschischen's moccasins have the pointed tip that marks them as Chippewa. Has their discourse ended? But after a moment Pemitschischen does a surprising thing: he takes off one of his necklaces and holds it out to her.

In spite of Consolation Susanna feels that she must look at him, and when she does he is looking straight back at her. His eyes are lined with the fine wrinkles of someone who laughs and enjoys it. He says a few words in Chippewa, and the young man next to him translates: "Accept this gift as a promise of new friendship on this day and all the days to come." Then Pemitschischen places the necklace in her hand. His fingers are warm on hers.

"Thank you," she says, bowing her head. She looks at the necklace. It is very pretty. Small strips of leather strung with white beads hang from the main strand, and in between the strips of leather hang eight bleached bones, polished and creamy, like milk.

A ripple of pleasure mixed with embarrassment runs through her. She wants to say more than thank you but she doesn't know how. She is honored that he has noticed her in this way, and surprised that he would seek to make reparation even though he is not responsible for what happened. He is still watching her, and when she looks at Brother Graves again he signals for her to put on the necklace. It comes down to her last rib.

"*Wanishi*," she says in Delaware. She does not know the word for thanks in Chippewa.

"Well," Consolation says later, when they have finished serving. They've left the men to their speeches and are standing outside the Meeting House. "My dear, how surprising."

Johanna nods. "A great honor was given to you." Carefully she lifts the necklace to look at it more closely. "These little beads are whelk. From the east," she tells them.

"And what are these?" Beatrice asks, touching a bone.

Susanna fingers the necklace. Evening is falling and the air smells of coming rain. Above the village, dark clouds are pushing against one another as though each one wants to claim the same small space. A storm is coming. Maybe more than one.

"Turkey hen bones," she says.

Eleven

After the Chippewa leave it rains for three days without stopping. A heavy wind keeps everyone inside, and it is so dark that even at midmorning candles are needed. Seth stays in the Brethren's Choir contemplating the tedium of seclusion with insufficient tasks. The upstairs room is crowded and smells like sleeping bodies, of which there are many, and the downstairs fireplace smokes. Seth stays downstairs, but on the side of the room farthest from the hearth.

He does what he can, mends his bridle, writes a few letters, but on the third day he can think of no other task and finds himself reading the Proverbs. There is always a Bible at hand.

The way of a fool is right in his own eyes, he reads. He thinks of himself. Perhaps he was a fool to come here, but how would he know? It certainly felt natural to pursue his own happiness, as recent statesmen gloriously and shrewdly have proclaimed is his right. That Susanna Quiner is tied to his happiness he has no doubt. But to move to Philadelphia? What would he do there? He pictures an ironworks shop hemmed in on both sides by other shops, the constant noise, horses everywhere. Perhaps it would not be so bad. The point is, he doesn't know.

Outside he can hear the storm's wind gathering force again. When he looks out he sees that the ground is covered with green branches ripped from the trees, some of them as thick as his arm. In one corner Brother Witt, a slate on his lap, is going over the letters of the English alphabet with two Seneca men. Seth puts down the Bible. He hasn't been back to the chapel since he heard the Ottawa speak of his conversion. It occurs to him now, watching Brother Witt and his pupils, that it might be the very meeting of these two people—white and native—that makes him so uncomfortable. As though the two sides of himself could stand up together and declare that indeed a whole can be made from them. He does not know if that is really possible.

He takes from his pocket a letter he received from Cade a week ago and rereads it.

> We have heard the British are selling their land for a farthing to Belgians and French alike in the hopes of raising money for a new army. Some say they are planning to invade again. England has not entirely given us up. And so I've decided conclusively to join a militia. There are several in Kentucky that will provide you a uniform if you provide a gun. Amos is drunk all the time, worse than ever. No doubt I'll take to drinking too one day, if I don't leave. He is very angry with you and talks about fetching you back with a whip in his hand. I've reminded him you are much stronger now than you were at twelve.

It goes on a little longer, but it is the postscript that interests Seth most:

> I've adopted Aurelia's hens and have built a new henhouse closer to our cabin. But today I found two eggs in the scrub—they have not yet taken to their new home. When I leave for Kentucky I will take a hen with me as some do dogs. Fresh eggs, that will be my contribution to whatever cause I fight for.

It is a comfort to see the familiar scrawl, even the inkblots, of which there are many. The militia will be a good place for Cade. Seth can see that Aurelia's death still weighs on him, as indeed how could it not? But he has no doubt that eventually Cade will find a new woman and make his own, new life. The life of a soldier-farmer perhaps. Or might he persuade Cade to follow him to Philadelphia? It is then that Seth realizes he has made up his mind. He still cannot picture that life but somehow he has made up his mind.

Brother Witt laughs at something one of the Seneca has said and pats the man on the shoulder. The rain is now beating down sideways with a fury. It's as if the earth has pulled back its own curtain to reveal its true nature: uncontrolled, unordered, unplanned, a thing apart from man whether native or white. Somehow he must get word to Susanna. Perhaps he can send a boy with a note? *I agree to your proposal. Let us go to Philadelphia.* The brethren would not object to a short note, surely. *Let us go to Philadelphia and be married.* As he gets out his writing paper and quill a great sadness comes over him that he does not understand, and does not wish to examine.

On the third day of the rainstorm Meera appears at the Sisters' Choir holding a small wet sack in her fist. Susanna sees her dark head turn as she comes up the narrow staircase and at the top she pauses, looking around. Her square, defiant way of standing makes Susanna think again of a warrior. A very small warrior. She calls to Meera and moves her blanket over to make room for her.

"I have been sent here like the servant I am," Meera announces. She tells Susanna that her foster mother Nushemakw has banished her from her small cabin in the married people's section. Nushemakw's husband has come to see his son, and there is no room anymore for Meera's hammock. But Nushemakw still expects Meera to come to the cabin every morning and work— sweep, mend, cook the traditional food that Nushemakw cannot get at the Bell House, and take care of the baby. You must still be my daughter and do your duty to me, Nushemakw told her.

Meera says, "Nothing has changed. She talks of me as her daughter but uses me as her slave."

"Maybe one of the brethren could help?"

Meera's face grows darker. "I asked Sister Consolation to petition for my release, but she told me that the brethren heed the wishes of the parent, not the child. But Nushemakw is not my parent! She is my captor! And I am not a child."

Susanna looks down at her sewing and tries to think of a suggestion. She is mending a torn collar and pulls on a loose stitch. The room is crowded with women sitting cross-legged on blankets on the floor, knitting or darning while they wait for the rain to stop. She can hear the wind whining down the chimney. Despite the storm, Beatrice has gone to the store as usual. Discomfort always spurs her on, Susanna thinks sourly.

She gives up on the stitch and puts in another one to cover it. "Don't talk to Consolation. She makes everything into a bad business. She's been encouraging my sister to remain here as a missionary. And now Beatrice has gone to a special service without telling me, and they drew lots for her."

"I have witnessed this custom," Meera says.

To Susanna, it seems like a child's game: small pieces of paper marked with a tick or a minus are rolled up inside of goose quills, and then with some ceremony the applicants choose one of the quills from the basket.

"Beatrice drew a paper with a tick on it. Now she may formally join the community. They have given her a new name, Benigna. *Benigna!* I cannot get used to it."

Meera shrugs. She has her own worries. "I will be gone before they next draw the lots," she says.

"Gone! Where will you go?"

But Meera just cocks her head. After a while she says, "I heard you received a gift from the Chippewa chief."

"Would you like to see it?" Susanna lays aside the torn collar and opens her grain sack. She sets the necklace down on her blanket, and Meera looks at it without touching. "You must keep it in a cedar box," she says. "To preserve its strength."

"I don't have a cedar box."

"They will have one in the store. Especially when you travel, that is very important."

"Meera, what did you mean when you said you'll be gone soon? Is that really true? Are you planning to leave?"

Meera nods.

"But where will you go?"

For a moment she thinks Meera won't tell her. But then Meera says in a low voice, "There is a tribe to the north by the Place of Cold Water." That's Lake Erie. "They are the uncle tribe of my people, my real people, the people of my mother and father. Last month when Nushemakw was pregnant and we were traveling here we came upon a group of them. One invited me to their village. Follow Injured River until it meets the larger river going north, he said. And then follow that to the Cold Water."

"Injured River! But that would mean going through the Black Swamp! You don't want to do that."

"I am not afraid of getting wet. My name is Meera. That means Walks Through Water. And I have been to the Swamp before, it is nothing."

Susanna picks up her sewing again. She doesn't believe her. "When have you been there?"

Meera tells her about a certain kind of fish in its southern brooks that Nushemakw's people eat in the summer. She claims that the danger is only if you go in winter when the ice is thick and the rivers don't move. Or in spring, with the floods.

"Natives go into the Swamp all the time, we only spread rumors to keep white people out. It is like all land: if you know its ways you can live on it. The men I saw, my uncle tribe, they are Wyandot. All the time they go back and forth along the rivers of the Swamp. They travel in flat canoes. What do you call them? These are good when the water becomes shallow."

"Skiffs."

Meera lowers her voice to a whisper. "If I go by skiff the journey will take me only two days. I can take one from the brethren. They have little need even of one, and yet they have many."

Susanna is still skeptical. "Did Nushemakw see these men? What does she think?"

"Do not ask Nushemakw about them. If she thinks I am planning to leave she will tie me up. Anyway, they did not speak to her, only to me. Her tribe is not a friendly one to them. And they had captives that they did not want to share. White captives."

Susanna looks over at Meera quickly, her needle stopping upright in the cloth.

"White captives? You mean white women?" A line of sweat pricks the back of her neck. "White women?" she asks again.

"Yes, white women," Meera says impatiently. "Captives. Two or three, I'm not sure. It was a large group."

Susanna is staring at Meera's small face. A month ago, she cal-
culates. That would fit. But it couldn't be them. They were killed.
"What did they look like?"

"We had just come from the river to the west. They tried to
hide them from us."

"But what did the captives look like?"

"I saw only one clearly," Meera says. She looks down for a moment and touches a bone on the Chippewa necklace. "She had the
red hair, like you."

"The girl lies," Beatrice tells Susanna. "She is lying."

Her mouth is sticky and she swallows, trying to moisten her
tongue. They are in the store with Sister Johanna, and Susanna is
sitting in front of the Franklin stove trying to dry herself. Outside
the wind is howling and rain beats on the store's sloping roof. Beatrice was astonished to see Susanna bang open the door in all this
weather. She is wet from head to toe and her moccasins—
Aurelia's moccasins—are covered in mud. Beatrice still feels a
spurt of irritation when she looks at them.

Johanna, who is also sitting on a stool near the stove, is watching her. Beatrice walks over to the water cask and takes a drink.
She isn't sure what she feels most: insulted, angry, or amazed at
the girl's audacity. When she rehangs the dipper she sees that her
hand is shaking. She hopes that Johanna doesn't notice.

"She heard why the chief gave you his necklace," Beatrice says.
"Everyone is talking about it. And so she decided to make use of
the story for her own purposes."

"What purpose would that be?" Susanna asks.

"To leave Gemeinschaft, of course. She needs help to do that, especially if, as you say, she plans to go by boat."

"Miriam has never liked being here," Johanna puts in. "I have known her since ten years. Always she has a hunger for someplace else."

"Her name is Meera," Susanna tells her.

Johanna looks at her from under her eyebrows, chin down, as if reassessing her worth. "The woman Nushemakw comes only when she is hungry. With Meera, as you call her. I know them both. They have no loyalty to this place."

"Why do the brethren let them come back if they are just going to leave again?"

"We are Christians," Johanna says mildly. "Hope is like food to us. We need it, and also we enjoy it."

Susanna shifts around on her chair as if looking for something she dropped. "But what if she's telling the truth? At the very least we should try—"

"You would go into the Black Swamp?" Beatrice asks. She cannot picture Susanna there with all the mud and slimy water, the dead trees, and the stories of fantastical creatures like swamp wolves. Not that Beatrice believes those stories, but she knows Susanna does.

"Meera says Indians go into it all the time. They talk ill of it only to keep white settlers out."

Johanna cocks her head. "I don't know if this is true."

"I have to find out if they're alive. We worked it out, it will take only two days if we go by boat. Two days! Surely I can spare that. Beatrice, what if they are there at that village! What if they escaped?"

"It's a fool's errand," Beatrice says. She begins rubbing the store counter although it is already polished to a gleam. She can feel something coming up, an ache somewhere, her ankle? She rubs the wood harder. "And it's a lie. You must accept that they are dead. I don't want it to be true either, but we have to move forward."

"Then help me do that! Tell me what happened."

"I already told you. They were killed." She does not look up.

"Beet!" Susanna goes over to Beatrice and stops her hand as it moves over the counter. For a moment the rain pounds violently on the roof as though the sky has decided to hurl down everything left in its arsenal all at once. How did Susanna manage to run here in all this rain? Beatrice feels trapped.

"Beet," Susanna says. "Please tell me what happened. Please."

Beatrice looks at her. From this angle she can see something of Penelope in Susanna's face: her nose and forehead. It might be a relief to tell the story but she isn't sure she deserves relief. *When comforts flee...*she looks over at Johanna, who has never once asked her about it.

But Johanna now says, "Sometimes it is good to tell."

She sits down where Susanna was sitting in front of the Franklin stove and wishes she had tea or something hot to drink. Instead she holds on to the bit of chamois rag she was using to polish the counter. She doesn't know where to begin so she just starts talking, looking at the wall behind the stove, the gap where the pipe isn't quite wide enough for the hole they made for it. Shaves of wood curl off the wall where the surface was imperfectly planed. She opens her fist and draws out a bit of the rag so she can hold on to it with both hands.

"At first they tied us all up together," she says, "but when we were far enough into the trees they untied us so we could run faster. We were all worried about Aurelia. She got more and more tired. At first the Potawatomi did not seem to notice, they were busy sending scouts back to see if anyone was following us. Sometimes they made us stop and be very quiet while Koman listened, but it's hard to be quiet when you're hurting for breath. Koman was one of the leaders. The other leader, I don't know his name. He had a white scar running down the side of his face. We called him the scarred Indian." She pauses. "That one hated us," she says.

She twists the rag around her finger. "In the beginning Penelope thought we were heading toward Risdale, but after a while it felt like we were going in circles. There was some disagreement between Koman and the scarred Indian. Finally we stopped at a place where three streams met up together, and they had us make a shelter out of tree branches. I thought...I don't know what I thought, that maybe we would sleep there? Sleep and then keep going in the morning? It all felt so wrong, I couldn't make any sense of it. They were arguing more and more, and Koman left, I don't know why. I don't know if he planned to come back. But that's when the scarred Indian took Aurelia."

She stops for a moment. In her mind she sees with unusual detail the inside of the shelter again, the roughness of the branches, how it was hard to turn without getting your dress caught on one of them. *Shelter,* she thinks ironically.

"The scarred Potawatomi figured out Aurelia was ill even though we all tried our best to hide it from him. But she was so brave, Susanna. He took her away...and of course I hoped..." She twists the rag in her hands again. "You know what happened. He came back with blood on his hatchet and he lifted it up to show us, almost gleefully, and Penelope said, don't show him any fear, he's a devil. But how could we not be afraid? He had us all get out of the shelter and stand before him. He held up his hatchet and said, 'See this blood? This is the blood of your sister. This blood is lonely, it wants a companion. You,' he said, and he pointed to Naomi.

"I was holding her hand and I could feel her whole body go stiff. And in that moment I thought...I thought that this was much more terrible than dying, to be forced to watch first Aurelia and now Naomi go off with this devil. I heard myself saying, 'Take me instead.' Maybe I thought there was a chance he would only kill one more of us. Maybe I thought Koman would come back and put a stop to it. I'm not sure what I was thinking. But the scarred Indian just laughed at me. 'You then,' he said. 'The others can wait on their fate.'"

Beatrice's eyes fill with tears. "I'm sorry," she says. "I'm sorry. I didn't know. Susanna, believe me, I thought I was saving Naomi. I really thought I was saving her. Instead I took her place. The Potawatomi was taking me off to trade me, not to kill me. He had come upon Brother Graves and Brother Anders in the forest. Brother Graves did not know, was not told, that there was more than one captive. And when I realized what was happening it was too late."

Susanna says, "Penelope and Naomi were alive when you left?"

"It should be Naomi who is here. He meant to trade her and not me."

"But then how do you know they were killed?"

"Because I looked back and I saw another Potawatomi pushing them off. I saw their backs as they were being led away into the forest. Like Aurelia."

"But being led away is not the same thing as being killed!"

Beatrice makes a fist around the rag. "Why are you making this harder for me? I heard gunshots, Susanna. I was confused when I saw Brother Graves and I didn't think fast enough...I would have pleaded for them but I didn't think fast enough. And then there were shots. Two. One for Penelope and one for Naomi. Companions for Aurelia's blood," she says bitterly.

The wind shifts and for a few seconds the rain beats so sharply against the window it sounds as though someone is throwing pebbles at the glass. For a moment Susanna stares at the streams of water snaking down the wet pane. She feels a sharp twinge under her ribs as though something has pierced her. The feeling is hope. She tries to keep her voice gentle.

"You heard gunshots, Beet," she says. "You saw them being led away, and then you heard gunshots. But you didn't actually see them being killed."

"I *heard* them being killed."

"But the Potawatomi took a hatchet to Aurelia. Why would they shoot Penelope and Naomi?" She looks over at Johanna, who is frowning in thought. "What do you think?"

Johanna hesitates, and then she says, "It seems, well, not quite right. To waste powder and shot on a woman. Forgive me, I am thinking like a Potawatomi."

"But why else would they shoot?" Beatrice asks.

Johanna hesitates again. "I don't know."

The wind dies away for a moment and Susanna thinks about what Meera saw, a red-haired woman with a group of Wyandots. But that doesn't make sense, either; they were taken by Potawatomi. How does one determine the truth of a story? And yet she has never been especially motivated by truth. Luck and superstition—this is what she relies on, much to the dismay of her sisters, who do not. Johanna lifts the lid to the water cask and fills a cup.

She passes it to Beatrice, who takes a sip. Beatrice has always been drawn to hardship, Susanna thinks. She wants to do big things: run a trading post in a remote settlement without a man's help, die in her sister's stead, convert natives to a Christian life. The idea of sacrifice appeals to her. But not to me.

Outside the rain is thinning but the sky is as dark as ever. Johanna suggests they go back to the Sisters' Choir before the next storm hits. Beatrice looks at Susanna. Her face is soft, not the face of the overbearing older sister from a month ago, or even this morning.

"I just want forgiveness," she says.

Susanna gives her a handkerchief. "Maybe there's nothing to forgive."

Beatrice hands Susanna her crumpled rag and wipes her face with the handkerchief. Then she stands up and looks for her shawl. She will be all right, Susanna thinks. She will be fine here.

"Beet," she says. "Do you have any cedar boxes on the shelves? I need one for the Chippewa necklace. To carry it in."

Maumee River Valley

Twelve

Back in Severne each sister had a dream but they were all different dreams.

Penelope married a man whom, she found out too late, she couldn't abide. Thomas Forbes. When he was irritated Thomas's breath grew bad and he was irritated often. At night coming in from the fields he never asked Penelope how she fared, he only looked for his supper. On the one hand Penelope understood that this was because he was bone tired from breaking ground all day, but on the other hand she could not help but feel lonely. She missed living with her sisters. She missed the chatter and noise. She was supposed to do whatever Thomas Forbes told her to do but he spoke to her so curtly, and she found she had too much pride for such plain commands. When Thomas died after being kicked in the head by his horse, she tried to remember the boy she'd wanted to marry but even so she could not cry. The other farmers called her hard-hearted and began the rumors that she was barren and cold.

Her dream now is no longer the dream of marriage. In her dream she does not have to marry ever again. She wants to run a store in Philadelphia with her sisters. She prefers Philadelphia because, after Thomas Forbes, Severne became the place of her failure. She dreams of leaving.

She is almost too dazed to take in the irony of this as she stumbles along the forest path that takes her farther and farther away from Severne. She is tied by the wrist to a native woman, who pulls her sharply whenever she trips. They turned west out of Thieving Forest and almost without a pause in the trees entered the next forest, this one with darker ferns and a rockier path. If it has a name she does not know it. Vines hang down from the elms on either side of her and roots as hard as stone push up through the ground. Walking is a test of avoidance and balance. The thick tree canopy casts them into a prolonged twilight, and Penelope can get no sense of passing time. She and Naomi have been separated, each tied to a different woman. They are no longer with the Potawatomi. They have been traded to the Wyandots for a few muskrat skins and a horse.

It came about suddenly. Just as the scarred Potawatomi was leading Beatrice away, another Potawatomi with small round cheekbones like early apples told Penelope and Naomi to come with him quickly. A band of Wyandots and their horses had been spotted nearby. The Potawatomi carried one of the sacks with the Quiners' belongings over his shoulder, and he said to them in English, "Your sister traded for a horse but will be lucky to get one muskrat skin for the two with me now."

In this way Penelope learned that Beatrice hadn't been killed. She is grateful for that at least.

As they walked into the forest the Potawatomi signaled for them to be quiet, and he packed his rifle as they walked the last few yards, disturbing a family of bobolinks that scurried for cover. They came out of the trees to see twenty or so Wyandots sitting on tree stumps and rocks. One man was rearranging the bags on a horse and turned his head in surprise. The Potawatomi raised his rifle and shot under one horse and then over another one, perhaps to show how little he cared if these animals lived or died. A tactic. The horses shied and tried to take themselves off but the Wyandots caught them by their manes and stood possessively next to them, two to a horse. After a long negotiation—during which Naomi's arm was repeatedly squeezed and Penelope had her loose hair fingered by several of the women—the Potawatomi ended up with the largest horse and an armful of pelts. He then pushed Penelope and Naomi toward the Wyandots, and Naomi fell over an exposed root into the mud.

Everyone laughed. She stood up, blinking, the left side of her dress smeared with black.

About two dozen Wyandots make up the group, more women than men, plus a handful of children. The women are slender and attractive with dark hair and light coppery skin. Quite a few of the men have plucked all the hair from one side of their head and wear skin kilts decorated with the Iroquois symbol:)(.

Penelope was given to a thin woman with a long, beakish nose who wears a necklace of dyed porcupine quills. Every so often the woman strides ahead and then jerks Penelope up by the arm in a show of power. Naomi is with this woman's sister or daughter—it is hard to guess their ages. They both wear wrap-around dresses and share a dog for protection. Toward the rear of the group the horses walk without riders, their rumps slapped by one of the three men who guard them if their pace becomes too slow.

In Severne the Wyandots are said to be horse thieves. But the farmers called all natives horse thieves. Penelope's main worry is this: how can she and Naomi prove their value? Only if the Wyandots believe that they are useful will they be fed and kept alive.

When they come to another clearing, the women begin to search for groundnuts. Penelope and Naomi are untied and told to help. Penelope wants to impress them by finding more nuts than anyone else, but her Wyandot mistress keeps scolding her for straying too far. When she thinks no one is looking she hides one in her pocket.

Back with the others she empties her apron of nuts and is pleased to see that Naomi has found a good many as well. Out of the large pile Naomi and Penelope are given only one each. They eat them quickly, and then Penelope licks the inside of the shell. One man laughs at her.

"*Gwi gishgama*," he says, and pantomimes a big belly. He thinks she is fat? Penelope blushes and looks at Naomi, who looks back without expression. Both of their dresses are torn almost to shreds. Penelope's armpits are wet with sweat. For her part she thinks these Wyandots odious and uncouth. They use no water pouches but drink straight from puddles with their hands.

As the sun is setting they come to a stream too fast and deep to wade across, so the men fashion rafts by cutting down dry saplings and overlaying them with brush. When Penelope and her mistress are settled on one, two men sitting on the bank push them off with their feet. But by the middle of the stream the raft is a good three inches under the water, and although it does not sink entirely Penelope's legs get soaked to the bone. By this time the sun has sunk below the horizon and she cannot make out if the vines on the opposite bank are grapes or poison ivy.

They disembark, abandon the raft, and walk only far enough to get clear of the line of scrub along the water. This is where they will spend the night. The women begin peeling dry bark from the birch trees to make little shelters. Their dogs, excited and hungry, run back to the stream bank and stand there barking.

Naomi and Penelope are told to build a fire and carry up water. They are made to understand that they will do their mistresses' work for them every day: fetching water, making the fire, cooking. If they do all this to their mistresses' satisfaction then they will be fed.

"We will starve to death, then," Naomi says in a flat voice. She has finished her chores but not quickly enough and has been given no food. Her red hair has come out of its braid and is hanging loosely down her back.

Penelope puts her arm around Naomi's shoulders. They are sitting a ways back from the fire, farther away even than the dogs. A few bright stars are out, and bats swoop in jagged circles above their heads. She gives Naomi the groundnut she has been saving. Taking care of her sister is now her first responsibility. She pulls off her wet stockings and stretches them out beside her to dry. She tries not to despair although there is no chance of escape and nowhere, in any case, to escape to. They might run miles in any direction and find nothing but more wilderness. She thinks of Severne, a long way behind them.

"We must submit to them entirely and do what they tell us. Maybe some opportunity will come." If we live long enough, she thinks.

Naomi lays her head against Penelope's shoulder. "I'm so hungry," she says.

It is no good wishing she had something more to give her but Penelope wishes it anyway, feeling in her pocket as if some morsel of corncake or nut might still be lodged deep in its corner. Can it really be that just this morning they were all in their cabin? And now one sister is surely dead and the rest have been traded around like horses. Penelope thinks of Susanna. She is all right at least.

Penelope kisses the top of Naomi's head. Back home Naomi usually ate her supper quickly in a rush to get back to her violin, but she has no violin now. They are sitting on the moist ground, and one Wyandot woman passing by takes pity on them and gives them a blanket to share. Some hours later, when the camp is still and there is no sound except for the rushing stream behind them, Penelope wakes to find that Naomi has thrown off her portion of the blanket and is sleeping on her side with one arm over her head, just as she always slept at home.

⁂

The next day the Potawatomi attack.

They come in the morning after most of the Wyandots have bathed in the stream and are drying themselves and their clothes near little campfires scattered around the clearing. A layer of cottony clouds is spread out above them, peeled back in one spot like someone starting on an orange. Penelope feels stiff and bruised all over. When she checks her stockings she finds bits of debris sticking to them but at least they are dry.

On impulse, she shows them to a young Wyandot woman nearby. She asks, "Do you like?" Like all of her sisters, she knows some Iroquois from working in the store, and the Wyandots speak an Iroquois dialect, Wendat, with a few Algonquin words mixed in and once in a while some French.

The woman, shorter and younger than Penelope with a thick cloud of loose dark hair, comes over to feel a stocking. She runs a cupped hand down the length of it. Her heart-shaped face reminds Penelope a little of Aurelia.

"*Skanotawa*," the young woman says, signaling with her hands to show that she is smaller than Penelope.

"I can ravel them out and knit them to fit you," Penelope says. She mimes what she will do. "But you must help me find my knit bag. *Ajera.* Bag."

The knitting bag, she hopes, is in the sack of their goods tied to one of the horses, part of the trade. The young woman has to speak with two older women and a man before she is allowed to untie the sack.

"I wonder if we could get your violin, too," Penelope says while she and Naomi watch the young woman go through their belongings. "You could play something."

"It isn't there," Naomi says. "The Potawatomi kept it. Besides, I don't have my bow anyway."

"Maybe you could fashion something, a flute or a drum..."

"A flute! You must be mad. What would I do with a flute? Just because I play the violin doesn't mean I can play the flute."

The problem is that Naomi is not much good at anything other than playing her violin. Back at home almost every task she did had to be done over again by someone else. She undercooked beans and made watery butter and her stitches were always uneven and loose. Even Susanna can sew a better seam than Naomi. Penelope watches the young woman take out their mother's blue pieced bed quilt, their candlesticks, a bag of tea. Soon the Wyandots will knock down their bark shelters and bank their fires and be on their way. Her mistress will no doubt start looking for her, if she isn't looking already. Several loud birds call out to each other. Later Penelope recalls that a couple of Wyandot men stood when they heard that and looked toward the stream, which is half-hidden by trees and brush.

At last the young woman comes to the knitting bag and she holds it up to show Penelope. But before Penelope can even nod, a rushing sound comes up from behind her like a sudden, fierce wind sweeping through the trees. She turns to see a group of men running toward them waving hatchets and knives.

Her first impossible thought is that white men have come to take her home. But that lasts less than a second. These men aren't white. It is the group of Potawatomi from yesterday. Everything becomes chaotic as shouting breaks out from several areas at once. Two or three Wyandot men begin herding the women and children to the other side of the clearing where they can escape into some woods, while others engage the intruders. Penelope's throat seems to close up in fear and she has to push her breath to get it out. She reaches for Naomi's hand just as Naomi is reaching for hers.

"We must stay together."

She's not sure if she says this or if it's only something she thinks. She tries not to look back as they run with the other women toward the trees. Although the gunshots are not frequent—reloading takes time—the arrows are flying nonstop. Before they get to the end of the clearing there is an earsplitting sound and the woman running on the other side of Penelope falls, her skull split open by gunshot. Blood spurts up the side of Penelope's dress and later she finds bits of skin in her hair. A whiteness comes over her like a spell. Her legs are moving but she feels herself fading. She makes a noise and stumbles but Naomi pulls her forward before she can fall to the ground.

"Stay with me," Naomi orders her.

They enter the woods and stop beneath a huge oak tree with dead limbs intermixed with living. For a moment Penelope bends over with her hands on her ears, thinking she is going to be sick. The men's cries are horrifying. After they catch their breath they move deeper into the woods, but what tree anywhere could protect them? Now Penelope stops and really is sick, and afterward she does nothing but take a step back. It is Naomi who wipes her mouth for her on the sleeve of her own dress. Then they stand pressed together looking back through the trees in the direction of the fighting. Penelope's arm moves with each breath Naomi takes, in and out. Her own breath leaves in spurts, and when she inhales it feels like a gulp.

Then, just as suddenly as it started, the sound of fighting is over. Gradually the noises of the forest—birds, insects, a brief knocking on wood—resume. Only now Penelope notices all the women sheltering under this tree or that with their children. No one moves. After a little while an older Wyandot with pockmarked skin comes with his hands raised to signal their victory.

As they make their way back to the clearing, Penelope sees the young woman with the heart-shaped face crouching between two trees, still holding Penelope's knitting bag. Penelope looks down at her hands. She is still holding her stockings.

Back at the clearing the women scatter to help the wounded. The air smells of gunpowder and blood.

"They must have been following us all this time," Naomi says. She means the Potawatomi.

She goes from body to body and Penelope follows her. They are searching for the scarred Potawatomi. Without saying it aloud, they both want to find him among the fallen.

Sure enough there he is, lying dead on his back. His eyes are open to slits and there are two arrows in his chest, one with a broken shaft. The scar down the side of his face is in shadow. Blood trickles out of his ear.

Penelope stares at his face. This is the man who killed Aurelia. She doesn't believe in fate but she feels avenged.

"Do you think he wanted us back?" she asks. "Do you think that's why they attacked?"

Naomi looks at her in surprise. "They just wanted more horses," she says.

The Wyandots spend the rest of the day in the same clearing tending the wounded and burying the dead. Naomi and Penelope have been given the task of breaking up walnuts and mixing them with water. Naomi's fingers feel empty without her violin. She picks up the shallow wooden bowl and begins grinding kernels. The women are burying the dead west to east while the men cut up a horse that was shot by mistake in the fighting. The stench is terrible.

"My legs ache," Penelope is saying. "And my back. And my shoulders. Everything aches."

Naomi says, "You sound like Beet."

"But my aches are real."

They smile at each other—they are too hungry to laugh. If at first they felt a slight thrill from surviving the battle and seeing their enemy dead, that thrill is gone and they are left with their empty stomachs and their aches and pains and worries. Naomi's arms feel heavy but her head feels light, as if emptied of all her thoughts and dreams as well as the music she kept so carefully stored there. Everything is gone, that's how it feels. Even music cannot help her.

Her sisters would be surprised to learn that Naomi's dream is not the dream of giving concerts or teaching the violin. She does not want to play for anyone else, and she certainly does not want to listen to others play badly for her. She thinks of music as her own private world. No, her dream has always been much more mundane: she wants to marry. But she wants to marry a man who, as she puts it to herself, understands music. This is her way of describing a person who can experience more than just the scrabble of livelihood. She wants beauty in her life. She wants a companion who can appreciate beauty and mystery: the sound of Haydn, the sound of birds flying in after the winter, the sound of a narrowing creek. It's hard to explain to others and in general she does not even try. Only her father, she thought, understood.

She sits on the ground pounding walnuts with Penelope until a woman with dried blood on her hands comes to take their bowls. With a short spoon she begins feeding the mixture to an infant in another woman's arms.

"Why are they feeding that to a baby?" Penelope asks.

"Its mother must be dead," Naomi guesses.

She watches the baby struggle to suck the spoon. Here in this wasted clearing there is no beauty whatsoever. The afternoon sky has turned dark and the stark trees around them are good for neither fruit nor wood, just scrub put down to block the view. The Wyandot women work hard and their hard lives show in their faces. They have nothing, Naomi thinks, except the battle of living one more day. No beauty. No music. She looks down at the hard, permanent calluses on her fingers. And what does she have? Her dream of marriage seems as far off as Sirus and Ellen, as far off as the sun.

A short while later, a tall Wyandot comes over to question them about the band of Potawatomi: how many of them are there, how many guns, are there women and children among them? He speaks broken English and a little French. His name, he tells them, is Tawakota. Naomi can see he is a leader by the way the others address him.

He leans over and touches a spot on top of her lip.

"*Qu'est-ce que c'est?*" he asks.

"A mole," Naomi tells him. She does not know the Iroquois word. The mole is light purple, unusual, and people often remark on it. "I've always had it. *Je l'ai toujours.*" She does not want him to think she is ill. She knows too well what would happen then.

Tawakota turns away and directs two women to cook the slain horse. This will take some time, so he must think another attack is unlikely. In the evening, Penelope and Naomi are given none of the cooked horsemeat but are allowed to drink some of the broth. Afterward Penelope's mistress gives them two worn deerskin dresses to wear in exchange for their aprons. Their old dresses are badly torn and stained with blood and dirt, but Penelope tucks them into her knitting bag anyway. She pulls out her needles and begins to make over her stockings for the young woman with the heart-shaped face.

Before they go to sleep, Naomi braids her hair into one long plait and binds the end with a rubbery piece of grass.

"You'll never look like an Indian with your red hair," Penelope says. Naomi knows she is trying to tease her, to lift her mood, but she answers, "I don't want to look like an Indian."

What she wants is to leave this gruesome place that smells of death and find something of beauty. All afternoon a sheet of clouds covered the sun, stretching out like a shroud over the earth. A hard, hungry life—is this her fate now? Her music is gone for good.

❧

In the morning they move on, beginning what Naomi later thinks of as their march through the mud. The ground grows spongier and the stream banks bleed into the surrounding grassland, making everything soggy. Although they are skirting the Great Black Swamp, Naomi feels as though she is falling into sludge every other step. They are still heading west. In the afternoon they wade across a rill so cold that she reels a little when she first steps into it and loses her footing. A few nearby men laugh. *Tau-tie-yost,* one says. He mimics her falling and they laugh again. Soon everyone is calling her *Tau-tie-yost.*

"Why do they call you that?" Penelope asks later, when they have stopped to rest.

"It means clumsy."

"But you're not clumsy!"

She is clumsy, they both know it. Both of her shins are badly bruised and there are stinging cuts up and down her legs from when she fell against a nest of nettles. Only when she stands still playing music does she feel graceful. Now she's like a sailor who can't find his land legs.

They walk for days without stopping except to sleep. Penelope finishes the stockings for the young Wyandot woman and takes Naomi's stockings to make for someone else. Naomi watches her, wondering how she has the energy after walking all day. She wants to do nothing but eat and lie down. Penelope knits in the evening, after she has done all her chores and most of Naomi's. Half the time, more than half the time, Penelope starts Naomi's cooking fires for her. Naomi's hands just can't seem to do what she wants them to do. She takes meat out too soon and lets the fire die. None of the Wyandots like her knitting. In exchange for the stockings Penelope receives a bowl of samp, cooked corn porridge, which she shares with Naomi. They spoon it up using two sticks.

"I wish I knew where we were going," Penelope says. "Mud, mud, mud. That's all there is."

"We're going to Hog Creek," Naomi tells her. This is what the natives call the Ottawa River. "I heard some of them talking."

"You can understand what they say?"

"Back at the store I learned Iroquois pretty well." She smiles slyly. "I thought if you knew, you would make me work at the counter even more."

Some of the Wyandots are smoking hemlock, and the thin, tangy scent wafts over with the wind. Naomi listens to them chatting. Language is like music to her, she can hear a word once and somehow understand it and remember it later. It doesn't help to think too much about it. It's like knowing where a melody is going the first time she hears it. Often she knows where the notes will land before they get there.

"What else do they say?" Penelope asks her.

"They like our hair, but they wish we didn't smell so bad."

At the end of the second week they come to a brook so fast and full that even traversing it on rafts seems dangerous. Two scouts are sent to look for a better place to cross. After only a few minutes one comes back and speaks hurriedly to the leader, Tawakota. Naomi is crouched on a rock over the brook cupping up water when her mistress pulls her roughly back behind the trees. A moment later she sees four Indians approaching, not Wyandots. Perhaps a family? One woman is heavily pregnant. Naomi spies some early berries among the scrub, greenish yellow, not quite ripe, but she picks them anyway and pockets a few for Penelope. When she looks up through the trees again, the foreign Indians are gone.

They find a better crossing but stop on the other side because the men come across fresh elk dung. A few of them go off with their dogs to track the animal. Penelope is now sewing a shirt for Tawakota's young son, and Tawakota comes over to tell her that if an elk is killed he will give her a bowlful of meat for her work.

But the men come back without the elk and in need of new arrowheads. Naomi is shown what to look for, a kind of chert that is abundant in this place, but everything she finds is discarded by her mistress as unusable. She doesn't know why. After a while she stops looking and just stands in the canary grass watching the Wyandots' dogs running around. The Wyandots are good to their animals. They might kill a horse for food but they would never kill a dog. Dogs chase game and sniff out berries. Naomi thinks: they have more use than I do.

She wishes for the first time she were more like Penelope.

That night she sleeps on a piece of limestone outcropping thinking it will at least not be damp, but when she wakes every muscle in her body aches. She looks around the campsite with its palette of gray and brown, at all the gaunt figures bending over various fires, and at the small bark shelters hastily put up last night only to be pulled down again now, at sunrise. There might be some beauty somewhere but she is unable to see it. The wind blows it all away. It is so gusty that even Penelope is having trouble with her cooking fire and can't help Naomi. Naomi's fire never flames. Her mistress scolds her severely and sends her away without food.

They pull down the bark shelters and begin that day's march. It occurs to Naomi while she's walking, feeling both hungry and sore, that not only has her music failed her but it has betrayed her. Because she can do nothing else.

Late in the afternoon they come to a stand of oak trees and the air grows thick and dark. Naomi allows herself to lag a little as she looks for berries or mushrooms or nuts, anything to ease the raw emptiness in her stomach. She hears her mistress calling her, *Tau-tie-yost!* But she ignores her. As she stops to re-braid her hair, her fingers feeling comfortable in this task at least, she spies a twig with tiny, hard, butter-colored buds. She picks it up and twirls it between her fingers: yellow fairies dancing on a stick. She thinks of her mother, who loved to tell old Scottish tales with fairies in them, and of Susanna, who loved to hear them. When she looks up again, something in the distance sparkles.

It is the Ottawa River. Hog River. Naomi can see it through the trees, and she realizes that she's been hearing it for a while now without really noticing. She slips the twig of hard yellow buds into her moccasin and then makes her way quickly down the path until she is standing next to Penelope on the sloped bank looking down.

The river is fast and wide, and its color changes in spots from blue to green. The Wyandots' dogs run down the bank barking, excited by the power of the current. The light is changing rapidly as white clouds race across the sky, and the drooping willow trees along the bank seem to change color along with it. Naomi can see men dragging canoes out of a marshy inlet where they had been weighted down with heavy stones and covered with reeds. Their movements are precise, like dancers. Later she will learn that the boats have been hidden there for weeks while they conducted their trades. Now the men examine the hulls and then begin to rub them down with the rough sides of skins. Above them the sky is a vast purple field.

Is this where all the beauty has been hiding, Naomi wonders, all bunched up into this small stretch of sky and river, a magnet pulling whatever is good away from all the other places they walked through? She puts her arms around herself, feeling lighter. She has to hold herself down. If she looks at the river in just the right place, the color of the water is the same dark blue as her father's eyes.

"Where are we going?" Penelope asks her mistress, who is standing next to them. Her mistress shakes her head, not understanding.

"*Tuh-tish-yuh?*" Naomi asks. "*Tundi?*"

"*Yadata*," the woman replies. Naomi translates for Penelope: their village. Penelope's mistress gestures toward two women who are packing hide bundles into the first canoe.

"*Yes-tse kwa-oh*," she says.

We return.

Thirteen

Paddling down the river, in spite of her best intentions, Penelope begins to daydream about food: apple slum and roasted goose and baked sugared beans and all the ways Ellen used to cook corn—hominy, johnnycake, and cornbread with the corn kernels soaked in milk first to make the batter moist. Thinking about food is painful and she knows she shouldn't indulge herself. But it is better than constantly worrying about Naomi, which she would otherwise do.

They are heading toward Lake Erie, which the Wyandots call the Place of the Cold Water. Their village lies a few miles to the west of it. Six men ride the remaining horses along a deer path near the bank, their legs dangling loose without stirrups. After the first bend in the river Penelope never sees them again.

She listens to the birds calling out as they paddle downstream mile after mile, a song taken up and carried and lost as the birds change along the route. She wonders if Naomi hears any comfort in their music. They are in two different canoes, each with her own mistress, and in Penelope's case, a dog. Penelope does not see the river as beautiful, not at all. It would sweep them off and drown them if it could.

If at first she thought canoeing would be easier than walking—she is sitting, after all—that notion is quickly dispelled. After only a few hours her hands at the paddles grow swollen and red, and her forearms begin to ache.

"*Tatsa-tah-tai-no-teh*," her mistress says from behind her. Hurry up.

She cannot see Naomi's canoe. She tells herself that she should not be annoyed with Naomi because she cannot knit properly or build a proper fire. She knows how Naomi is. And she knows it is her job as the oldest to protect her, to save Naomi's life as well as her own. But how can she do this when Naomi herself contributes so little? She lied to Naomi about being clumsy. Of course she knows Naomi is clumsy. They all knew that.

The insects are intense and soon her knuckles are puffy with bites. How she wishes she were more like Susanna with skin made of stone.

"*Tatsa-tah-tai-no-teh*," her mistress says again more sharply. The little dog with its long matted hair is curled up into a tight black ball at the bow. She would like to stretch her legs but there is no room. When she looks down at her hands she sees they are bleeding.

"Look!" she says to Naomi later. They have stopped in a narrow clearing above the riverbank and will camp here for the night, although there hardly seems to be enough room for them all. Pin oaks grow right down to the river on either end, their roots in the water, and women are setting out wet clothes to dry on the surrounding brush.

Penelope holds out her hands. The fleshy tops of both her palms are torn and swollen and red. Pus runs from several of the blisters.

Naomi draws in her breath. "What happened?"

"Paddling with that hard paddle! My mistress pushes me, she never lets me rest."

"Mine aren't nearly so bad, maybe because of my violin. The skin on my hands is harder. Yours will toughen up."

"I can't even bend my fingers. How will I knit?"

They look at each other, worried. If she can't knit, they'll get no extra food. They both know this.

"I can't understand why they feed us so little! We're their property. They bought us to do their work. Why starve us to death?"

"Look how little they eat themselves," Naomi says. "They don't have much."

"But what if we get sick?"

They both know what will happen if they get sick.

The wind picks up and blows harder against them and the air begins to smell of rain. That evening Naomi does Penelope's chores as well as her own, and Penelope cannot help but be dismayed at how poorly she does them. But later, after her mistress dismisses her, Naomi goes down to the river. When she comes back she says to Penelope, "This might help." She wraps wet oak leaves around each of Penelope's hands.

"Hold them in place," Naomi instructs her. "I've seen the natives do this."

"When?"

"I don't know. Back when we were walking."

It is odd what Naomi notices. Can't she notice how to start a fire? Penelope holds the leaves down with her thumbs. After a while her hands do start to feel a little better.

Still, she won't be able to knit for days. She's not even sure if she will be able to close her hands around a canoe paddle. For the first time she can imagine how Naomi feels, trying and failing to light a fire. Penelope isn't used to feeling useless. She doesn't like it.

"*Na-ho-ten-ye-sa-yats?*" Naomi says to a woman sitting near them.

"*Oyanoga.*"

Naomi repeats, "*Oyanoga,*" and then asks her something else.

"What are you talking about?" Penelope asks.

"Her name is Oyanoga. I'm asking her if she has any food she would trade."

She holds out a button from her old dress. The buttons are an ordinary brown, but Oyanoga nods. "I'll give you one," Naomi tells her, holding up one finger. They settle on two, and in exchange Naomi receives some boiled goose meat.

The sun has set. With the last of the remaining light Naomi finds a tree with dry, loose bark and she peels enough strips to make a bed for herself and Penelope. She spreads them underneath a short willow tree and wedges some thicker strips of bark among its lower branches like a roof. When Penelope's mistress sees the structure she laughs, but it is better than lying out in the open. Penelope huddles underneath the tree next to Naomi and they eat the boiled meat, careful to save some for later.

"Shall I tell us a story?" Penelope asks. She used to do this almost every night, tell her sisters a story as they lay in bed, Penelope and Beatrice in one and Naomi, Aurelia, and Susanna in the other. Their feet touching for warmth. She hasn't told a story since they left Severne.

"How about Aunt Ogg Falls into the Cistern?" Naomi suggests, yawning.

Penelope cups the palms of her hands and holds them carefully against her thighs. She can see the cloudy sky through the willow branches. The story is funny and mostly true, which is how she likes her stories, but she feels Naomi fall asleep before Aunt Ogg even gets out to the garden. Around them on the narrow bank people are talking to each other and laughing or scolding their dogs. Some time later the rain begins. Penelope wakes when a piece of bark falls on her shoulder, and in her half-dream state she thinks, "Then the roof caved in..." as though she were telling someone another story, the story of her decline. She gets up to wedge the bark back in place, her hands stinging when she uses them. Finally, when she can do no more, she lies down again.

It is pitch black. Everyone is sleeping. She can hear the river behind the rain. She thinks about food: pork chops and new peas and sliced tomatoes with a sprinkle of sugar. If she closes her eyes she might be back in Severne breaking up salt so they can sell it in paper twists at the store. The creaking trees could be the roof beams in their cabin. Or even their old house on Walnut Street in Philadelphia. The rain could be horses clopping along on the cobblestones outside.

But she is not in a city. She doesn't know where she is. Her hands throb with pain and she has the feeling that she will never see Philadelphia, nor any other city, ever again. When at last she falls asleep again she dreams she is walking through a walled town while strangers look down at her from the battlement. Someone shouts a warning and for a moment she is afraid, but then to her delight small loaves of bread begin falling down around her like rain.

⚬

Naomi gets up early the next morning to make another poultice for Penelope's hands. It is still raining and the sky is as dark as sunset. Afterward she goes to see if she can trade another button to Oyanoga for food but she is told that Oyanoga is ill with a fever. Flashes of lightning appear up and down the river like spears. Several men with their hair hanging loose pull the canoes farther up the bank and weigh them down with muddy stones. Today they will not go on the water.

Naomi goes from shelter to shelter looking for food until at last she finds an old woman who gives her muskrat meat in exchange for only one button, a better deal than she reached with Oyanoga. She is pleased with herself. She goes back to their shelter where Penelope is patching up what passes for their roof as best she can.

Penelope is happy about the meat. "How many buttons do you have left?" she asks.

"Eight or nine."

"And I have ten. Perhaps they'll do us until my hands heal."

No one ventures out if they can help it. Naomi spends much of the day trying to make their shelter more waterproof or fetching sodden leaves for Penelope's hands. The next morning the dark sky is unchanged, but at least the lightning storm is over so they set out on the river again. The scrubby brush that lines the riverbanks does not change for many miles. But around midday there is a break in the landscape and a mass of rock rises like a tabletop above the water. Here they stop to eat and look for chert. As Naomi pulls her canoe up and wedges it between some bushes, she smells a foul scent in the air: weeds and mud and, when the wind shifts, some sort of carcass nearby. The men search until they find the dead animal, an elk, several days old. By now even the vultures have abandoned it.

A man who is traveling with Oyanoga cuts off the elk's horns and hooves. Oyanoga is still ill. Unable to sit upright, she lies stretched out in her canoe as if it is her coffin.

Although Naomi tries to help the women look for chert she notices that many turn when she approaches, and when she speaks to them they do not answer. But at least Penelope's hands are looking better. The blisters are beginning to harden. Naomi climbs down the northern part of the rockface to submerge more oak leaves in water, where a large Wyandot woman with very broad shoulders and a barrel chest is crouching to fill her water pouch. When she sees Naomi, she quickly goes up the other side of the rock, a harder climb, her pouch swinging behind her.

"Why are the women keeping away from me?" Naomi asks her mistress when they are back on the river.

Her mistress smiles a smile that is amused rather than kind.

"See you as witch," she tells Naomi. She is at the stern, navigating with her paddle.

"A witch? Why?"

"Give Oyanoga buttons, Oyanoga get fever. Oyanoga brother take elk feet to cure. He say you are witch turning to wolf at night. In day, clumsy in woman shape."

"That's absurd," Naomi says.

"Wolf whiskers come out there." She points to the mole above Naomi's lip.

Naomi turns around and puts her paddle back in the water. She is shocked and hurt. She has enjoyed speaking Wendat to the Wyandots and trading with them these last two days. For the first time she hasn't felt quite so useless. But she knows about their fear of witchcraft. Sirus used to say they were worse than the Puritans. Once when he was hunting with Old Adam they saw an old woman running in a scattered, haphazard way as if trying to put off her scent. Later, three Wyandot men asked Old Adam if he had seen a wolf in the shape of a woman.

The soft rain comes down steadily as though marshaling itself out to last as long as possible. Naomi wipes her face with her hand. She can smell the rancid bear grease that her mistress uses on her skin as lotion. The river is as brown as the scrub trees. The brief glimpse of beauty she'd seen on the river was only a mockery, not a promise as she thought. If she had argued to go to Philadelphia they might be halfway there by now. She could have broken the tie. But instead here she is: a wolf, a witch. She pulls her paddle up out of the water and changes sides.

That evening Penelope and Naomi stand in a crowd to watch an old man bleed Oyanoga, hoping to save her life. He affixes a sharp piece of flint onto a short stick, presses it against her bare arm, and with a grunt pushes the flint into her skin. To cup her blood he uses a hollowed gourd. When he decides that Oyanoga has bled enough he wraps wet leaves around the wound and then lifts her arm to blow on it. He makes a sign with his hands that looks, to Naomi, very much like the sign of the cross.

Oyanoga shakes all night but the next morning she is able to sit upright, and by the afternoon she can paddle her canoe. However, the old woman who gave Naomi muskrat meat is found dead the following day. That night Naomi's mistress ties Naomi to a tree after sunset, so she won't be able to attack them while in wolf form.

❧

Penelope thinks about food more and more often and with growing details: the color of pork, the texture of hominy. She knows that instead of letting her imagination run this way, she should be coming up with a plan. She needs to do something now that they are calling Naomi a witch. But what can she do? She has no idea how long they have been with the Wyandots, how many days on foot and how many in a canoe. Maybe it doesn't matter. When she asks how far away their village is, a shrug is the answer. At least her hands have toughened up. She begins to knit again at night after she has finished her chores and before exhaustion sets in.

She sits close to Naomi, who is now tied securely to a tree every evening.

Not everyone believes that Naomi is a witch. Tawakota, the leader, does not believe it. This is fortunate, for the rest can do nothing without his leave. Naomi's mistress argues that anyone can see that Tau-tie-yost never takes on wolf shape, but of course she does not want Naomi killed since Naomi does chores for her every day.

Some believe Naomi's mistress, some do not. A powerful witch can choose not to change her shape if it suits her.

"How can you tell if someone is a witch?" Penelope asks her own mistress.

"Make circle of fire, she walks west to east. If cross, woman. If stumble, *day-hudah-ki.*" Witch. She looks at Penelope and nods. "Witch killed," she says. "Woman not."

But they call Naomi Tau-tie-yost, There She Stumbles. Surely they must know she would fail that test.

"Sister cannot make good fire. Cannot make *urica.*" Stockings. "Don't know good chert. All like witch, not woman."

"She is not a witch, I promise you!"

Her mistress shrugs. "Tawakota not know," she says. "Wait." Penelope is not sure if she must wait, or if Tawakota is waiting. For supper, her mistress gives her a piece of dried fish folded over like paper.

"Eat," she says. "But not giving to sister."

She watches as Penelope puts the dried fish into her mouth, but when she looks away Penelope takes it out and hides it in the palm of her hand. She is the oldest. Naomi is her responsibility. She must come up with a plan. She thinks of the little fish they used to catch at a stream near their cabin. They were no longer than a thumb. Sirus didn't know their name so he called them silveries because of their color. Ellen would fry them by the dozen in buttered breadcrumbs. She served them with cornbread or with eggs and bacon. Or fried up with hashed potatoes for breakfast.

She has to stop thinking about food.

Their river meets up with a larger river, and then a larger one after that. As the days go on, Naomi grows more quiet and withdrawn. She no longer tries to speak Wendat with anyone and she does not try to barter for food. The spark Penelope noticed when they got to the river has vanished. One evening, after a particularly long day canoeing, Penelope is shocked to see Naomi's bleak, inward expression as she pulls her mistress's boat up the bank. It reminds her of a neighbor they had back in Philadelphia who was not ill, but who died anyway after her child died of yellow fever. She just turned her face to the wall and stopped breathing.

"I caught a fish," Penelope tells her that night when they are collecting pieces of bark for their beds. "I boiled it when no one was looking." She holds it out. It is the size of a small pickle. "Do you remember the silveries Mama used to fry up?"

Naomi looks at the fish as though it were a stone. "It's strange, but I'm not hungry anymore. I think I'll lie down."

"Eat this first. Please, Nami. I took a great chance getting it, I stole some meat for bait. If they find out they'll flog me..." She doesn't know if this is true but she will say anything.

Naomi chews the fish slowly as if even eating is now a chore. The weather has turned warmer and a blue mist rises from the mud. Penelope brings her some water.

"It's hard to find a clear stream around here, so much algae, and the weeds. But look at the gourd I found. Doesn't it make a good cup?"

Naomi lies down on her bark and blinks, looking up at the clouds.

"What are you thinking about?" Penelope asks.

"Hmm. You know, I don't suppose I was thinking anything," Naomi says in a dull voice.

It's as if her body is a loose sack around her, she cannot pay it sufficient attention. If this keeps up she will die. Penelope makes herself imagine the worst, hoping this will spur her brain into action. All she can think of is running away but they can't run away. Where would they go? What would they eat? Could they find enough berries, could they fish? She thinks about breakfast, egg pudding and oatmeal and jam.

The next day the murky river widens as if approaching the sea. They are on the Maumee now, Penelope reckons. From time to time she can see fish skimming along only a foot under the water, ugly specimens with bulging eyes and whisker-like barbels. In the afternoon the two lead canoes bank on the eastern side of the river, beneath low willow trees. A few Wyandot men stand in the shallows waving everyone over. They are the ones who determine when and where the group lands, when they eat, and when they rest.

Penelope and her mistress paddle over and the men pull up their canoe. Although the river ahead looks clear to her, the Wyandots are preparing to portage through a break in the trees. The carrying place, her mistress calls it.

"Why are we not taking the river?" Penelope asks, shouldering the wet bottom of the boat.

"Hush," her mistress says.

When everyone is on land the men on the bank untie their canoes and begin to walk in pairs, like everyone else, carrying their boats between them. As Penelope walks she looks for Naomi but cannot find her among the throng. Now she grows anxious. Did they make their decision? Did they drown her in the river? Each time she glimpses someone who might be Naomi but turns out is not her anxiety worsens. But when at last they stop to rest she spies Naomi up ahead holding the front end of her canoe. She stumbles as she sets down the boat, which makes her mistress speak to her sharply.

Penelope exhales the breath that has been tightening in her chest and lowers her end of the boat. They have stopped in a muddy acre of land dotted with standing dead trees with branches bleached as white as bones. A drowned forest. Beneath the trees are pools of the same fish she saw in the Maumee. But here the fish are dead and half-rotting. They must have somehow swum up from the river and then couldn't get back. Her nose fills with the ripe odor of plants that feed on mud to no purpose, for nothing can eat them. They will only grow until they become too wet themselves to live, and then they will begin their soft, slow decay.

"They are talking about white men," Naomi says when Penelope catches up to her. "A fort nearby. That is why we left the river."

But even this potential piece of good news does not seem to stir up any life in her. Her eyes are dull and she speaks without inflection. She looks around as if the world is nothing more to her than a picture book she is paging through idly, having nothing better to do.

Penelope takes hold of her hand and squeezes it. "White men! Nami, that's good news. Perhaps we can go to them. Make our escape! Did they say where they are?"

"I can't, my head aches. You go. You can come back for me." She says this without the least hint of hope in her voice.

"You need some water," Penelope tells her. "Wait here."

Naomi needs more than water but water is all that Penelope can offer. Carrying the gourd she now uses as a cup, she makes her way toward a little rivulet no wider than a grass snake is long.

The land around it is muddy and rank, and the air is so humid that even the insects can hardly raise themselves. Her clothes seem to cling to every hollow on her body. But just as she is clearing algae away with a stick to get clean water, she sees a group of people come out from behind the dead white trees. At first she thinks they are Englishmen because the men are dressed in English clothes—white shirts and neck-cloths and white sashes around their waists. One woman wears a short fur cape. Penelope's heart begins to race. But they are only more Wyandots. She sees their faces as they come closer.

This time no attempt is made to hide Penelope and Naomi. Penelope doesn't know if this is because these new people are from their own tribe, or because by the time they see them it is too late. The tallest man calls out a greeting in Wendat as he walks though the wet grass and stops to talk with Tawakota. After a short conference, Tawakota follows the man and his company back through the dead trees, signaling for the others to follow. They leave their canoes and walk a short distance to a place where an outcropping of flat, brownish-yellow stones rise up like slanted shelves. They are warm from the sun and, more important, they make dry seats.

For the rest of the afternoon the Wyandots rest and eat and talk among themselves. The new women go from rock to rock as if making social calls. Penelope can only understand one word in ten. But her mistress, pleased with something—perhaps just the change that new people bring with them—gives Penelope a large piece of fried cornmeal. No one notices when she gives half of it to Naomi.

Naomi says, "They are calling them The Rich Ones."

"The new group?"

"Apparently they are going back to the same village. But people are wondering where their canoes are. They don't like them exactly I don't think, but they envy them. They like their clothes. The tall man is called Hatoharomas. That means something like, He Draws Wood from the Fire."

"Naomi, I had no idea you were so good with languages. When we get back you must start French or German." She wants Naomi to think about the future. Naomi is someone who needs a dream.

"It's easier to understand than to speak. And I'm not getting much practice speaking." She says this with no bitterness. "I learned a new word this morning, *tsi-day-heska*. It means frog. At first I was confused because it's the same word as stooping."

Penelope takes her hand. She is rambling, but at least she is speaking.

"They scatter frog parts when I sleep," Naomi tells her.

"What?"

"To keep the witch-wolf away."

Penelope is shocked. But sure enough when their mistress calls them to retire she looks carefully on the ground until she finds, half buried, the leg of a frog. She puts it in her knitting bag. Tomorrow she will roast it for breakfast.

"Maybe I can untie you for a while when everyone is asleep," Penelope says.

"I don't mind anymore. I've learned to sleep without moving."

"Don't you feel cramped in the morning?"

"I don't feel anything," Naomi says.

That night Penelope can't sleep. When will Tawakota decide his people are right, that Naomi is a witch who should be burned or drowned, she wonders? Whenever the next bit of misfortune occurs, she guesses, and that might be anytime. This is a hard life, a life full of misfortune. People leave Philadelphia to escape yellow fever only to die, like Sirus and Ellen, of swamp fever in Ohio. Farmers are kicked in the head by their horses or felled by trees in a storm. Whole tribes are brought down by smallpox or chickenpox or the blue cough. Women die in childbirth no matter where they live. She thinks of Aurelia somewhere in Thieving Forest with a tree stump as a headstone. Did anyone find her body? Would they bring her back to Susanna? Where is Susanna now?

Penelope hopes she's found her way back to Philadelphia, where she has always wanted to be. Susanna never liked Ohio. But no place is safe. You make your choice and take on those risks, Sirus argued before they set out for Severne. That year the yellow fever had been particularly bad in their neighborhood. She herself, a child prone to sore throats, had nearly died from it. But after that she never had a sore throat again. Beatrice used to claim, half joking (but also half bitterly), that Penelope had passed her sore throats on to her.

The night air is warm and still and the frogs belt out their deep, plaintive cries like lost cows. Naomi is lying very still beside her. Not too long ago, Naomi's calm acceptance would have irritated Penelope, but now it brings on a kind of frozen feeling in her chest. If she turns her head she can see sparks from a dozen small campfires flickering like so many fireflies, and although she wants to believe that she can steal out and soundlessly pull a canoe into the river and paddle it alone until she finds this fort, this company of white men, she knows that she will be detected before she even puts a paddle tip to the water. The boats are guarded like gold. There might be white men out there somewhere, Penelope thinks, but they cannot help me.

She checks again on Naomi, who at last has fallen asleep. She gets up carefully and stands for a moment looking around. Then she takes a few steps trying not to make noise. With her blanket over her head she might be any Wyandot woman, and she picks up her mistress's kettle. If stopped, she will say she is fetching water. She does not know where Hatoharomas has set up his shelter. She passes a few shadows, men talking to each other in low voices, and smells their hemlock smoke. A fat yellow moon is rising.

As she makes her way through the encampment she sees a cluster of lilies growing near a wet hollow. It is the kind of lily her mother loved, a ditch lily. Perhaps it will bring her luck. She thinks of Susanna again. Sirus used to say that if there were any luck to be found then Susanna would find it. But to be lucky you must believe in luck. Penelope has never before had to rely on something so changeable. Her own abilities have always been more than sufficient.

When she straightens up she senses someone behind her, but before she can turn a warm hand comes up over her mouth and another around her throat. Her heart jumps.

"You are far from your mistress tonight," a man's voice says in English.

She moves instinctively but his grip tightens.

"Why do you lurk here?" he asks.

He is standing close behind her, his voice like breath in her hair. She can smell dirt and smoke on his fingers. His grasp is firm, but not violent. He lifts his hand away from her mouth so she can speak.

"I am looking for you." Her voice comes out in a whisper.

"Who are you looking for?"

"The man they call Hatoharomas."

"And how do you know that is me? Are you a witch like your sister with eyes behind?"

"No one has yet spoken to me in such good English. It stands to reason, you must be from the group who arrived today."

He takes his hand from her and she turns around. He is still wearing an English shirt but has changed into hide leggings. A string of beads hangs from his neck. Now that she sees him, she feels less frightened. She doesn't know why.

"Why do you look for me?" he asks.

"I come to beseech you. Please, buy my sister and myself. Take us to Sandusky where you can trade us for gunpowder. I know you will get a barrel at least."

It is not the eloquent speech she planned but it is all she can manage at the moment. She tries to gauge his reaction but he looks at her with no expression. His white shirt shines in the moonlight. He is handsome, she notices, with his straight nose, his prominent cheekbones.

He is assessing her, too. Finally he says, "Come with me."

He leads her to his bark shelter. She is confused by his good looks and gentle voice, at odds with his tight hold on her arm. A light seems to be rushing up her body. No, not a light, sharper than that. As they walk the smell of wet moss becomes stronger, and later whenever she smells moss she will think of him.

At his shelter a woman is sitting on a skin feeding sticks to an already healthy fire, and she moves to make room for them. It is the woman with the short fur cape that Penelope noticed earlier. Hatoharomas does not introduce her. His mother? Penelope wonders. On her arms she wears many copper bracelets, which jangle every time she adds another stick to the fire. After he settles himself on the blanket, the woman takes up a long clay pipe, lights it with a twig, and hands it to him.

Hatoharomas draws from the pipe and then passes it to Penelope, motioning for her to sit down beside him. She hasn't smoked a pipe above twice in her life, although she likes the smell. Her husband Thomas Forbes smoked one. The great thing is that after she smokes for a while, passing the bowl back and forth with Hatoharomas, she does not feel so hungry.

For a while Hatoharomas just smokes, says nothing. A dog barks nearby and someone hushes it. At last, looking at the fire, he says, "I am told you traveled first with Potawatomi. I wonder, how did you come to be with them?"

It is possible, she thinks as she tells him the story, that Hatoharomas might have known Sirus. There are not many white trading posts in Ohio. And everyone liked Sirus. But Hatoharomas makes no acknowledgment when she says her father's name.

"And so you and your sister the witch are the only family remaining," he says when she finishes.

"She is not a witch!" Penelope says. "Naomi is very talented, very gifted, a musician. An artist. If you could hear her on her violin..."

"What is a vie-lin?"

"Like a fiddle. Sir, please. Naomi is delicate. She needs to live withindoors with her own people. We are not far from Sandusky. You could take us there and collect a reward."

"You plead for your sister."

"Yes."

"But not for you."

"I plead for both of us."

Sparks from the fire fly up and dissipate in the night air. Hatoharomas puts his hands on his thighs, palms down. "Your sister's mistress has offered to sell her to me this very day."

The way he says this does not make it sound like a victory. Penelope waits. She feels her pulse throb in her neck.

"But with you, your mistress will not part."

So. They want to get rid of the witch and keep the one who can knit tight stockings. Her insides turn over but she makes herself say, "We stay together. We're sisters."

"Would that I could always go with my brother! But this is not the world's way."

"I will pay you over their price when we get to Sandusky. And I can knit for you, sew. I will trade you something. I will trade you this kettle," she says, lifting it up.

"Your sister for a stolen kettle?" he asks.

"I will be your servant, then. I am a hard worker."

"And if I need no servants?"

She is bargaining with an empty hand, she knows this. She's moving her pieces across the board one after the other even though she has no queen and no knight, nothing but pawns, and even the pawns are dredged up and created on the spot out of pure will.

"Then take me as your wife," she says.

As soon as the words leave her mouth she is horrified, but she won't let herself think about it. She is the oldest. She has to do what she can to save her sister.

"And if I have already a wife?" Hatoharomas asks.

She opens her hands. "I have heard Wyandots sometimes take more than one wife."

At that, surprisingly, he laughs. Then for a long time he does not speak. He smokes his pipe and passes it to her but she waves it away. A sick feeling is rising from her stomach but her eyes feel wide open, held taut by small tight threads.

"This evening as I ate my meal I considered what to do and yet finished eating without deciding," he says at last. "But now I have decided. I will buy your sister as you wish."

"And me?"

"As I said, you were not offered, and I will not ask. This is as much as I can do."

So they will be separated. But then how can she make sure that Naomi will be all right?

"Do *you* think my sister is a witch?" she asks.

Hatoharomas laughs again. "If I did, I would not buy her."

He promises her that he and his mother will be good to Naomi. He says they will all meet up again at their village in a few weeks. "There I have more power."

Penelope looks at her hands, thinking that if this man does not believe that Naomi is a witch, then it is better that she go with him rather than stay here. Safer. If that word can be applied to anything about their situation.

"You will not be unhappy with my sister. She is..." What can she say about Naomi? For some reason she does not want to lie to this man. "She was my father's favorite."

"Not for her knitting," he says with a smile.

But she cannot match his gentle levity. "No. Not for her knitting," she says seriously. "But Naomi is strong. And she understands..." What? She thinks of how Naomi looked for the scarred Potawatomi to make sure he was dead. She knew that it was important for them to see with their own eyes the end of his story. And she has an instinctive understanding of the Wyandots that Penelope lacks. The moon has moved behind the trees. Although Hatoharomas is facing her she cannot make out his expression. His eyes are dark hollows but she can tell he is listening.

"She understands something...something more than the rest of us." She feels a lump rise in her throat. "She is a musician. An artist. It's hard to explain."

Hatoharomas says, "She sees more in the world than you or I."

Penelope nods. That's part of it.

Hatoharomas stands and gives her his hand. "I too once had a sister like this."

❀

Naomi is awake when Penelope returns. "Where did you go?" she asks her. "I was afraid for you!"

Penelope crouches down next to her. Naomi is holding the twig with yellow flowers that she keeps in her moccasin, the buds by this time as dry as pebbles. Mosquitoes hover above her other hand, the one tied to the tree. They bite, drawing blood. With some difficulty, Penelope unties the knot and throws the rope from Naomi's arm.

"Look what I found." She holds out a tuber that Hatoharomas gave her before they parted, to seal their agreement. It is a long, sweet edible that Sirus used to call a Jerusalem artichoke. A patch of them grew wild near their barn. "Eat it all. I have another one for the morning."

"But where have you been?"

"I've been to see the man Hatoharomas."

"What? Why?"

She tells her about their meeting. She tries to keep her voice even. "Hatoharomas doesn't believe you're a witch. It's better that you go with him than stay here."

Naomi is silent for a moment. Then she says, "This is the end."

"It's not the end! Don't say that! Hatoharomas is better than these people here."

"You believe him to be a good man?"

"I do." She hopes so, at least.

Naomi says nothing.

"I think this is for the best, Nami, I truly do. You must leave. These people are dangerous to you. But listen to me, now. This is a second chance. You must make yourself useful. Ask them how they build their fires, and watch them. Make them teach you."

"I'll try."

"And look Nami, I found something else," she says.

Naomi looks at what Penelope puts into her hand. "A ditch lily," she says with some wonder. "Are they early this year?"

Penelope tries to calculate how long they've been gone but she can't. Weeks? A month? Tomorrow everything will change again. She does not want to wake up to the day when her sister is traded away from her. Naomi is her favorite sister. Did she know this before? Whether she knew it or not, it seems all too clear now that she is about to lose her. Naomi carries her own world within her, Ellen always used to say, and that is true. Penelope doesn't understand music and for the most part she thought that Naomi wasted her time playing—or worse, did it to get out of chores. She thought her parents were indulgent to let her. All the same, now that that piece of Naomi is gone, completely gone, the surprise is that Naomi herself is still the same. Her music was indicative of something deeper—this is what she tried to tell Hatoharomas. She isn't sure if she just saved Naomi or not.

She lies down next to her and takes her hand. "Do you want me to tell you a story? Or are you too tired?"

"I'm not tired. And I know which one I want. Our Journey Here."

This is a story Penelope often tells: how they came to Ohio from Philadelphia. For a moment she is quiet, gathering the story in her mind. With her thumb she feels her sister's long, slim, strong fingers, the fingers of a musician.

"Sirus Quiner was a shopkeeper," she begins. "And his father before him was a shopkeeper, and his father's father. As far back as anyone can remember the Quiners have been shopkeepers. They sold general goods and lived on Walnut Street in the city of Philadelphia, but one day Sirus got a yearning for space."

The Great Black Swamp

Fourteen

Meera blesses their journey by scattering tobacco leaves in the water before they leave in the skiff. It's very early in the morning, almost still night. The wind sounds like an animal looking for its mate, but the rain has finally stopped and everything smells wet and fresh. Susanna looks up into the dark sky. Four bright disks shine there like suns. A good sign, she tells Meera, although she doesn't know if it is or not.

Meera has brought food from the kitchen. "Enough for two weeks," she says.

Two weeks! "You said it would take us only two days."

"Always you must prepare for longer," Meera tells her. Something about the cloth bundle seems familiar and Susanna takes it from her to look. It is a black shawl turned inside out. When she opens it, tiny fragments of mirrors glint at her.

"Consolation's shawl," she says.

Meera nods. Her little face holds a look of pride. "It will fetch a good price in trade."

Susanna feels a childlike pleasure at this little theft that extends to the journey itself, as if they are only playing a game. She does not want to think too much about what lies ahead. They push off, leaving the flat bark roofs of Gemeinschaft behind them. Susanna can smell the pine gum that the brethren used on the skiff's seams in place of tar, along with a pervasive scent of wet wood.

They navigate easily downstream, letting the current do most of the work, and the moist, still air seems to wrap itself around her shoulders. She's wearing the split skirt Liza made for her and Aurelia's moccasins and the deer collar from Old Adam. Her grain sack is stowed next to Meera's bundle of food. Last night she gave Ellen's wedding ring to Beatrice: "For safekeeping, or if you need money."

Beatrice pushed it over her finger knuckle. Then she took it off and put it in her pocket.

"They might not be there, you know," she said. There were tears in her eyes. Susanna hugged her tightly.

"I know. But they might be."

Hard as it was to leave Beatrice, she could not deny that she was relieved to be going, and she packed everything she owned in a matter of minutes. When they left Philadelphia, she tells Meera now as the boat carries them downstream, it took them almost a month to load their wagon. Tools and inkpots and iron pans and window glass. Blank leather ledgers. Nails. Anything they couldn't make themselves, which was plenty. Every morning Sirus changed his mind about what to bring, and Ellen had to rearrange the loaded wagon so the girls would still have a place to sit. On the very morning of their setting-out, Sirus impulsively bought a small hand mill, and that turned out to be the smartest thing they brought since it meant they could grind their own grain.

Susanna puts her oar into the water to push them away from a fallen tree with a dozen sparrows perched on a high, dead branch. Above them, the sun rises behind a hazy web of clouds. They are going west on Injured River, named for some forgotten injury done to some forgotten Indian. This will lead them to Fish River, and Fish River to the Maumee. The sounds are familiar river sounds: frogs, birdcalls, the gulp of the current as it falls over rocks. She pulls up her oar and lets it drip over the side of the boat.

"It took us only seven weeks to get to Ohio, since that year the spring was so dry," she tells Meera. "At first we spent the nights in taverns along the way, some of them with only bundles of straw for beds." Later when there were no more taverns they slept in their wagon. One evening, she said, they came upon an Indian and his wife who were living in a small house built entirely from tree branches. Susanna was only seven and felt a little afraid—these were the first Indians they had ever seen in their lives except once on the street near the open market, a woman who wore a gingham dress. These Indians dressed in skins and hide shoes sewn across the top. They were very small, the man the same size as the woman, and smiled all the time. They fed the Quiners great portions of venison steak, which Susanna had never tasted before, and afterward the Indian woman sang for them.

"In the morning my father gave them two pewter spoons as a parting gift. I remember they were very pleased about that."

"Where was this place?" Meera asks.

"Near the Allegheny, I think."

Meera says, "Oneida people." She speaks confidently, but how she can know, Susanna wonders? By her own account Meera has never been east of the Sandusky.

Their trouble begins not long after they stop to eat. Meera ties the boat beneath a stunted tree half submerged in the river while Susanna unpacks some food. They sit down in the shade and are just cutting slices of cheese when Meera makes a sudden movement, grabbing Sussana's arm.

"Someone on the river," she whispers.

They crouch behind the tree, hidden by its leafy branches. Meera grabs the side of the boat to keep it from rocking into view.

Susanna listens hard but can hear nothing out of the ordinary. However, a moment later a skiff like theirs comes around the bend. Two white men are rowing hard. Men from Gemeinschaft? It takes Susanna a moment to recognize Seth, and then her heart seems to twist and at the same time expand. She should have sent him a note before she left but they had to be secretive. Nushemakw would never willingly let Meera go unless she herself had no more use for her, and the brethren would honor her wishes. Plus they planned to steal a boat.

Seth and the other man—Brother Lyle, she sees now—steer their skiff into the middle of the river. Brother Lyle leans over the bow and puts one hand in the water to push away some debris while Seth rows for both of them, looking first toward one bank and then the other. As their boat goes by Susanna feels a sudden urge to call out to them: here we are! But she doesn't. Later she will wish she had. That was her chance.

Only after the boat disappears from view does she realize she is holding her breath. Meera whispers, "They are looking for us. The man who is in love with you."

"We stole a boat," Susanna reminds her.

"How long will they look?"

Neither one had seen what supplies the men carried. Do they mean to spend the night? If not, Susanna and Meera could wait here for them to turn around and go back to Gemeinschaft. On the other hand, why waste time waiting? They could leave Injured River here and begin portaging to Fish River.

Meera says, "Since the two rivers do not meet we must portage sometime, the only question is where."

Susanna did not know about this portaging. She thought that they would be in water for the whole of the trip. She looks for a break in the foliage beyond the river. It's hard to see much beyond it.

"When I come with Nushemakw," Meera tells her, "we leave the river a little ways ahead where it feeds into a small lake. But Injured River snakes around so much. At best it only saves an hour or two of walking."

She draws a map in the dirt. "Here, we are. Here"—a line to the north—"is Fish River."

In the dirt, it seems a short distance.

At first the skiff feels light on Susanna's shoulder, or at least light enough. More difficult is finding the next level step. But soon enough the land evens out and they find a rhythm to their walk. They carry the skiff through wet meadows and between stands of trees, and then more meadows and more trees, marking the sun for direction. Heavy oaks spread their branches like nets catching the light. For almost a hundred years, Susanna's father once told her, after the Iroquois had driven everyone out, Ohio was absolutely empty of people. One hundred years. The land to the south is being cleared and resettled, also to the north along Lake Erie, but here the overgrown landscape feels everlasting.

After a while the ground begins to feel spongy underfoot. It's getting wetter, more swamplike.

"This isn't the real Black Swamp," Meera says. "When we get closer to Fish River you will see its true heart."

Susanna has never seen the Great Black Swamp let alone step foot in it, but she knows it is huge, over one hundred miles east to west extending like a sideways fang from Lake Erie all the way down to Fort Wayne. Underneath the water lies rich, black loam—good farmland if it could be drained, which most people

196 | MARTHA CONWAY

doubt. But although they pass trickle after trickle of water and some fairly wide brooks, the afternoon lengthens with no sign of a river. After a while the empty country begins to feel oppressive. Or worse: an illusion. Sounds follow them from behind, probably only frogs or insects but with the skiff on her shoulder Susanna can't turn around to check. Late in the afternoon they come to a meadow full of long brown grass that bends in the wind like the lush fur of an animal, tall enough for something to hide in. Here they find a few pawpaw trees in fruit. Ellen used to make some very good jelly out of pawpaws, but these are not yet ripe. Still, Susanna picks one and puts it in her pocket.

"Where is Fish River?" she asks. "Could we have missed it?"

But Meera says it is impossible to miss. "Maybe we entered at the longest point between the two rivers. We should stop to make camp. Then we can come to it first thing in the morning."

That's fine with Susanna. By now her shoulders are aching and there is a hard knot like an apple at the base of her spine. They find a spot in a little clearing with a small creek running through it and a pond shaped like half a heart. The ground is slightly higher here, and it is bordered on one side by a thicket of black ash trees.

"When the sun sinks," Meera says, "more mosquitoes will rise. We must light a few fires to keep them away."

Smudge fires. Back in Gemeinschaft the brethren used to light them at dusk. Meera begins to cover the boat with leaves and sticks to hide it. Susanna does not see the point of that, considering they are the only people within miles. She finds a dry spot to sit down.

"You can start the cooking fire," Meera says.

Susanna picks at a callus on the palm of her hand. Part of her would like to stretch out right now and go to sleep but she doesn't want to stand up to go get her blanket. Plus she's hungry. "I've never built a fire outside."

"I will teach you. First fetch kindling."

Susanna doesn't move.

"No thicker than your thumb," Meera says.

"I know how to find kindling," Susanna tells her. She rises reluctantly. As she brushes off her skirt a movement flashes to her right. "What was that?" She peers at the dense thicket of ash trees, squinting her eyes.

"What?"

"I thought I saw someone. A child."

"A child?" Meera stands up quickly to look. "What did the child look like?"

"I don't know. I only saw a movement. Thought I saw," Susanna corrects herself.

Meera frowns. "Maybe the Little Warrior."

"Who is that?"

A spirit, Meera explains, who appears in the form of a child dressed in war gear—eagle feathers and paint. "He comes to those alone in the forest to warn them of danger."

Susanna's heart begins to beat faster. "But we're not in the forest," she says. "And there are two of us."

They are both staring at the trees. At last Meera says, "Could be bear here."

Susanna swallows. "I'm not fetching any kindling," she tells her.

They eat a cold supper of cheese and day-old biscuits. A long pink streak forms in the sky where the sun has been, and as if on a signal insects rise out of the grass and seem to multiply. Meera pounds damp sticks into the ground and lights them with the tinder and flint that she carries in one of her pouches. They both peel dry bark from nearby trees to sleep on, and drag them into the middle of the smudge fires.

Susanna sits down on the piece of bark and puts her arms around her legs. She rests her cheek on her kneecap. Will they sleep like this, then, surrounded by smoke and fire? Is this safe? The smoke makes her eyes tear and she closes them. She wonders if Seth is still looking for her. Probably by now he has turned back. She wishes they found the river already. Off in the distance she can hear a lone wolf calling out and she thinks of her mother: "Tonight the sprites and fairies will keep us company," she used to say when they slept in their wagon on their way to Ohio.

The sound of braying comes closer. Now Susanna is no longer sure that it is a wolf. She opens her eyes. Meera is standing with her hands on her hips looking at the trees again.

"What is it?" Susanna asks.

The cicadas, which were loud a moment before, suddenly stop altogether. The sound grows nearer. It sounds like bells. Susanna stands and tries to see what she can through the trees.

"*Kshikan nati*," Meera says in Delaware. Get your knife.

But before Susanna can take a step, a large group of men come out from the trees. No, not all men, Susanna realizes. Some are women with children on their backs. A tribe of natives, maybe twenty of them. Meera holds out her hand to keep her still but Susanna couldn't move if she wanted to. Her legs suddenly feel like two heavy stones. She has never seen anyone from this tribe before, of that she is certain. They are small and very ill clad, all them hunched with the kind of stoop that a poor diet creates. Their faces are wide with dark round eyes and the men wear small shell decorations woven into their matted hair.

Two of the men are carrying sticks tied with small silver bells. Between them stands a man with warrior paint on his face. He is carrying an older man on his back. The bell ringers give a final shake of their bells and the older man slides down from the warrior's back. He raises his hand in greeting.

"*Gloucheecheechee*," he says, or at least that's how it sounds to Susanna. The smudge fires flicker between them. Susanna looks at Meera, who is standing as still as a cat.

"I do not speak this language," Meera tells him in Delaware.

The chief shakes his head at her.

She says the same thing in Iroquois, and then in English, and then in another language Susanna doesn't recognize, but each time the chief shakes his head. He wears a small smile on his face but to her mind that does not mean he is friendly. The fact that there are babies and women, though, that is a good sign. It's not a war party at least. Although the chief is not the tallest he stands the straightest. Pockets of skin under his eyes sag toward his cheeks, which give him the look of a schoolteacher wearing round glasses.

He makes a gesture, spreading his fingers, and begins to speak for a long time in his incomprehensible language, nodding all the while. When he finishes he looks at the woman to his left, who then begins to walk toward them. Meera and Susanna press closer together and Susanna takes Meera's arm as if to tether herself, but the woman only wants to give them a gift: two green feathers. Surprised, Susanna looks down at hers. She knows of no bird that carries such colors. She tries and fails to breathe in deeply.

"Thank you," she says, almost without enough breath for the words. She starts to lift her dress to curtsy when she remembers she is wearing a split skirt.

The woman copies Susanna, touching her own skirt, a sheath of untanned elk hide. Meera is watching the chief. Susanna sees that he is pointing to his mouth.

"They want food," Meera says.

"We can't give them food. We need it for ourselves."

"We have enough for twelve days. The journey will take only two."

"But we are already delayed! Who knows how many more times we will be delayed!"

"We are delayed because of you. Because of the man who loves you."

"He doesn't love me. They came for the boat."

Susanna is aware that the chief is watching them. He begins pacing back and forth moving a small object—a pipe?—end over top between his fingers. Consolation's shawl is behind them with all their dried venison, their biscuits, their crackers, their cheese, their dried fruit. Susanna is carrying dried bear meat in her grain sack. Meera says, "We should give them the bear meat."

The chief stops pacing when he sees Meera opening the sack. The meat is wrapped in a linen napkin, and at first he seems to be more interested in the cloth than in the meat. When Susanna sees how many people he has to feed and how little they gave him, she feels ashamed. By this time the children have all slid off their mothers' backs and are staring at Susanna and Meera, but without fear. Nor is it confidence, exactly. She isn't sure what it is.

One child comes toward her, a girl. She stares at Susanna intently. Maybe she has never seen a white woman before? There are stories back home about Swamp People, but they are giants who travel from tree to tree like squirrels. Nothing like this small girl. Her thin arms and distended belly upset Susanna, and she bends down to give the child the green pawpaw that she has in her pocket. The child has beautiful dark eyes with an adult's expression. Her heart-shaped face reminds Susanna a little of Aurelia.

After a moment the girl reaches out curiously to touch Susanna's collar.

It is the collar with the deer tail that Old Adam gave her. Susanna has forgotten she was wearing it. Without thinking, she unties it and hands it to the child. The child looks down at it seriously, stroking the tail with two fingers. When she starts to hand it back, Susanna shakes her head and the child smiles broadly.

Meera says, "That is good, a gesture of peace, they will like that."

The wind shifts, blowing the torch smoke away. The chief calls to the girl and she brings the collar over to him. Is he going to keep it for himself, Susanna wonders? But he just examines it and then hands it back. He says something to Meera and Susanna and points to the sky, and then to the east. The night is clear and warm. They shake their heads, not understanding. He motions for them to come with him, and they shake their heads again. Finally he spreads his arms as if finishing their conversation. With a gesture Susanna cannot interpret, the chief says something to the warrior, who leans over and hoists him up on his back. The bell ringers begin ringing their bells, and the people return to the ash thicket and are gone.

Or most of them are gone. One woman remains: the one who gave them the feathers. She makes no attempt to conceal herself, but sits down facing them just beyond the torches. Her expression is unreadable in the deepening twilight. She keeps very still. Only her loose hair lifts now and then in the wind.

"Why does she stay?" Susanna asks.

Meera says, "I don't know."

On the one hand it seems clear that the woman—Susanna calls her Green Feather, since she must call her something—does not mean them any harm. On the other hand, maybe she does.

"Maybe she wants to steal our food while we sleep," Susanna says.

"They could easily have taken it already by force."

By this time night has set in fully although the moon is not yet up. They can no longer see Green Feather but Susanna feels certain she is still there.

"You see it is a good thing I hid the boat," Meera says.

When the moon rises they see her figure again with her back toward the trees. She sits cross-legged, her hands in her lap. Will she stay the whole night this way? Why does she stay? Susanna cannot make out her face, whether her eyes are open or closed.

They decide they must keep watch. Meera takes the first one. Susanna stretches out on her narrow piece of bark convinced she will never fall asleep, but in no time it seems Meera is pulling on her arm.

"Susanna, Susanna look."

She doesn't mean look at Green Feather, which is what Susanna first thinks. She is pointing to the sky. A flash of light illuminates the tops of trees to the east. After it dies it appears again a moment later like someone is throwing a lantern's light to and fro. There's no sound except the mild wind. Green Feather is still there, still sitting. She too is looking at the sky.

"Lightning," Meera says. They cannot see the line of it, only the brightening treetops where it throws its light, and then for only a few seconds. But why is there no sound of thunder? For a while Susanna and Meera watch the lightning silently flare over and over again behind the trees. In its light they can see branches waving in the wind.

"Somewhere the *pate-hock-hoo-ies* are hard at work," Meera says. "The rain spirits." She guesses that the storm must be miles and miles away since they can't hear it. Susanna feels a hair near her mouth and she pulls it off and then gathers her blanket more securely around her. She feels no urgency to leave. Anyway, where would they go? Not in the trees in a lightning storm. But the wind is rising. After a while Meera says, "I think that it's moving this way."

Susanna holds her breath. Finally, the faint sound of a thunderclap. The wind picks up significantly and one of their torches blows out. The next time Susanna looks over at Green Feather, she is standing.

"Look, she is beckoning to us," she says to Meera.

Green Feather shouts and beckons again. Half a second later a thunderclap sounds loudly overhead. Susanna, startled by how fast the storm has suddenly traveled, says, "We have to go."

The wind begins pulling wildly on their hair and skirts. Susanna grabs the blankets while Meera snatches up their bundles of food and supplies. At the last moment Meera remembers her iron kettle.

They follow Green Feather into the ash thicket, Susanna for her part not caring now that a tree might be struck by lightning, so eager is she to get out of the wind. But what Green Feather wants, it turns out, is to show them a cave. It's down a little ravine, more of a stone outcropping really, but a shelter nonetheless formed by a huge piece of rock jutting out like a rooftop over a sunken piece of land. Standing at its entrance Meera peers inside. Green Feather says—shouts, really, because of the wind—a few words that Susanna takes to mean, It's all right. It's safe. The rain starts coming down in small hard drops.

Inside, the cave is dank and smells like limestone and animal dung. It doesn't extend very far back, but it is high enough for them both to stand up. The bones of a small animal lay scattered in the dirt. When Susanna turns back around, Green Feather is gone.

"Where did she go?"

Meera looks out. The rain is falling hard and fast now, and with almost no pause the lightning strikes again and again. Susanna can see debris flying in the wind and thinks that she has never seen a storm to match this one. The air is loud with the cracking sound of tree branches splintering and falling. Suddenly they both gasp and draw back at the same time as lightning strikes a tree not twenty paces away. The tree lights up like a lantern and then throws out sparks. Afterward, a strong burnt smell wafts into the cave.

Now hailstones begin to shower down. The noise, if possible, becomes even more terrific. However, the lightning is moving away, and the hail soon follows. The storm is passing as suddenly as it came. Susanna can see little piles of ice on the ground—the hailstones. The rain has nearly stopped entirely when she sees Green Feather walking among the dripping trees with two or three other women. They pick up the hailstones and put them into sacks of some kind. Where did they shelter? Is there another cave? Susanna asks Meera what they're doing.

"Collecting water," Meera tells her.

"But they live in a swamp!"

Meera casts her a look of disbelief or disdain. "Clean water," she says.

All at once Susanna is deeply exhausted. She moves away from the entrance to stretch out on the floor of the cave, wrapping her blanket around her. Has it really been less than a day since they left Gemeinschaft? She can feel the gravelly dirt of the cave floor against her head but she is too tired to look for dry leaves to use as a pillow. At least, she thinks, I have a good story to tell Penelope when I see her tomorrow, or the day after that.

Fifteen

In the morning they remember the boat.

They rush back to where they hid it. Fortunately Meera covered it with heavy branches, so the wind managed to drag it only a little ways off. But it is overturned and the oars, stashed underneath it, are missing. After a long search they find only one, and it is split at the top. Although at first it doesn't seem as if the boat itself suffered much damage, when they heave it over they see a dent on the bottom of one side that could easily develop into a rupture.

Susanna moves her hand over it. "If we pound the dent, the surface might break," she says. "And we have no means to fix it."

"Holes can always be mended. It is the oar that worries me. We must fashion a new one. Did you bring a whittling knife?"

"A *whittling* knife? No, I didn't have a *whittling* knife with me at the mission."

"Do not make fun. You are very ill prepared. Luckily I thought." Meera takes a small knife from her bundle.

"Why did you ask me for one if you have one yourself?" Susanna asks peevishly. Traveling with Meera, she can see now, will be like living with her sisters: the constant disappointment in her and subsequent little lessons. She is so tired of people telling her she is not good at this or that. But after a while, perhaps to make up for her irritation, Meera says, "It is good you gave the girl that collar. That is why they showed us the cave."

Susanna doesn't see how Meera could possibly know that, but she decides not to contradict her. Credit of any kind is good.

The morning sky holds a strange greenish light—an after-effect of the storm—and the ground is as wet as it can be outside the boundaries of a stream. When they hoist the boat up onto their shoulders it feels heavier to Susanna, and her moccasins sink with each step. There is no sign of the Stooping Indians, as she now thinks of them. As they walk she tries to catch any sound of a rushing river and silently curses the birds that chatter endlessly, drowning out other noises.

After a while they come to a shallow pond filled with straight, yellow trees that branch only at their tops. They wade through the water carefully with the boat floating between them. If the pond were a little deeper they might get into the boat, but it never gets deep enough. On the other side is a stand of swamp oak entwined with vines so dark they look black. To Susanna the trees seem like a positive boundary, one she does not want to cross.

For a while they put off the moment and sit on a rock to rest. They eat the last of the cheese.

"When do you think will we find the river?" Susanna asks.

"Soon we will hear it."

She wonders if she should just turn around here and go back. A failed bet. She can always try to enlist the aid of the brethren to get to the Wyandot village. Only Meera would be out of luck, forced to stay with her foster mother in a place that she hates. Still, Susanna cannot make up her mind definitely, so when the cheese is all eaten she once again hoists the boat up onto her shoulder. They enter the woods by way of a little deer path that looks surprisingly used—do the Stooping Indians come this way? Soon the tree canopy closes above them and her eyes adjust to the change in light. But they have not gone more than a dozen steps when Meera, who is in front, stops abruptly.

"What is it?" Susanna asks.

"Carefully. Put down the boat."

The undergrowth on either side is so thick that they have to lay the boat straight down on the path. Susanna looks around, trying to see what Meera has seen—ripe berries perhaps?

Then she sees. Leaning up against three young trees are three long wooden boxes. Inside the boxes are three dead bodies.

Susanna draws in her breath and crosses her arms quickly in front of her. Three bodies of three white men, each wearing a muddy blue uniform. Scouts? Certainly it is not unusual to see soldiers traveling in threes. They often came through Severne on their way to scope out new territory. Although the bodies have been disfigured, Susanna cannot bring herself to look away. Each of them has paint on their faces, one side red and one side black. Their ears and noses are pierced with bits of thick reed. One wears a shift of painted deerskin that is tied like an apron to his uniform.

Something else catches Susanna's eye. She takes off her bonnet and covers her mouth and nose, and then bends over one of the bodies. Someone has stuck a feather into the pocket of the uniform. A green feather, exactly like the ones the Stooping Indians gave to them.

She pulls the feather out. As she turns it over her vision seems to narrow.

"They did this," she says. "They killed these men."

Meera takes the feather and examines it.

"This is a warning," Susanna tells her. She is scared now, truly scared.

Meera says, "To us they were kind."

"I think we should go back to Gemeinschaft."

"To Gemeinschaft! No, I will not go back."

"Listen, Meera. I can ask the brethren to come with us. I can plead for your case. You can still go to your people up north, only you'll be protected. Think on it! The brethren do carry guns for hunting, you know. They believe in self protection."

"Sometimes it is safer for women to travel alone."

"That is certainly not true!"

"It is true," Meera insists. "We are not warriors, not soldiers. Not a threat. Listen to me. I know these kinds of people. They live their way as they have for hundreds of years going from one food to another depending on the season. They know the passing of time only by what grows and what swims. But make no mistake, they will protect their land and themselves. A uniform is enough to tell them this person is a danger. As women we are not a danger. But what do you think would happen if we came back with soldiers?"

"Not soldiers. Missionaries."

Meera shrugs her shoulders as if to say: they are the same. "They showed us the cave," she reminds Susanna. "They did not have to do that. To us they are friends."

"You cannot be sure how long friendliness will last."

"We gave gifts to one another. That is a promise of goodwill."

But no matter how much they argue, neither one can convince the other that the Stooping Indians will or will not hurt them. It has to be the Stooping Indians who did this. It is too much to believe that more than one starving tribe could live in this mossy wasteland. And yet Susanna does not even know that for certain. How can she determine the right course of action? In any case, Meera refuses to return.

"I would be a prisoner," she says. "Nushemakw will not give me another opportunity to run away. She will see to that. Anyway, I feel sure that the river is just on the other side of these trees."

Susanna looks at the bodies. What a desolate place to die. And after death, to be mocked with paint and piercings. She hates this wet, spongy land. Every tree seems to be watching them. The truth is, she doesn't want to go back to Gemeinschaft either, but neither does she want to go on.

"If they wanted us dead, we would be dead," Meera tells her.

Not a comforting thought.

The woods lead to a small dry clearing scattered with mounds that look almost like sand. After they set down the boat, Susanna bends down to touch one. It *is* sand.

How is this possible? She lets it run through her fingers.

Back before the mastodon left, Meera tells her, the Black Swamp was made up of six ancient lakes. So Nushemakw's people say. They claim that one lake is still here, hidden and full of magic. "The person finding it will become great with power but also bewitched, unable to leave."

The clearing, surrounded on all sides by woods, is bowl-shaped and smells like the wet trees. But there is no sign of a river. Susanna's initial stab of disappointment turns to worry. Are they lost? Not yet but soon, if they keep going, they might be. She should turn back but she doesn't want to go alone. She never wants to go alone, that is her problem.

"We've been going northwest, but now we must turn fully west," Meera says firmly.

A blue haze seems to float in the air. Meera decides to climb a tree, hoping to catch a glimpse of Fish River. Meanwhile Susanna takes off her moccasins and scrunches her toes. They are still wet from wading through the shallow pond. She hears the faint trickle of water nearby and pulls her tin cup from her grain sack. She follows the sound to a stream almost hidden by a thick line of plants with brown fanning leaves. On the largest leaf a small frog hides quietly. Looking closer, she sees it is dead.

Meera comes up beside her. With one hand Susanna shades her eyes. "Did you see Fish River?"

"I saw to the west the red maple that grows along its banks. We are close."

Susanna looks down at the dead frog. Nothing has changed. From here she can probably find her way back to Injured River. But when she takes a step she feels a sudden sharp pain on her ankle.

"Oh!" she cries out. Something golden rustles away in the grass.

"A snake," she says. "It...I think it bit me!" She drops to the ground.

Meera turns quickly. "Where did it go?"

"I don't know. Oh!" She can see fang marks above her ankle-bone and the skin around it is turning red. All in a moment every limb of her body seems to stiffen. "Oh! It hurts." But Meera has run after the snake. A few moments later she returns, her face ashen. "A yellow *shixikwe*. It makes its way to water after attacking, else it dies."

Susanna is still on the ground, cupping her ankle with both hands. "Is it bad?" she asks, rocking backward. It feels very bad.

Meera crouches down and gently takes Susanna's hands away from her foot. She looks at the bite without touching the skin. "The poison is inside you," she says. "Try not to move."

She makes a travois with her blanket, maneuvers Susanna onto it, and pulls her toward a nearby stand of sycamores. The sky has become a curious shade of yellow-green, and a hazy rain begins, as soft as fog. Susanna lifts her face to it, hoping for some relief. Her ankle throbs.

"My nose feels strange," she says. She looks up at Meera's face, which is pinched with worry. Meera says there is a plant she's seen used, she doesn't know the English name, but she will look for it. Susanna watches her disappear into the trees. Her tongue begins to quiver and she touches her lips gingerly. She doesn't want to be alone but at the same time she is aware of some new barrier rising up between herself and the rest of the world, as though some important change is happening but only to her. Her nose feels like little bubbles are popping inside.

She realizes she's going to be sick. Leaning out as far as she can away from the blanket, she empties her stomach. Meera returns as she finishes, and wipes Susanna's mouth with a cloth.

"I'm sorry," Susanna says. "I was afraid to move." Is she slurring her words? Her tongue feels very thick in her mouth.

Meera says she will dig a hole for her to be sick in, but first she must drink. She puts a cup of water to Susanna's lips.

"*Wanishi*," Susanna says in Delaware. Thank you. Then she leans over and is sick again.

The afternoon turns into bouts of vomiting followed by rest followed by yet another bout. Her thirst is unquenchable. Meera makes a poultice from a long smelly shaft of bugwort she found, pulverizing its knotty roots with a rock. She mixes the powder with water and crushed leaves from another plant, making a kind of wet cake. When she lays it over Susanna's foot her ankle feels better, but soon afterward a sharp pain punches her in her middle. She crawls off the blanket and pulls off her skirt to relieve herself. Looking down, she sees with horror that her urine is filled with blood.

"Everything is coming out of me," she wails.

Meera gives her something sour to drink. After she finishes it Susanna falls into a heavy sleep.

When she wakes it is dark. Meera is shaking her arm. "I built a shelter," she is saying. "Can you walk?"

A low, bright moon casts a sharp shadow behind her.

"I thought I should try not to move?"

"By now the poison has run where it will."

Susanna puts her two hands to the ground. She says, "But I can't feel my legs."

Meera drags her again by the blanket. Fortunately the shelter is not far off—a little structure made out of thin sticks woven over a framework of thicker branches. It is the length of Susanna's body, wide enough for them both to sleep in, and open at either end. But when Susanna lies down her nose begins to bleed and doesn't stop for some time. Her bowels still ache but the pain in her ankle is gone. She has no feeling there at all. Through the branch latticework of the shelter she can see broken fragments of the night sky. Clouds come and go and the moon grows smaller and smaller. The morning takes a long time coming. The air keeps getting colder.

Sixteen

When there is no sign of Susanna on Injured River, Seth leaves Gemeinschaft and returns to Severne. There he learns that Cade has left for Kentucky almost two weeks ago, and that Amos is dead. And not just dead, but brutally killed. One of the farmers, needing help with a wagon wheel, found Amos's body three days ago propped up against the cabin door.

One of his ears was missing and his face was painted black. He was naked and all of his weapons were gone. Some Indian did it, but why? A couple of farmers took it upon themselves to bury him, not knowing if Seth was coming back or not. That was yesterday. Seth missed the funeral by a day. But he does not go over to the small walled plot where the settlers have chosen to bury their dead. He does not want to see Amos's grave.

Inside, their cabin smells like blood. There is a dark stain in the corner where the planks of wood have run out and the floor is bare dirt. Is this where he was killed? Then dragged outside? A few things are obviously gone: the iron tongs, the longest hammer, and a mirror that once hung over the basin and pitcher, their only decoration. The room feels like defeat. Seth looks at the ceiling. Has it always been so sloped? Even the walls seem darker than he remembered and strangely, considering Amos erected the cabin only six years ago, in a state of decay. Seth knows he should do something, get his things together, see what he can sell to any takers. Maybe meet Cade in Kentucky. But he stands in the empty room as if listening. He knows Cade will never come back. Seth could sell the rest of his father's tools without too much effort. Maybe someone would even want to take up the trade, one of the farmers tired of being outdoors all day. Every settlement needs a blacksmith.

One thing is certain, though: it won't be him. Amos always talked of leaving the trade to his sons. Cade didn't want it, but Amos never saw that. Seth pours some water into the basin but it sat too long in the pitcher and the smell of sulfur is strong. He should go out and fetch more water but instead he just puts the pitcher back down. A feeling is pulling at him but he can't think what.

The other settlers have gotten nervous—trouble with the natives, they're saying. John Johns, one of the farmers who buried Amos, told Seth that he was going to carry a rifle with him the next time he plowed. But Seth isn't worried about natives. That isn't it. Something to do with Susanna? He needs direction. A task. The slope of the ceiling is permanent, there is no fixing that now.

He goes outside to get some fresh air and that's when he sees the Indian crouching near the cabin. A Potawatomi. He isn't hiding but he isn't making himself too visible either. The long rye grass rises behind him, and Seth realizes that he would only be seen by someone coming out of his cabin: himself.

The man stands. "*Bozho*," he says. Greetings.

The man is taller than Seth and broader but his hands hang to his sides, empty. His only knife is tucked into his belt. Seth can see that he is not here to threaten him.

"*Bozho*," Seth replies. He knows Potawatomi from Amos's late night rants after hours of drinking.

The man is looking at his face. Then he looks at Seth's arms and legs, his shoulders, and back to his face. "You are Potawatomi," he says.

Is this a question? "I have Potawatomi blood, but also German. Mostly German."

"Face is Potawatomi. Father is Potawatomi but does not have face."

"Did you know my father?"

He says, "I did not sanction his death." For a while he says nothing more. Seth waits, curious. Sanction is an interesting word to use. For a moment he wonders at his own coldness, and then lets it go. Amos was not an easy parent to live with. Thank God for Cade, his ally.

"I am here to see if you seek revenge," the man finally says.

At that Seth looks at him quickly, warily.

"I am here peacefully. To parley," the man says.

Seth looks around. No farmers in sight, all of them out in their fields probably. There is not much to Severne: a couple of plank walkways, a half dozen yellow buildings, and that's it. That's the settlement. Behind him the ground is so flat you could see a man riding in from nearly a mile away. Also that man could see you.

"Let's go into my cabin," Seth says. "This place is too open."

But the Potawatomi does not move. "If you seek revenge I am beholden to help."

This surprises Seth. "Beholden! But I have never seen you before. We have no connection."

"Both Potawatomi."

Seth pushes his damp hair off his forehead. The day is very humid. He tells the Potawatomi that he believes his father was engaged in some wrongdoing. What he means by this is that he does not think revenge would be a fitting response.

"Do you know who killed him?" Seth asks. Immediately he wishes he could take it back. Better not to know. They still have not moved from their spot in front of Seth's cabin. The wind when it reaches him is hot. The man doesn't answer. An insect lands on his arm but he still does not make a move. Seth asks him what his name is.

"Koman."

"Koman, let me offer you some food inside. It is too hot to speak here without shade. I do not seek revenge, but I would seek your aid. I am looking for a woman. Her name is Susanna Quiner. She's gone into the Black Swamp."

Koman searches Seth's face. Then he says, "Red hair?"

Seth nods.

Koman crosses his arms in front of him. His hair blows forward in the hot wind. "I will aid," he says.

Seventeen

At night wild creatures call out in human voices and she is convinced that the Stooping Indians are coming in a pack to kill her and pierce her ears. When she opens her eyes a full white moon is close to her face. So that is why she feels so hot. A moment later, the moon is gone. It is daylight and Green Feather is massaging her leg. Green Feather says, "*Gloucheecheechee*," in a very soft voice. Susanna licks her dry lips and searches her mind for an answer. "*Merci*," she says finally.

She dreams she is walking through Thieving Forest in search of something vitally important only she has forgotten what. When she looks up she can see a single tree branch angling down as if pointing to her head. It places her in the world and gives her solace: you are still here. In the morning Meera urges her to drink some foul liquid from a cup, which she spits out.

"Look over there," Meera tells her.

On the opposite end of the clearing, men and women are dropping down from tree branches. In the cold gray light they look like ghosts.

"It is where they sleep," Meera tells her.

Susanna watches them drop, breathing through her mouth. Is she dreaming again?

"They share the night with the birds," Meera says.

Whenever Susanna thinks back to this time she can still feel the soft tug on her scalp as the children braid and decorate her hair. They love her hair, probably its red color, and they thrust their little fists into it whenever they can.

When she is able to sit up, one of the men carries her on his back away from the sycamore trees so she can get more sun, which is important for healing, Green Feather says. Her right leg is getting stronger but her left leg, the one the snake bit, still has no feeling. It is swollen and yellow and her toes are like little sausages. She cannot so much as bend her knee. When Meera or Green Feather helps her stand she turns into a wading bird, up on one leg. Looking down, her foot seems like something attached to somebody else.

A week goes by and still she can't move it. At night she is carried back to her little shelter but during the day she sits up against a tree stump in the sun with a skin over her lap, dozing or watching the Stooping Indians at work. The women make little reed hammocks that they sleep on up in the trees, or look for nuts and roots. Meanwhile the men hunt, using short bows that they handle with astonishing accuracy. By this time all the food that Susanna and Meera have brought with them from Gemeinschaft is gone. They are dependent on whatever food the Indians can find. Every morning the men bag birds nesting in the Swamp, each one tiny, hardly a meal for a child, and they also snare small rodents and snakes. They save the bones and the children pound them into powder, which they mix into hot water and drink.

Susanna takes a sip. It tastes like chalk.

Slowly she sleeps less and remembers more. Her sense of smell returns. But she still can't move her left leg. One afternoon after they decorate her hair, the children play a game pretending to cure her. The girl to whom Susanna gave Old Adam's collar plays the part of a priest or doctor. She blows on Susanna's leg and chants some words.

She is the chief's daughter, Meera tells Susanna. Her name is Light in the Eyes. She wears Old Adam's deer collar every day, although it is too large for her and droops over her collarbone. The chief himself—they call him Gosi—visits Susanna wearing a cape made of muskrat skin that Susanna sometimes sees the children playing in. He bends down to touch her leg, moving her kneecap as if that is indicative of something, like testing if a roasting chicken is done. Then he stands to consult with Green Feather, rolling between his fingers the small wooden object she saw him holding that very first evening. It isn't a pipe, as she thought at first. It looks like a wavy snake.

When he leaves Susanna asks Light in the Eyes about it, pantomiming a snake on the ground. All of her communication feels like an exaggerated performance, a play, all signs and pantomimes. The children especially like to act out little speeches for her, telling her every day what the men have found to eat.

"Not snake." Light in the Eyes shakes her head. Her eyes sparkle with mirth. She waves her two hands gently. Then she makes a motion as if she is drinking.

"Water?" Susanna asks. With her fingertips she pantomimes rain coming down. Light in the Eyes nods. Do they pray to this figure? Susanna wonders. Do they worship the water? Light in the Eyes is watching her, still smiling. She has a sweet, heart-shaped face.

A thought occurs to Susanna. "Is there special water somewhere? Something that will cure my leg? Heal it?"

She is growing more and more anxious. But Light in the Eyes just smiles and touches Susanna's hair, which that day has been braided into five or six braids with long golden leaves at the ends.

Susanna immediately feels ashamed of herself for asking about magical water, something a child might ask for. She is glad that Light in the Eyes did not understand, and nods to her as she feels the ends of her braids, crinkling the leafy decorations: yes, this is good, I like this.

One morning Green Feather massages Susanna's injured leg with a new kind of oily plant resin, and afterward she consults with Meera in a mixture of Iroquois and signs, also a few words of her own language, which Meera is learning.

"Ask her when my leg will be healed," Susanna says to Meera.

She wants a number: two days, a week. But Meera tells her she must be patient.

"We will keep you comfortable," she says. "Don't worry."

Don't worry? She looks at their faces, are they hiding something from her? She wants to ask if she is crippled now but is afraid that they will not say no strongly enough. Meera and Green Feather crouch on the ground. Green Feather picks something up. She laughs.

"What? What?" Susanna calls out.

Meera turns.

"What are you saying about me?"

"Nothing. We'll be right back."

They disappear into the woods. When they come out again their arms are linked. Is it her imagination, or does Green Feather look a little like a grown-up Meera? Susanna finds herself spinning a tale: this is Meera's tribe, not her uncle tribe but her real tribe related by blood to Meera's real parents. Meera is waiting for the right time to tell her. She will be traveling with Green Feather now. And since Susanna cannot walk she will have to stay behind.

Susanna tries to bend her knee but without success.

They approach her, smiling. Meera is holding something in her hand: a purple root. It is still wet from whatever stream they dug it up from. Beside her, Green Feather touches her mouth: for you to eat.

"Gnaw on this," Meera says. "Green Feather found it. It will help your muscles strengthen and also ease the pain in your stomach." She hands it to Susanna and then turns. "Now she wants to show me the plants for your poultice."

"Don't go off with her, please!"

"Susanna, she is helping you. She is showing me how to heal your leg."

She owes her life to Meera and Green Feather, and yet she's conscious that she is nothing to them. Not sisters, not kin. No natural ties bind them together. Every day the men bring back fewer birds. Soon no doubt they will have to leave this place to find more food. When that day comes, if she cannot walk, Susanna will not be able to go with them. Will Meera leave then, too? Susanna looks down at her leg, willing it to move. What if she is left to die in this place alone and unburied? Her bones taken by vultures? Her hair used for nests? She touches the puffy skin above her ankle. Blood runs through it, muscle lies underneath, but the leg itself is asleep. Just a bone to pick at, she thinks.

❦

A few days later there is a great commotion: rabbits have been spotted in another clearing, smaller than this one but with the same dry patches of sandy dirt. It lies to the east not far away, and the Stooping Indians begin preparing to go there.

For a moment Susanna thinks: It's come, they will leave me now. But as if sensing her anxiety Light in the Eyes comes to tell her that Gosi has instructed two men to make a bier for her. They carry her to the new spot while Light in the Eyes walks alongside them. Today we will catch many rabbits, she tells Susanna, and eat them, and spend the night in new trees. We will dance, she says, and pantomimes dancing.

The trees droop over them, heavy with leaves. Summer is passing. Behind them, Meera and Green Feather are carrying the brethren's skiff. Susanna can hear them laughing. A thread of worry winds itself around her heart and tightens. Meera never laughs with Susanna.

The new clearing is hotter and flooded with insects, and yet all the Stooping Indians seem happy and excited. They busy themselves finding clubs or small round rocks. When everyone has a weapon they stand in a circle and keep very still as they wait for a rabbit to come out of a burrow. Meera stands next to Green Feather with a rock in her hand.

At last a rabbit emerges. Two men drive it toward Green Feather, who is nearest, and she throws her club at it. It veers off to another person, who throws a rock. Then another hits the rabbit and another and another until the rabbit can no longer run. In this way twenty-two rabbits are killed: a feast.

The women skin the rabbits and the men cook the meat in large hollowed-out gourds filled with hot water. They save everything: fur, bones, teeth.

"Why don't they have kettles, do you think?" Susanna asks Meera. "It's obvious they sometimes trade with other tribes. They have whelk beads, and Green Feather knows some Iroquois."

"Probably they would rather have food. Besides, then they would have to carry the kettles from place to place. Have you noticed they take almost nothing with them?"

They have only their rough clothes and their hammocks made of reeds. Sometimes Gosi's attendant puts out a collapsible stool for the chief to sit on; it is made from whittled swamp oak with a hide seat. This is their only piece of furniture.

"They leave nothing behind them but leaves and sticks," Meera says, "which will disappear into the earth. When the white man comes for this land they will believe it was empty. No one will ever know they were here."

"Why would white men want it? It's just swampland."

"If it is there," Meera says, "men want. Women do not want so much."

Well that's not true, Susanna thinks. She wants plenty. Maybe not miles of land but at least a safe place to live with her sisters—a roof and four walls. And to walk again. That most of all. She'd seen cripples in Philadelphia make their way slowly down the street, dragging their bad leg behind them. But she can't even go to relieve herself without help.

When it comes time to eat Light in the Eyes brings Susanna her share of rabbit in a watery broth. Susanna uses the wooden bowl and spoon she brought with her from Gemeinschaft, and when she is done Light in the Eyes washes out the bowl and fills it with drinking water, which they share. Two men go around the little clearing lighting smudge torches. They will sleep here tonight, Light in the Eyes tells Susanna, but first there will be dancing. She sways to demonstrate.

While they wait for the music to begin, Susanna listens to Meera and Green Feather talk to each other in a mixture of words and pantomime. The four of them are sitting together on blankets but Meera keeps her head turned away from Susanna.

Light in the Eyes takes her hand and pats it. Then she pats the collar around her neck. Susanna agrees, it does look handsome.

She smiles at her and says in English, "Hello. Hello. Hello." She makes Light in the Eyes repeat it: "Hello-ello-ello." Susanna is thinking that if the white men come as Meera says they will, Light in the Eyes will fare better if she knows some of their words.

At last the bell ringers ring their bells and the men begin drumming on upside-down gourds. A young man steps forward and begins blowing into a reed flute. At first everyone just listens, and then a few get up to dance. Susanna is surprised to see that they all begin dancing the same dance in synchronized movements: legs together, a bend of the knees, a sway from left to right. The music gets faster and the dancers raise their arms. More people get up to dance. When the chief enters the circle, a man with a goose-wing whistle calls attention to him.

Their movements become more and more joyful, a celebration. Bending, swaying, stepping forward and back—Susanna does not understand the timing, but it is beautifully executed in absolute unison. Now even the smallest child is dancing. Later, when she arrives at the Wyandot village, she will see the same dance but there only the men are allowed to dance it.

Green Feather has pulled Meera up with her, and Light in the Eyes is dancing, too. A young boy with a tiny reed flute steps up next to the flute player, who puts his hand on the boy's shoulder and nods. The boy raises his little flute to his mouth. Unexpectedly, tears come into Susanna's eyes. Here are these people, she thinks, practically starving, with nothing, and yet look at them dancing, making music, full of joy. God himself could not help but look down on them with every pleasure in his heart.

Light in the Eyes sways and then she looks back at Susanna.

"Help me stand," Susanna asks her.

Light in the Eyes helps her up. Susanna stands for a moment trying to find her balance. The dancers go on dancing, oblivious to her, but Green Feather and Meera come over and she gives them each one arm and then looks down at her leg. She concentrates. At first, nothing. But she keeps looking at it and finally, painfully, slowly, she shuffles her left foot forward. It feels puffy and stiff but she moves it. It moves. On either side of her, Meera and Green Feather both tighten their grip from either excitement or caution. She tries to move her foot again. She cannot put weight on it, or not much, but she can at last shift it forward with the greatest of effort.

"You walk!" Light in the Eyes cries out in her own language, but her meaning is clear. She makes a little hop and begins to dance around her. "You walk! You walk! It was the *chimwa*!" she cries. The rabbit.

Eighteen

Meera tells Susanna there are rapids where Fish River meets the Maumee and she must tie her grain sack to her back so it won't fall out. But looking down at the river Susanna has a hard time believing it can stir up enough white water to trouble them. It is so clear she can see whiskered fish swimming along the pebbly bottom. They put in their skiff at a narrow point between two willow trees and then turn to say farewell.

"Hello, Chimwa," Light in the Eyes calls out, meaning goodbye. She has been calling Susanna *Chimwa*, rabbit, ever since Susanna began to walk again. She is convinced that she herself healed Susanna's leg. When the rabbits were first spotted, Light in the Eyes petitioned her father, Gosi, to let her select the one Susanna would eat. She declared that the right one would cure Susanna's lameness. The rabbit she chose was not the largest but it was the hardest to kill. Twice it nearly escaped the circle. It had special strength. Afterward, men and women came up to congratulate Susanna and to hear, from Light in the Eyes, the story of the rabbit.

Two of the men have repaired their skiff and fashioned new oars, and although Susanna watches Meera closely for any sign that she wants to stay with Green Feather, Meera just steps carefully into the skiff and sits down, clutching its side with one hand as it rocks. She holds her body very stiffly and looks at Susanna: Ready?

Susanna lifts her oar with a heavy heart. She wishes she had her turkey hen bone, or even some tobacco that Meera could scatter on the water. She wishes Light in the Eyes and Green Feather could come with them, but there is no room in the boat even if they could persuade them to leave their people.

She puts a hand on her heart, which is how the Stooping Indians say thank you, and then waves good-bye.

"Hello! Hello!" Light in the Eyes calls out as the boat moves away. Gosi lifts his hand in farewell, as does Green Feather, who is standing up to her ankles in the river. Meera waves once and then turns her head sharply. Her mouth, Susanna notices, is drawn very tight.

Susanna keeps her arm raised. She turns around so she can see them as long as possible. "Goodbye!" The corners of her eyes are wet. She will never see Green Feather or Light in the Eyes again.

When they are out of sight Susanna turns back around and after a moment she stretches her leg, which is still a little stiff. The river moves steadily north in the wet landscape, and for a while they just let the boat drift. When Susanna looks down she can see two fat fish swimming beside them. One looks up at her with an open mouth full of teeth, and she has her first moment of uneasiness. A sign, she thinks, but of what? The boat floats on through a patch of reeds. Fish River is placid and easy, nothing to worry about. An easy boat ride downriver to the Maumee. Susanna moves her leg into the sun and scrunches her toes in her moccasins. She can see larger trees coming up ahead that will close off the sunlight.

But very soon after they enter the trees, the river tips a little to the east. According to Meera, Fish River flows west and northwest. A slight hiccough, a curve that will adjust itself? They take up their oars as if that will make a difference. Susanna wills the river to turn back toward the Maumee, but stubbornly it does not. If anything it veers even more decidedly to the east.

"Are you sure this is Fish River?" she finally asks. "When did you last go down it?"

"A few summers ago. After Nushemakw married the second time."

Three years? Four? So much could have changed. A dry, hard wind begins blowing down the river, making steering more difficult. They stop to rest and to eat a few strips of the dried rabbit meat Green Feather packed for them. Susanna crouches over the river to wash up. Although the water is still clear, she can't see any more fish. A river called Fish River should have more fish.

The longer they stay on the river the more easterly it flows. Finally Susanna lays her oar across her lap and turns to look at Meera. "This isn't Fish River."

Meera's face tightens into a stubborn expression. "Green Feather said it was. She said this will take us to the Maumee."

"Meera! We're going east! We need to get on the first river going north and then find one going west."

"But she knows this land, we do not."

"All she said was that this river will take us to the Big River. But maybe she meant the Sandusky."

By this time the white water is increasing and the wind brings with it a scent of minerals and mossy stone. Up ahead they can see the river bending to the east even more.

"Meera!"

At last Meera shrugs but her face is still tight. "It's possible she was thinking of the Sandusky," she concedes.

The first river going north that they come to flows so fast they cannot steer the skiff into it in time, and the second is too shallow. The third is also fast but at least it is wider. They manage to turn into it rowing harder than Susanna has ever yet rowed. Wet, triangular rocks protrude from the banks like fangs. But at last the current slows, and for a little while they drift, resting their arms, and letting the current do their work for them. However it soon becomes apparent that they must pay attention to these jutting rocks. They are getting larger and no longer confining themselves to the edges of the water. The current picks up its pace again, and Susanna is splashed from head to foot as the skiff turns sharply. Meera shouts an instruction she cannot decipher. She is trying her best to keep the boat away from the rocks. Should they get out of the water and portage until it is calmer? She pushes her oar against a jagged rock as dark as a bad tooth. Where can they bank?

But it is too late. All at once the current races harder as the river narrows and turns, and the boat, hitting a confluence of rocks, tips over.

Meera shouts as they are dumped into the water. The boat turns over on top of Susanna and she struggles to get out from beneath it. The smell of wet wood fills her nostrils as she pushes up the skiff's side while at the same time being pulled in the opposite direction by the current. Later she thinks: if I had only hung on! But she is too intent on getting up to the air to think of anything else. At last she manages to get her head clear and she gulps at the air. Her grain sack is still tied to her back, but Consolation's shawl with the kettle and all their food inside is drifting away—she catches it by its fringe. The water is up to her chin and feels like cold, wet silver. Where is Meera? At last she spots her on top of a flat rock near the bank dripping wet and stretching her hand out for Susanna.

Susanna begins paddling with one arm, the other wrapped around Consolation's shawl, her head barely above the current. The heavy, wet shawl with the kettle inside threatens to pull her under, but somehow she gets to the rock and Meera gets hold of her arm and helps her up. Meanwhile the boat, with strands of velvety weeds hanging across its hull, is coming toward them. Susanna knows she has to catch it. She gets on her stomach and leans over the water. As the boat bumps its way over she manages to grasp its slippery edge, and the tips of her fingers work at finding some leverage. But before she can find any the current pulls the boat out of her grip and it rocks onward down the river.

She scrambles down onto the bank. For a moment a jumble of rocks near the river's edge catches the stern of the boat and Susanna thinks she has another chance. She looks down to see grassy underwater plants bobbing in the current like thin snakes as if to say, Go on, Go on. She steps in and begins to wade toward the rocks, but just as she is nearing it the current wrestles the boat away again.

"Stop!" Susanna calls to it irrationally.

Meera is standing on the bank with her back to the wind.

"We might still be able to get it," Susanna says, wading back to her. "It could get caught again."

She stops to catch her breath, and when she does she realizes she cannot possibly keep walking with any kind of speed. Every muscle in her bad leg aches, and with the wind blowing against her she is even colder than she was in the water. She looks at Meera. There is a long gash down the side of her face, making a line of blood like an arrow to her mouth. She is holding Consolation's wet shawl against her stomach. Susanna is afraid that she will say they cannot continue without a boat. But how can they go back without one, either? She is afraid Meera will say, This is the end.

But Meera just stares at the place in the river where the boat disappeared. There is a glazed look on her face. She doesn't say this is the end.

"This is your fault," is what she says.

—❦—

They follow the river slowly, stumbling over the stones and tree limbs that are scattered along the bank. Meera will not speak to her, even after Susanna cleans the gash on her face. At every bend Susanna hopes to see their skiff caught on a rock but eventually the river turns and they are obliged to abandon it. If they head due north they will get to the Maumee River or Lake Erie eventually, and the Wyandot village is not far from where the two meet. But if they let themselves circle around following this stream or that they might be lost in the Black Swamp for weeks.

Susanna reties her grain sack more firmly to her back. Most of their food has fallen into the river, but she still has their kettle and their blankets and Meera has a bundle of rabbit bones in one of her pouches for soup. While they walk they must keep particular watch for anything edible: berries, plant greens, roots. She tries not to think about her aching leg.

The trees spread their branches like great wings blocking the sun. Mud sucks at her moccasins. They are in the true heart of the Swamp now, as Meera would say. Late in the afternoon they come upon small pools of oily water floating in patches: petroleum, which her mother used to call Seneca oil. Meera scoops up some in the cup of her hand to put into one of her pouches.

"Good for sore feet and sore bones," she says.

This is the first thing she's said for hours. To encourage her, Susanna says, "My mother used the oil to treat chilblains."

"Chilblains? I don't know this word."

"Little swellings on your feet. You get them from the cold or the wet. Bigger than blisters. Beatrice used to get them a lot on her heels."

Meera nods. "That is sore feet," she says with the authority of a doctor.

They pick dandelion greens for their supper, and after they eat Meera scouts around until she finds four young trees arranged in a rectangle with no trees in the middle. She ties two thick branches to the trees on the longer sides of the rectangle, about a foot off the ground, and then she collects long sticks to arrange across the two branches, making a kind of platform. She has some rope and her hunting knife. Everything else they have to search for on the ground. When the rope runs out they cut vines to use as twine.

"This will be our bed," Meera says. "We will make one every night."

Susanna lies down on it. It is not very comfortable, but at least it keeps them from sleeping on wet ground. She can't see the stars or the moon or anything else through the thick canopy of tree branches above them. The air feels wet when she breathes it in.

"How far do you think we've gone so far?" she asks Meera. "I mean, since Gemeinschaft?"

"Perhaps ten or fifteen miles."

Ten or fifteen miles! The Black Swamp is forty miles north to south at least. How will they manage to travel twenty-five miles without a boat? The foolishness of her venture strikes Susanna again with all the force of false pride. They will never get out. She will never see her sisters or anyone else ever again. She will die here, and her last meal on earth will be boiled dandelion leaves without salt. A swarm of pinhead insects hovers over her face and although she swats them away they only come back.

"If you move about they are worse," Meera says. But it makes no difference whether she moves or not. They have found her, and they are not going to leave.

❧

Now, every day, they walk. The days become weeks. They carry no food since they eat every morsel they chance upon and wish for more. Their packs are lighter, that is the only good thing. But they wade through so much standing water that they have to stop again and again to pick leeches off their legs. At night Susanna becomes adept at making raised swamp beds, but even so she never feels completely dry. Sores form on her arms and legs that will not heal because of the damp. Her fingernails become as soft as skin.

They keep to the north, using the sun for direction. Somewhere Susanna loses one of her mother's gloves, and the other one she uses to dry her feet at night. She can feel the wet seeping deeper and deeper into her skin, saturating her bones, the muscles of her heart. She imagines tiny wet spores lodged beneath her ribcage or flowing alongside the blood in her veins, a part of her now. If they come to dry ground, Meera finds a tree shadow and stops to mark the tip of it with her knife. They count out the seconds to make a quarter of an hour as the shadow moves from west to east, and then they mark the tip of the new shadow with a stick. Standing with Meera's knife on their left and the stick on their right, they face true north. But if they can't find a shadow they have to guess and trust their luck.

Are they walking in circles? Conflicting signs are everywhere: whole spider webs, good; broken fern leaves, bad. The constant wind through the low swamp trees is like an approaching wave that never breaks. Sometimes the trees end abruptly and they come into a small, wet, grassy prairie where swamp swallows swoop like bats hunting for insects. One afternoon Susanna hears a bugle call in the distance. At first she thinks it is just her hunger playing tricks on her, but then it sounds again.

Meera says, " *Wapiti.* White deer."

Elk. "I thought they were all gone," Susanna says. "With the buffalo."

"They live where the grassland and trees come together. But their meat is not as good as the red deer. Also have tough skin, hard to kill."

Meat would be manna but they find no way of getting any. Meera fashions arrows from branches of swamp oak but they all have splits or kinks and she has no straightening tool, so the arrows shoot off crookedly in ways she cannot compensate for. The best they can hope for is to stun a small animal long enough to kill it with their hands. But where are the small animals? Susanna gets excited when she sees a dead mouse lying up ahead on a fallen log, but when she gets there it turns out to be only a narrow gray leaf with a long stem curling out behind it like a tail.

Meera says, "This is like the time when we were traveling and my family went many weeks without food. Sometimes I licked cold stones for the mineral taste. We ate moss from the river. We looked for fish but found only moss."

"I'm surprised Nushemakw didn't leave you if there wasn't enough food for you all."

She wasn't with Nushemakw, Meera tells her. This was with her real parents. "We walked across a shallow pond and there were fallen tree logs on the bottom and my mother kept slipping on them. My father carried me on his shoulders. We saw a stand of pawpaw trees on the other side. That's why we were going there. I was crying, and my mother and father thought it was because I was afraid I would fall, but it wasn't that, it was because I was so hungry and the pawpaws were so far away. I was so little that my father could hold my two legs across his chest with one arm. He told me that I always either cried or talked, that was my way. He said when I was older I would feel pleasure in silence, but that right now silence frightened me."

The air is misty and wet. They are walking among cattails with edges as sharp as knives. Susanna cannot see an end to them.

"Did you ever eat the pawpaws?" she asks.

"At the other end of the pond, Nushemakw's tribe was waiting for us behind the trees. They pointed their arrows at my people and killed everyone except for me and one boy."

Susanna stops walking and looks at her. "Why?"

Meera shrugs. "We were enemies."

"What happened to the boy?"

Meera doesn't know. But when the battle was over, someone gave them both a pawpaw and also some meat. "I did not miss my parents at first. I was so eager to get food. I don't think I really understood until later." For a while they walk in silence. Then Meera says, "That morning, before we went across that pond, I talked to the trees. I told them how hungry I was. Then my father spotted the pawpaws. The trees heard me. And my father was killed."

Susanna looks at her quickly, but Meera keeps staring straight ahead. She is so small and thin. Susanna wishes she could give her something. Food or comfort. Preferably food.

"The trees don't care about our hunger," she tells Meera. "I'm sure about that."

The afternoon spills into evening with almost no change of light until suddenly the sun is gone, it is night. The next day they walk for hours without finding anything at all to eat, and Susanna begins to feel very light-headed. She worries that she is walking more and more slowly, and tries to pick up her pace. For a moment she thinks she sees Aurelia in the distance, the particular color of her hair, but it is only a tree in early turning. Still, the idea takes hold of her.

"Susanna, whatever are you doing here?" Aurelia would certainly ask her.

"I'm going to find Penelope and Naomi. They need my help."

"Your help! Susanna, you astonish me, you do. Even if you could help them, how do you propose to find them? You have no sense of direction, you know you do not. If someone says east, you turn south. We've told you this often enough."

"I don't know. But here I am. I can only keep going."

"Well I wish you luck! Truly I do! Now I, as you know, have a very keen sense of direction. I've developed it because of my birds. Those hens are smarter than anyone gives them credit for. If a wind comes up in the east they..."

A small, fine rain begins to fall. Susanna wipes droplets from her face with the sleeve of her dress as she listens to Aurelia prattle on about her birds, a speech so familiar to Susanna she could recite it in her sleep. She feels her usual spurt of irritation— Aurelia always leads the conversation back to herself. Then she catches herself and feels ashamed. Poor Aurelia. Tears come into her eyes.

"It does no good to pity yourself," Meera says sharply.

"I'm not pitying myself!" Susanna says, and then all at once she is. If they had gone to Philadelphia like she wanted she might be sitting down right now with Lilith and Aunt Ogg for supper. Cold ham, hot tea in china cups. Her hands would be clean. Raindrops would not be trickling down her face.

"I'm hungry, too," Meera tells her.

Susanna wipes the rain from her eyes. "I know," she says.

⁂

The rain comes down for five days without a break, and then six. The clouds remain so heavy that they cannot use the sun for direction. Food becomes even harder to find. At night they are now too weak to make swamp beds but instead lie down on fat logs, sleeping as still as snakes so they will not tumble off onto the wet ground.

"I think we're walking in circles," Meera says on the seventh day.

They are sucking on reeds to try to fool their stomachs, but Susanna's stomach is not fooled.

"Do you think we should stop and wait for the sun to come out?" Meera asks. The rain has tapered off at last but the clouds are still thick overhead.

"We need to find food. Maybe a stream where we can catch a fish."

But when at last they come to a sunken brook its waters are muddy and shallow and without fish. They sit down to rest on a log so decayed with age and rain that it threatens to fold up wetly in the middle. Susanna looks at the sky through the canopy. The trees are still dripping but the clouds are finally moving off.

Oh well. Maybe finding food doesn't matter, she thinks. Maybe I can just sit on this wet log for the rest of my life. Her mind has begun to feel like something suspended, a bird asleep. She rubs her thumbs over her fingernails, their softness almost mesmerizing in their oddity. At last Meera rouses herself and goes to a nearby tree. She pulls back the bark here and there until she finds what she is looking for: a couple of dark green insects as long as a man's longest finger. Meera takes one and twists off its head and eats the body. Then she plucks the other one off the tree and holds it out to Susanna.

Susanna hesitates. Then she takes it and twists off its head.

Inside her mouth she presses the insect sideways and tries not to taste it, but a bitter and woody flavor comes up anyway. She thinks of the Bible: eating manna from heaven, which she'd been told was some sort of insect. But manna sounds pleasurable and this is not. This is more like a chore. She swallows and holds her hand out for another. They each eat four of these insects and then they chew the bark from the tree. Afterward Susanna feels strong enough to look for wild onions, which they eat slowly, making them last, and Meera lights a couple of damp torches to keep the mosquitoes away.

For a moment she turns back to look at Susanna, and Susanna is shocked to see how much older her face seems, like an old woman's. Her eyes are set back deep in her face, and her cheekbones rise prominently around them. That is hunger.

"Meera," Susanna asks, "why did you not stay with Green Feather?"

"Why did you not stay in your home in Severne?" Meera counters. She looks down at the ground.

"I know you considered it. You thought about it."

She wants Meera to say, because I wanted to go with you. But Meera doesn't say that. She pushes one torch deeper into the soggy ground, making adjustments.

The wind picks up and blows against the torches. A plane of smoke rises and then flattens like a tabletop.

"That was not my place," Meera finally says. "My place is with my people. My uncle tribe."

"But what if you don't like them? You don't even know them."

"Like does not matter. They are my people. Once I have faced my seven demons I will find them."

"Seven demons?" This is new to Susanna. "What are the seven demons?"

"Different for each person. My first demon was the pond with the fallen logs. This place we are in is number seven. At the end of it I will find my guardian spirit. Green Feather was not my guardian spirit."

It seems to Susanna that if ever there was a guardian spirit, Green Feather was that. But Meera seems convinced it will be someone from her uncle tribe.

"Was Sister Consolation one of your demons?" Susanna asks.

A shadow of a smile crosses Meera's face. "I vanquished her when I took her shawl."

Susanna tries to count up her own demons but it feels as though she's met with more than seven already. Her head begins to ache again and she closes her eyes. A moment later a hooting owl comes swooping down from the trees and over the brook, and as she turns her head to watch it she remembers that seeing an owl near water is an omen of death.

Aurelia sits down beside her.

"I'm worried, Susanna," she says. "This is all so unlike you."

"I know," Susanna says. "I'm worried, too."

"I'm amazed you even started this journey. Because now of course you can't go back."

"It seemed simple at first. All I had to do was get to Risdale. And then to Gemeinschaft. I don't know how I got here."

"You were tricked by that girl."

Susanna looks over at Meera. She has fallen asleep sitting on the ground with her back against the wet decayed log. Her head bends awkwardly against her shoulder. But Meera didn't trick her. Susanna wanted to come. She needs her sisters, that is the truth, although she worries that they don't feel the same way about her.

"Tell me, are they all right?" Susanna asks Aurelia. "Penelope and Naomi?"

"How should I know?"

Suddenly there is a commotion in the trees. A bright, fast creature storms out of the underbrush running for its life: a young elk. *Wapiti.* Meera wakes with a jerk and stands up. She reaches for her knife but the elk is followed closely by two fast wolves. There is hardly time to see them before they disappear behind more trees, but Susanna can hear their progress by the crashing of branches.

"Let's go," Meera says.

They each pull up a torch and follow the sound of the chase. Soon Susanna hears the unmistakable cry of a creature in pain. She follows Meera through the trees as fast as she can, branches lashing her shoulders. The wolves have brought the elk down in a muddy strip between two large trees. When Susanna and Meera get there, the elk is still alive with one wolf at its neck and the other at its middle. Its eyes are like clear water. It raises and lowers its head, fighting to the last. A young male.

Susanna can't stop watching the wolves as they eat it. Beside her she can hear Meera breathing through her mouth. Each of them is still holding a lit torch, and the idea comes to Susanna that soon the wolves will not be so hungry. Perhaps they can chase them away.

And so it happens. The wolves, first one and then the other, break off for a moment to sniff the air.

"They know we are here," Meera whispers.

"Maybe we can shoo them off with our fire."

"Yes, we must frighten them." But she waits, looking at Susanna, and so Susanna is the one who takes a shallow breath and makes the first lunge toward the beasts—mangy, stringy fellows, all clumpy fur and teeth.

"Shoo! Scat! Scat!" She waves her burning branch at them. Her heart is beating fast but she gives herself no time to consider her fear. Meera is only a half a moment behind.

"Off! Be off!" Meera shouts.

The wolves rear away from the burning branches but each manages to pick up a bit of fallen meat to hold in its mouth as they trot a little way off through the underbrush. When they are far enough away, Meera begins quickly to skin a section of the carcass while Susanna holds both of the torches. What Meera said before is true: tough hide. But soon enough she is able to get to the meat. Her hands are shaking and blood streams from her fingers as she cuts piece after ragged piece. They hear the wolves begin to snarl. They are ready to eat again, and feel bolder. Susanna sees four gleaming eyes among the trees. She waves the torches and they retreat a few steps but not as far as before.

Soon these wolves will be joined by other wolves. Susanna knows that they must be gone by then. When they have cut as much meat as they dare they leave in the opposite direction, making a long loop back to their camp. Susanna builds up a little fire and Meera cuts a few slim green boughs and then douses them in the muddy brook so they can use them as skewers. Their hands are covered in blood and gristle. Susanna is so hungry that she starts to eat her meat too soon and vomits before she can properly swallow. But eventually the meat is cooked through, and she makes herself eat slowly. It tastes as good as anything she has ever eaten, even without salt or bread.

"We should sleep up in the trees tonight, with the rest of the meat," Meera tells her.

They can hear more wolves howling and fighting. Meera finds two trees with horizontal limbs a good ways up from the ground. Up in her tree, Susanna wraps her arms around the massive wet branch, too exhausted even to worry about falling. She rests her cheek against its rough bark. The moon is higher and smaller now. She can feel her heart beat against a raised knur in the wood.

What would her mother say if she could see her? Aurelia is right, she has changed beyond recognition. Susanna closes her eyes. She lost something a long way back, and it's more than just her mother's glove. But she's gained something, too. Stealing meat from the wolves was her idea, and she was the one who rushed at them first. In the distance, she can hear them snap at each other like her sisters quarreling over some triviality. Is the porridge burning? Whose turn is it to feed the pig?

"Good night, Susanna," Meera calls softly from her tree. "Don't fall off your branch. I don't think there's enough *wapiti* for them all."

The next morning Susanna is awakened early by the cold and by an uncomfortable stiffness throughout her body, particularly her neck. She's hungry and thinks instantly of the elk. How weak they were last night! They should have been more aggressive with the wolves and taken a larger share of the meat.

A low mist rises from the ground as Susanna climbs down out of the tree, thinking she will go back to look for anything she can scavenge. It's very early and Meera is no doubt still asleep. However Susanna is not altogether surprised to see Aurelia sitting among the ferns at the base of her tree.

"Where are you going?" Aurelia asks her.

"To look for bones. For soup."

"Well I might as well go along, too," Aurelia says, standing up. She pats down her dress. "Gracious, what a strong smell this place has. I don't know how you can stand it! But of course they say that one can get used to anything by and by, and a good example of that I suppose is you, Susanna. Just look at you, sleeping up in a tree!"

As always, Aurelia can lay down sentence after sentence without seeming to take breath. Susanna only half listens as she picks her way through the trees. Everything looks different in the pink light. Is this where they turned?

"And eating that deer after the wolves got hold of it!"

"Elk," Susanna tells her.

But as usual Aurelia pays no attention to a correction. "You are like a vulture now, Susanna, you are, yes, or one of those terrible creatures the Black Swamp has created, half of this and half of that. Like the swine wolf I told you about. Now, as it turned out, that swine wolf was a good creature, he really tried to help me, so I suppose the lesson there is...what is the lesson? Well, I suppose the lesson is that you never know how events will shape a creature. But I beg you, heed my warning, I mean to say, scavenging

from wolves! You are already losing part of your person and be-
coming part of something else. Half person, half something else.
But what, I wonder? A bird of prey? An Indian?"

"An Indian is a person," Susanna tells her, offended.

"Oh, you know what I mean." Aurelia laughs.

"Indeed I do not," Susanna says as stiffly as she can.

"Oh, your pride! Penelope really used to shake her head over
you and your fussy ways. How you hated Severne. Susanna, goodness, I've just figured it out! Your problem? You are not satisfied
with where you are. That's it! Never satisfied. And that's why
you've found yourself here in this desolate bog. It has nothing to
do with Penelope and Naomi. You are not going someplace, you
are leaving someplace else."

Is this true? Susanna looks up at the mist settling among the
tree branches like soft fur. Certainly she never hid the fact that
she did not want to live in Severne. And she did not want to be a
missionary, either, but no one could expect her to want that.
Could they?

"I don't believe it," Susanna says. But maybe she does.

"Over here," Aurelia tells her. "There it is."

The elk carcass lies in the mud among the twigs and old leaves,
nearly picked clean. All the organs, the rib meat, the shank—
gone. The head is turned north with spaces where its eyes had
been, and a few small feathers are crushed into the hollows between bones. So the birds have come, too. Aurelia stands with her
feet apart looking down at it, her small nose wrinkled. She would
never do what Susanna has done. She is still pretty, her hands
smooth and white.

"Aurelia, please don't leave me," Susanna suddenly says.

"Oh, you don't need me. Now Susanna, when you get out of
here make sure to cut yourself a new dress, and mind that you

make it soft, cut it out of some nice, soft material, so you can feel the wind. That's what I miss most, the feel of wind on my skin."

"Susanna!"

She turns her head. Meera is coming out from among the trees with her blanket over her head, carrying Consolation's shawl and Susanna's grain sack. She comes up beside Susanna and looks down at the elk.

"There's nothing left," Susanna tells her.

Flies cover the carcass and the bits of gristle left on the bone shimmer blue. Meera opens her pouch and they both look at the meat they still have. It is such a small amount. Susanna looks back at the elk. There is nothing to salvage.

"We won't get out of here, will we," she says.

Meera says, "That's not true."

"You'll never meet your guardian spirit. We'll die here. We'll starve."

"We will not starve."

"We're starving now."

"After you eat some more meat, you'll feel stronger," Meera says. "We've been hungry for too long." She stops and lifts her chin. "What's that? Do you smell that?"

Susanna turns her head and catches the faint scent of hickory smoke. Another illusion? But Meera smells it, too. It's coming from the east where the trees are ancient and thick, mostly bur oaks with cracked lined faces like old men watching everything but keeping their thoughts to themselves. They walk toward the smell and Susanna is surprised to find that the bur oaks do not lead to more trees but instead form the outer edge of a little clearing. A grassy brook runs along one end, and above that stands a large garden encircled by a wattle fence. But where is the cabin or hut? The smoke is coming up from the shade.

"Who's there?" a voice calls out in Delaware, although Susanna could have sworn they've made no noise. She follows the sound of the voice to an old squaw standing between two great elm trees with a reed mat in one hand and an English hunting rifle in the other. She is Crow, Susanna guesses, or part Crow, with a wide nose and full lips. When Susanna begins to walk toward her she switches to English. "Don't come any closer."

"We are travelers in need of food," Susanna says. "Will you help us?"

Silence.

The squaw is wearing a long deerskin tunic painted with decorations—deer antlers and a moon—over a pair of English trousers. Her hair is long and dark and frayed at the ends, worn loose. She might be fifty, sixty, seventy years old. It's hard to tell with natives. When Susanna takes another step the squaw drops the mat to hold the gun in her two hands, not pointing it directly at her but not too far off, either.

"I am Susanna Quiner," Susanna says. "From Severne, Ohio, and before that, the city of Philadelphia. And this is Meera."

"She your slave?"

"Not my slave. My..." What is she? "We're traveling together."

"Tell her to put down the weapon."

Meera places her knife on the ground between her feet and shows the squaw her open palms. "*Welankuntawakan*," she says. Peace.

"We're traveling north," Susanna explains. "We got lost."

"Of course you got lost. You shouldn't have come."

Does she live here by herself? Susanna wonders. But that is impossible. Her husband must be out hunting or tending to the— what, pigs? Sheep? Hard to imagine sheep in a swamp, but it is equally hard to imagine an old woman standing with a hunting rifle in front of a large, well-tended garden. A noise as familiar as Aurelia's voice makes Susanna turn her head.

Chickens.

"Are those Dominicos I hear?" she asks, taking a chance.

The squaw shifts her rifle. "You acquainted with Dominicos?"

"My sister raised them. Said they were the best breed for intelligence and hardiness."

"Fine mothers, too. Not all raise their young so unselfishly." She cocks her head at Susanna and rests the butt of her rifle on the ground. "All right. I'll give you some food and one night's sleep, but then you must be on your way."

"Thank you, grandmother," Meera says.

The squaw snorts. "I'm not your grandmother. I'm English. You can call me Omie."

Nineteen

Back in Severne Penelope often told her sisters a story in bed at night, either true or made up, but if she ever conceived of telling a story about a white woman living alone deep in the maze of the Great Black Swamp who hunted on her own, built whatever needed building, and needed no man's help (Susanna can imagine how such a story would appeal to Penelope), she probably would never have dreamed up a woman so talkative as Omie. Once Omie puts down her rifle it's as if a spark has been touched to dry sticks, and the flow of words begins.

"Grow my vegetables there," she tells them, showing them the garden first. "Some are under those vines to keep the birds off, see that? And over here just flowers. Inside you'll set your eyes on a beautiful sight, all my little darlings in pots and jars, some growing wild around here, some I put in from seed. You found me by my smoke, no wonder. When I first came I took more pains to be invisible but I've grown less careful with fires as I like my meals to be hot each one. No one around anyway, I've not seen a person since..." She stops to think. "Don't know, actually."

Although Susanna is looking for it, she does not see Omie's hut until they are ten paces away from it, surrounded as it is by trees and undergrowth. Its outer walls are lined with bark, and it has a straight, well-formed chimney constructed of small gray stones no larger than a child's fist.

"Every autumn I pull new bark for the walls," Omie tells them. "I do love that smell."

She directs Susanna and Meera to wash themselves using a bucket of water by the door and hands them a sliver of soap so dry and rutted that Susanna has to work it a full minute before it gives up any lather. Afterward Omie gives them each a cloth to dry themselves with. For a moment Susanna just holds hers. It has been a long time since she's held anything so dry.

Inside, it's true, flowers stand everywhere: daisies, swamp roses, purple coneflowers, and clusters of what her mother used to call turkey-foot grass. They are arranged in hard clay jars on the floor all around the room like wallpaper that starts at ground level and grows to life against the log walls. The cabin is undivided, just one large room that smells like green plants and smoke. Three windows without glass bring in the light, and Susanna notices clever shutters on hinges to close them up. A rough three-legged stool stands by the hearth, and that is the beginning and end of the furniture.

Omie sits down on the stool and stirs the fire embers with iron tongs and then pours a bit of water into a standing kettle. She tells them to eat slowly and not too much at first. "You look near death."

Clearly she came here from somewhere carrying iron tools and supplies, but where, and how long ago? As Susanna puts the soup-spoon to her mouth she feels a sigh escape her like it's from her whole body. Squirrel. For a while she forgets her questions and just eats. Meera, sitting across from her on the floor, is holding the bowl up to her chin and Susanna can see she is also trying not to gulp it down in one swallow. Susanna bites into a boiled potato and then with her tongue presses it into a warm grainy mash on the roof of her mouth. She's almost forgotten that sensation.

"I'm no stranger to hunger," Omie is saying. "Back some years, before I came here. Famine of '90, but ye'll not remember that. All we had was sap porridge, that's cornmeal and maple tree sap. After that was gone we ate snow."

"Where was this?" Susanna asks politely.

"I'll not tell ye," Omie says sharply. "I'll not go back."

She glares at Susanna. Then she abruptly changes again. "Let me give you a touch more." She tips half a ladle of stew into Susanna's bowl, the rest into Meera's. "My father gave me a hundred acres of land as a wedding gift, all hills and rocks. From *his* parents, two sheep. Look at this." She takes from the mantel a pair of hand millstones. "When I left I packed them out with me. Grind my own grain. Ever have johnnycakes fried in bear oil? A little honey on top. I like honey. Just follow the bees back to their home when I see them, I can't be bit nor stung. That's why I don't get swamp fever."

"You don't ever get swamp fever? I don't either!" Susanna says. Until now she thought she was the only one. She is strangely pleased to find something in common with this odd woman.

"Can insects bite ye?" Omie asks.

"Not mosquitoes. But swamp fever comes from plants, you know, not insects. It comes from their gases."

"Gases from plants? Puh!" Omie scoffs.

After they've eaten, Omie takes them to the side yard to show them her chickens.

"Here my lovelies, here my own," she calls.

It's here that Susanna begins to realize why Omie still has the habit of speech: she talks to her hens. No doubt, when alone, she talks to her flowers as well. Each hen has a name and curious markings painted on their feathers like the markings on Omie's tunic: rings, purple moons, a star. Only the two roosters are left unmarked. They perch on top of a henhouse made of boards pulled from crates or barrels or both and then nailed and roped together. The door is made from barley straw.

"Aye, it looks a mishmash but it holds," Omie says about the henhouse, holding one chicken loosely in her arms. "Good scratch about. Times I give them a little crushed grain too, if I have it."

"My sister mixed wood ash into their feed," Susanna tells her. "Said it made their shells stronger."

"That interfere with the hatching?"

"She's lost only two chicks in the last two years."

"How many does she have now?"

"She doesn't...she recently died."

"Then who's taking care of her hens?"

"I don't know." Susanna feels a pang of guilt. Aurelia asked her to do that. But isn't it strange, she thinks, that Omie is more concerned over the fate of Aurelia's chickens than Aurelia? Later Susanna tells herself that Omie is a woman without kindness.

Omie has brought out with her a large knotted net, tangled and full of holes. She sets her hen down and shakes out the net. "Help me with this. And you too, Little Pea," she says to Meera. Last night she saw a flock of passenger pigeons fly overhead and she figures more are on their way.

"Like to catch some for supper. But I have to mend my net or they'll fly right through it."

She spreads the net on the ground, and Meera and Susanna help her to untangle it. When it is lying straight out they begin to mend it with odd bits of string and rope.

"How is it that this land isn't wet?" Susanna asks her.

"Limestone not too far underneath," Omie tells her. "And it's on a little rise as you can see. I chose the spot smartly."

She takes up her knife and cuts a worn piece from the net, measures it against her thumb, and then cuts a new piece to match it from her scraps. She makes a pile of the worn pieces, perhaps intending to mend them later, while Meera and Susanna tie the new pieces to the net with small tight knots. All the while Omie talks and talks, sometimes to Susanna and Meera, and sometimes to her birds.

"My father raised flax to sell but kept some back for our clothes. I had a new dress every year. A little bit of cleared land, that's all we had, and right beyond was the wilderness. Hard to imagine now, but how I feared it as a girl. Hated to go into the woods even for kindling. Father worked the land with a hand hoe. My husband, he mostly talked down the neck of his whiskey bottle. It was his right to beat me but he took on that responsibility a deal too often."

Is this why she came to this lonesome place, Susanna wonders? It seems a hard thing to have to live alone like this. She never would.

"Why do you paint your birds?" Meera asks.

"For the powers. Stars for might, moon for understanding, rings for their ability to heal the cramp. I mostly use pokeweed berries but there's a lichen I sometimes mix in, cuts a nice shade."

"Can you tell if a venture is unlucky?" Susanna asks her.

"I can tell your venture is," Omie says with a laugh. "Else you wouldn't be here."

But she shows no curiosity about them or why they have come. She sits on a little tree stump with her knees spread, the part of the net she is working on pulled up onto her lap. Her fingers are thick but nimble, and her hair webs around her shoulders like a shawl. When the net seems good enough, Omie puts her hands flat on her thighs and pushes herself to standing.

"At sunset is when the birds fly," she tells them, shaking the net out. "We'll catch a few then and make us some good pigeon pie."

⁕

They set out just as the last line of bright sun is sinking out of view, Omie leading the way with her gun broken over her arm. Where does she get her gunpowder, Susanna wonders as she follows her. For Omie is preparing to shoot the birds as well as net them. The sky is filled with flat, distant clouds outlined in pink and purple, and the air smells like wet leaves.

"See that pair of sour gums yonder?" Omie asks. She points to a pair of trees on a little rise. "The birds like to fly right between them. I set the net among the lower branches because my climbing days are past, but if you could get yourselves up top we could affix the net higher and catch all the more."

The branches of the two trees extend toward each other like people holding out their arms before an embrace. Susanna climbs one and Meera, holding the net, climbs the other. When they get high enough Meera throws Susanna one end of the net, and they pull it to stretch it out taut between them.

"Tie it fast, now," Omie hollers up. "Pick a good bough. Then climb down a ways and fasten up the middle same as the top. I'll get the bottom." She sounds happy. "Yuh! Don't sway so, you'll break yer neck!"

Susanna feels tree sap stick to her fingers. She is still not strong and she worries about Meera, who is climbing down even more slowly than she is. On the ground, Omie hands each of them a long stick with a blade tied to it, a kind of spear. As she examines the tip a sound swells in the distance, or maybe just the feel-

ing of a sound, and she looks up to see a dark cloud of birds coming into the clearing. They make no noise save their wings, which
are long and elegant, and they lift slightly as they approach the
trees like a preacher making the start of a slow blessing. The first
of them fly well above the branches. But as the flock thickens,
some of the birds are forced to fly lower down until at last one
flies right into the net.

Its surprised cry is like the soft gasp of a woman. Omie cocks
her gun and puts her eye to the finder. A few more birds fly into
the net, and the first one breaks free. Soon the net begins to shake
as more birds escape and others get caught. Will the ties hold,
Susanna wonders? She sees Meera gripping her spear hard. Still
Omie doesn't shoot, even when part of the net begins to sag with
the weight. Finally, when the net seems ready to fall with all the
birds in it, Omie squeezes the trigger, taking the kickback into
her large shoulder.

At once a dead bird tumbles from the net. Omie quickly tamps
down more powder and lights the barrel and shoots again. Although she has to load between each pull she is quick at it and
seems to find her mark every time. Some birds fall without being
shot, and these Meera or Susanna spears on the ground. Feathers
begin floating up as though in defiance of the natural laws, and
the clean fresh smell of the summer evening gets lost in the tang
of gunpowder. Omie pulls the trigger again and again and the
noise is terrific. Susanna wants to cover her ears but she needs
both hands to spear the birds. It feels like hours before Omie sets
down her rifle.

"That's enough! Now leave off!"

But the birds are still flying, now the tail end of the cloud, now
the stragglers. Climbing back up the tree to untie the net is like
climbing an undersea plant: the caught birds make the whole tree

rock in their current. It takes all of Susanna's concentration to find a tie, cut it, and go on to the next. For some reason one bird, a late straggler, decides to alight on a branch of her tree, so close that she could touch it. She watches it blink its eye and sway slightly on the slim bough. Its long red plumage makes her think of a rare biblical bird, although there are more passenger pigeons, her mother used to say, than any other creature on this earth. In comparison, Susanna's own body feels monstrously large and inelegant.

Back on the ground again she looks at their take: six sacks full of birds. Susanna's mouth is already watering at the thought of the pies they will make. Each of them picks up two sacks and this time they walk around the back so that Omie can fetch more water from her well. From this side Omie's cabin looks less inviting, the roof more jagged, and the surrounding bushes even more overgrown. Just as Meera asks Omie what she uses for dough Susanna notices something leaning up against the cabin's back wall. A shadow?

A boat.

A canoe, a little one. It is leaning upright near a rangy blackberry bush picked clean of fruit, almost hidden by the branches. Susanna's heart begins to pound.

"Meera," she whispers. She points.

Meera's eyes widen as she takes in what it is. The canoe is old and probably needs repair. It looks like it has not been in water for years. But still: a boat. A boat would save them days, maybe weeks, of travel. A boat would get them out of the Black Swamp.

"Acorn flour," Omie is saying. She drops the water bucket by its rope into the well, a narrow hole covered by a plank of rotting wood. "Works just fine if you knead it long enough. We'll make a good many pies for you to take along with you."

"Omie," Susanna begins, but Meera puts a hand on her arm.

"Wait," she says in a low voice.

Back in the cabin they plunge the birds into the bucket of cold well water to make them easier for plucking, and then Meera and Susanna sit outside pulling out feathers while Omie mixes the dough.

Susanna's thoughts are racing. A boat would mean getting to the Maumee tomorrow, if the current is right. They could find a stream pointed north and not look back. She might even see her sisters the day after that. Suddenly they are so close that she fancies she can touch their hair. She imagines their faces: their surprise at seeing her, their gratitude.

Omie trusses the plucked birds and sets aside their livers, tiny as knuckles. She shows Susanna how to pound the livers with parsley and bear fat, and then she lays the mixture, which she calls forcemeat, at the bottom of the crust. She says something over the meat and adds a few small mushrooms. Susanna cannot make out what she says—a prayer? A spell? Maybe she's just reminding herself of the next step. And yet she's very like a witch, Susanna thinks, with her potions and special markings, her animal familiars, her web of hair. But the little pies, cooking in the iron bake kettle, smell delicious.

They eat them on their laps sitting cross-legged in front of the fire, which Meera has built up into a nice blaze. Outside the insects grow louder, and Omie gets up to close the window shutters.

"Omie," Meera asks casually when Omie sits down again. "Where do you get the powder for your shot?"

"Oh I get to the Maumee once a year. One of the river boatmen knows me, gets me what I need. Mark you, I'm careful to hide my tracks."

Omie licks her fingers and reaches for another small pie.

"Do you go on foot," Meera asks, "or by boat?"

Omie says, "You saw my boat did you, Little Pea? No I walk."

"Then perhaps you will trade us for your canoe?" Meera suggests in her gentlest voice. "It would save us many days of walking. We would trade handsomely for it."

"We have money," Susanna puts in. "We could buy it from you."

"Money! Puh. I've no need for that."

"Perhaps you would like my kettle then?" Meera asks. "It has a handle, unlike yours."

But Omie says hers does her fine.

"Maybe you would fancy a curiosity?" Susanna takes the Chippewa necklace from its cedar box. Omie touches the turkey bones as she listens to the story behind it.

"You lost your lucky bone? Aye, that is a misfortune. Better you had reached for that. Luck is more important than money."

But although she admires the necklace, she does not want to trade for it. Nor does she want the dinner knives, the cherry buttons, or Sirus's ax. When Meera brings out Consolation's shawl, Omie fingers the tiny mirrors and holds it up to look at her face.

"Breaks me up, don't it," she says, amused. "Eyes here, nose there." She gives it back.

"What can we give you?" Susanna asks. "Name it."

Omie appears to think, giving Susanna a moment of hope. "Don't really need anything," she says finally.

She tells Meera to fetch more water and gives Susanna a cloth to wipe their dishes, turning her back on the conversation. But now that Susanna has seen the boat, it feels too hard to give it up. She searches her mind for another argument. They've been delayed over and over. She has to get out, she doesn't have the strength to keep going, she doesn't have any more patience for leeches and mud, she has come to the edge of herself and what she is capable of, in fact she is over the edge. And what about Meera, a child still growing, who needs her food? Saving three days or four days or even a week—it makes a difference, Susanna thinks. Four days not spent in the Swamp would make a difference. Not to mention they might get lost again. They can't continue on foot. It's too difficult. She would rather stay here and paint chickens.

"Omie," she says desperately, "please listen. A boat would save us so many days! And we have no more food. We might get lost again."

"I go every year on foot. It's simple. And I'll give you enough food for the journey."

"You don't understand...these last weeks...if we'd had a boat..." Susanna swallows. Never negotiate by showing need, Sirus used to say. But she has nothing else except need.

When they are done cleaning, Omie takes something from a little box in the corner. She brings it over to show them, her eyes almost shy.

"Look at this."

It is a small, cheaply framed picture: a blank check printed with the words "Mechanics Bank of Baltimore" in swirly letters at the top. Underneath is a small line drawing of an elegant woman wearing a long tea gown and reclining on a sofa.

Omie touches the folds of the woman's gown. "Pretty, isn't she? I want to keep her nice so I just take her out now and again to look."

The fire snaps and then falls quiet. Omie, standing so close to Susanna that their arms are touching, seems large and soft. She unloosens the back of the frame and removes something from inside. A lock of hair.

"My babe," Omie says.

It is blond to the point of whiteness. A frayed curl. Omie's bent, red fingers look even redder holding it.

"Died the day before his first birthday. Found him in his cradle. Nothing for it."

"Is that why you left?" Meera asked.

"Puh," Omie says. "I left because my husband beat me at every turn and took to rye whiskey while he was at it. Called himself religious." She looks down at the lock of hair.

"What was your baby's name?" Susanna asks.

Omie closes her fingers over the lock. "That I'll not tell."

All these years living alone has made her both lonely and skittish, Susanna thinks, wanting to air her thoughts but afraid to give too much away. She gives Meera and Susanna two warm deerskin blankets and takes their torn ones away. A kind gesture. She isn't heartless. Susanna isn't sure what she is.

"Why won't you trade us the boat?" she asks her. She can't let the matter go. Disappointment is too slight a word for how she feels.

Omie shrugs. "I may yet want to leave."

That takes Susanna by surprise. But then she thinks about it. Omie has fashioned this home entirely by herself, a place of pride. She will never leave it but needs to believe that if she wants to, she can.

Omie rechecks the windows and the door while Susanna spreads her new blanket near the fireplace and lies down. Beside her, Meera does the same. Then she turns her head to look at Susanna. Her dark eyes do not seem as blank and hopeless as they seemed yesterday. That's a good thing. Susanna hesitates only a second, and then she rises above her disappointment and stretches out her hand. Meera takes it and squeezes it.

It's all right. They will be all right, even without the boat. They are dry after all, and their bellies are full, and there is a promise of breakfast in the morning without having to search for it first. After Omie spreads the ashes in the fireplace, she lies down on her blanket next to Meera. For a little while she is quiet. Then she says, "Never had anyone else sleep here before."

The room is warm and smells of roasted meat.

"Don't really like it," Omie says.

Yadata

Twenty

Koman carries with him a pipe for peace, a pipe for battle, and other pipes for other purposes, each one marked by the color of the feathers interlocked with human hair. White feathers mean peace, he tells Seth. When traveling, displaying such a calumet is vital to their safety.

It is propped up in the bow of the canoe with its white and black feathers leaning away from the wind. Once in a while a pair of blueflies land on it and take a short ride. Seth doesn't mind the blueflies, it's the mosquitoes that plague him. They bite through the paste of mint he applies every afternoon to his face and neck. At dusk he applies several coats, for they are at their most brutal then.

Sitting on the backs of his legs at the bow, Koman turns his head to observe a crooked line of beech trees growing down into the stream, their leaf tips drinking the water. Is he searching for something? Seth wonders. It is wet and hot and desolate, the land only fit for insects. They have not seen much in the way of game. Three days ago they took the Blanchard to the Auglaize and now are cutting up north on a smaller tributary that will meet up eventually with the Maumee. They are more than halfway across the Black Swamp, Koman calculated that morning. Water stands all around them in ponded hollows that sometimes bleed into the stream, and their main accompaniment, besides the insects, has been the scores of wood frogs piping out from among the milkweed and sedge grass. When the trees close up, which they often do, their canopy makes a dark vaulted ceiling. Then the frogs sound even louder.

Seth presses a wet leaf to his arm. Despite all his care, he has bites everywhere. The mosquitoes here are hungry enough to draw blood from a horse.

There has been no sign of Susanna and the girl she left Gemeinschaft with, but Seth is not worried, not yet. Susanna got a head start but he and Koman are making good time. Every day they go farther downstream with a swift current, and the water for the most part has been deep enough for the canoe. Only twice so far have they had to portage. At night they sleep with their feet toward the fire, Koman in a buffalo robe with the fur inside and Seth in a Scottish wool blanket. They rise early, before the sun, and Koman always stretches his whole body as soon as he awakens. Curious, Seth tried it himself and found it a satisfying way to warm up his limbs. Now he does it without thinking. Afterward they clean up their camp and leave without eating. An hour or so downstream Koman stops with the sunrise to trap a grouse or a couple of bobolinks, and they make a small fire to roast them. Seth boils water for tea, and Koman accepts a small cup but only to rinse out his mouth, never to drink.

The problem, one of the problems, is that neither one can guess which route north Susanna might have taken. Impossible to find her in the Black Swamp itself, it's too large. They will have to try their luck at the Maumee. Find out where she crossed, or, if she hasn't crossed it yet, wait for her to do so. Talk to the ferrymen. Talk to the other traveling bands of natives. Seth has brought with him many gifts: knives, a net that Cade used to use for fishing, blunted awls, gunpowder, hooks and eyes, sacks of tea.

And some cash for any white men. But for the natives, Koman has taught him to say gift, not trade.

"My grandfather's grandfather did not have the word *trade*," Koman told him. "His people went up north to exchange gifts, bringing tools they no longer needed and receiving beaver robes that the northern tribe no longer had use for. Each gift was already used, that was how it was. You gave what you didn't need anymore knowing it would be useful to another, and they did the same. That was how it was."

"Not so different from trading," Seth said. But after thinking about it, he wonders now if maybe Koman's grandfather's way is more honest. No underlying hope of getting more than you will give. Just looking to get something you can use. A gift. Koman has brought with him copper and crystals and shells from the Atlantic, all with some ritual significance. When Seth asks Koman what they mean, Koman says, "Telling won't tell story."

The trees close up into a leafy ceiling and the blueflies fly off the calumet. Seth can see a long horde of mosquitoes on the bank hovering in a throbbing, vertiginous line. He fancies they are looking for him. He paddles harder.

The next day he and Koman come upon a group of Miami paddling up in the opposite direction. The lead canoe also carries a white calumet, as well as three young pigs in a willow-branch cage. Twelve or fifteen men and women are traveling in six canoes, and each canoe carries a cage of pigs. The two parties land their boats on the riverbank, and Koman talks to the eldest Miami for several minutes. Then he comes back to Seth.

"We will share food with them," he says.

That morning they shot two turkeys for breakfast and ate only the wings of one. Now they cook the other one and share it with the Miami. One woman carefully picks out the bones and saves them with the gizzards in a cracked leather sack. The men are wearing trade blankets and beads like the Ottawas, and while they eat they talk to Koman. They speak quickly, not always in Pota- watomi, and Seth can understand maybe one word in five.

"Have they seen the women?" Seth asks Koman. "Say they are traveling in a flat-bottomed boat."

The men shake their heads. The woman who collected the bird bones looks at Seth. "Your women lost?" she says in English. "No good."

He tells her in Potawatomi that the two women are heading north. They are going to the Maumee. One has red hair.

"Many streams here." She shakes her head. "You are first *chmokman* I see."

A hot wind begins to blow, bringing with it the scent of damp earth. Some clouds drift across the sky and then seem to stop in a bunch. The pigs have fallen asleep in the heat.

"They are going to Gemeinschaft," Koman tells Seth when the meal is over. A boy fills a pipe with tobacco and brings it to him. He lights it and gives it to Seth. "Pass to the father after you," he tells him.

It is the calumet with the long white feather from the Miami's lead canoe. Seth is not much of a smoker, but this mixture is smooth and like Koman he pulls on it twice before passing it on. "They are Christian?"

"No. They hope to buy land near the village. One daughter once lived there as a Christian with her husband, but now she is dead. Last hunting season was thin, and the one before that, and the one before that. There are signs that this season will be the same. They blame the Delawares, skinhunters they call them. They have decided to raise pigs and cattle, if they can buy a few cows from the brethren. And if they find land close enough, they are hoping that the Christian Indians will watch their livestock when they are off on the hunt."

One of the sons says something to Koman, shrugging and smiling. When he smiles small wrinkles make an O around his mouth.

"Not enough wild meat anymore," Koman translates.

Seth watches them smoke. They inhale deeply and seem to enjoy the conversation. They don't have an air of despair. No feeling of tragedy. It's just a fact: not enough wild meat. So now they will do something else, something to augment the hunting. Pigs and cattle. Seth notices a long kind of flute on the smiling son's belt, which he has seen Old Adam use when he's fishing—it makes a certain noise to attract the fish. The Miami will do what they have to do to survive.

The son reaches over and feels the hem of Seth's trousers.

"What will you take for?" he asks.

The gray linen fabric is stained and ripped in one place, although that can be mended. Still, Seth is surprised. The Miami's leather breeches are much more useful for traveling in a swamp. More effective against the mosquitoes, for one thing.

Seth points to the man's own breeches, and they agree to trade. Wearing the breeches will mark him as Miami, or as one who trades with Miami. But he doesn't care about that. Even better would be one of their hide tunics. He would trade everything he had if it meant even one mosquito could not get through to his skin. He goes to his canoe and comes back with Cade's fishing net.

"This gift for you," he says. "For your shirt?"

Twenty-One

As soon as she and Meera come out from the trees that mark the end of the Great Black Swamp, Susanna sees the two Wyandot men fishing on the riverbank.

The men's poles are stuck fast in the sandy dirt, and they are squatting next to them playing a game with rocks—gambling?— and laughing at some mistake one of them has just made. Susanna's first urge is to turn around and escape their notice, but where would she run to? Back into the Black Swamp? She almost cannot believe that they have gotten free of it at last. She looks at the Maumee River stretched out before them, which is wide and green and dotted with slivers of islands like thin crusts of bread. Susanna draws in her breath at the vast pale sky above the water. It's been a long time since she has seen anything overhead except tree branches.

In the end Omie let them stay with her for three nights, but she never changed her mind about the canoe. Yet she was generous in her way, feeding them and washing their clothes and packing enough food for two weeks although she claimed the journey would take them less than half that time, even with crossing the Maumee. On the morning they left, she herself led them to the rill—to Susanna, indistinguishable from all the other rills they passed—that would lead them out of the Black Swamp. Omie lifted her hand in farewell as she turned without breaking her pace to go back. Besides pigeon pies, she gave them a jar of raisin wine and a good many bones for soup, wrapped up in a handkerchief. When Susanna drank the wine later, she fancied it carried the faint taste of flower stems.

They have come out of the trees to a spot where the Maumee turns, and the two men are on a narrow sandbar near its bend. Both of them are muscular and thin and wear only a small patch of deerskin covering their loins. Behind them lay two large cords of firewood. One stands to check his fishing pole, and Susanna steps back into the tree shadows. But Meera walks boldly past her down the bank.

"Wait," Susanna whispers, and reaches out to grab her arm. Too late. Meera walks toward the two men and after a moment Susanna follows, feeling both annoyed and protective. Why does Meera never consult me? she thinks peevishly.

Meera approaches the two men holding something out in her hand—four white beads—and she asks the men where they can find a boatman to cross them to the other side of the river.

"We are looking for the Wyandot village," she says in Delaware. "We were told it was to the north."

The older man looks at Susanna and speaks quickly in a low voice, a question.

Meera says, "She is my property."

Susanna has a moment's surprise at that. The younger man wears an affable expression, as if everything he looks at pleases him in a way that he did not foresee. When he opens his mouth, she sees that his two front teeth have been filed to points.

There is a boatman, the older one says, just a mile or so up the river. But he warns them that the man has moods and you never know where those moods might lead him—sometimes away from his boat for days. Follow the river north until you see a small dock, he tells them. If no one is there, sit down and wait.

"And the Wyandot village is on the other side?"

He gives her directions. Although he's a Wyandot, he doesn't say if he is from that village or not. Meera thanks him and gives him two more white beads, which he hands to the younger man.

"*Lennowayeh-hum*," Meera tells Susanna as they walk away.

"What's that?"

The men are eunuchs. Susanna feels a flush of shock as Meera explains it to her. "What? But why? Are you sure?"

"Did you not notice the bundles of firewood? They have been sent to do a woman's work. There was one in Nushemakw's tribe. It is not so unusual."

Susanna looks back at the men. "Was it a punishment?" The men, playing their game again, are squatting close together making their own shade. They do not look unhappy.

"Usually the men choose it themselves. I don't know why."

"But afterward...how do they marry?"

Meera shrugs. "Some have women as companions, some have men. The eunuch in Nushemakw's tribe lived with a man. He made beautiful little animals out of twigs and acorn tops, and was a skilled hunter. He taught me to shoot."

"What happened to him?"

"He died and was buried, the same as everyone else. Let us take cover, we need not walk in plain sight."

A line of beech trees comes down to meet the riverbank, and Susanna follows Meera into their shade. The eunuchs are strong, healthy men who have chosen to live this way. She tries to understand it. Meera is telling her about some of the hunting she did with the eunuch, a bear they tracked for six days, while they walk over piles of old leaves and fallen branches. Without a path it is hard walking, and even after their time at Omie's cabin their strength is not what it was. After a while they decide to stop and split the last pigeon pie and then they rest, each one leaning back against a tree trunk. Susanna feels herself drift into a hot doze. She is following her mother from room to room in their cabin, now a cave-like maze with dozens of doorways, but she cannot get Ellen to stop or turn around.

Something wakes her. She opens her eyes to see the younger eunuch squatting in front of her with the flat of his hands on opposite knees. He is wearing the same affable expression as before. She draws back reflexively, hitting her head on the tree trunk.

"Meera," she says. Her voice comes out high and scared, like a child's.

But he just smiles at her showing his pointed teeth, and says in English, "Not safe here to sleep."

His companion stands behind him with his arms at his sides. The cords of wood are tied high up on their backs, the way women carry wood, and the older one has a string of strong-smelling fish slung over one shoulder.

Meera gets to her feet. "We weren't...we just ate. We were resting."

"A band of Ottawa not far away," the older one says. "Could be mischief." He tells them they should climb a tree and wait for the Ottawa to pass.

"Did you see them?" Meera asks. "How do you know?"

The older one says something in Wendat and both men laugh. Meera translates for Susanna: "The smell."

They choose a thick, leafy buckeye with small orange flowers growing along the base of the trunk like tiny heads of flame. The older eunuch straightens the stems once they are up in the branches to hide their presence. From where she sits, Susanna can see the top of his head. It has been a long time since she's seen a group of men. Her palms, gripping the tree branch, feel slippery.

What would the Ottawa do if they found them? She's heard stories of prisoners who are burned, their hearts bled into a broth. But Liza Footbound told her that stories like these were lies. Still, she tries to position her feet so they cannot be seen from the ground, and Meera, a little higher up, does the same.

When they are satisfied that Meera and Susanna are well hidden, the two eunuchs shrug their wood bundles up a little higher on their backs. Then, like Omie, they walk on without a backward glance.

For more than an hour Meera and Susanna stay up in the tree. Susanna grows hotter and more uncomfortable with each slow minute. Perhaps the Ottawa have gone by without being seen, she thinks. Perhaps they found a path farther from the river. Perhaps the eunuchs lied. But in any case, when she notices that the sun is directly overhead, that the whole of the morning has passed, she decides that she cannot stay in that cramped position a moment longer.

She says, "I'm climbing down."

"Is it safe?" Meera whispers.

"I don't want to miss the boatman. I don't want to run out of food."

She has learned one thing at least: food must be considered at every juncture. The trunk of the buckeye is smoother than it looks and her grip slips coming down, causing her to fall on the orange flowers and crushing the eunuchs' careful work. She stands and holds her breath to listen, but can hear nothing except the sound of the rushing water and the same birdcalls they have heard all morning. Meera climbs down more carefully, and they make their way over to where the tree cover is heavier. They do not speak to each other, fearful of missing any warning sound of the Ottawa.

But they come to the ferry landing without seeing anyone. Through the tree branches Susanna spies a lopsided dock with mossy water lapping up to it, and a weathered gray shack up the shore. There the boatman sits against an unevenly nailed wall with his hat down over his eyes and a hunting rifle across his lap. He takes his time standing when Susanna calls out to him. He looks her over, and then looks at Meera, and tells them his name is Swale. He has long matted hair that reaches halfway down his back like a dark dirty web and he is swarthy for a white man. His arms and legs are fat with muscle, and when he speaks his voice is so heavy it could carry clear across the river. Yet for all of that he is barely taller than Meera. A strong, short man.

The ferry is tied up against the dock: a sorry-looking platform made up of wet gray planks nailed together without symmetry, and splintering everywhere. Swale loads Meera's bundle onto it with the manner of a man pitching hay.

"That's a pound apiece," he tells them.

"Will you take federal dollars?" Susanna asks.

"Aye, if it's minted these last five years."

She opens her grain sack to get Seth's purse. For a moment her hand gropes, finding nothing. She opens the neck of the sack wider and looks in. Still nothing. She dumps everything out onto the dark compacted sand.

"My purse," she says.

Her eyes run back and forth over her possessions. The purse has to be here. There is no other place for it to be. Meera kneels down and spreads the objects apart with her fingers, the ax and the dinner knives and everything else, but there is no way the bulky purse could be hiding underneath any of that. After a minute, the boatman throws Meera's bundle off the ferry and turns to go back to his shack.

"Wait," Susanna tells him. She looks at Meera. "The eunuchs. They must have taken it while we slept."

"They were very quiet," Meera says.

"And afterward they made us hide so they could get away."

"Your wench speaks English same as you," Swale interrupts roughly. She looks at his face, which is crossed with an expression she can only call judging. She realizes that she and Meera have been speaking Delaware to each other. When did that become their shared language?

"Bad enough you take one of them as your wife," he says.

For a moment Susanna doesn't understand his meaning, and then when she does she almost laughs. He thinks she is a boy.

Meera says rapidly in Delaware, "And you look like you were born of wolves and then abandoned by them for your ugliness and backward manner."

Swale glares at Meera, understanding nothing except that an insult was given. He thinks Susanna is a boy but that hardly bothers her, the lost purse is much worse. Her hair is short from cutting nits out of it, and ragged and dirty. She has no cap and her split skirt could be taken for unbecoming trousers. She is thin to the point of a stick. And why else would she have an Indian girl with her? People carry their own beliefs with them and then paint the world accordingly. That's what Sirus always said. But she won't bother to correct Swale—he might give them worse trouble if he knew. They aren't in the Black Swamp anymore, they're back in the world of men. Already they've met with thievery and insult and the day is little more than half over.

How will they get across the Maumee with no money? She looks down at her belongings scattered on the bank.

"Is there anything here you would take in trade?" she asks in English.

Swale leans over to examine what she has. Feathers. Dinner knives. Sirus's ax. Their kettle. Meera clutches their bundle of food, not on offer.

"Don't need feathers. I'll take everything else."

Meera says in English, "We will keep the necklace. You have no use for that." To Susanna, in Delaware, she says, "The Wyandots are allied with the Chippewa. They'll value the necklace of a chief. That will be enough for the ransom."

"But we need the kettle, too." In her pouch Susanna still has her mother's cherry buttons and the avian-head nail scissors, but Meera puts a hand on her arm. "*Punitu,*" she says. Leave it.

"But without the kettle, how will we cook?"

"We've fared worse," Meera tells her, and that is certainly true.

Swale poles them across the water and holds the ferry more or less steady as they disembark. Susanna hates to think of Sirus's ax in his hands but there is nothing she can do about that. He points out the wagon path that leads to the Wyandot village, a couple of hours' walk, he says. Then he spits not too far off Susanna's foot, his last gesture of disgust.

But Susanna doesn't care what he thinks. The day is still fine, with a thin string of clouds hanging overhead like a partially beaded necklace. For a long time she can still hear the Maumee behind them.

"Perhaps I should go into the village by myself," Meera says presently. "Just at first."

"Why would you do that?"

"I could find out if your sisters are there."

"You told me they would be."

Meera hesitates. Then she says, "If they are alive, I mean."

So that's it. Meera is protecting her.

"I want to hear for myself," Susanna tells her. She adjusts her nearly empty grain sack and keeps walking. Just behind her conviction that she will find her sisters at the village, there is the other conviction that she will not. A worry she has to resist. Her plan is very rough: she'll negotiate their freedom and then they'll leave. From here, it is easy to get to Sandusky, and from Sandusky they can get to Philadelphia. Her basic plan hasn't changed. Leave Ohio and go back East. They pass a maple tree with an unbroken spiderweb shining in the sun, a sign of good luck.

Eventually the brook widens and they begin to see the first signs of people: a partial footprint in the mud and broken branches set off together in a pile next to the wagon path.

"They no longer bother to cover their tracks," Meera remarks. "We are fully in their territory. Will you hand me the shawl?"

Consolation's shawl with the last of their food is wadded up inside Susanna's grain sack. Meera reaches inside and pulls out a small hard lime.

"Where did you get that?" Susanna asks.

"From Omie." Meera slices the lime in half with her hunting knife. Then she takes a fistful of her thick, dark hair and begins cutting it off.

"What are you doing? Your hair!"

"I must make myself humble." She scoops up some dirt and squeezes half of the lime into it. Then she rubs the dirt into her shorn hair.

"This is what the Wyandot do?" Susanna asks.

"It is what I do."

Her hair looks ghastly. Already the lime juice has altered its color in places. Why would Meera have to make herself ugly? Wouldn't her uncle tribe welcome her no matter what, like a lost daughter, a lost niece? Susanna is beginning to wish she had a better plan.

"If something worries you," Meera says, "say *scan-oh-nye.* That means peace in Wendat."

Her chopped-off hair makes her look like a stranger. "Why would something worry me?" Susanna asks. But her jaw tenses as she says it.

When the path turns they see the first faint plume of smoke in the distance. They are very close now. Perhaps someone from the village has already seen them and is running back with the news. They follow the path into a stand of birch trees with dark knobs running up their trunks like open sores, and two loose pigs come squealing toward them before veering off. Susanna feels her stomach constrict like a violin string quickly and expertly tightened. After a while the path opens up into a long, sloped clearing, and suddenly there it is spread out below them.

" *Yadata,*" Meera says in Wendat.

The village.

They both stop to stare. Susanna has never seen a settled Indian village before, only ones that have been abandoned. It is much larger than she had imagined. Below them is a wide, fast-moving stream with a bridge at one end, marking the entrance to the village. Beyond the bridge she can see scores of small huts and longhouses laid out neatly across the flat plain, and planted cornfields to the north. To the east, a palisade of sharp poles runs along the perimeter like a fence.

The summer day seems impossibly long but it is still only afternoon. Susanna can see dots of people working the fields. The chirping of cicadas rises and falls, and a bird calls out a question that not another one can answer. Two tall Wyandots, a man and a woman, are walking up the clearing toward them. The man carries a painted buffalo skin and the woman carries a sack and a long calumet pipe made of painted clay. The stem of the calumet is decorated with locks of human hair.

As the pair approaches, Meera drops to her knees and touches her face to the ground. Susanna is looking at the calumet for any red hair. She must have made a movement because the man steps toward her and puts a warning hand on his knife. Its blade is as long as her forearm.

She drops to the ground like Meera. "Peace, *scan-oh-nye*," she says.

The man comes no closer but keeps his hand on the knife. The woman says something to Meera in Wendat, which Susanna cannot follow, and Meera rises and begins talking. When she finishes, the woman calls to a child who is running across the clearing with a dog at his heels. She gives him some instruction. Then she and the man continue walking toward the stand of birch trees. When Susanna turns, she sees them sit down on the ground facing the path.

"They are not escorting us to the village?" Susanna asks.

Meera makes a noise of reproach. "They are meeting someone important, you can see by the gifts that they carry."

"Did they say who?"

"A band of Ottawa with their chief."

"Ottawa? So the eunuchs told the truth!"

A guttural scream comes from the trees. Susanna hears a group of men laugh.

"They are killing a hog for the feast," Meera says.

"*Hao. Owa-he*," the boy tells them. Come.

The clearing slopes down to the bridge and the village beyond it, giving the Wyandots long notice of anyone coming out from the birch trees. The boy walks ahead of them, his dog trotting briskly by his side. Everything is adding to Susanna's confusion: the huge size of the village, the couple taking scant notice of them, the news of the Ottawa. She can see animals—mostly pigs and cows—roaming freely between the longhouses and the woods.

"Where is he taking us?" Susanna asks. Her voice comes out as breathy as a whisper.

"To someone who will decide our fate."

"The chief?"

"There is more than one chief in a village," Meera says sharply. "I do not know which one we will see." She quickens her pace and Susanna tries to keep up.

"Why are you angry with me?"

"I'm not angry," Meera says.

She's anxious, Susanna thinks, like me. After they cross the bridge the land flattens and she can no longer see any farther than what is immediately in front of her: rows of huts made of bark and wood with deerskin doors, and women sitting on the ground before them with their work on their laps. It is crowded and noisy. She can smell roasted meat and corn, and animal skin, and smoke, and the faint odor of something unpleasantly sweet, like sewage. They pass a fenced enclosure for horses. "*Kupi kupi kupi,*" a man calls to the animals.

"We will be fine," Meera tells her. "In the past, Wyandots often used to marry my people. We are related in spirit. And the Chippewa also are special to them. They will honor the necklace you carry."

But her anxiety doesn't lessen—in fact it seems to get worse as they walk through the village. Women look at them casually without stopping their work, as though they are used to people coming and going, even white women and natives from other tribes. In contrast to them Susanna feels muddy and thin, like an animal in the wild. When they get to the center of the village the boy stops at a small building made of gray and white stones.

Susanna is surprised to see a stone building. Perhaps it was made by the French and then abandoned? So far she has seen no one with red hair.

The boy makes a motion—stay here—and goes inside the building. Susanna looks around at the nearby men talking or smoking or chewing on long, brown leaves. They look back at her curiously. A thick, ancient elm tree dominates the area, and most of the men are sitting or squatting in its shade. At last a very brown, very wizened man wearing a hide tunic and English trousers comes out of the building. Several peltries are drying on a wattle stand nearby and he takes a moment to rub his hand over one of them. Then he turns to look at Meera and Susanna.

He asks Meera a question. By this time Susanna's stomach is feeling pinched in the middle. She wishes they would speak Delaware instead of Wendat so she could understand them. The man says a few words to the boy, who clicks his tongue at his dog and they both run off.

"He has told the boy to fetch someone," Meera tells Susanna. "One of the chiefs. Perhaps the chief of tribal friendships."

"How many chiefs are there?"

"Often a great many. They don't always agree with each other. We must hope we are given someone sympathetic."

The wizened man turns to them. "*Skwaray-miha,*" he says sharply. Meera bows her head.

"He does not want me to speak English with you," she tells Susanna in Delaware.

Clearly he is some sort of petty official, Susanna thinks. The boy comes back with strips of leather in his hand, which he gives to the man. The man asks him a question and the boy seems to answer yes. Then the man turns to Meera and speaks to her. He has a nasally voice. Susanna gets the impression that he is not happy.

"You must tell him why I have come," she says to Meera in Delaware.

"I will," Meera says. She holds out her hands. "But first show him your hands."

To Susanna's surprise the man starts to wrap a leather strip around her wrists, and when she pulls away in protest, Meera says, "Huh! It is just a ceremony. What do you say? A symbol. Until our fate is decided. Look, he ties mine as well."

"What do you mean, decided? I've just come to bargain for my sisters. Tell him that. If they're not here, I will leave." The binding is tight, it doesn't feel like a symbol. "The Wyandots are friendly to white men," she says in English, looking straight at the official. "We are friends."

The man makes a sharp noise with his tongue, a rebuke.

"Do you speak Delaware?" she asks in that language.

The man says something to Meera.

"You must not address him," Meera says.

The men under the elm tree stand to let an old woman walk though. She is short and wears twenty or thirty strings of beads around her neck and a deerskin dress decorated with a pattern of small white and blue feathers. The skin on her face is stretched and folded into a permanent frown. She stops before Meera and Susanna and, like the official, looks them over carefully. Then she turns to the man, who begins to speak to her.

"This is the chief," Meera whispers. "He is telling her my tribe."

"The chief is a woman?"

"That is not unusual. There are many chiefs with different roles, both men and women."

"What does he tell her about me?"

"Of you he says nothing."

This is not good. "Please," Susanna says loudly in Delaware. "Let me speak."

But the chief does not look at her. She looks at Meera instead and asks her a question. Meera speaks a few words, and then says quickly to Susanna, "I will tell your story before I tell my own. You can see by this how I am a friend to you. Now take out your necklace."

With her hands tied it is difficult to take the necklace from the box but no one makes a move to help her. While Meera tells the story, Susanna holds the necklace out, but the chief barely glances at it. Finally, Meera moves her bound hands forward as if saying, and that is the end of that story. She tugs at Consolation's shawl, which she has tied to her waist. The boy unties it for her, and when Meera reverses it to show the tiny mirrors there is a cry of delight from the men watching. The old woman says nothing but takes the shawl.

"Did you explain about the Chippewa chief?" Susanna asks Meera. "How he gave me the necklace himself?"

The official grunts at her. She spoke in English again. But in any case Meera does not answer. She is busy pulling things out of her various pouches and offering them to the chief. Her knife, some white beads, the green feathers from the Stooping Indians, and then, to Susanna's amazement, Meera pulls out Seth's purse.

"My purse!" Susanna says.

The skin around Meera's jaw flushes dark red but she doesn't look at Susanna. She gives the faded black purse to the official, who counts the money inside. Then he puts it in the pile along with the other offerings. The chief bids Meera to come over, and Meera kneels before her. With her strangely dyed hair and her bony shoulders, she seems both humble and desperate. The chief unties the leather thong from Meera's wrists. Then she returns Meera's knife to her, places a hand on her head, and speaks softly for a moment. When she takes her hand away, Meera stands.

"Meera!" Susanna says. "Why did you take my purse? How could you do that?"

"It was not necessary for you," Meera says. But she still doesn't look Susanna in the eye. "You had the necklace. I had nothing. I needed a gift. And now I've been placed with a family in the north of the village, which means they are wealthy. That is good. Don't worry, I explained all about the Chippewa chief."

"You let me think those men did it! But it was you, you stole it!"

Meera says quickly, "If they think we are quarreling it will go worse for you."

How can it go any worse than it is already going? For a moment Susanna doesn't know what to do. The young boy begins to walk off and Meera follows him.

"Meera!" Susanna calls.

"Farewell, Susanna," Meera says. "Stay harmless." Then she rounds the tree and is gone.

Three black birds with white stripes like rings on their necks fly rapidly around the tree trunk as if in search of a fourth. *Kwe-kwe-kwe,* they sing. An omen of death? Despite the warm day Susanna's hands feel cold.

She turns to the chief and says in Delaware, "*Nuh-mee-suk. Ne-mah-kal-hu-kohena.* My sisters with the red hair. Are they here? I have come to you with my head bent"—she does not know the word for humble—"seeking an exchange for them."

The chief waves a hand as if all this means little to her.

"My sisters," Susanna says again. "Are they here? In exchange for them I give you this honored necklace from an important chief. He took it from his own person to give to me." She picks up the necklace with her bound hands and moves it closer to the old woman. "Please accept it as my gift."

By this time more people have gathered, both men and women, crowding around the stone building to watch. The old woman pays them no attention. She lifts up the necklace and, significantly, lets it drop in the dirt.

"We have quarreled with the Chippewa," she says in Delaware, "and no longer count them among our friends."

She calls to another boy—a smaller boy, without a dog—and gives him some instructions. The boy pulls Susanna to her feet. He speaks to her in Wendat, which of course she cannot understand. Susanna looks at the old woman. "But my sisters," she says. "Can you tell me where they are? Are they here? *Scan-oh-nye,*" she says. Peace.

The chief gathers up the gifts—the feathers, the beads, Seth's purse—and rolls them up in Consolation's shawl, preparing to leave. The boy repeats himself and Susanna looks down at him, a skinny minute of a child with nut-stained teeth. The official clucks at her and lays his hand meaningfully on the long knife hanging from his belt. Now the boy calls to her a third time, the same incomprehensible words, but this time he roughly pulls her forward.

"*Hay-tet. Hu-wahay. Huwae.*"

"*Scan-oh-nye*," she says again, looking from the chief to the official and then back. *"Scan-oh-nye. Scan-oh-nye."*

But they aren't listening. They are done. There is no sign of Meera, nor anyone else who might speak on her behalf. The birds with the white neck rings fly off their branch in perfect unison and she hears their wings flutter like tiny drumbeats overhead. She is hot and confused, and just like that terrible morning when she stood outside Amos Spendlove's cabin, she wishes more than anything else that she could go back in time and do something different. The boy tugs her again by the arm. What else can she do but go with him, her hands still tightly bound in front of her? It is in this way that she realizes she is now a captive herself.

Twenty-Two

Susanna is taken to a hut and left with two women who strip her of her clothes and examine her lean, dirty body. They give her the name Tarayma, which means, she learns later, Holding Mud.

It takes them a long time to scrub her clean in their large copper tub, and afterward she is given Wyandot clothes to wear: an unpainted deerskin dress that smells strongly of wood smoke, and long moccasins with stiff soles. They take Aurelia's moccasins away and Susanna never sees them again. One woman cuts off her hair to the nape and another pierces her ears. The earrings are made up of four small thin metal circles that hang one inside the other, like chains.

She tries speaking to the women in Delaware. "Have you seen my sisters? *Nuh-mee-suk? Ne-mah-kal-hu-kohena.*" We have red hair.

They take her pouch from her belt and shake it upside down. Ellen's nail scissors fall out as well as the two remaining cherry buttons. They pass around the scissors, each of them rubbing her thumbs over the bird-head fingerholes. One of the women gives her a spoonful of roasted corn. Then the same boy who led her here comes back to lead her away. He takes her to the other side of the village, where it is very dusty, and as they walk he explains to her in bad French that a family has bought her and that she must *plaisir* with hard work.

They pass longhouses with groups of women cooking in front of them, but the hut that the boy stops in front of is small and ill-made and there is no one outside. Inside, Susanna finds an old woman sitting cross-legged mending a basket. When she stands Susanna sees that she is not as tall as the others—the Wyandots are generally a tall people. This woman is small with a thin, angular frame and very white skin. She looks like she has been ill. Behind her, built into the interior wall, is a narrow shelf made from hides, a kind of hammock covered with a couple of bearskin blankets. The old woman is bent with age but not so bent as the Stooping Indians. Her face seems neither kind nor cruel. She assesses Susanna closely, feeling her forearms for muscle.

"Have you seen my sisters?" Susanna asks her. "*Ne-mah-kal-hu-kohena.*"

"*Astay-ta.*" No.

The old woman's name is Akwa and she speaks some Delaware, but it is her daughter, Akwendeh-sak, who will be Susanna's mistress, she explains. Akwendeh-sak has been working in the cornfield but soon returns with her two daughters, both of whom are older than Susanna. As soon as Akwendeh-sak enters the hut Susanna can smell on her the smell of plowed land and sweat—a familiar odor that exuded from every farmer who ever set foot in the Quiners' store. Like her mother, Akwendeh-sak pinches Susanna's arm. Her pinch, though, is meant to hurt.

"There is much for you to do, Tarayma," she says in Delaware.

It is the last Delaware she speaks to her. She is very bad tempered, Susanna soon discovers, and her hands are flat and hard. She sends Susanna to fetch water and then tells her to build up the fire and set the water to boil. The cooking fire is just outside the hut, and as she works Susanna keeps watch on the people walking by. But she sees no one with red hair and not a glimpse of

Meera, who is, in any case, by her account, living with a rich family on the other side of the village. Akwendeh-sak comes out with
corn and indicates that Susanna is to boil it in the kettle. Susanna
stirs it, not knowing exactly what to do, and when Akwendeh-sak
comes out later to taste it, she spits it on the ground. Then she
kicks the dirt in front of Susanna so that a cloud of dust hits her
in the face. While Susanna is shielding her eyes, Akwendeh-sak
begins to hit her arm with a stick. Susanna steps back but
Akwendeh-sak holds her by the other arm and gives her a swat
across the back. She is shouting in Wendat.

"I know Delaware, can you tell me in Delaware," Susanna says
but Akwendeh-sak doesn't hear her or doesn't care. What is perfectly clear, however, is that if Susanna does not do her chores to
Akwendeh-sak's satisfaction, she will be beaten.

By now her stomach is tight with hunger. At least in the Black
Swamp there was no smell of roasted meat to mock her.
Akwendeh-sak's hut sits on a crowded, noisy spot where two
dusty paths intersect. People are everywhere. They don't seem to
be looking at her but still she feels watched. Clouds of insects
hover over her.

On the ground near the cooking fire she spies the stick that
Akwendeh-sak beat her with, and she picks it up and throws it
behind the hut. But there are other sticks, a forest full. She sits on
the ground and tries not to cry. She thinks of what Meera said,
"We've fared worse." For a while she lets herself be angry with
Meera. That at least feels better than self-pity.

A young boy with a round, pleasing face runs down the path
carrying a dead rabbit. He wears a too-long tunic and woolen leggings dyed green. Perhaps because of the smile on his face, Susanna calls out to him.

"*Mi-chewakan?*" she asks in Delaware. Food?

The boy stops to look at her. Then he puts down the rabbit and draws out three hulled nuts from his pouch, which he gives to her.

She thanks him, and then says, "Have you seen my sisters, with the red hair?"

He smiles and nods and then shakes his head no. *"Astay-ta, astay-ta!"* he shouts. *No, no!* Susanna steps back quickly, gesturing for him to go. She is afraid that Akwendeh-sak will hear and come outside. As the boy skips off he swings the rabbit by its hind legs, and she eats the nuts quickly before anyone can take them away.

⸻⧓⸻

Her days fall into a pattern: she wakes before dawn and fetches kindling from the scrubby, picked-over woods, brings the bundle of wood to the hut, and then goes to the stream for fresh water, carrying two full buckets awkwardly up the long path. After that she builds up the cooking fire and boils water and corn in the kettle to make samp porridge for the women. It's heavy work and the skin on her fingers—so bony they are bent out of their natural shape—often bleeds. Most days Akwendeh-sak is displeased with her labor and hits her or, if Susanna manages to get the cooking fire between them, throws sticks at her head. Susanna learns to pass over the most sharply jagged sticks when she fetches kindling but still blood runs from her arms from tiny punctures almost every day. Akwendeh-sak ties a rope to her wrist so she can tether Susanna at night and whenever she wants to during the day. When Susanna fetches kindling or water the rope dangles from her wrist, marking her as a captive as surely as her shorn hair and the rings in her ears.

Escape is impossible. There are people everywhere who watch her. And anyway she is too hungry to think about anything other than how to get more food. Sometimes in the morning Akwendeh-sak gives Susanna a spoonful of the porridge but sometimes she forgets or is angry at her and refuses. After breakfast she and her daughters leave for their plots of land where they work all day, while Susanna helps old Akwa—mostly sewing or mending hide garments. Susanna is always hungry but Akwa is a little cowed by her daughter and will not give her anything without Akwendeh-sak's leave.

One morning, after Susanna has been there for over a week, Akwa takes her to a small trading house in the center of the village and leaves her outside to wait. Akwa needs a certain ingredient for a poultice she is making for one of her granddaughters. The rope dangles from Susanna's wrist but she is not tied to anything since there are no trees immediately nearby. That morning she burned the samp porridge and as a result was given nothing to eat. Her stomach feels raw and angry. To distract herself, she tries to remember what Naomi was playing on her violin that last morning, the morning they were all taken. She is just trying to pull out the melody when the boy with the green leggings comes running down the path.

He stops when he sees her. He squeezes the outside of one of his pouches and then shrugs: no nuts today. She smiles back: that's all right. He has a dark smear of dirt over his chin that makes him look as if he's been eating chocolate. Then he says something in Wendat that she now understands to mean, Come.

"Hay-tet, hay-tet," he says.

Akwa is still bargaining inside. Susanna has a moment's hope: maybe the boy knows something about Penelope and Naomi, maybe he will take her to them. She follows him, her heart beating hard even as she tells herself that she might be wrong. And she is wrong. He doesn't take her to her sisters, but stops instead at a curiosity: a large enclosure with a bear inside. The bear is fully grown, with one torn ear and eyes as bright as a child's. It is sitting like a short fat man with its legs stretched out before it. One side of the bear's pen is fenced by the palisades that surround the village, sharp spears like prison bars, and a bowl with dried blue corn stands on the ground just inside.

Susanna looks at the bear's food, and then she reaches through the spears and takes a small handful. The dried corn is tough and hard to chew. The boy watches her as she eats it, saying nothing.

Susanna swallows with difficulty. "What is your name?" she asks the boy in Delaware.

"Tako," he says. Later she finds out it means squirrel.

At that moment Akwa comes around looking for her and scolds her fiercely, shooing Tako away. She continues to scold Susanna so much as they walk back that Susanna is afraid she might tell Akwendeh-sak, who will certainly beat her. But back at the hut Akwa busies herself making the poultice from the root she has obtained, and when Akwendeh-sak returns all the talk is about her daughter's finger.

That evening Tako comes by Susanna's hut, this time carrying a string of small silver fish. He gives her one and calls her by her Wyandot name, Tarayma. How did he learn it?

"Thank you," Susanna says in Delaware. *Wanishi.* Then she says, "I like your green trousers."

She is not sure how much Delaware Tako understands, but he pushes one leg out to look at it and then nods as if he has only just now decided that indeed the trousers are good. How old is he, she wonders, eight? Nine? Something about his dark, upturned eyes seems familiar. After a moment she realizes that they remind her of Seth Spendlove.

"Tako," she asks. "Have you seen anyone in the village with red hair? Hair like my hair?"

Tako chatters for a moment in Wendat.

"Say again?" she asks in Delaware.

"*Oui, non! Oui, non!*" Tako shouts.

"It is my sister with the red hair," she tells him.

Tako runs off shouting, "*Oui, non!*" and laughing. When he has gone Susanna puts the little fish into the cooking fire embers, but one of Akwendeh-sak's daughters, the one with the hurt finger, comes out just as Susanna is checking it and she takes it and eats it herself.

The next day Susanna finds Tako sitting alone on the stream bank when she goes to fetch more wood at midday. Although he pretends at first not to see her, she has the feeling he's been waiting there for her.

"*Hay-tet,*" Tako says. Come with me.

The sun is directly overhead. Akwendeh-sak is away at her field and will stay there for hours. Akwa might scold her for being slow but she has never yet hit her, so Susanna follows Tako up the streambed. After a while Tako ducks in between two saplings bending toward each other and enters the woods. Here is the best firewood, he signs to Susanna, and it is true. It is farther from the main path and not so picked over. After she has a good pile of wood, Susanna, in no hurry to leave, takes the time to pick some small, sour blueberries while Tako teaches her a few Wendat words: berry, wood, squirrel—*tako.* He points to a squirrel climbing the trunk of a maple tree, its tail sweeping up after it.

Quietly Tako puts his hand into his leather pouch and draws out two small stones and a buckskin thong—his ammunition and slingshot. From this distance it seems to Susanna a foolish attempt, but Tako fells the squirrel with the first stone and they hear a thump as it falls on the ground. Tako pushes around the pile of leaves until he finds the body while Susanna, using his flint, makes up a small fire with as little smoke as she can manage. Tako nods when he sees it, and when he next looks at her she sees that his estimation of her worth has increased. This amuses her, and pleases her, too.

Together they pull off the skin, cut up the soft meat, and roast it on sticks. Then they eat up every bite. Afterward Susanna feels some discomfort—she is now used to only a mouthful or two of food at a time—but that is an easy enough price to pay for the meal.

"You will look for my sisters, with the red hair?" she asks when they part. He laughs, shaking his head. She does not know if he understands her or not.

After that Tako meets Susanna every afternoon at the same spot at the streambed, always when Akwendeh-sak is away in the fields. Akwa never says anything about Susanna's absences, and Susanna tries never to stay away too long. The Wyandots' forest is brighter than the forests in the Black Swamp, the trees are not as tall or as thick, and sunlight breaks through their branches easily, warming Susanna's head like a blessing. But like the Black Swamp it is quiet. There are no squealing pigs or barking dogs, no hatchets ringing out, no shouting quarrels. Akwendeh-sak is not screaming at her: *bad fire, bad porridge!* Instead the trees hold, like a sack, the soft noises she has come to appreciate: frogs and birds and pecking creatures, the wind rustling through heavy summer leaves, an insomniac owl. Sometimes a man, a sentry, appears and speaks a few words to Tako. Other than that they are alone.

She helps Tako trap little animals and they make tiny fires to cook them. It is almost like playing house, but to Susanna it doesn't feel like playing since it is all that she can do not to eat her share in one bite.

Tako says, "Tarayma, let me show you, it is easy." His little hide pouch is a store of tools: the buckskin slingshot, small round stones, horsehair, deer sinews, sharpened bits of rock, a flint. He takes out a length of horsehair and ties it into a slip noose, and then hangs the noose over a little trail where they saw a mouse run the day before. After that he bids Susanna to keep very still. When a mouse finally emerges and runs into the noose, Tako quickly pulls the string tight. Although the mouse fights as violently as a panther, Tako eventually prevails. After they cook and eat it he gives Susanna one of the mouse's tiny teeth. He demonstrates its use by scratching himself up and down his arm with another tooth, his wide face nodding: yes that feels good.

It isn't the method of trapping that is hard to learn, but the patience. Sometimes they try to bring down larks and other slow birds, and once Susanna thinks she sees a wood vole among some rotting logs but it is gone before she can get to it. Besides trapping, Tako lets Susanna practice shooting with his slingshot. One day he rewards her with a slingshot of her own that he has made for her. She is very pleased and thanks him as many times as he will let her. When she leaves the woods she folds it up and hides it inside her moccasin so that Akwendeh-sak will not see it and take it away.

Every day when they part Susanna asks Tako about her sisters. Part of her feels better (the food and a friend), and part of her feels worse (Penelope and Naomi must not be here, Tako would have told her). The asters and dogbanes are beginning to bloom: the last flowers of summer. Soon it will be fall, and then winter. Whenever she thinks about running away she remembers the sentries who check up on them in the woods, and the lookouts stationed along the palisades every evening. The leather strip marking her as a captive dangles from her wrist. She would be identified in no time, brought back, and beaten.

But she is learning how to survive here. And she is not so hungry every day. That is something. That is good.

One evening Akwendeh-sak's daughters decide to stay with their mother for the night instead of going into their own huts to sleep, which means Susanna must sleep outside. Their husbands will be at council far into the night, Akwa tells her, so they prefer to stay here. A great meeting is taking place. The Ottawa who arrived the same day as Susanna have been joined by others: more Ottawa, a band of Potawatomi, and two bands of Miami. Susanna is learning more Wendat, words enough for some comprehension, but she still prefers Delaware. She has not spoken English for weeks. There is no one to speak it to.

Akwa gives her two blankets and Susanna lies down on one and covers herself with the other, her feet toward the smoldering cooking fire. A strong breeze ruffles the tree leaves, and then stops, and then ruffles them again like a woman trying to make up her mind. The wind is higher and cooler than it was a week ago. Summer is turning. Her hidden slingshot rubs against the skin of her ankle but she likes the feel of it. It is her only possession. She wonders, as she does from time to time, how Meera is faring. The village is large and they live at opposite ends, so Susanna is not surprised that she hasn't seen her—or only a little surprised. She is still angry with Meera, but like the wind her anger feels a bit higher and cooler than it was last week.

"Tarayma," someone whispers.

She pushes herself up. By the light of the moon she can make out a small shadow of a boy: Tako. But someone is behind him, another figure, someone taller. A man? She jerks away as long arms come down around her.

"Penelope," the figure whispers in her ear.

It is Naomi.

Susanna quickly puts her arms up to catch her. "Nami," she says. A feeling bursts inside her like sparks of light, maybe more than one feeling. "It's me, it's Susanna."

A second of silence. "*Susanna?* But...?"

They embrace hard and for a moment can say nothing. Naomi's smell is different but not the feel of her arms. Susanna starts to cry, a hiccough in her chest that erupts into a gray cloud of feeling. It comes out of her whole body and envelops the night air. Naomi pulls back and looks at her face.

"Susanna! I can't believe it's you! I thought the boy meant Penelope. In fact, I didn't believe him at all at first, I was so stupid."

"Where is Penelope?" Susanna asks, trying to swallow and stop crying and talk at the same time. "Isn't she here?"

"They sold her to a fur trader up north. A Frenchman. A Canadian." Naomi combs her fingers through Susanna's cropped hair. "What have they done to you?"

"And they pierced my ears, too! But my hair is the worst."

Naomi says, "Luckily you've always had a perfectly formed head."

They laugh, quietly. It feels good to laugh. Susanna hiccoughs again and wipes her face with the back of her hand.

"Let me come under your blanket," Naomi says.

They sit under the pounded hide blanket with their arms around each other as close as they can get. In the moonlight it is difficult to make out Naomi's features but her face seems round enough, not pinched with hunger. Her soft red hair is in two plaits with beads braided into them. There's no rope on her wrist, and no chained earrings in her ears. Her voice sounds just the same. But something is different.

"I never in the world imagined the boy meant you," Naomi is saying. "I thought maybe Penelope had been traded back. We were on a fishing trip until a few days ago, and when we returned, here was this boy I didn't know telling me about a sister with red hair. Only because he persisted...and then I had to wait for nighttime. But tell me about you. How did you come here?"

Susanna doesn't know how to answer. She begins crying again. Every feeling she has ever had in her life seems to be rising up and fighting each other for dominance.

"Shhh, it's all right now, Princess," Naomi tells her gently. "Wait. Here." From her pocket she takes a piece of fried cornmeal and gives it to Susanna. In that moment Naomi reminds Susanna of Beatrice, who could be so consoling when someone was ill, whereas Naomi was a terrible nurse, always looking for an excuse to get back to her violin. But of course Naomi doesn't have her violin anymore. Maybe that's what is different.

"We all thought you escaped!" Naomi says.

"I did. That is, they didn't take me. I came here myself looking for you and Penelope."

"You came here by yourself? But Susanna, how astonishing!"

"I had help. An Indian girl...but that's over. Now I'm a captive like you. Naomi, I've made such a mess of things. How will I ever get you out? And then we have to go get Penelope from that fur trader, but I have nothing to trade for her, they've taken it all!"

"Hush, don't, it's all right. You don't have to worry about that tonight," Naomi says. She draws Susanna closer to her. An owl hoots nearby. "Princess, I have to go. My family might miss me. But I'll arrange something. Is your Wyandot family good to you?"

"They hit me and won't feed me. I have to scrape the bottom of the kettle for my supper."

"I'll try to have you traded to another family."

"You can do that?"

"My family is wealthy...they have some power. And they're kind."

"Meanwhile I've been treated like a slave," Susanna says bitterly. "Nami, let's leave this place together right now! You must know the woods around here, places to hide."

"It would never work. They know the woods much better than we do. And you're in no condition to run. Just look at you—a ghost of a child." A phrase of their mother's.

Susanna looks up. The stars seem to pulse for a moment. "That seems so long ago, doesn't it?"

"Another life," Naomi agrees.

The owl hoots again and Susanna realizes that it isn't an owl at all, but Tako. He is sitting on the ground some ways off, a rock in the shadows.

"I must go," Naomi tells her. "Tomorrow I'll see that you're moved closer to me. Remember, you have me now." She rearranges Susanna's blanket over her thin shoulders and kisses the top of her head. "We'll get you a thicker blanket, too," she says.

Twenty-Three

Naomi follows Tako through the village although she does not need him as a guide. She has only been gone for a month. When she gets to her longhouse she lifts the bark door and makes her way carefully to her blanket, stepping over many sleeping people, including Nadoko, her foster mother. Nadoko partially wakes and says without raising her head,

"*Hat-kah-keta?*" What are you doing?

"*Aja-yai-haw. Iskwanyo,*" Naomi whispers. I went outside and now I have come back. But Nadoko falls back asleep even as Naomi is speaking.

Naomi settles herself on her blanket and looks up at the bark ceiling, trying to breathe evenly. Smoke holes are scattered along the far end, and near them the bark has turned black with soot. Her heart is still beating hard with surprise and something else—what? Something she does not want to examine too closely. How did Susanna find her? Why did she come here?

The answer to that last, of course, is that Susanna thinks Naomi is a captive and needs her help. Naomi is strangely irritated by the thought, although she knows she's being unjust. She was a captive once, but now she is not. Now it is her choice.

When Naomi first went off with Hatoharomas and his mother Nadoko, she wasn't thinking about choices, for she had none. She was just hoping to live out the day. She'd been traded for a dozen silver brooches, about half the price of a good horse, and she felt both lucky and despondent. Lucky because Hatoharomas—whom his family called Hato—did not think she was a witch, and despondent because she felt in her bones that she would never see Penelope again, no matter how many times Penelope assured her that they were both heading to the same village and would meet up again in a matter of weeks. But in this case Naomi was right. By the time she arrived at the village, Penelope had been sold to a fur trader who wanted a wife. A white man called Boucherie.

From the first, the difference between Nadoko and Naomi's old mistress was marked. The canoes Hato and his group had hidden were miles away, and they made their way to them carefully through forests of hugely tall poplars and trees that Nadoko called "sugars," all of them intertwined with so many vines that scarcely any sunlight could penetrate. Naomi often stumbled, but each time, instead of scolding her, Nadoko helped her up and asked if she needed to rest. She fed Naomi peas and bear meat, though not in the same dish—that, Naomi learned, was unacceptable—and taught her how to skim clear water out from a layer of algae.

Remembering Penelope's advice, Naomi tried to learn from Nadoko. She asked questions that her old mistress would have laughed at: how do you build a fire up quickly, or tamp it down without letting it go out altogether? What kettles do you use for fetching stream water, and what kettles do you use to cook with? What food should never touch one another, like the bear meat and peas?

Naomi wondered if Nadoko's patience with her came from ignorance—perhaps she thought all white women were as backward as Naomi?—but Hato was equally patient, and he knew white people. He spoke very good English from living outside a British fort for a year. Once, when they were walking across a stream with white rocks on the bottom, Hato took her by the arm to keep her steady. And when Naomi made her first samp porridge by herself he complimented her greatly, although it was not nearly as creamy as the porridge Nadoko regularly cooked up.

What will Susanna think of me now? she wonders. She's shared pipes of tobacco with Nadoko and Hato, and when their tobacco ran out they smoked red sumac bark that Hato ground into powder. She speaks Wendat easily and has learned how to cook animal rough—the diced organs—in fire embers, and to eat the dish with pleasure. She has learned to look at the world as Hato looks at it, and this perhaps is the greatest change. This is the change she will have the most trouble explaining.

By the time they came to their canoes and embarked on the river, Naomi felt almost comfortable with Nadoko and Hato. There were others in the group—Hato's younger brother Detsukwa, and several cousins. They divided up into the four canoes, Naomi with Nadoko. But unlike her first group, this group was not in a rush. They lingered, enjoying the journey. For five days there was not a spot of rain, only blue sky and trees that seemed golden at their tips as the canoes snaked north along a jagged vein of the Great Black Swamp.

Every day Hato called to her from his canoe to look at various things on the shore: a grebe with a new chick on its back, a wild boar with two striped babies. At night they pulled their canoes up over the bank and camped in clearings bordered by tall bluestem, where they gathered wild grapes, eating some of them and boiling the rest into syrup. When Naomi took off her moccasins to bathe her feet one night, the dried twig of yellow buds that she found so long ago, when she was still with Penelope, fell out. Hato picked it up and gave it back to her. A few days later when she woke up she found twenty twigs with fresh yellow buds in a bunch beside her head. That was when she understood he was wooing her.

He gave her a polished panther's bone, a whelk shell, and a necklace with one blue feather. Naomi made honeycakes out of oak flour, and gave Hato the biggest one. Being apart for so many hours in different canoes began to feel intolerable. In the evenings, after they ate, Hato took her hand gently. He kissed her at night after the moon had risen and in the morning when the air was still damp.

One evening Hato gave her a smooth white stone like a wild bird's egg, which even now Naomi keeps in her pouch. It is a stone from the river, Hato told her, where they first touched, when he held her by the arm to keep her from stumbling. The stone was a pledge: when they got to the village, he told her, they would marry. Naomi ran two fingers along the stone's smooth surface. She had nothing of her own to pledge except the twig with the dried yellow buds that she kept in her moccasin. So she gave him that.

A few days later, Naomi happened to be alone among some trees one afternoon, not far from the riverbank where the others were resting. It was a muggy day, the sun veiled by thin lace clouds. She was looking for food but she didn't know precisely what. She wanted to make something for Nadoko and Hato. Maybe she could find some early apples. But the ground was wet and spongy, not the sort of place where apple trees grow. As she stepped around a shallow pool of gray water like an unreflective mirror, she noticed that a few small fish were trapped in it. She crouched over to look at them. At this particular angle they appeared purple, and she thought Hato might like to see that. As she was getting down onto her elbows to look more closely, she heard a noise that she first mistook for a frog piping nearby, but the noise went on and changed, forming itself into words. English words. A man was speaking English in a low voice to someone else, who replied in a slightly higher, nasally voice.

For a few moments Naomi could see nothing, and then the two men came into view. They were soldiers, or maybe scouts. They wore blue uniforms and hats that were slightly too large for them. They looked scarcely older than Mop. What were they doing so far into Indian Territory? All soldiers have two things in common, Sirus used to say, lice and the flux. Naomi watched the men squat to relieve themselves, and one scout was close enough so that she could see his trousers down about his knees. They continued to talk to each other calmly, as if disinterested in the business they were doing here in the woods.

All she had to do was stand up and they would see her. They would take her back to their camp or their fort—wherever they came from. One had red whiskers and the other one, the one with the nasally voice, laughed at something with a pitch like a woman's. Naomi breathed into her chest and crouched farther down. Maybe she should approach them about Penelope, direct them to her. But how could she do that without being taken herself? And if they saw her, they would make her come with them. They would have no scruples about killing Hato or anyone else in their party. A squirrel jumped out from somewhere, startling the two men, and the man with the red whiskers cursed. A rustle of leaves, twigs breaking, and they were gone. When Naomi returned to Nadoko and Hato, she said nothing about them.

And now here she is trying to sleep in Nadoko's longhouse, turning over and pushing her hot feet outside the blanket. She enjoyed those long days spent out among the white rocks and the bluestem, fishing from the riverbank or stitching the side of a moccasin while Nadoko showed her how to angle the needle. They stayed in the village for only a few weeks before they left again to go on a fishing trip. Hato and Nadoko prefer to spend much of the summer away from the village, but now the time has to come to start preparing for winter, Nadoko told her. So they have come back.

She does not miss Severne. She loves her sisters, but she does not miss living with them, all their noise and quarreling. Perhaps this is the uncomfortable feeling that seeing Susanna has brought up. Without realizing it, she thought that that life was over. And she was glad. She sighs without meaning to, and Nadoko opens one eye, a habit of hers that Naomi still finds unsettling. One of her dogs is lying behind her legs, wound up like a ball of dark yarn.

"*Ekwa-toray-shay*," Nadoko says quietly. Let us both sleep.

Naomi is good to her word. The next morning a young boy leads Susanna up to the northern end of the village to live, and Akwendeh-sak is given a bolt of cloth for the trade.

Susanna's new mistress is an old woman called Onaway who is some sort of relation to Naomi's foster family—an aunt or an older cousin. Naomi's foster mother, Nadoko, exclaimed over Susanna in Wendat and squeezed Susanna's two hands in her own with apparent pleasure. Susanna can see at once that she is wealthy, just as Naomi said. She wears a dozen copper bracelets on each arm and she tells Susanna proudly—Naomi translates for her—how she owns many European items: spades and umbrellas and shawls. Nadoko is especially proud of a short fur cape, which she wears every morning over her deerskin dress.

That first morning they stand outside Nadoko's longhouse with the sun pouring down on their heads. Nadoko touches Naomi's arm, and then Susanna's arm, and then her own arm. Here we are together. But Susanna is not sure how pleased Nadoko really is that she has joined her family. There is a look about her—not sly exactly, but maybe secret. As though she is thinking something else.

Although the father of Nadoko's children is dead, he had been a senior chief in the village and people respect the family. Nadoko has two grown sons, Hatoharomas and Detsukwa, and a daughter who died the previous spring of the blue cough. Naomi is a replacement for this daughter. They are all tall and handsome, well dressed, and, Naomi tells Susanna, clever in business. Their longhouse is the largest in the village, made of slabs of bark over pole frames that extend back almost into the trees. It is big enough for four or five families to live in comfort. Inside there are hammocks for the men to sleep on, and the women use the space underneath them to store wood. They hang their food jars and clothing and anything else they want kept away from the mice on thick poles that rise up to the roof. The mats and skins that serve as flooring give the room a slightly animal smell, not unpleasant, that mixes with the smell of smoke and cooked meat.

At first Susanna is a little in awe of the large space, the plentiful food, the many possessions. Nadoko's younger son often carries an unfurled brown umbrella—like his mother, he is fond of English goods. He is called Detsukwa, which means fishhook, because of his long crooked nose. The older son, Naomi told her, is named Hatoharomas and called Hato. This month he is training boys in a lodge at the uppermost corner of the village, and so is not living in Nadoko's longhouse. For a few days nothing more is said of him.

Susanna's new mistress, Onaway, lives at the far end of the longhouse away from the cooking fires, which worsen her cough. Other than her cough she seems healthy enough despite her age. Although Onaway has three grown daughters and two grown sons, they live elsewhere with families of their own and can no longer help their mother. She is happy to have Susanna do her chores. Most of the work is the same—fetching wood and water, building up a fire, boiling corn—but here she is properly fed and Onaway does not throw sticks at her. Meera said that the wealthier families live here in the north near the head of the stream, and indeed everyone seems to have clearer skin and newer clothes. Susanna does not have to walk so far to find kindling, and even the stream seems brighter and moves at a quicker pace. She no longer has to wear a rope attached to her wrist, and she is not tied up at night. But she moves everywhere with a crowd of women, not only Onaway and Nadoko and Naomi, but other women as well who are somehow related to Nadoko. Susanna is never left alone with Naomi. Is this by design? She wonders if Naomi has already formed a plan to leave, and what that might be.

"The Wyandots have a proud history," Naomi tells her one morning outside Nadoko's longhouse, after Susanna has been living there for almost a week. "Nadoko has told me many stories about them. They are one of the oldest tribes. Holders of the council fires."

They are sitting with Nadoko and Onaway pounding corn. Although the afternoon is warm, the light is no longer lengthening into summer but rather backing away. Huge white clouds seem to dip down into the village itself. Is it late August, Susanna wonders? Early September? She is getting impatient to leave, but still has found no chance to talk to Naomi alone.

"They believe trade is more important than war," Naomi is saying. "Also—you'll like this, Princess—women here are prized since they alone have the gift of foresight. Can you imagine the farmers back in Severne believing that?"

"I did not feel particularly prized by Akwendeh-sak," Susanna says. She pounds the corn in her wooden mortar bowl a little too hard and a few kernels fly up over the rim. Carefully she picks them out of the dirt and looks at Onaway. Akwendeh-sak would have thrown a stick at her, but Onaway pulls the mortar closer to Susanna and shows her how to hold it up a little so the rim makes a kind of wall. Onaway knows no Delaware or English, so they communicate mostly by gesture. Her warm fingers remind Susanna of Ellen. She has the same gentle touch. Naomi is grinding her corn neatly and efficiently, Susanna notices. When did she learn to care about food preparation?

"Women in general are treated very well here," Naomi continues. "They harvest their own fields, sell their own crops, and keep the profits. They hold positions of power in the village. Nadoko has herself appointed several chiefs."

"Why are you telling me all this?" Susanna asks sharply.

"It's interesting," Naomi says. "I think it's interesting, at least."

Susanna pounds the corn harder. After a while she says, "I've been trying to work out what seems different about you, Nami. I mean apart from the clothes. I realize that it's that you're not carrying around your violin. Do you miss it?"

"No," Naomi says. She moves her own bowl clockwise and begins pounding again. "I guess you think that's strange."

"Don't you?"

Naomi doesn't answer. Soon it will be time to fetch wood and begin building up the cooking fire, but for the moment they can remain in the sun's warmth working the corn and enjoying each other's company. Susanna feels a twinge of guilt for speaking so sharply to Naomi. Naomi is just making the best of a bad situation.

"I did wonder about the bear," she says, trying to repair the conversation. "You know, the one in the enclosure with the crooked ear?"

"Oh yes, the bear." Naomi turns to Nadoko. *"Hanone,"* she says. She tells Susanna its history: some hunters found it as a cub wandering in the forest alone, without a mother, and they brought it back to the village where the boys played with it and taught it tricks. It is now fully tame. At night the bear sleeps in its pen but sometimes during the day the children lead it outside to play.

Nadoko begins speaking, and Onaway and Naomi both stop to listen. When Nadoko pauses and nods in the direction of Susanna, Naomi says, "She is telling a story. She wants me to translate for you. It's about a Wyandot man and his wife who were traveling from one village to another when they were captured by a company of bears. The bears took the couple back to their mountain and put them in a beautiful cave with lots of nut trees and other food nearby."

The bears told the couple they must not leave, Nadoko continues, but every night the man tried to escape. However, each time the bears found him and they beat him until every bone was broken, or they gave him diseases that left his body limp. But the following morning the bears always showed his wife how to cure her husband, until she knew as much as they did. And when that time came, the bears released the couple, saying, "We are friends of the Wyandot. Now we have shown you how to cure yourself when sick or injured. Bring this knowledge back to your people."

Naomi translates Nadoko's words almost without pause. Out of all of Susanna's surprises, this is perhaps the greatest: Naomi's fluency in another language. Although she is smart, Naomi was always lazy about schooling. She could barely be bothered to learn her times tables.

"Why did she tell us this story?" Susanna asks when Nadoko has finished.

"Nadoko and her family are from the bear clan. She is very proud of that. By telling the story the Wyandots keep the bear clan sacred."

"I think she wants to warn us against running away."

"Careful," Naomi says. "Most people here know more English than you might think."

Nadoko stands up abruptly. She spreads her arms and speaks to Naomi pointedly, an instruction that Susanna does not understand. Then she goes into the longhouse. Onaway is leaning back against a tree trunk. She has fallen asleep in the sun.

When Nadoko comes back out she is holding something in her hands. A basket. She looks at Naomi and waits.

Susanna looks over at Naomi, too. "What? What does Nadoko want?"

Naomi picks up her bowl and sets it down beside her. "Susanna," she says, and then stops. She tries again. "Susanna, there is something I must tell you. It was a surprise to me, too. But I've changed."

"You've changed? What do you mean?"

Naomi hesitates again. Then she says, "I'm in love."

"What? How can you be in love?"

"I'm in love with Hato. Hatoharomas. Nadoko's oldest son."

Hatoharomas? For a moment Susanna cannot speak from amazement. "But that makes him your brother!"

"Susanna, don't be foolish, of course he's not my real brother."

"But I don't understand. I thought you would want to leave. To play your violin again."

"I feel, indeed I have long felt, that that is no longer my fate."

"But what else could you do? You've never liked doing anything else!"

Naomi says, "I have married him."

"What?" Susanna stands up. She feels an urgent need to move, to do something. She looks at Nadoko who surely cannot follow their conversation, but who nods nevertheless.

"I fell in love with Hato, I betrothed myself to him, and now we are married."

"But Naomi, he's an Indian!"

"Oh Susanna, don't be so closed minded."

"What about home? What about our store?"

"I know it's hard to understand, but I like living with Hato and Nadoko. I'm learning so much. And I don't miss my violin at all. Not at all. Don't you think that means something?"

"No. I don't."

"Susanna, I know this is difficult." Naomi stands and tries to take her hand but Susanna pulls it back. She feels as though she's been holding on to her self-control as one would hold on to the end of an icicle, trying to climb it like a rope, and now it's slipping out of her hold.

"Difficult?" she says. "This is nothing, this is easy. I don't have to fight with wolves for meat, I don't have to wade through miles of bog and pull leeches from my legs over and over. All of which I did for you. For you! For you and Penelope. And now you tell me, now you say..." She is stuttering with emotion. She wants to shake Naomi hard. Nadoko is watching her closely.

"Susanna..." Naomi says.

"How can you want to live with the people who did all this to you?"

"They weren't the ones who took me."

"And what about me? How will I ever get back?"

Onaway makes a soft snore. Naomi looks at her and says quietly, "You don't have to leave. We could find a place here for you, too."

By *we* she means herself and Nadoko. Susanna swallows hard, not trusting herself to speak.

"Susanna. Listen to me. It's a good life here. You may not think so now, but you'll see. When you have experienced more, and can see what I see."

But here is the problem exactly. Naomi has always seen the world differently. No matter how much Susanna wants to—and at the moment she wants to not at all—she knows she can never be like Naomi. I see things as I was taught to see them, she thinks bitterly. White women do not work in the fields. White women do not fall in love with Indians. Naomi is right, I am closed minded, and moreover I'm foolish and misguided. I counted on luck when I shouldn't have, and now I'm paying for it. What is luck anyway except self-delusion? And I've been deluded my whole life. I can't change the smallest particle of myself. I'm not Naomi.

"Nadoko wants to give you a gift," Naomi tells her. Susana turns to Nadoko, who is pulling something out of her basket. Susanna can't read the expression on her face but she knows she must feel triumphant. She has won the prize: Naomi. Nothing in the basket can make up for that.

"I don't want it," Susanna says.

Twenty-Four

That night Susanna can't sleep for thinking about all the many ways she's miscalculated. If only she'd stayed in Severne. If only she'd never asked Old Adam to help her. In Risdale, Liza Footbound made a very generous offer to let her live and work there—why didn't she take it? Then came Gemeinschaft, another disaster, a mirror of this one. Both of her sisters have found another life without her. They haven't appreciated her efforts. But hasn't that always been true? As for Meera—that was her biggest mistake of all. Back in Severne the farmers used to say that friendly Indians are more dangerous than open enemies. Of course, those farmers were fools.

She shifts on her blanket and looks up at the neatly crisscrossed rafters. She came all this way for nothing. What if you do what you think is right, for yourself or someone else, but it doesn't make a difference? she wonders. What if all the right action in the world still results in pain and disappointment? Maybe she's just meant to live alone. To go home by herself.

Of course, she can't go anywhere now. For all of Naomi's help, she's still a captive.

She listens to Onaway breathing heavily next to her. At least Onaway has taught her how to keep an outdoor cooking fire hot, and how long to boil meat, and how to mash peas to her liking. She does not beat Susanna for not knowing all this beforehand.

They work together side by side, and eat together, and sleep head to foot.

Chores, food, rest. Susanna can almost appreciate that simplicity now. Perhaps she was foolish to think that life could be anything else, that in Philadelphia her days would be different.

In the morning when she is cooking porridge in the big kettle outside, Tako comes skipping along throwing a stick into the air and catching it. He still visits Susanna every day although she can no longer escape with him into the woods—there are too many people watching her now for that. But Susanna makes sure to give him some food whenever she sees him. She ladles porridge into a bowl and Tako leans against a huge gray boulder to eat it.

"You like new mother?" he asks.

Susanna turns back to stir the porridge, which does not need stirring. "She is not my mother," she says. "But yes. I do like her. She is good to me."

"Kettle bought last winter," he tells her. "Very shiny!"

The way he says this makes her laugh. "You like shiny?"

"New is good. Bad is old," Tako says. He finishes the porridge and wipes his hands down his green trousers. Something on the gray boulder catches his attention. "Tarayma, *regardes,*" he says, picking it up.

At first she thinks it's a shell of some sort. But then she draws in her breath. It is one of her mother's cherry dress buttons.

She takes it from him and rubs her thumb over the cherry shape, trying to imagine how it got on the boulder. "This used to be mine. I mean my mother's. My first mother's. Where did it come from?"

Tako looks up at the sky as if it came from there, and then grins. A joke. Could he have brought it himself? It fits with his childish crush on her. But he runs off before she can question him further, throwing his stick in the air and catching it as he goes.

Susanna looks down again at the button. Perhaps Naomi negotiated with Akwendeh-sak for it? A conciliatory gift after their quarrel? But Susanna is not sure if Akwendeh-sak was ever given the button. The women who bathed her and pierced her ears took the buttons from her...and after that? They were gone, that's all she knows.

When she shows Naomi and Nadoko the button they both express genuine surprise.

"Mama's button!" Naomi says. She passes it to Nadoko, explaining what it is. Nadoko fingers the little stem, and then hands it back.

"You didn't trade for it?" Susanna asks Naomi.

"I didn't know about it. Where did you find it?"

"On that rock. I thought maybe you put it there, to surprise me."

Naomi frowns. "That is odd."

Susanna rubs it between her fingers. Maybe it was Meera, feeling remorse. But Meera never feels remorse.

"Are you ready?" Naomi asks.

She's carrying two baskets of uncooked corn and hands Susanna one of them. Today they are going to the boys' school so that Susanna can see Hato, although she cannot actually meet him since women are not allowed to talk to the boys or their teachers during their training. They will deliver the corn to them and watch the boys train from a distance.

The day is not as warm as yesterday, and the trees are shedding large yellow leaves. Nadoko promises it will be a great treat to watch the young boys at their games, but Susanna has already made up her mind to dislike Hato. She is still mad at Naomi. She rolls Ellen's button around in her fingers and then puts it into her new pouch—this is the gift that Nadoko gave her yesterday. It is a pretty pouch, decorated with small blue and yellow beads, and it is useful, but Susanna doesn't like it.

The lodge is at the far end of the village set off by itself. While they walk, Nadoko gives them each a handful of small, dark blueberries to eat. They pass women harvesting a line of hemp growing along a wattle fence, not a proper field but nevertheless land that can be used. After that the grass grows taller and there are no more people about. Susanna eats her last blueberry and flicks away the stem, as tiny as an eyelash. She wonders again how late in the summer it is. But then she thinks: What does it matter? I can't get away by myself.

At last they come to a long meadow with a large bark lodge with two chimneys at its easternmost end. This is where the boys eat and sleep during the month of their training. The men have chosen the heartiest boys from the village, Nadoko is saying while Naomi translates. She explains that during the time of schooling they are completely isolated from everyone else.

"We are allowed to grind their corn but not cook it," Nadoko says.

The noise of the village is long behind them. The women stop behind a short fence and put down their baskets. The boys are in the clearing playing a wrestling game: pairs of them wrangle over a skunk skin on the ground; the first one who touches the skin with any part of his body loses.

"The training helps them become great hunters and fighters," Nadoko says as they watch. "The white man has no school such as this."

She lifts her chin. She is proud of her son, the teacher, and of the boys of her village. The boys' faces are serious as they wrestle, intent on finding an advantage. They are twelve or thirteen years old, Susanna guesses, just this side of manhood. Heel-sized mud holes with spoonfuls of rainwater inside dot the ground, evidence of weeks of such games. A young man, maybe twenty years old, watches and acts as judge. He does not speak to the women and he does not look over, but Susanna feels sure he is aware they are there.

"Hato," Naomi says.

Susanna says, "I guessed."

Hato is wearing deerskin trousers and a white shirt, and he holds a spear with a sharpened flint on one end. He is tall and good-looking with even features and a strong, straight nose. After the boys win or lose at wrestling, they select spears from a pile near Hato and begin to throw them at each other.

Nadoko speaks rapidly. Naomi smiles as she translates: "When Hato was a boy with short hair, he was the best spear thrower in the village. Even better than his teacher." Naomi pauses, watching him. Then she says, "Well, she is his mother. But it is true that he is very skilled. Once I watched him fell a buck through the trees with one arrow."

But Susanna is watching Naomi, not Hato. Naomi is wearing the faraway look she used to get when she was deep inside her music. A look of concentration mixed with something fey. The violin pulled up at an angle, her fingers working hard over the neck. Sometimes when she was playing something particularly difficult she would lean forward with one leg pushed out in front of her, and later in bed she'd complain: why is my leg sore? After she got herself into a certain state she didn't notice anything else. Penelope used to say that their parents indulged Naomi but Susanna, when she was younger, felt a little in awe. What would it be like to be able to close yourself off so completely, to be in your own imagination so far, that even your senses, your hunger or discomfort, didn't bring you out?

Nadoko takes the baskets of corn and starts toward the lodge, telling Naomi and Susanna that they should stay to watch more. She will deliver the corn to the man there, the cook, and then return for them. Naomi goes back to watching Hato. Her hair is in a long braid down her back but wisps of it near her forehead blow forward in the wind. From this angle she looks beautiful.

"Nami," Susanna says. "You can't stay here, you know."

For a moment Naomi says nothing. Hato claps his hands and the boys put down their spears and form a wide circle around him. When they are assembled, Hato pulls a piece of meat from a basket at his feet and pierces it on the end of his own spear. Then, quickly, he throws the spear at one of his students. The boy catches it and pulls off the meat. This is his meal. The boy throws the empty spear back to Hato, who does the same thing again, now whirling around to choose a boy behind him.

"You can't be an Indian," Susanna says.

"I'm not an Indian," Naomi answers without taking her eyes from Hato. "I'm a woman who is married to a man who is Wyandot. Like someone who marries an Italian, or a Welshman."

Susanna feels a sweep of annoyance. "You know it's not the same thing."

"Why not?"

"He's a Wyandot, Nami, not a Welshman. Our lives are entirely different."

"How is your life so different? After everything you've told me, the Black Swamp, your friend Meera."

"She's not my friend. And that was all temporary. When I leave here I'll live like a white woman again. I want to go back to that."

"Well I don't."

"Well you should!"

Naomi laughs a short laugh. "Why?"

"Be reasonable. It's a hard life here."

"Harder than Sirus and Ellen's?"

Susanna looks off at the lodge. Nadoko is still inside. How can she persuade her sister? "Naomi, Indians are completely different from Christians." This is what the farmers always said. "We don't understand their ways. How can we live with them if we don't understand them?"

But Naomi is able to read her thoughts. "Those farmers are just ignorant, you know that."

"About some things..."

"And intolerant."

"It's not intolerance, it's..."

Naomi waits: what is it, then? Susanna feels her position slipping further. "Just look at how they live! Even here in a settled village. Why don't they build real houses? We've shown them how."

"You think I need to live in a house to be happy?"

"Yes! A brick house! A proper brick house! Or stone." What is she saying? She sounds foolish even to herself. Susanna puts a hand on her pouch and tries to feel Ellen's button through the thin, pounded hide. The wind blows hard against them for a moment and Naomi wraps her arms around her body. Susanna looks at the boys in their little hide breechclouts and bare feet. She wants to sound as if she is just being reasonable.

"People are different, Nami. You have to accept that."

"I do accept that," Naomi says. "It is you who do not."

Susanna presses her lips together. Soon it will be too late in the year to travel. She needs Naomi. She can't escape on her own.

One by one her sisters have abandoned her. Even Meera. Susanna could almost make herself believe that there never was a band of Potawatomi but instead her sisters all went willingly into Thieving Forest by themselves, like a nightmare you might have as a child: you wake up to find that everyone has left, your house is empty, and you are alone.

Hato is still spearing meat and throwing it to the boys, but one boy is taken off guard and can't reach it in time. Susanna watches as the spear sails past him, bounces once, and then falls flat among the grass. The boy looks younger than the others, smaller and disadvantaged.

"Now that one will go hungry," Naomi says.

In the morning Susanna finds another cherry button on the rock.

This time she pockets it and does not tell Naomi. Somehow Tako must have found out about the buttons, that's the only explanation. And he's doling them out as gifts to win her favor. Susanna looks for him while she sits outside the longhouse with Onaway grinding hickory nuts, which they mix with sugar from tree bark to make hickory milk. Onaway wants to give Nadoko the milk as a gift. Later they plan to start parching corn to store for the winter. Back in Severne the farmers said that when food is scarce Indians eat horses' ears and entrails. They boil old bones and then drink the liquid. What will happen when it snows? Susanna wonders for the first time if Onaway will be able to feed her all winter.

"What do you eat in the winter besides corn?" Susanna asks Onaway as they work, but she doesn't know enough Wendat to make her meaning clear and Naomi is inside with Nadoko.

The clouds are low and gray. Several parties of men have gone off to hunt—the first of the season—even though corn is still growing in the fields. It has been a long summer, which according to Sirus means that autumn will be short. When Susanna looks up again she sees that the clouds are all bunched together: a storm piling up. Women begin making their huts ready for rain, bringing skins and kettles inside. For a moment, Susanna thinks she sees a flash of green trousers near the trees. Tako?

"I'm going to fetch more kindling," Susanna tells Onaway. "*Ndata-skwija.*" Twigs.

The sky grows brighter for a moment before it settles into a more permanent gloom. She wants to ask Tako directly about the buttons, but when she gets to the trees he's not there. She can smell the sharp tang of the coming rain so she quickly picks up a few sticks and turns to leave. A gust of wind presses hard against her clothes and something sweeps over her, a premonition. She peers through the trees but sees no one. Their branches are beginning to wave harder in the wind.

"Susanna," someone whispers.

She drops the twigs and whirls around. A man steps out from behind a tree. An Indian. She doesn't recognize him. How does he know her real name? Her heart starts beating hard against her ribs.

"Susanna..."

Someone else is with him, another man. An oriole's nest hangs like a low pouch from the branches, partially obscuring her view, but as he comes closer she hears a sob coming out of her mouth as though it's been waiting a very long time to leave her. The other man is Seth.

He's taller and broader than she remembers, and his dark hair is loose around his shoulders. He's wearing a hide tunic and trousers, and small dry leaves stick to his sleeves. Probably she shouldn't run to him but she isn't thinking. He catches her and holds her tightly.

"Are you all right?" He pulls back to look. "Are you hurt?"

"How did you know to come here?" she asks. And then, "Beatrice," she answers for him.

"I thought you must have gotten lost in the Swamp," Seth says. "I talked to every ferryman on the Maumee just about, paying for news of a red-haired woman. Finally one told me he had crossed a red-headed boy with a little Indian wife. I had almost given up."

She can hear the rain start falling. It's in the tree branches above them, caught in the foliage. She's holding both of his hands in hers and wants to tell him about everything that happened to her in the Black Swamp, but a noise redirects her attention.

She's forgotten about the native. He isn't a Wyandot. She isn't sure what he is. He's wearing the plainest hide trousers and tunic imaginable, as though deliberately hiding any affiliation to his tribe. She thinks to herself: I must be quick. Neither man is Wyandot, and if they are caught here in their woods they'll be killed. So she begins telling Seth instead about Naomi, how she found her but can't persuade her to leave. He listens with that intent gaze of his. Why did she treat him so badly? As for his father selling their wagon and then lying about it—does it really matter? That was a long way back on the river, as Sirus used to say. The rain quickens and a few drops begin falling through the leaves.

"Perhaps it's just despair?" Seth suggests. "Maybe if she knew that escape was possible?"

"I don't think so. She thinks she's in love. But he's an Indian. How can she hope to be happy?"

Seth turns away slightly at that and looks down at her with an expression she can't read. She waits, not sure what he is thinking. At last he says, "They've cut your hair."

So that's it. She's grown thin and unattractive, she's forgotten that. The wind shifts the branches above them and suddenly the rain comes down heavily, soaking her shoulders.

"I'm a slave here," she tells him.

***

Back in the village the rain stops everything for a while. The women come in from their fields to wait out the storm inside, knitting or mending. Onaway says nothing when Susanna returns with no kindling. She dries Susanna's hair and face with a worn Englishwoman's shawl that she uses as a towel and, twisted, for shooing off dogs. They can hear the rain pounding on the roof like a giant drumming his fingers.

Nadoko's longhouse is large enough to have several fires, and it is dry despite the smoke holes in the roof. Onaway presents Nadoko with her gift of hickory milk in a small birch container, a *mokuk,* which has a yellow flower design embroidered on two sides. Nadoko takes a sip of the milk, nods her pleasure, and passes around a cup to share. Meanwhile Naomi and Susanna pull their blankets over to a corner to do their work. When Nadoko's cup comes to her, Susanna takes a long sip. The milk is very good.

"Where is Penelope exactly?" she asks in a low voice, handing the cup to Naomi. Everyone is engaged in some task and pays them no attention. Susanna is trying to knit stockings for Onaway using two long heron bones as needles, and Naomi is making thread from the sinews of an elk or deer, breaking the strands apart and then twisting two strands tightly back together.

"I told you. She was sold to a fur trader. A Canadian called Boucherie. He lives on the River Raisin."

"Where on the Raisin?"

"That's all I know. Why?"

"I saw Seth Spendlove," Susanna whispers. "In the woods not an hour ago."

Naomi looks up quickly. "Seth Spendlove! No, that cannot be."

"It is." She tells Naomi how Seth was among the party that went to Gemeinschaft, but she does not mention his marriage proposal. She wants Naomi to believe that Seth has come for both of them. She wants to make it hard for her to refuse to go.

"He has a plan. He will contact me again through his friend, an Indian. It's complicated. But I trust him."

"Susanna, think about this a moment. If you leave, they will come after you. You are considered Wyandot property now. And if you're caught you might even be killed."

"But this is our chance! We can leave together! Now that there is a way, you surely don't want...surely you would come with me, wouldn't you?"

Naomi keeps her eyes on her thread, frowning as if encountering some difficulty there.

"Are you listening to me?" Susanna asks.

"Yes," Naomi says in a calm voice. "I am listening to you. It is you who won't listen to me. I don't want to leave."

"You can't mean that. Look at the way you must live!"

"When you are in love, you want to stay with your beloved. It's that simple. And I like this life. It suits me."

"But Hato is an Indian! He's bound to treat you badly!"

Naomi's cheeks flame. "That is not true. That is not true at all. That is a white man's misconception. The women in this village own their own land, they own everything they farm. What white woman has ever owned land? What white woman can sell or trade without first consulting her husband or father or brother? It's different, yes. And in many ways it's better. Quite a few of the women in the village here are very powerful. Respected. They hold important positions."

Susanna thinks of the chief who decided her fate when she first arrived. She thinks of Meera. "Indians betray you."

"No," Naomi says. "Or at least no more than anyone else. Look at me, look at how well I am treated. I found a good family. And if I could be happy, if I can trust them after everything that's happened to me...Listen, Princess. I wasn't going to mention this yet, but Nadoko and I have talked. She might be able to find a husband for you. With your red hair you would be prized, even given your...your current status."

As a slave, Susanna thinks bitterly. She throws her knitting down beside her. Tears of frustration come into her eyes. "If I had known that I would have to *convince* you all to come back with me, any of you, I would never have stepped foot outside our cabin. You can never make a Quiner girl do anything she hasn't already thought of doing herself—isn't that what they said back in Severne?"

"Susanna, you're upset." Naomi lifts the thread she's been working on and examines it. "And now Nadoko is looking at us. We'll talk about this later. I should make her some tea."

"Make Nadoko tea? What's become of you, Naomi? You used to be so...so...independent."

"Lazy, you mean."

Susanna can't help but laugh although she is still irritated. "Yes, that's what I was thinking."

"You're right, I was lazy. But I've changed. Don't you think that these last few months might have changed me? After everything I've been through?"

"What about me? What about everything *I've* been through?"

"I can see you've changed," Naomi says. She gives her a sly glance. "For one thing your hands look awful."

Susanna laughs again. But this is exactly what I miss, she thinks, being able to laugh in the midst of a quarrel. Who else can you do that with except your sisters?

"Please come back with me," she says. "Please, Nami. This is not your place."

"You're wrong about that," Naomi says.

Twenty-Five

Seth and Koman shelter from the rain in the Wyandot forest having nowhere else to go. No one would mistake Koman for a Wyandot except from a distance. In a thicket of oaks they find two hollow trees, each big enough to fit a sitting body. Koman gives Seth the larger one and folds himself up inside the other, disappearing from view. From his own hollow Seth watches a pool of water form outside like a sudden idea. It's barely past noon but feels like evening. Muddy debris floats by him, broken branches that smell like wet bark. He thinks of how Susanna smelled when she was in his arms. She was glad to see him, at least. She smelled like green trees.

He must have slept. When he opens his eyes again the rain has stopped. He can see the silvery light of the sun but not its body, and the sky is the color of a woman's summer dress. Climbing out, he sees Koman walking toward him, his moccasins caked with mud and his hair wet. He has been to the village, he tells Seth, scouting around.

"I saw the *Neshnabek*," Koman says. The band of visiting Potawatomi. "One man I know. I spoke with him. He will vouch for me."

"So we go into the village?"

"Better than here. There are scouts, we will be found."

"They'll accept me?"

"I will paint your face like a captive."

They are speaking to each other in Potawatomi. For the past two months they have traveled together, made fires and cooked together, hunted for food, and paddled up and down the Maumee asking every ferryman they could find if he had crossed a white woman with red hair. The ferrymen were to a man isolated and unfriendly. One man was pleasant enough in voice but held a knife between himself and every person he came across, while another called himself Wolf and wore an odd cape made out of an assortment of furs. Most of these men, Seth figured, would eventually drown or get killed by another man's hand. If they looked strangely at a white man and a Potawatomi traveling together, Seth and Koman did not show that they noticed.

They kept to their initial agreement: Koman did not say who killed Seth's father, and Seth did not ask. He would not avenge Amos's death. In a twisted sense he feels responsible for it. He never gave Amos the money for the Quiners' horses and wagon. Of course, twist the rope further and the responsibility loops back again to Amos. Cade would be as unlikely as Seth to avenge Amos's death. Both of them—he believes he can vouch for Cade— would stop just short of saying that Amos had it coming. It did not positively have to happen this way, and yet like the ferrymen, wasn't Amos bound by his drinking and his lies to come to a violent end?

"How will we get her?" Seth asks Koman. "And how will we all get away?"

"We will look about once we are settled. Someone will give us shelter. We will say we came with the traveling party and my friend agrees it is true. Only we are late, because of you."

Koman smiles. He is enjoying this as one might enjoy a hunt or any good game of strategy. "They are negotiating peace with these men and will give us a good place. Then we listen, pay attention, look about. Wait for a distraction. A feast, a game...we will know."

"What tribe will you say I am from?"

"You? A mixed breed, a little of everything. One sees it in your face." He opens one of his pouches. "Are you hungry? It is good we go into the village. This is the end of the venison."

Once, a few weeks back, they lived for five days just on whortleberries and ginseng, which grew wild on a little island on the Maumee. When they came upon a band of Wyandot trapping deer, Koman offered their help in exchange for some of the meat. The way they felled the deer was new to Seth: the men made a kind of enclosure out of great wooden stakes, nearly half a mile long. It was covered with branches, closed on two sides, and got narrower as it went on. Seth and Koman helped the men drive deer into this trap, which was so barricaded that once the deer entered they could not get out. Seth ran through the woods with the other men beating deer bones together and imitating the cries of wolves to frighten the deer into running. After three days they caught ten does and four bucks, and hung most of the meat to dry. One deer was roasted on the spot, and Koman and Seth were given a haunch. They saved the fat to use as butter.

The hunt was exhilarating, and, Seth thinks, he did not do too badly at it. Koman has taught him new ways to trap and how to make a fire that cannot be seen from a distance. He taught him to notice the minute signs of other travelers—broken branches, a slight crest in the mud—and to gauge how long ago they had passed. Koman claimed that bird calls varied if there was a wolf on the prowl or if the bird was just searching for a mate, and Seth learned how to listen. He learned to use reeds and little else now to catch a fish. His arms and face have gotten very brown. *What dost thou in this world? The wilderness for thee is fittest* *place...*To pass the time Seth taught the poem to Koman in Pota-watomi. But he is not thinking anymore of Susanna when he re-cites it, he is thinking of himself.

"Night soon," Koman says after they have eaten. The day seems to have spent itself away in rain, and what little sunlight filtered down after the storm passed is now fading. "Let us go."

"What about my face?"

Koman finds a few red berries and begins crushing them with his thumb into his palm, making a red paste. He'll smear the paste on half of Seth's face, and on the other half he'll smear a black paste, marking him as a captive. Meanwhile, Seth gathers his things and puts them one by one into his dark gray pack. Money, some dried fruit, their small kettle for cooking.

Will Susanna forgive me once she knows everything? he won-ders as he tucks in his last bag of tea. He is his father's son, he can never forget this. And in truth he is proud of that lineage now, in spite of Amos. Amos was not proud, maybe that was his problem. Petty, self-serving, secretive, and ashamed. That was his father.

"I will make you as pretty as a girl," Koman tells him, putting a reddened thumb to Seth's cheek. Seth laughs. Koman's dry humor is still a surprise. It reminds him, strangely, of Susanna's father Sirus.

"If you can, my brother," Seth says. "If you can."

While Susanna waits for Seth she decides to gather as much food as possible to take with them when they go. Of course she needs to do this stealthily. But she has the new pouch from Nadoko and a plainer but larger pouch from Onaway, both of which close up tight with a drawstring. She can hide food away and no one will see.

As she helps Onaway cut rabbit meat into thin strips to dry for the winter, Susanna wonders if Seth will go to one of the chiefs to petition for her release. The Wyandots are famous negotiators. What will they trade her for? Akwendeh-sak received only a bolt of gingham cloth, so maybe her value is not very high.

With a short knife she cuts the rabbit meat in the same direction as the muscle, following Onaway's example. Afterward they hang the strips over poles to dry, and cover them with a piece of cheesecloth so that insects can't lay their eggs in the meat.

Three days pass, and then a fourth, and there is still no word from Seth. Of course, negotiations take time. A soft rain begins to fall, the kind of weather that Sirus used to call Irish weather. She has not seen Tako in several days but she heard that a second group of hunters left, many of them boys on their first trip, so perhaps Tako went with them.

When the strips of rabbit meat are sufficiently dry, Onaway takes them down and shows Susanna how to beat the meat until it flakes. To this they add melted bear fat and some crushed berries to make pemmican. When no one is looking, Susanna takes a fistful of the pemmican and puts it in her pouch. Later that evening when she fetches kindling she sees a nuthatch hiding seeds in the bark of a tree. After it flies off she picks one seed out with her thumbnail. It tastes sour and does not split when she bites down on it, but she takes another seed and eats that, too. Although she lingers in the woods as long as she dares, there is no sign of Seth or his friend.

By the next afternoon the light rain has stopped, and Naomi and Susanna go outside to do their needlework. Around them, women are throwing skins on the roof of their huts to dry them.

For a while Naomi sews in silence, but when Nadoko and Onaway go into the longhouse, she looks sideways at Susanna.

"Nadoko and I saw the bear yesterday," she says. "It was performing tricks for bits of dried fish. It looked just like an enormous dog."

Susanna has forgotten about the bear. "What will happen to it during the winter? Will it be fed?"

Naomi assures her that the bear will be fine. "But listen, Princess. While we were watching it, Nadoko told me something. She may have found a husband for you."

Susanna feels a sudden heat rise to the top of her head. "A husband? Who?"

It is Nadoko's other son, Naomi tells her, Hato's younger brother. Detsukwa.

"Fishhook?" Susanna could not be more surprised. "But he is..." He's ugly and a certain smell surrounds him—many foods disagree with his stomach, Nadoko explains all too often.

"He's courteous to women and attentive to business," Naomi says. "You could do worse."

Susanna looks to see if Detsukwa is among the men talking outside the longhouse. She tries and fails to picture herself holding his hands, embracing him—she cannot even remember him looking at her, that's how little he notices her.

"I'd prefer to stay with Onaway," she says.

"Onaway is old. And at least married to Detsukwa you won't be treated like a servant."

But Susanna thinks differently. Who would treat her well now that she has been a slave? Tarayma, they call her. Holding Mud. Seth once saw her as a wife but that's over, she's changed too much. But what else can she do? Naomi said running away was impossible. The men are fast and know every inch of their land. But marriage to Fishhook? That seems impossible, too.

"Detsukwa is considering her proposal," Naomi continues. "I believe they are bargaining."

At that, Susanna stops working and stares at Naomi. Something pounds for a moment behind her eyes. "*Bargaining* for me? She's *selling* me to her *son?*"

"Susanna, this is a good thing. At least he did not refuse outright." She stops to feel the tear in the tunic she is mending. "They are a family of business," she says, as if that explains it.

"But Seth—"

"You have to consider that Seth might not be successful. Believe me, I would be very sorry if anything happened to him, but we have to face the truth. If the Wyandots discover him in their woods they will kill him. And how can they not know who's in their territory? They have scouts all around. Listen to me, Princess, Detsukwa was very good to me on our canoe trip. He'll make a fine husband, I'm sure of it. If all goes well you could be married within the month. No longer a servant."

"If Seth is...if Seth can't help me, I'll go alone. I'll leave by myself. I'm not going to marry Fishhook. I don't love him. I don't even know him."

"You can't run off! You wouldn't get half a mile away. And even if you did somehow get back to the Maumee, how would you get home? You don't know what it's like to live in the wild."

"I do know."

"You couldn't do it by yourself, I mean. Susanna, you can't even tell north from south!"

Susanna colors. "Yes, I can. And I have some food, and also a slingshot..."

"A slingshot!" Naomi laughs at her.

"Well I won't marry Fishhook."

"He's not so bad. Be realistic, Princess."

"Stop calling me Princess!"

Their voices rise and several women look over. Then, as if to underscore their argument, heavy drums start beating: Bomp bomp *boom.* Bomp bomp *boom.* The drumbeats are coming from the center of the village, and they go on and on. Nadoko comes out of the longhouse and looks toward the sound with her arms folded in front of her, and all the other women stop what they are doing and look, too.

Susanna's first thought is that they have found Seth, and a chill runs up her arms. Wouldn't they drum like this to announce a hanging? Or worse, burning a prisoner alive? But a few moments later a group of little boys run up the path shouting:

"Ononharoia! Ononharoia!"

The women look at each other, and Nadoko quickly pulls on her short fur cape and then gestures to Susanna and Naomi.

"What is *ononharoia*?" Naomi asks Nadoko as they hurry down the path.

It is a ritual for curing the ill, Nadoko explains. Someone must be petitioning the chiefs for the ceremony, and the drumming has started up to mark the event. Everyone is going to the center of the village to see who it is. Women throw blankets around their shoulders and step onto the path, while little boys cut through the trees and in and out between the bark buildings.

Not an execution, then. But Susanna's heart is still racing as if slow to catch up with her logic. They pass the pet bear in its cage lying in a corner where sunlight has cut through the bars. His food bowl is empty but he looks fat and well fed.

"Over here," Nadoko says.

The sound of drumming intensifies as they round the large elm tree that stands in the heart of the village. In the small clearing behind it, a woman is sitting in an enormous basket holding on to its two sides. She is dressed all in red, and her dark oiled hair hangs loosely over her shoulders. Men and women are standing on either side of the basket. They are Wyandot but not, Nadoko says as she stares at them, from this village. According to the practices of *ononharoia* the ill woman would have been carried in the basket, her attendants singing as they walked.

"But why bring her here?" Naomi asks. "Why not cure her in her own village?"

"*Ahntenyai-teri,*" Nadoko says. I don't know.

One of the village chiefs comes to talk to the ill woman, and Nadoko bids Susanna and Naomi to move closer so she can listen. The questioning goes on a long time, and Susanna, who cannot follow what they are saying, finds herself looking around at the crowd. She sees a group of Ottawa and Potawatomi, the visiting warriors she's heard about. Behind them, across the clearing, she can see Detsukwa holding his prized possession, the brown umbrella. Although he doesn't look at her, for the first time she fancies that he is aware of her.

Then a figure catches her attention. There, behind a group of women—is that Meera? A short, stocky girl. Susanna tries to get a closer look. A moment later the crowd shifts, and Meera—or whoever it was—has gone. Meanwhile the drummers carry on, never varying their beat. Bomp bomp *boom.*

"The chief is satisfied with her answers," Nadoko says finally over the noise. She tells them what she has heard: the woman suffers from weakness of the bone. She has tried many cures but nothing has helped. Three nights ago the moon appeared to her in the form of a beautiful woman, who told her she would be healed if she returned to the village where she was born.

"You can see that she is dressed in red like the moon," Nadoko tells them, "which is made of fire."

Ononharoia lasts several days. The villagers will give the ill woman gifts, and in exchange she will interpret their dreams. Afterward, a feast to celebrate. And then she will be cured.

"What if she isn't cured?" Susanna asks.

"She will be cured," Nadoko insists. "Within a month, she will walk by herself."

A month, Susanna thinks. About the same time she is to be married—if all goes well, as Naomi said. Susanna looks across the clearing at Detsukwa again. This time he looks back.

Naomi feels bad for speaking so plainly to Susanna. She remembers what it was like to be treated as a servant. But Susanna is unrealistic. She's just not being practical. And Naomi can't help thinking that even as a servant she is treated much better here than Naomi was treated back on the Maumee. She's fed. No one thinks she's a witch. No one scatters frog parts near her while she sleeps, hoping to curb her powers.

They walk back to the longhouse past a line of women skinning and gutting three stags, and a moment later Naomi hears the squeals of pigs being slaughtered. Susanna walks looking down at her moccasins. Is she pouting?

She must be persuaded to think realistically about her choices, Naomi decides. She has to grow up. I grew up. She can see in the distance a great cloud moving west, almost but not quite cleft in the middle. Sometimes she likes to think that she really is a witch, and she conjured Nadoko and Hato out of the misty fog that day to rescue her. She still doesn't understand why she felt, almost from the first, easy in their company, or why she finds pleasure here in this crowded village with its packs of dogs and snorting pigs. There are many things she's surprised by. Her interest in how Nadoko makes clothes or meals and, once she concentrates, her own success at doing these things. Back home the only thing she was good at was her music. Here, Nadoko is constantly picking up things Naomi has made to praise them.

Of course the biggest challenge will be having a baby. She has not told Nadoko the rumors about her family. Naomi knows she's not barren. She is not. Nevertheless there is a woman she sees secretly in the southern part of the village, who gives her a strengthening potion in exchange for firewood. It tastes like sour milk and cinnamon.

The ragged frog legs did not curb her powers, they only hardened her against other people's ideas about her. This is what she tells herself.

Inside the longhouse everyone is putting on their finest clothes for the *ononharoia.* Nadoko is wearing so many silver bracelets that they clink together like wind chimes. She has oiled her hair with sunflower seed oil and fingers some though Naomi's hair too. Naomi likes the feeling of being made pretty by someone else. If only Hato were here! The new moon is next week, and he'll be back then. This year's training will be over. She's desperate to see him, to hold his hands and smell his smell, to press her lips against the spot on his neck she likes. She wants to hear what he has to tell her of the world, what he has noticed, which is always something unexpected. He surprises her. She likes being surprised.

Onaway gives Susanna an embroidered shawl to wear but Naomi thinks the embroidery down the front of her dress is the most beautiful in the room. The pattern is made from yellow and green beads, and only when you stand off a ways can you see what it is: a bird's head. Naomi runs her hands down along it and tries without looking to distinguish the tiny rows with her fingertips. Nadoko made it for her daughter, the one who died of the blue cough, but the girl never grew tall enough to wear it. It fits Naomi perfectly.

Nadoko clucks at her in approval. As she adjusts one of the sleeves, her bracelets ring with the movement.

The ill woman does not arrive until late in the evening, dressed in her red clothing and supported by two young girls wearing plain hide dresses with colorful waistbands. They walk down the length of the longhouse, passing so near the fires that they seem to walk right through them. Nadoko, who is the most important person in the longhouse, gives her their presents: white ribbon, four segars, and a mokuk with embroidered purple flowers on all four sides. Then the woman announces that anyone who wishes can come up to her one by one to tell her their dreams, and she will determine their meaning. After she seats herself one of her attendants covers her with a long raccoon-skin robe, although the longhouse is very warm from all the fires and the bodies.

Susanna does not go up to her. For one thing, she does not know enough Wendat, and for another she not allowed to, as a captive. Anyway, all her dreams are the same: slogging through mud and cattails in the Black Swamp, and worrying that she has lost sight of the path. But Nadoko takes her turn with the woman, and then Naomi does too. From where she sits Susanna can hear the woman's high, light voice speaking to her sister. The sound but not the words. There is a musical quality to her voice, and in spite of her bone illness, or whatever it is, she moves her arms gracefully as she speaks. When Naomi returns, her eyes are wide and unfocused, as though she can see through the bark wall and out to the world beyond.

"She did not guess my dream," she whispers to Susanna. "But she knew something about me. She knew I would have a child."

Susanna draws in her breath. "What?"

"She said that by the first snow I would feel his life. *His* life! Susanna, it will be a boy!"

"A boy? But that's impossible." No one has given birth to a living baby boy on her mother's side of the family for at least three generations.

"It's true," Naomi says fiercely.

The longhouse is cramped with people, and hot. Two young girls stay by the fires to keep them built up, and Susanna feels a thread of sweat run down the knobs of her spine. She stares at Naomi. This is her dream, she realizes. To be in love, to marry, to have a son. But it will never come true. At least not the son.

"Naomi," she says. She looks at her sister's flushed, pretty face and feels a wave of tenderness, a wish to protect her from disappointment. She takes her hand.

"I'm glad for you," she says.

"Those farmers just hated us, to say such things," Naomi tells her. "What do they know about babies?"

"They don't know beans from bird's eggs, as Penelope used to say."

"Susanna, think of it, if you marry Fishhook we could have babies together!"

But Susanna doesn't want to think of the babies she might have with Fishhook. Only Naomi would be able to conjure up a world where they would be lovely. A small white feather, detached from somebody's clothing, floats toward them at a slant.

"I've found what I wanted," Naomi says, watching the feather drift down.

"What do you mean?"

But the ill woman has finished interpreting dreams now and is trying to stand. Two of her assistants help her, and when she's upright she says something in an important-sounding voice.

Naomi bends toward Susanna. "She is going to tell us all her last desire in the form of a riddle. Whoever solves the riddle gets a prize."

"What's the prize?"

"The winner can choose her own prize," Naomi says. She listens to the woman and frowns. "I don't really understand it. She says a thing alone, or maybe she means single. Something unique, but not unique."

The woman repeats herself: a thing unique but not unique, a thing alone and not alone. Tomorrow there will be feasting and a dance to celebrate the woman's cure, but the excitement for this night is over. Before they leave, the woman's attendants hand out gifts: white beaded bracelets for the women, and for the men, small beaded necklaces. Naomi shows Susanna her bracelet. The white beads are irregularly shaped but pretty, and she runs her fingers over them. As a captive, of course, Susanna did not receive one.

She gives Naomi back the bracelet. "Tell me the riddle again," she says.

All the next morning Susanna tries to guess the riddle, but in truth she has never been very good at solving riddles. Sirus used to tell them at supper sometimes, and Beatrice usually guessed before Susanna could even work out all the parts to it. But Nadoko confirmed what Naomi said, that anyone who solves the riddle could name her own prize.

The drummers begin drumming again as soon as the sun rises, and they continue without stopping while the women cook food for the feast. It will take place in the clearing just beyond the old elm tree near the center of the village. Late in the afternoon Susanna walks down with Nadoko, Naomi, and Onaway, all of them again dressed in their finest clothes and jewelry. A feasting hut has been erected—four slim poles and a bark roof—and the drummers sit cross-legged in front of it, pounding on covered kettles in their laps. Women holding buckets of dyed grease are painting their faces, and one man laughs as a woman bends over him but without missing a drumbeat. Next to him two men hold tambourines on long sticks with stones or pebbles inside, which they shake or turn or strike on the ground.

For a while Susanna stands with the others watching the musicians, and they discuss if they want to go into the feasting hut now or wait a bit. The clearing is already crowded. Some men are wearing traditional Wyandot costumes—sleeveless tunics, embroidered breechclouts, and leggings that stop above the knee—while others wear English coats with brass buttons. All the women are wearing long decorated dresses like Naomi's.

Naomi and Nadoko decide to go into the feasting hut while Onaway stays with Susanna who, as a captive, cannot go in. There are a few logs rolled out as seats, and Susanna helps Onaway to sit down on one. Her eyes are bright and happy, and curve like little crescents when she smiles. She must have been very pretty when young, Susanna thinks. She looks at each passing face but she does not see Seth or his friend and she does not see Meera. She also looks for Tako. The afternoon is unusually warm and the air carries the scent of cooking meat and smoke. She notices a group of men standing off to the side playing some game, and she watches them for a while. A pair of painted bones is placed in a bowl and then tossed up into the air. When the bones come down the men look at them, and then there is much debate and some arguing before they are tossed again.

The ill woman and her two attendant girls are sitting in a little three-sided gazebo made of willow branches not too far from the feasting hut. Today the woman is dressed all in white and her hair is dyed vividly red. Susanna spots Detsukwa nearby among a group of men. He catches Susanna's eye and nods to her but does not smile. Their first hello.

Suddenly she has an idea. "I'd like to guess at the riddle," she says to Onaway. Onaway does not understand her at first, but when she does she cocks her head and lifts her shoulders as if to say, Well all right! As if this will be just another entertainment to enjoy.

The gazebo smells like roses, and Susanna notices pink petals scattered on the ground as they enter. The ill woman turns her face toward them and Onaway speaks to her. Then it is Susanna's turn. She puts her palms forward in supplication.

"*Tiyeme-dutay dasya-nay.*" My language is of the Delawares.

The woman nods. "*Dinaytay-ri.*" I know it.

The girls in their beautifully embroidered waistbands look at Susanna calmly. She cannot guess by their expressions whether they know the answer to the riddle or not. She begins speaking in Delaware:

"I am a white woman with red hair. Unique in this village but not in the world. I am alone here, but if you consider the whole world I am not alone. Therefore I am the answer to your riddle. Unique and not unique, alone and not alone."

But the ill woman begins shaking her head even before Susanna has finished. "The answer is not a white woman," she says.

Susanna's heart sinks. "A white woman with red hair?"

"You are the only one with red hair in this village?"

She thinks of Naomi. "I am...I am the only captive with red hair."

"It is not you. I did not know of you. You have not guessed the riddle correctly."

The woman turns her face away. Some of the red hair dye has stained her neck and Susanna stares at the spot. She could be lying. She could have changed the answer now that Susanna has guessed it. Susanna wants to stay and press her point but Onaway takes her arm.

"A white woman like myself," Susanna repeats. "The answer fits the question!"

Onaway begins to lead her away, patting her arm. She looks at Susanna's face and Susanna can feel her sympathy but that only makes her feel worse, her hope crumpling up in a wad. Then all at once everything crumples.

Seth is dead. And her chance to guess her way out of captivity is gone. She walks out with Onaway into the clearing where a few young boys are running around lighting torches, but as far as Susanna is concerned the celebration is over. She helps Onaway sit down again, thinking: Somehow I'll have to run away on my own.

She feels a push from behind. "Hello!"

"Tako! I've been looking for you," Susanna says. Despite her disappointment a nugget of pleasure comes up when she sees his face.

"I went with the hunters. Brought down a deer."

"By yourself? Really?"

"Well..." he shrugs, pulls a face, and says a few words in Wendat that she takes to mean, Why not? There is a familiar line of dirt along his jawbone. He looks very young.

"Tako, listen. I wanted to ask you about this." She pulls one of the cherry buttons from her pouch.

Tako looks at it, nodding solemnly. "*Tudedi,*" he says. Button. Then he grins at her as if making a joke.

"Did you give this to me? Did you find it and leave it on the rock? Or did someone ask you to leave it there?"

"*Oui, non! Oui, non!*" he says.

She tries several ways of asking him, but he makes each of his answers into a joke. Finally, she gives up. "This *tudedi,* it is for you," she tells him. She wants to thank him, to tell him—what? How much he helped her? But he would only make a joke of that, too. So instead she just repeats, "For you."

Tako closes his fingers around the button and laughs. Then he skips off between bodies in the crowd and is gone.

Onaway says something to Susanna and points to four men wearing traditional Wyandot dress, who are beginning to dance in front of the drummers. This is the oldest dance, Onaway tells her, and the most important—sacred, Susanna understands her to mean. As she watches she thinks it looks like the same dance that the Stooping Indians danced after their rabbit feast. The same dips, the same swerves, except now only men are permitted to dance it. She thinks of Light in the Eyes, and of the small boy learning to play the flute. In this village there are more rules, but there is also more food. But even so she would rather go back to the Stooping Indians than stay here. If she could find them.

At last Naomi and Nadoko return from the feasting hut, and Naomi presses several strips of spiced pork into Susanna's hand.

Her fingers are slim and strong and Susanna can still picture them curved up over taut violin strings.

"Nami," she says. "I've been wanting to ask you. What was that last song you were playing on your violin that morning, back in the cabin?"

"The day we were taken?" Naomi stops to think. "It must have been Bach. *Sleepers Awake?*" She hums a few bars.

"Yes, that's it! I was trying to remember."

"There are things I've wondered, too. Where was Aurelia? Somehow she wasn't in the cabin with the rest of us when they came in."

"No, she snuck out to feed her hens."

"And what was Beatrice doing?"

"Burning the porridge?"

They laugh. "We shouldn't make fun," Susanna says.

"I know, I know," Naomi agrees. But she's smiling. Beatrice always burned the porridge. Always.

"Here," Susanna says, pulling the last cherry button from her pouch. "I want you to have this."

"No, no," Naomi tells her. "You should keep that."

"Please, Nami."

Naomi hesitates, and then she takes it and hugs Susanna. Her hair, her clothes, even her neck smells Indian. The dancers begin a new dance and now women and boys are allowed to join in. Nadoko leads Naomi into the circle, and Susanna watches them appear and disappear among the dancers.

Naomi is someone else now, she has to admit that. Even if I stay here, she thinks, that will still be true.

Suddenly there is a commotion: the ill woman is being carried out of the gazebo. With a flourish the drummers stop drumming and the woman's attendants help her to sit in a special chair in front of them. One girl, not an attendant, walks behind the others carrying something on a large wooden slab. More meat for the feast? But instead of going into the hut, the girl presents the platter to the ill woman.

Naomi and Nadoko hurry up to them. "Can you see from here?" Naomi asks. They help Onaway to stand and move closer for a better view. And then all at once Susanna can see what is on the platter: it's the head of a bear. The Wyandots' pet bear.

She turns to Naomi. "It's the bear!"

Even from this distance she can make out its one crooked ear. Its fur looks darker, especially at the bottom where it is wet with blood. Its eyes are open. Something—a rock?—is keeping its jaws apart, and Susanna fancies she can even see a sliver of tongue. But even more astonishing: Meera is the one carrying it. Susanna can see the side of her face. She looks very solemn.

"How could they do that?" she asks Naomi. "That bear was a pet."

Naomi's expression doesn't change. "It wasn't a pet."

"They kept it in its own pen!"

"Yes, like Saul, or any other farm animal."

"Saul was a pig, this is a bear!" Susanna looks at Naomi, and then at Nadoko, and then at Onaway. None of them seem the least disturbed. Nadoko says something to Naomi.

Naomi turns to Susanna. "The bear is being honored. He is part of an important day. The girl with the platter must have guessed the riddle and the bear was the answer. Something unique and not unique—I understand it now. The bear is unique in this village but not in the world. She is clever, that girl."

"She's the one who traveled with me through the Black Swamp."

"That one? But she's so tiny!"

Susanna looks around: doesn't anyone feel the way she does? Only she can't tell what she feels most: pity or horror or fear. Naomi is wrong, she thinks, that bear was a pet. It was tamed and taught tricks. And then they killed it for a mere fancy, a riddle. Somehow that one fact seems more important than all the others. She can't help but feel that her status is not much higher than a pet bear's. Anything could happen to her here. Anything. The fact that Meera is connected to it makes it only feel worse.

"*Yawi-tsi-no-ha daya-nos,*" Nadoko says. "*Notsi-raya-gyahac. Hao-she-e.*"

"The girl will cook the head and the woman will eat from it," Naomi translates. "And then she will be cured."

Susanna watches the woman go into the feasting hut, and when she is gone the drummers begin drumming again. After a while people turn back to each other, laughing and talking. It's getting to be twilight now, and men have begun drinking whiskey out of glass jars. Nadoko pulls her little fur cape closer around her shoulders, gesturing that it is time to go home.

Susanna is glad. The day has been a failure. But as she turns she hears a shout behind her: a fight is breaking out among the gamblers. They've gotten much closer since Susanna last looked, and there are more of them now, at least twenty, mostly Wyandot but also some of the visiting Ottawa and Potawatomi, too. The nearby crowd not involved seems collectively to take a step back, but the gamblers are spreading out, some of them waving their arms and others pushing whoever is closest. One man is knocked over and falls toward Naomi. Quickly Nadoko puts Naomi behind her, but in a moment the fighting is everywhere. Although Susanna is only a step or two away from the others, men keep pushing between them and she can't get back. A bit of silver flashes to her right: the blade of a knife. She jerks back to avoid its sweep, and when she looks again she sees something rippling out of a Wyandot man in front of her. At first she thinks it's cloth or, what is it, a snake? He's been slashed across the middle and his insides are falling out in a long rope. Blood spurts out as he holds his body together and tries to walk, either in shock or hoping to get away. But the man who cut his belly now grabs him by his hair and slits his throat, and a strong scent of skunk oil rises up as he falls to the ground.

Blood is everywhere. In a panic, Susanna pushes harder to reach Onaway just as another Indian falls against her. She can't see his face but she can smell grease paint on his skin. One of the drummers?

"Onaway!" Susanna calls frantically.

"Tarayma!"

Onaway stretches out her thin arm to Susanna but the Indian who has fallen on her is now holding her hard by the forearm. As she struggles to get free she hears the sound of a knife being unsheathed and all at once her skin feels like a taut sack around her.

She tries harder to pull her arm away. "Onaway! Naomi!"

But the man is holding on to her tightly. She twists around trying to get out of his grip, her heart fluttering as fast as a bird's. Where will he cut her? She tries to protect every part of her body at once. But instead of using it on her, the man holds his knife out like a warning to others as he pulls her away. The drums go on faster than before, faster even than her heartbeat, and she can hear the tambourines rattle like a thousand snakes. She kicks him and falls backward and regains her footing and falls again. A bush scrapes against her hand and she tries to grab it and hold on but he pulls her away. Her vision cuts up and down between the sky and the well-pounded earth that smells strongly in one place of urine. She kicks out again and falls and he pulls her to her feet. In the darkness she still cannot make out the face of her captor, and even when he says in a low voice, "Susanna, it's me, it's Seth," she still cannot understand who it is, this Indian, and how he knows anything about Seth Spendlove.

The River Raisin

Twenty-Six

After she finally understands that it is Seth himself who is dragging her away, Susanna stops struggling and tries to match him stride for stride. His hand on her arm feels warm and firm, and they cross the darkening village as though making the start of an X. Most of the villagers are still at the feast but a few old women are turning kettles upside down or shaking out blankets. No one looks at them.

When they get to the stream they stop to catch their breath. Seth bends to wash the greasepaint off his face and Susanna holds her stomach. Her breath comes out in hard punches. Ribbons of stars are forming above their heads and the bats swoop down erratically. She watches Seth splash water onto his face and she notices again his straight, even nose and his smooth hair. His skin looks even darker in the dim light.

"You're Indian," she says.

Why had she not seen this before? Why had no one seen it? Back in Severne they said he was part Italian or Hebrew or Gypsy. Never Indian. Well, his father and brother looked as German as they could be, maybe that's why.

"Potawatomi," Seth tells her. "My father's mother."

"Amos is half Potawatomi?"

Even though they are facing each other the darkness takes a layer of communication away. All they have is a tone of voice, and how much tone can there be in a whisper? Susanna doesn't know how she sounds to Seth. Surprised? Surprised and not surprised somehow. Maybe she did know.

From the other side of the stream a man signals to them. "Koman," Seth says, and that is the beginning and end of his introduction. They cross the water using an old footbridge that Susanna didn't know about. Midway across her foot slips but she regains her balance quickly, half jumping half running as she keeps up with Seth. Koman takes her hand on the other side, helping her off the narrow plank. He has a gray pack with him that he gives to Seth as they run up the short clearing and into the woods.

By now Onaway would have alerted the men about Susanna's capture. Seth urges her to run faster. But they are barely in among the trees when a noise makes Susanna look over her shoulder: two Wyandots are already behind them. Koman, who is last, turns quickly and puts a knife up into the first man's belly. The second one lunges for Seth.

Susanna falls onto the ground, her only idea for protection. Face down, eyes closed, she breathes in the scent of dry leaves. She thinks of the dry smell of her father's barn, a small unpainted outbuilding, trying not to think of all that could happen to her. Naomi was right, they found her at once and now they will kill her. She hears a grunt and clenches both her fists, waiting for the first blow.

"It's all right Susanna," Seth says finally. He helps her up by the arm. "They're dead."

Up on the path she looks for the bodies but they are already hidden, rolled out of sight. Koman speaks quickly in a low voice as Seth translates. "In a little while, maybe very soon, another party will come looking for the first one. We must move fast. Once we get to the Maumee we will be safe." The Wyandot will not follow them across the river, Koman believes, since the river marks the end of their territory.

"But I'm not going to the Maumee," Susanna says. "My plan is to go to the River Raisin. That's where Penelope is. She was sold to a fur trapper called Boucherie."

Even as she speaks she realizes that she is throwing out a kind of challenge: Seth can come with her or not, but either way she is going. Inside one of her pouches is the slingshot Tako made for her, and in the other one is all the food she's stolen. This is all she has in the world. Four months ago this might have stopped her. But maybe not. Her past self sometimes surprises her now that she knows more. She hopes Seth will come.

Koman says, "It is difficult. The village lies between here and the Raisin. But they will not be searching in that direction. That is an advantage."

"How many days' walk to get to the Raisin?" Susanna asks.

He holds up two fingers and then says in English, "One if run."

A great many streams run between the Wyandot village and the Raisin: Ottawa Creek, Plum Rill, Bear Creek, Old Woman Creek. Whichever one they find will lead them to the river. Koman will stay behind and make a false trail. He will fight if he has to. He draws a map for Seth in the dirt, but when he straightens up he is looking at Susanna. Something in his manner reminds her of her father. He looks her straight in the eye without shyness and without dominance either. She wonders how he met up with Seth.

"Why are you helping me?" she asks.

His expression seems to leave his face with his breath. He is still watching her, but now he looks thoughtful. He says something in Potawatomi.

"In reparation," Seth tells her.

"Reparation? Why?"

Koman draws a knife from his belt and holds it out in its sheath. "For you," he says in English. "Take it as my gift."

After they part, Seth and Susanna loop around to the north taking care to keep a good deal of woods to the east of them, while Koman goes south toward the Maumee. In the darkness Seth cannot find a path so they walk straight through the thick layer of dead leaves that litter the woods. When she moves behind him to avoid a fallen tree trunk, Susanna notices that he is holding his arm.

"What is it?" she asks in a low voice.

"From the fight." Without stopping he pushes up his torn sleeve to show her in the moonlight: a long knife cut just under the crook of his elbow. He has a handkerchief pressed against it.

"We must clean it," she tells him.

"Let's get a little farther first."

The night air is full of blind insects that bump up against them as they walk. Every once in a while Seth stops to listen. The trees make no noise, not even the occasional creak, and the wind has died off. The air feels unnaturally warm and still. Susanna glances at Seth from time to time thinking of how they played on the stream that one summer when they were little, pretending a footbridge was a boat and they were going over the falls. Sometimes she steered but then he had to call her captain. They saw river rats slinking up the banks and ate bread and butter that Ellen gave Susanna folded in half like paper. She doesn't remember what they talked about, but she remembers talking quite a lot.

After what seems like a long time walking in silence, they come to a clearing ringed with flowers like round white biscuits. They sit down on a damp log to rest and Susanna takes a closer look at Seth's wound. His breath comes out in a stream. "Is it painful?" she asks, but he shakes his head no. The knife sliced the skin a long way but it is only deep at one end, near his elbow. If it were day she would find a patch of trillium to make a paste for it. As it is all she can do is wash it with the cold water in Seth's pouch and wrap it up again with his handkerchief, hoping the cloth is clean. He has another shirt in his pack, he tells her, a cloth shirt, if she needs to cut a new bandage.

"Why did Koman give me his knife?" she asks him.

"It's a long story." Seth tucks in a loose end of the handkerchief and rolls down his sleeve.

"Tell me."

He looks into her eyes as if there might be a way out of this conversation if he searches there hard enough. An owl hoots above them and they both tense, knowing it could be one man signaling to another. But after a moment they see the owl fly down and extend its claws to pluck something from a pile of leaves, its wings flapping hard as it tries to turn and lift at the same time with its catch.

"Let's keep walking," Seth says.

She tries to count their paces but loses the number after two hundred. She watches the moon grow smaller and smaller. When the night noises fall off for a moment, Seth stops again to listen. Susanna closes her eyes but can hear nothing behind them, no twigs breaking, no sign that anyone is following. When they start up again Seth says, without preamble, "It was Amos. He wanted your store."

"What do you mean? What was Amos? Everyone knows he wanted our store."

"Yes but I don't think you all realized how much he wanted it."

Back in Virginia Amos had owned a dry goods store himself. Everyone knew that, too. However now Seth tells her that he never got over the fact that Sirus set up a store in Severne first, before Amos got there. Instead of accepting his fate or leaving to start a store somewhere else, Amos stayed in Severne year after year building up his bitterness. When Sirus and Ellen died he thought this was his chance. He became overly confident. The daughters would leave, he boasted to his sons, and he would have their store for a song.

"But the day that Beatrice told him you all were staying in Severne, something broke in him. I could hear him talking to her just outside the cabin. There was a tone to his voice but I didn't know what it was. A shrillness. Afterward he went out into Thieving Forest and got foully drunk. Worse than usual."

That must have been when he came up with his plan. Give the Quiners a fright. Get them running to Philadelphia. Amos found Koman and his half-brother, who were up the Blanchard negotiating with some Miami for horses. He picked them because they were Potawatomi and he knew their language. He gave them money and said there'd be more once they took the women away, and that he would meet them in Thieving Forest where he'd pay a ransom and take the women back.

"Then he pulled your wagon and team from your barn and had Cade and me sell them, which also got rid of us for the day. If I'd known..."

Susanna glances at his face but it's too dark to see much. The pieces are coming together but she still cannot see the whole picture. She thinks she remembers Aurelia saying that name. Koman. The one with the swine wolf. But there was no swine wolf with him on this trip. She tries to keep following the story as Seth speaks, though what she really wants to do is stretch out among the brittle leaves and go to sleep. She wants to wake up to find that parts of the story never happened.

She thinks of the man with the face painted half red, who saw her hiding behind the maple tree but let her get away. That must have been Koman.

Amos was supposed to meet the Potawatomi at a given place in the forest, Seth tells her. He was supposed to make a show of negotiation with the money from their horses and wagon. His plan was to buy the women back, and in return they would give him their store.

But Amos never came. Why he decided to renege on the deal was anybody's guess. He got greedy. He didn't count on Susanna being left behind. His sons bypassed his cabin and went straight into the forest without giving him the money he meant to use to pay the Indians. Whatever the reason, Koman's band circled around and around, waiting for him to show up. Later, someone found an opportunity to come back and kill him.

"They found Amos..." Seth stops. He doesn't say how Amos was found. "It was clear that he was killed by a native. In revenge for deceiving them."

"Koman?"

"Not Koman. But that's all I know."

A wind rises gently, as if not entirely willing to commit even to this first step. The moon has sunk behind the trees, which means she cannot read Seth's expression. Amos planned all this. It's hard to believe.

"I'm sorry," Seth tells her.

She understands what he means. "You're not your father. I don't hold you responsible." And she doesn't. For a long time they say nothing more. With the moon gone, the morning seems somehow further away. It occurs to Susanna that maybe Seth followed her all this way out of shame for what his father did, some need to make it right, like Koman, and not as she thought out of love. All at once her weariness hits her like a stone.

"I need to rest," she says.

An aching in his arm keeps him awake after Susanna falls asleep. They are lying between three logs that form a broken triangle around them. Seth pulls his blanket up and looks at Susanna's face. Her expression is firmly set as though whatever she is dreaming takes all her concentration to maintain.

There is no question about it, she has changed. And not just her short hair and the rings in her ears. He's changed too. He wonders what she thinks of him now.

He must have slept. When he opens his eyes again Susanna is looking at him with that direct look he remembers from childhood and he feels it in his heart. Her face is only an arm's length away from his own.

The air is blue and cold, neither morning nor night. They talk about the Wyandots, whether they are safe now.

"I'm not sure where their territory ends," Seth says, "but I don't think it extends all the way here. If they haven't found us by now we're probably all right. My guess is they are staying to the south and combing every inch between their woods and the Maumee."

"I'll make a fire then," Susanna says, and she pushes herself up. "Small. Not too much smoke. I want to boil water for your cut."

How much sleep did they have, three hours? Susanna uses his flint to light a few sticks and then she boils water in his kettle. She finds some trillium and makes a paste. As she touches his arm, turning it slightly to look at it, he feels himself holding his breath. She tells him it looks all right to her but she covers every inch of it anyway with the paste, and then bandages it up carefully with strips she cut up from his extra shirt. His arm feels much better after that.

She says, "When I was looking for the trillium I saw what looks like a little den. Do you have a piece of twine with you?"

She catches a small wood vole and they skin it together, slicing it down the side and then pulling on it from either end. She cuts the meat up and cooks it in the kettle. While they eat she keeps looking at him in an obvious way, waiting for him to say something.

He says, "Needs a bit of salt," and she laughs.

"I haven't yet learned how to trap salt."

He watches her bury the fire ashes and cover the spot over with leaves. He isn't sure if she wants to show him what she can do, or if she wants to do it for him. They don't speak about Amos or anything else that Seth told her last night. The morning chill is dissipating but he can already tell that it will be cooler today than it was yesterday. In this country, autumn can wash into winter overnight.

Around midmorning they finally come to a stream that should lead them, if Koman was right, to the River Raisin. Susanna picks up a few nuts from the ground and puts them into one of her pouches.

"Roasted, they taste like corn," she tells him.

He looks at her sideways, and then picks up a long dry stick and touches the ground with it, testing its bend. "I was thinking to myself that you've changed," he says. "But now I don't think you have."

She looks at him, surprised. "What do you mean?"

"You're still a Quiner. You speak with that Quiner...authority."

She grimaces. "Pride, you mean."

"Maybe." He's smiling.

"Well, I've had to learn a few things."

"So I see."

He's strangely moved by her little neck and her cropped hair and the set of her shoulders. Although she is thinner, she is very strong and easily keeps pace with him. In his pocket he feels the ring he bought so long ago. Its presence comforts him. It's a pretty ring. If he can persuade her to take it, it will look nice on her finger.

He plants his walking stick on the ground and lets himself move a little closer to her. To his great happiness, she does not move away.

———※———

Susanna walks alongside Seth feeling strangely pleased. She woke up that morning knowing instantly where she was and how she got there. No question but that her senses have sharpened. She liked waking up in the fresh air, the scent of moisture coming out of the earth, no bodies crowding hers in the longhouse, no smoke from the cooking fires getting into her eyes. How did she bear it, living with all those people? She could never live in a city anymore. Not even Philadelphia. That dream is gone.

They walk above the noisy stream among just enough trees to make shade. Once in a while Seth's arm brushes hers. The first time it happened she felt a tingling sensation. As they go along Seth describes a deer hunt he went on, and she tells him about trapping animals in the woods with Tako. The way he listens is Indian but his easy humor, that reminds her of Sirus. Late in the afternoon the deer path leaves the stream's edge and ventures farther into the woods, although they can still see sparkling glimpses of water through the branches. Some time later the path ends in a small, natural clearing so beautiful that Susanna and Seth both stop at the same moment to stare.

"Oh," Susanna says.

Hundreds, maybe thousands of tiny flowers spread out before them like an embroidered bedcover, purple and white and yellow, the buds almost stemless, their faces no bigger than knuckles. Their colors change as the sun moves in and out from behind clouds. Susanna and Seth sit down on an old nursing log in the midst of them and Seth takes an apple from his pack. He peels it perfectly in one long peel, a lucky sign. She accepts a chunk of apple and the wind presses on the tiny flowers as though something invisible is stepping among them. Seth tells her how once, at the very beginning of their trip, he and Koman saw four deer leaping together across a clearing like this one. They leaped from one end to the other in perfect unison, he says, like dancers going across a stage.

"You've seen dancers on a stage?"

"A troupe, if you could call it that, came though our town in Virginia once on their way to the capital." He gives her the last of the apple and throws the core away with a long, strong throw. "But the deer were more graceful. They had just come from the river and their legs were still wet."

Susanna holds the last apple slice in her hand. She says, "You came a long way to help me."

"Longer than I expected," he says with a smile, but she is not joking.

"You came to make amends."

"In part."

He wipes the blade of his knife on his trousers and looks at her with what she takes to be sadness or maybe fatigue. She cannot understand why it makes her heart billow out like a muscle made out of impossibly thin fabric. Back in Severne she liked to walk by his shop but she didn't like to go in because of Amos. Sometimes Seth would be outside working, a heavy hammer in two hands. Everyone went to him when they needed something fixed. If he was outside Seth said good morning or good afternoon and she replied the same. It occurs to her now that what she liked was just seeing his face.

The wind begins pushing harder on the flowers and Susanna sees clouds gathering to the east. A storm coming on. They find the stream again and follow it until they get to a dry rise of land with a patch of scrub woods to the right. Some of the trees have hollows, but none are big enough for a person to sit in. Their only choice, besides getting soaked, is to build a twig shelter and wait out the rain inside it.

Seth builds a fire while Susanna searches the woods for bendable sticks. As she works on the shelter she sees herself through his eyes: a woman in a hide dress weaving branches into the arch of a frame. Her hair is short now and she prefers moccasins to boots. Her arms are very strong and her hands are chapped from so much outdoor work. She is good at building fires and finding food, and she can walk just as long and as far as he can. How did she become this person, she wonders? But the answer is obvious—necessity—and that's the answer every time.

"I hung up our food," Seth tells her when she returns. "In case of bears. And there's hot water for tea. Wait."

He pulls a few small twigs out of her hair. When his fingers brush the top of her ear she feels herself blush.

"There," he says.

She steps back quickly without looking at him. As they are drinking their tea—the last Seth has with him—the rain begins to fall. Two minutes later it seems as though someone has overturned a hundred buckets at once. They abandon the campfire for the shelter and sit inside facing each other. They can stretch out their legs if they want to, but they will have to curl up if they want to lie down.

"I should have made it larger," Susanna says, wrapping her arms around her bent legs. "We might have to sleep here."

"It's fine. It's very well constructed. No terrible leaks." He looks up. Then he smiles. "Yet."

Up close his face seems flushed and his eyes are so dark they look wet. He is still smiling but something in his expression turns sad. When he moves his elbow he touches her leg. She looks down at her knees. She doesn't want to meet his eyes. She has the thought that if she looks at him he will be able to see everything she feels.

"The canopy is very thick here," she says. "The trees will offer a lot of protection." She makes herself breathe evenly, as if that will steady her heartbeat. The air is moist from the rain.

"Susanna," Seth says.

She squeezes her legs and looks up at him. He is wearing the same expression she has seen off and on all day, only now she realizes that it is not disappointment, as she feared, nor weariness, as seemed likely, but rather patience.

He says, "All his life Amos hid his Potawatomi side. I've decided I'm not going to do that."

"All right," she says. "Why should you?"

"A hundred reasons. You know them as well as I do."

"Who cares what the farmers think. They don't know beans from bird eggs, as Penelope likes to say."

"I care what you think."

The way he says this surprises her. "Do you think I hate Indians?" she asks.

He is silent. Then he says, "In the Wyandot village, in the woods, you said to me, how can Naomi be happy married to an Indian?"

"I don't think I said that."

"You did."

"Well, I was mad at her."

Seth shifts a little. "I thought...after everything you've been through, what you saw, what happened. You might have some strong feelings."

"I do have strong feelings, but they're not always consistent. Some Indians in the Black Swamp saved my life. Meera, too. She could have abandoned me there but she didn't. Also there's Tako."

Seth moves a little closer, cradling his bad arm. She waits for him to reply but he doesn't.

"I'm not always logical," she tells him. "My imagination is very good. I can believe all sorts of things that maybe aren't true."

He still doesn't speak. Their toes are touching, nothing else.

"In a strange way I think that's helped me," she says.

At that he smiles his lopsided smile. His dark good looks make him seem, to her, more substantial than other men, as if he thought more, considered the world more closely. He leans forward and puts his hand on the tip of her ear and caresses it. Then he brings his mouth down on hers. His lips are cool from the night air and firm and altogether lovely. All of her feelings gather on her face and light seems to come off her skin like tiny spears from the inside. Her heart is a painfully sharp rock in her chest. She bends closer to kiss him again. He went down Injured River on a boat looking for her, and when he didn't find her, he went home. Now he is here: a miracle.

Somewhere above them an owl declares something, waits a moment, and then declares it again.

"Why did you come after me?" she asks. "Was it because of your father?"

"I was hoping you needed me."

She thinks of her sisters. "I know that feeling," she says.

They scrunch closer, pressing together, their feet intertwined. They are in a tiny space but are doing everything they can to make the space between them even tinier. The warmth she feels is his warmth. She likes his gentle wit, his patience. He can fix just about anything. He can tally long numbers in his head. He can find her even when she thinks she doesn't want to be found. And now here they are in a forest, a place she once despised, but now it feels like just another room in a house. Her hair is shorn, she is thin, she has no proper clothes, but he doesn't care and neither does she. Outside she can hear the rain moving off. She feels for his hand.

"But I guess you were doing all right without me," he tells her.

She kisses him. She wants to keep kissing him, and also she wants just to look at his face.

"This is better," she says.

-※-

Later that night, while Susanna sleeps, Seth pulls her blanket over her shoulders and then crawls outside to check the sky. His arm is beginning to throb a little. He builds a small fire although it is hard finding dry sticks and they take a long time to catch. He sees that the flames will not last long. But he sits beside it anyway, warming his injured arm. From far away he hears a couple of wolves starting up, a string of thin howls as if just testing their upper registers. Probably too far away to worry about, but he should have his gun handy in any case.

For the moment, though, he doesn't move. He can feel her sleeping just a few feet away. This is something he has wanted to do for a long time: watch her sleep. He never in his life imagined it might happen out here, miles away from any proper town or village or settlement, in a stick-and-leaf hut like his great grandmothers made for their men. But he doesn't mind that. There is a burning feeling in the back of his throat and he swallows, trying to coat it. He can't find a comfortable position for his arm. He wants to be alone by the fire to steep himself in the sudden gift of her, to stay with the surprise, which he still only half-believes in. He also wants to go back to watch her sleep, but he puts off the moment in order to savor it.

-※-

Susanna is dreaming of the white moths she saw when she was with Meera.

It was their last night in the Black Swamp but they didn't know it, and they'd stopped to camp in a meadow full of short yellow grass. They drank raisin wine and shared a pigeon pie, and just as they were finishing Meera said, "Do you smell that?"

Susanna looked around the clearing. Something was moving in the wind but there was no wind, and then she realized that what she had taken for yellow grass wasn't grass at all but rather small budded flowers that bloomed at night. While they were eating, the flowers had opened into tiny yellow mouths. A moment later Meera pointed to a cloud of white moths flying into the meadow.

The moths were tiny, each one barely the size of a fingernail, and their wings looked to Susanna like small bright eyes in the twilight. While she and Meera watched, the moths spread out among the yellow flowers, dipping and lifting and dipping again, gathering pollen like a woman bringing a needle up and then down. Everything in the meadow seemed to be watching them; even the owls stopped calling out. When they finished, the moths rose up and re-formed their cloud and drifted back into the trees like an enormous white beating heart.

Meera and Susanna had smiled at each other then, amazed at their good fortune to see all this, and they fell asleep with the sweet scent of the flowers still in the air.

Now, in Susanna's dream, the white moths have come back. They settle on her arms and shoulders, and on Meera's too. Meera is standing next to her laughing with pleasure. A strong sweet smell rises from the ground.

Susanna wakes with a warm feeling up behind her ribs. Seth is sleeping beside her and she wants to wake him up at once, right now, and feel his arms around her.

"Seth," she whispers.

But when he opens his eyes she can tell at once that something is wrong. She pulls her hand out from under the blanket to feel his forehead, which is burning.

"Let me see your arm," she says.

He is lying with it cradled over his chest. Underneath the frayed bandage the wound has turned yellow and ugly. An infection, but how? She tells him to lie still, that she is going to get water to clean it. Also she'll look for more trillium. She tries to keep her voice even.

"Wait," he says. He struggles for a moment trying to put his good hand in the opposite pocket of his breeches. "Last night. I forgot. This is for you."

In the palm of his hand lies a beautiful gold ring with tiny seed pearls circling a larger, rounder pearl. She picks it up to look at it, and then she puts it on her finger. Her hands are rough and red, her jagged nails have arcs of green dirt beneath them. She pulls the ring off.

"It will be ruined out here," she says. "Best if I keep it in my pocket for now."

"But you'll keep it?"

She kisses his hot forehead. She can tell he is struggling to keep his eyes open. "It's a beautiful ring," she tells him.

He closes his eyes. "We can go to Philadelphia. I don't mind that."

She starts to assure him that she no longer wants to go to Philadelphia. "Hard enough at the Wyandot village. All the people and the noise..."

She looks down. He is asleep.

The first bird of the morning calls out. She pulls the blanket up around his shoulders and tucks it in at the bottom. For a moment she can't think what to do next although she has already outlined it: clean the wound, apply a new salve, dress it. She wants there to be more, something she hasn't already done. Even in sleep Seth is holding his wounded arm carefully. His eyelids flutter and she thinks of her dream, the white moths in the meadow. Not everything wild is harsh and ugly, Susanna reminds herself. But it is difficult to remember that when you are sitting next to a wounded man who might die of infection in spite of your best care.

When she crawls outside she spies the remains of a campfire— Seth must have made one last night while she slept. So his arm was bothering him then already? A moment later something else catches her eye. There, on a flat rock, a rock very like the one near Onaway's longhouse, lies a shiny metal object.

Scissors. Her mother's good nail scissors with their elegant avian finger holes.

For a moment she feels swept clean of thought like a tide going out. She goes over to pick up the scissors. They are polished and cold. She closes her palm over the blades.

"Meera," she calls.

Several birds begin chattering at once.

"Meera, come out."

When Meera steps out from behind a blackened tree, what Susanna notices first is her dress. It is not a plain hide dress like Susanna's—the clothing of a servant—but decorated with beads along the hem and sleeve. The beads are brown and white and shaped like teeth, and she wears dark woven bracelets on both of her wrists. She is no longer pinched thin.

"Meera. What are you doing here?"

"Those people in the village, they were not my people," Meera says.

"But I mean to say, how did you find us?"

Meera shrugs a long shrug. "You leave a trail as though painting it."

Twenty-Seven

When Meera hears about Seth's arm and his fever, she immediately sets to work making a new poultice using trillium and a dark purple root that she digs up from the stream. She says she will take care of him. But Meera says a lot of things.

"They made me stay inside all day," she tells Susanna. "They watched everything I did. They betrothed me to a boy as short as a goat but not nearly so handsome. They let their dogs lick their spoons to clean them."

"Didn't I say you might not like them? Didn't I warn you?"

Meera shrugs, a tiny concession. They are sitting beneath a tree with two wide, exposed roots like the arms of an armchair as they make the new poultice. Meera is using a rock to pound the purple root into flakes, and Susanna mixes the flakes up with water and trillium to make a paste.

"But how did you know where to look for us?" Susanna asks her. "Why didn't you go to the Maumee, like the others did?"

"I knew there were two sisters. A long time ago I asked where the other one was."

She leans over to tip more flakes into Susanna's bowl. Susanna looks down at the top of Meera's dark clean hair. It is parted carefully down the middle from her forehead to her nape in such a straight line that Susanna thinks that someone else, a woman, must have parted it for her. Meera was the only one except Naomi who knew that Susanna would seek out Penelope, but that doesn't explain everything.

"How did you get my mother's scissors?"

"The answer to the riddle was so obvious I thought I would have to share the prize with many people. But it seems I was the only one who guessed it."

"You asked for *scissors* for your prize?" Susanna suspects that this is Meera's way of recompense but it isn't enough. "You were the one who stole my money. Not those eunuchs. You."

Meera does not look up from her work. "You had the necklace. I had nothing."

"The necklace was of no value to them."

"I learned of this later." Meera turns the root over and begins pounding the other side.

That's it, that's all that Susanna will get. Nothing like an apology. When she stole the money, Meera thought the Chippewa necklace would be sufficient for ransom. She didn't cross Susanna on purpose. And when she found out her mistake, she managed to obtain the cherry buttons and leave them for her.

"Did you know about Seth?" Susanna asks.

"Of course."

"You were following me."

"Only that once. After it was discovered I was never left alone."

"And Tako? Was he helping you?"

"Who?"

When the poultice is finished, Meera and Susanna sling up Meera's blanket between two trees to make a hammock. They want to get Seth off the damp ground. When they wake him up he looks at Meera and calls her by name. That's a good sign.

He says to her, "You've grown."

"Can you lean on me?" Susanna asks. "We're taking you to your new bed."

He holds his head stiffly, like an old man. "That's good," he says. "Because my old bed was beginning to smell..."

"Step carefully here."

"...of dry leaves."

When they get him in the hammock Meera says, "I stand no taller than I did before." She gives him a tin cup with two fingers of greenish liquid inside. "Here. Gargle but do not swallow."

Seth swirls the mixture in his mouth and spits it onto the ground. After Meera applies the new poultice to his arm she wraps a clean bandage around it.

He says, "I think you're taller."

"I am the same," Meera insists.

"Whatever you say to her," Susanna tells Seth, pushing the hair back from his forehead, "she'll contradict." His head is not as hot as it was before, but it is still warm.

"I fear you don't like me, Meera," Seth says, looking at her.

Meera presses her lips together, not enjoying the joke. Seth smiles at Susanna and then closes his eyes. Soon his breathing softens. Meera says quietly, "He will sleep off the infection."

"How do you know?"

"I can tell by the color of his wound."

But Susanna is still worried. They need disinfectant. Boucherie makes liquor, and he also will probably have clean bandages and cloth for a sling. The cabin is only half a day's walk from here, maybe less. Susanna can go there while Meera stays with Seth. It isn't the perfect solution but there is never a perfect solution. Meera picks up the shredded root and puts it in her pouch, and then she begins to gather a few sticks for a fire.

"I'm still angry with you," Susanna tells her.

Meera wipes her hands down her sides and looks at Susanna. Her face is rounder now but somehow not as childish. Seth is right. She seems older. "It turned out badly for both of us," she concedes. "But our fates are tied. I understand this now. My guardian spirit rests with you."

Meera's guardian spirit—Susanna has forgotten about that. Does this mean she has met her seven demons? She looks at Meera's face but Meera has already turned away to gather more wood. The morning light is on the other side of the trees but it is creeping closer. Already the day feels well underway, the events set in motion. Whatever else, Susanna reminds herself, Meera is practical. She will do what is needed for Seth. She feels for Koman's knife on her belt. She doesn't have room anymore for pride. Seth's temperature is down, he is sleeping, that is good. The hammock hangs low to the ground with his weight. He will probably sleep all day and then wake up hungry at night. Maybe she will even be back by then. She opens his gray pack and looks at his remaining supplies. What should she take along with her? She needs to be practical, too.

The last part of her journey. Or is it the last? Each time she has set out she thought it was the last, and so far she's been wrong every time. She remembers the shock that she felt when she found Aurelia, and how in her confusion she thought Thieving Forest would never end. But maybe she was right. All these trees still look the same. And even after she finds Penelope—if she finds her—they still have to get back to Severne.

She heads north following the streambed, which sinks into a kind of snaky gutter between the trees until the exposed water is barely an arm's length across. As she makes her way alongside it she tries not to worry about Meera and Seth, but that feels false. She tries to clear her mind of hope but that feels false, too. Penelope might not be there, she tells herself. So many things could have happened. The forest thickens until the path by the stream is buried under skeletal leaves, and when the stream itself disappears, absorbed back into the forest floor, she stops and closes her eyes. She listens.

In the wild you must see with all your senses, Old Adam told her. He said, Lose your dread.

Birdsong, wind, the creaking of trees, something pecking on soft bark, and then she hears what she wants: a low roar of water to the north. She opens her eyes. A charm of magpies cries hoarsely in the tree just in front of her, scolding each other or her. One is looking down at her from a knobby branch, his eye like a dark black seed. There's no path left for her to follow, but that's all right. Magpies are a good sign for travelers. She thinks this is true.

As she walks toward the sound of the river the net of foliage above her becomes greener and denser, and when she at last gets to the bank the trees are leaning over the river coloring it mud brown with their shade. She scans the sky for chimney smoke. Boucherie's cabin is to the east, according to Koman. But a huge, fallen oak tree half in the water obstructs that direction, and the bank on the other side is crowded with oaks entangled with the wild grape vines that give the Raisin its name. The natives call it Nummasepee for its abundant sturgeon, but looking down Susanna can see nothing but small pointed chevrons on the water's surface made by the wind.

She begins to pick her way over the fallen tree, and then over the flat mossy stones that begin where the tree ends. It is rough going, and once or twice she has to get down on her hands and knees. She can feel the sun's heat on only one side of her body. The bank is littered with rocks and broken timber and shrubs growing right out of the water, and her progress is slow, slower than she expected. From time to time she looks for signs of smoke.

The fact that she sees none doesn't mean anything, she tells herself. But she's worried now, she can't help it.

After the river turns, the bank levels out into a stretch of dark wet sand. At one end, four small black shapes shiver in movement. As she gets closer Susanna sees that they are buzzards, and that they are picking at something in the sand.

A body. A man's body. The buzzards are feeding off its neck.

Her breath stops tight in her chest but she makes herself keep walking. It is Boucherie, and she will find Penelope's body nearby—she says this to herself as though somehow believing it will make it not come true. The birds look up as she approaches but do not so much as lift their wings, so she makes a loud noise and swings her arms forward at them. At that they jump off a few yards, letting their wings rise once or twice before committing even to so small a distance, and then they each turn one eye to watch her.

The dead man is a native, not a Frenchman. Not Boucherie. And there is no sign of anyone else. He is face down wearing a hide tunic and trousers and plain ankle-length moccasins. His right arm is twisted at an odd angle behind him. Susanna covers her nose. Just behind him is a cut path with a blaze of three stones on either side to mark it. This must be the path to Boucherie's cabin. Koman said it was well marked. For a moment she is tempted to go down the path and just leave the body behind her. But it does not seem right to leave the man so exposed. She remembers her own fear that the Stooping Indians would leave her behind for the buzzards. She does not wish that on anyone.

They are still watching her, four ugly, skinny birds with their feathers hanging crookedly about their necks like drunk old men dressed up in dirty finery. One of them, the largest, takes a step toward the corpse. Susanna flaps her arms at it again. She sees a large rock lodged in the sand near the path, and gets the idea that she might tie the body to it and push it into the river, where it would sink. But the rock proves unmovable, so instead she just digs a shallow pit in the sandy dirt as best she can, using a dinnerplate stone for a spade. The man has been shot, she sees as she rolls him over into the pit. She covers the body with sand and stones and heavy branches. Then she reties her pouch to her belt and checks Koman's knife in its sheath.

As she makes her way down the short path she wonders for the first time what sort of man this Boucherie is. He traps animals and makes liquor, that is all she knows. At the end of the path there is a small cleared space with a cabin at its far end, and the sight of it does nothing to allay her anxiety. It is small and built flush to the ground with no porch or steps, and it leans a little westerly. There are narrow slits for windows and the door fits so crookedly to the frame that she can see spaces as big as her hand. No smoke is coming from the stone chimney, and there is a stringy spiderweb over the few sticks near the door that might be taken for a woodpile. No sign of people.

On the one hand, Susanna feels that nothing on this earth could induce her to go inside that dark, empty hut. On the other hand, she might be able to tell whether Boucherie and Penelope planned to return. Maybe she could even find some supplies, clean bandages and liquor for Seth's wound. But the sight of a small cross made out of oak twigs and stuck into the ground near the cabin makes her stop again. A grave? The mound in front looks much too small for a person. Still Susanna feels a watery sensation in her insides, as if her stomach has begun the slow process of turning to liquid.

But it would be foolish to come all this way, she tells herself, and not at least look inside. She pushes against the splintered door gingerly, thinking maybe it will be locked. Hoping so.

It isn't locked. As it opens a wave of musty odor comes at her and she looks down at the floor, which is made up of planks of rotting wood thrown down here and there as if someone meant to do more someday but never has. A shaft of light marks a knothole in the rough wall, with a puddle of water beneath it. Holes in the roof? She looks up.

"I have a gun," comes a voice in the corner.

Susanna pulls in her breath. She looks all around, her eyes trying to adjust to the darkness. "Penelope?"

A pause. "Who's that?"

"It's me, it's Susanna."

Nothing, not even a rustle. Is it Penelope? There is something odd about the voice. She hears the cock of a gun.

"Don't shoot, please, it's only Susanna. It's only me."

"Hutay-ee is not here," the voice says. It *is* Penelope. Susanna takes a step closer and stumbles on the edge of a wooden plank. She puts her hand to the doorframe to catch herself but something foul meets up with her there—bird feces? Also cobwebs and the dry skeletons of leaves.

"Don't move," Penelope says.

"Can't you see me? Let me come closer so you can see that it's me. Let me pull open a window shutter. It's Susanna. Susanna, your sister. Don't shoot."

"I don't know who you are," Penelope says. "So you can just take your chance."

Now Susanna can make out a table, a stool, and a figure sitting by the fireplace holding a long, old-fashioned pistol. Even from here she looks unkempt: her hair partly loose over her face, her dress bunched up and stained. There is a sour smell in the room. Penelope moves her head forward like the buzzards, one eye out, keeping watch on Susanna.

"All right then. I'm just going to stand right here and let you look at me," Susanna says. "I won't move. I'm leaving the door open to let in the light. Just look."

Another pause. "Susanna?" Penelope ventures at last.

"Yes!"

Still Penelope does not alter the direction of her gun.

"Listen Penelope, I'm going to walk over to you now. Please put down your gun. I'm your sister. Susanna."

Penelope's eyes are like holes. She bends to put the gun on the stone hearth but makes no move to stand. She allows herself to be embraced by Susanna. "He left the pistol unloaded in any case."

Susanna does not want to let go but Penelope shrugs under the embrace. The sour smell is stronger. Susanna steps back to look at her. Her face is thin and her chin has a few white pimples on it. She is wearing an ugly brown dress with no collar and with hooks and eyes down the front instead of buttons. Some of the hooks are missing.

"The dog died," Penelope says. "Hutay-ee went off to get a new one."

"Who is Hutay-ee?"

"The savages call him that."

"Don't use that word," Susanna says.

"What word?"

"Savages."

"Whyever not?"

There is something not right about her. Maybe from hunger, maybe from something else. She is not altogether right in her mind. Susanna feels a wave of dread go right through to her bones. A muskrat skin is stretched upon a board in the corner of the room, its guard hairs partially plucked. Susanna wants to let in some air and she pulls the plank away from one of the windows, but the cabin's squalor is even worse in the light. Bird feces and dry leaves have settled everywhere, and she can hear mice as bold as the sun running across the loose floorboards. When she goes back to Penelope she notices several old bruises on one side of her face. Her lip has a silver scab over one corner.

Penelope lifts her arm to show her something else. A rope leads from her wrist to an iron hook built into the stone fireplace wall. "He ties me when he goes."

"Why would he do that?"

It does not take long to cut the sorry, frayed rope. Penelope rubs her wrist, which is peppered with rope burns. Her breath is very bad.

"Have you been sick?" Susanna asks. The sour smell is vomit in the bucket beside her.

"I'm always sick. I'm pregnant."

"You're...but you can't be!"

"Not by Boucherie. He's a rogue. I won't have his child. No, it was Thomas Forbes come to visit me."

Thomas Forbes—Penelope's first husband, a man who's been dead for over a year. Susanna takes a breath and says carefully, "Penelope. Thomas died when his horse kicked him in the head. Remember? You told him the horse was a bad one. You told him to sell it. Do you remember that, Penelope? But he didn't listen to you."

Oh yes, Penelope agrees, but she goes on to explain in great detail how it is that Thomas Forbes was able to visit after being kicked in the head. It has to do with the particular way the horse struck him, not affecting his heart and nether regions. He is much more vital now than before, she tells Susanna. But Susanna is to stay quiet about this. It is a secret.

"If the rogue knows he will be angry."

She still speaks in her quick, intelligent way but her eyes dart all about the room in a confused manner. Susanna says, "How long have you been alone?"

"Two days? Or thereabouts."

Boucherie left her water, she says, and a bowlful of porridge. Did Susanna see the little grave out front? She doesn't know what happened, she found the dog one morning as stiff as the wood plank beneath him. A great misfortune. They need a dog. Everyone out here in this godforsaken country needs a dog, she says. And since Boucherie was setting out to buy more cornmeal for mash he thought he might as well get another pup if he could at the same time. That's a good business, Penelope tells Susanna, making mash. But the rogue doesn't want her to steal his money and run off, so he ties her up. Penelope speaks as though this is a most reasonable thing to do.

Susanna gives her a handful of pemmican to eat and some fresh water. "I saw a dead man near the river. I think he was shot by a gun. A native."

"Kwase?" Penelope frowns. "That's Boucherie's partner. He went with him to fetch the dog. Did he have a broken nose?"

"I don't know. The buzzards got at him."

"A sour meal for them," Penelope says with her old superior air.

"Hey-uh," comes a deep voice behind them. "Who in Christ are you?"

Susanna's heart jumps and she turns around quickly. A short, square-shaped man with a thick beard is standing in the open doorway. He is carrying a long black-and-white pup that looks too young to be taken from its mother and, over his shoulder, a sack of what Susanna takes to be cornmeal. He wears a rough woolen hat dyed red and a burlap scarf around his shoulders. But although he has never seen Susanna before, his face holds no look of surprise. The way he stands seems to project the conceit that he owns everything: the cabin, the air, even the thoughts of those around him. Susanna's heart starts beating hard. She knows this kind of man.

"I'm Susanna Quiner," she makes herself say calmly. "Penelope's sister." She holds out her hand but he doesn't even glance at it. "You must be Mr. Boucherie."

"My little sister," Penelope tells him. For a moment she sounds almost normal. "We call her the princess."

"What is that you're wearing?" Boucherie asks Susanna. He speaks English with a strong French accent.

"What do you mean?"

"What happened to your clothes?"

She forgot that she was wearing a hide dress. "I was a captive," she tells him.

"Yes, we all were for a while," Penelope says. "Although Susanna, you weren't...you escaped?" Now she looks confused.

"Close your hole," Boucherie tells her. He drops the sack of cornmeal on the floor and then the pup. The pup struggles to his feet and tumbles about looking for something—water, probably. He is panting.

"Ran off?" Boucherie asks. Susanna nods. "You came all this way without weapons?"

"A knife."

"Let's see it."

She pulls Koman's knife from its sheath and shows it to him. He brings it over to the uncovered window to look at it in the light, holding it at a strange angle. As he tilts his head Susanna realizes that there is something wrong with one of his eyes. When he turns back, she sees that a thin milky glaze covers the iris.

"*Bon.* Nice blade. But the handle isn't to my liking. Too Indian," he says.

Susanna puts out her hand but he doesn't give it back.

"I'm not one that holds women should carry weapons," he tells her.

Her face burns. She's been tricked. She's been tricked even though she knew from the start what kind of man he is. The kind who takes pleasure in showing another person up.

"I'll need it for my return journey," she tells him.

"Will you now." Boucherie looks at her steadily. "Well. I could use a meal before you go. She's not much of a cook, your sister. Nor much of anything else. A bad coin spent." He wets his bottom lip with the tip of his tongue. He is staring at Susanna. "But I'll get my money back somehow, don't you think?"

He pronounces "think" like "tink." Susanna presses her palms against the sides of her hide dress. She tries not to panic. If she doesn't return Seth and Meera will come looking for her. But in the meantime—what? Boucherie picks up the sack of cornmeal and takes it to a cupboard built into the far wall. After he throws it in he turns to face her again. Every movement feels aggressive. The way he is standing seems to highlight the strength of his arms. This is on purpose, she knows. He wants her to feel afraid. She can say this for him, at least: there is no pretense, his whole game has started up right away.

"Know anything about mash?" he asks.

"Not a thing."

"That's to change."

The dog has found his way to Penelope, who lifts him onto her lap. "What will we name you, then?" she asks. She gets her own tin cup of water and lets the pup drink from it.

"Don't spoil it, Docia."

Docia?

Penelope says without looking away from the pup, "He calls all his wives Docia."

"How many wives does he have?" Susanna asks.

Boucherie pulls off his red cap and runs his hand through his hair, which is as bushy as a squirrel's tail. "Well let's see. The first Docia, and then the one I replaced her with. And now that one there, your sister, that's three. I like the name Docia. That's why I picked the first one. Where did you get the knife?" Trying to catch her off guard. But Susanna is ready for this one, at least.

"I stole it. What happened to the other Docias?"

"Died in childbirth," Penelope says evenly. "I'll probably die too." She doesn't look up from the dog. She might have been saying, I like this one's coloring.

"They didn't have to die," Boucherie says. "Squaws don't die. They could be out in the middle of the forest when their pains start and an hour later, *bon* a healthy *fils* in their arms. The first Docia died out of spite. Second one, too. This one is probably too stupid to live."

At that Penelope looks up and her eyes meet Susanna's. For a moment, the old look of pride. But she says nothing. Susanna thinks of the bruises on her face. Restraint is a hard lesson for a Quiner.

"Where are the babies?" Susanna asks.

"One died being born," Boucherie says. "The other I hated the sight of."

Susanna's throat goes dry as different scenarios involving the second baby fly across her mind, each one more gruesome than the last. Boucherie is watching her closely. He is like an animal before pouncing: assessing the situation, waiting for the right time to move. He breathes heavily through his mouth like a short, hairy wildcat with sideburns that become a beard and neck hair.

Susanna considers her words carefully. "I know you paid handsomely for my sister. It is my intention to reimburse you. And then I'd like to talk to you about what I can give you for her..." She rejects the word freedom as too incendiary. "What I can give you as payment so she can go home with me. We have a store. It is too much for me to take on by myself, but the two of us...Well, what do you say, what is your price?"

"Twenty-five federal dollars. That's what I paid for her. You can give that to me now."

She has that, at least, but not much more. Money she borrowed from Seth. She puts it on the little stool near the drying muskrat skin, not wanting to touch his hand.

Boucherie makes no move toward the money. "The rest I'll take in work," he says.

"How much work?"

"Couple of days, I'm thinking."

"I was planning to leave today."

"It's too late for that," he tells her. He grins. "You're safer here with me."

Trouble comes to those who bring it upon themselves, her mother used to say, and here is a man who carries that burden joyfully, hoping to bring it down at every turn. Susanna's mouth feels gummy and she tries to swallow the stickiness away. He intends to keep them both.

"That's settled," he says, wiping his hands up and down his trousers. "Now. You make up a fire and cook my supper and clean up some. In the morning we'll see—what is it you *yanquis* say?— we'll see where we stand."

Every instinct tells her that he will let neither one of them go, not ever, not until they both die in childbirth or he gets rid of them himself one particularly unlucky day. Koman's knife is stuck in his waistband. The question is: will he kill her right now or make sport first? She is glad that she had the presence of mind not to mention Seth or Meera. But when will they start to worry? How many days can she last?

"What will we call you, eh? How about *la petite Docia*," he suggests, and laughs. "Petite Docia. That I like."

"Miss Quiner will do."

"Go get that kindling Petite Docia, and then scrape something together for my supper."

She says, "I won't answer to Docia. I'm not your wife."

Boucherie smiles with true pleasure. "*Bon.* I was hoping you'd be like your sister."

The sudden silence in the room feels like a well with no bottom. Susanna doesn't look at Penelope, only Boucherie. His expression says: I will enjoy winning this game. She thinks about Tako's slingshot in her pouch. But she doesn't have ammunition. From the corner of her eye she sees a few loose stones near the hearth and she takes a step in that direction just as Boucherie comes at her, holding Koman's knife out like a spear.

She turns on her heel and pushes him toward the stone fireplace, where his head connects with a crack. Surprised, he makes a deep-throated noise. Susanna runs to put the table between them. Behind her is the cupboard with the cornmeal. She pulls the cornmeal out but he comes at her quicker than she thought, so when she heaves the sack at him it connects too closely without the weight she'd intended. The meal scatters everywhere.

"*Merde!* You bitch!" He pronounces it like the tree, beech, a soft landing like a snarl. The table is between them and they circle around it. His head is bleeding. The loose hearthstones are on the floor near Penelope, and Susanna tries to make her way over to them but Boucherie, as if reading her mind—he owns her, he owns her thoughts—gets there first. But instead of grabbing a stone as she expected, he turns toward Penelope and thrusts Koman's knife at her belly.

Susanna shouts, "Penelope!"

Penelope turns but the blade still catches her in the side. Boucherie pulls it out with a grunt. He straightens up and makes no more moves toward Susanna. Indeed, he faces her with his mouth twitching. His version of laughter.

"*There* is your sister," he says.

The blood from his head wound is running down the side of his face. He wipes his temple with the back of his hand.

"Now go make the fire."

Penelope puts her hands on her belly. When she lifts them up her palms are red with blood. Wildly Susanna casts her eye about for something to use to stanch the wound, a rag or shawl, but all she can see are hard objects. She feels for her pouch and pulls it from her waistband. With a quick motion she empties all the contents onto the floor: the food, the remaining money, Tako's slingshot. Then she pushes the pouch against Penelope's wound. The cut is neither long nor deep, but there is a lot of blood. Meanwhile coins from the pouch begin rolling in every direction, and Boucherie looks around after them. But something else has fallen, too: her mother's nail scissors. When Boucherie turns to follow a rolling coin, Susanna grabs the scissors and tucks them up into her sleeve.

She says to Penelope, "Keep pressing this against you," and she pulls her sister's hands over the pouch. She then turns to Boucherie, who is stuffing coins into his pockets. "Do you have anything I can make into a bandage for Penelope?" The dog is curled up against the wall near the door, shaking.

"Docia," Boucherie corrects her.

Susanna swallows. "Docia. I need to bandage her wound."

"First the fire," Boucherie says. "Then my supper. Then you can look at her cut." He makes a wave with his hand, mock gentlemanly, as he steps away from the doorway. "You'll find kindling in a stack outside. If there's none, get you more from the woods."

"But she could bleed to death!"

Boucherie shrugs. "*Bon.* I have a new Docia now anyway."

She looks at Penelope. Her hands are red with blood. Is she in shock? Susanna prays that she will at least keep her hands pressed against her wound so she won't bleed to death before Susanna has a chance to wrap it. But Boucherie will delay her endlessly in this game of mastery, she understands this too well. Making the fire, cooking, cleaning up, and then...he's made it clear that he thinks of her as his new wife. He would take her in front of Penelope and make it as gruesome as he could. Even now he is watching her with wet lips.

"I can't help you," Penelope says sadly.

"I know," Susanna tells her.

Boucherie is still eyeing her in his animal way, and he returns Koman's knife to his belt without looking down. Is he planning to grab her as she passes? Susanna moves toward the door warily, hoping she can keep out of his reach, but just as she's about to pass him Penelope scrapes her stool back as if to stand up and Boucherie's eyes flick toward the sound. In that moment Susanna pulls the nail scissors from her sleeve and plunges them into his good eye. She is surprised to feel the surface resistance, and surprised too at the vehemence and anger she feels the moment the blade touches his body, as if her emotions have been triggered by the act of her revenge and not the other way around.

Boucherie makes a guttural noise and puts his hand to his face. It takes only a second to pull Koman's knife off his waistband, another second to step away as he blindly swings his arms out at her. Then she pushes him as hard as she can across the room. When her heart starts up again—it has stopped for a minute at least—she looks at Penelope, who is sitting very still but with her hands, thank God, still pressing the pouch against her wound. Boucherie's burlap scarf has fallen to the floor and Susanna grabs it and wraps it around Penelope's middle clumsily, still shaking. Her mouth is too dry to speak. But Penelope raises herself without direction, leaning hard against Susanna, and as Susanna takes her arm to help her it seems for a moment as though she is the older sister and Penelope is the younger one who needs her. She puts her other arm around Penelope's waist and with their inside feet first they step out, a mirror image, toward the door.

Boucherie is sliding over the scattered cornmeal on the other side of the room. Blind as he is, he is still trying to get back to them, to put them in their places.

"Wait," Penelope says at the doorway.

Boucherie falls again and swears in French. He's pulled the scissors out and is holding his hand over his bleeding eye.

"The dog," Penelope says.

Susanna looks at the pup, a shivering little ball near the door. She scoops him up, holding him with one arm under his belly.

"What about Ellen's scissors?" Penelope asks.

Susanna doesn't look back. "They've found a good use," she says.

Twenty-Eight

They return to Severne by water. Penelope makes a nuisance of herself with the dog, refusing to put him down and yet unable to carry him for long, until finally Seth fashions a collar out of deer hide and ties a rope to it that she can use as a leash.

"He went all that way for a new pup," Penelope keeps saying. "He'll come looking for it. I know him. He won't give it up."

But Susanna knows he won't be looking for anything. She feels cold and warm at the same time when she thinks of what she's done. Boucherie will die alone among the mice and bird feces, bleeding out from his eye until there is no blood left. She tries not to think about it, but she does.

They walk through the forest following streams to the Maumee, and in all that time—two and a half days—they meet with no incident. Either the Wyandots have given up looking for them, or they are lucky. They travel by night. Susanna has brought back no alcohol for Seth's wound and no bandages, but thanks to Meera's nursing his arm is healing fine. At first Penelope refused to speak to Meera—"I don't like Indians," she announced calmly—but then she forgets and speaks to her anyway. Susanna tells herself that Penelope will grow more lucid the farther away from Boucherie they get, and that turns out to be mostly true, although for the rest of her life Penelope will have her moments, as she calls them. A touch of melancholia, as she says.

"Make us a fire," she says to Meera the first evening. "My heart is cold with damp."

Meera says, "Watch how you sit. Your side must not open." For she has taken on the task of cleaning and dressing Penelope's wound, making fresh poultices twice a day and finding certain plant leaves to crush into water, which she lets no one but Penelope drink.

"Penelope, we can't risk a fire," Susanna tells her. "Remember we're in Wyandot territory now. We should not make our presence so obvious."

"Well that's just foolish. We need a big fire to keep ourselves warm. I'm the oldest, I know best what to do. Seth, you make it."

"In truth your sister builds a better fire than I do," Seth tells her.

"Who, Susanna?" Her old scoffing voice.

Meera says, "If Boucherie sees smoke, he might follow it to get to the dog."

Penelope pulls the pup closer. She has named him Tripper because he often trips over his own large paws. "No one must know about him," she says. She touches the space between the dog's eyes and watches his ears twitch in two different directions.

"That's right," Susanna tells her. "And no one will know."

Great gold and red leaves fall onto the brittle carpet of the forest floor. Silver maple, black ash, oak, basswood, elm. Susanna falls asleep among them and wakes when the moon is up. She and Seth take turns on watch while Meera takes care of Penelope. The next afternoon Seth lifts his arm out of his sling and flexes his fingers. "All good," he says. When no one is watching, he kisses her.

When they finally get to the Maumee it is a few hours before dawn. Seth looks for the canoe that he and Koman hid but it is no longer there. Koman has gotten to it first.

"Hopefully he is far away by now," he says to Susanna.

"Do you think we will ever see him again?"

"My guess is no."

A sharp wind blows the water east to west, and they walk until they spot the ferryman's barge tied up on the opposite shore. Penelope keeps looking back into the trees with a worried expression. She picks up the dog and puts him down again.

"When will the ferryman come? The rogue fears water. He will try to fetch the pup before we cross."

"Once we cross, is the dog safe?" Susanna asks.

Penelope nods. "The rogue fears the water," she says again.

"Wait here," Susanna tells her. She goes into the trees and looks around until she finds a hazel tree with short curling branches like overgrown fingernails. She breaks off a twig and brings it to Penelope. "Anyone who wears hazel in her cap will meet with good fortune," she says.

"More of your superstitions! You haven't changed at all." Penelope feels the side of her head. "But I have no cap."

Susanna breaks the twig and puts one half in Penelope's hair, and the other half she wedges in the dog's deer-hide collar. "There now. We don't need caps."

The ferryman is the same one, Swale, who crossed Meera and Susanna so many weeks ago. Just after dawn they see smoke rising from his chimney, and then Swale comes out to the river carrying a bucket. They wave him over. Seth gives him two English pound notes for their crossing, the last of his money, and Swale tells them of a trading house a mile or two south, a cabin in an abandoned settlement surrounded by a stockade. There they might find someone who can take them upriver, he says.

The Maumee is vividly green and weedy, and Susanna almost falls asleep watching the ferry pole bring up stringy wet plants and then disappear into the water and then bring them up again. It's a rocking, soothing motion, and Swale is adept at keeping up a rhythm, even graceful. Seth comes to stand next to her. He touches her hand with his pinkie and she puts one arm around him, and then the other, encircling him, not caring who sees. She rests her head against his chest. Swale does not seem to connect her with the boy he crossed before.

When they get to the opposite shore, Susanna spots Sirus's ax by the side of Swale's shack. The handle is already split but the blade looks well cared for, and although they barter hard Swale will not trade for it, not for anything they have.

At the stockade they fare better. Inside one of the old cabins, a dark-haired Irishman named Patrick Carey has set up a trading post. He agrees to take Seth's musket and three of Meera's bracelets in exchange for taking them up the Maumee. He has but one boat and cannot sell it, but he can land them at a bigger trading house where they might purchase a skiff for the rest of their journey: Beaver Creek to Hammer Creek to West Creek to the Blanchard River, straight up through the heart of the Great Black Swamp. A fortnight will see you through to the end, Patrick Carey tells them.

Two days up and two days back, Susanna thinks. How could I have been so foolish to believe that? It is October already, or later. The sun seems a long way off. Like Penelope, all she wants to do is put as much distance as possible between herself and the Raisin. Penelope still has the hazel twig stuck in her thick, golden-red hair. It will be there for days, and when it falls out Susanna will find her another.

By the time they begin rowing their skiff up the Blanchard, certain truths have come back to Penelope: one, that Thomas Forbes did not visit her in the night to give her the child growing inside her, for Thomas Forbes is dead. The babe is the rogue's. But Penelope is a Quiner, and with all the spirit she has in her command she wills the child to be one hundred percent Quiner too. The child will be a girl, and she will have red hair. Penelope is determined.

She is still sick sometimes, midmorning usually, and once in a while in the afternoon. When she is sitting upright she wants to lie down but when she lies down she waits and waits for sleep. In the skiff she holds Tripper on her lap. He is very good when they are on water but when they pull to shore he wants to run. She is never comfortable until he is safely tied up again. Meera says she will watch him but how can she watch him all the time? Of course, Indians have special talents that white men do not. Penelope knows this for a fact. It is because whites eat too much salt, her old Wyandot mistress told her, and so have lost certain powers.

Another truth: she will never have to set foot in the rogue's smelly cabin again. The bucket of morning sickness, the animal skins tanned and stretched out for days at a time, the empty jugs of alcohol that still retain their cloying odor. And his odor.

"You cannot think how closely I had to smell him," she tells Meera when they are stretched out waiting for sleep. Meera's hands are very gentle and she makes Penelope a good bed every night out of tree bark and leaves.

"White men do not smell good," Meera agrees.

"He was not a man, he was a devil. He had warts on each one of his knuckles. He held me by the hair when he touched me and afterward he slept with his fisted hands crossed over his neck. Then I could plainly see: wart, wart, wart, wart."

"You must try to forget," Meera tells her.

They meet not a single person until they come upon a preacher on horseback near Pike Run. His name, he tells them, is Reverend Forbes, but he is no relation to Thomas Forbes, Penelope's late husband. They share some food with him, and Penelope finds herself telling him the story of her captivity and escape. He is intrigued, and takes out a small leather-bound notebook and a pencil to take a few notes.

"This gentleman found you?" He nods toward Seth.

"No, my sister Susanna."

He says, "The gentleman is more believable."

He wants to write a sermon about her tale. It will be a comfort to women he says, and when it is finished he promises to mail her a copy. She tells him to send it to their store in Severne. "I'll not leave it again," she says solemnly, as if he's asked her to swear to it.

Back on the Blanchard, water sprays up the side of her face. She grows colder and colder the further away from the rogue she gets, but this, she decides, is a positive thing. Even the cold of a grave is better than that cabin—a third truth. She is sorely tired of squirrel meat, which they eat day and night. If it were up to her they would eat venison instead. She would be a good shot, she is sure. She would be a great hunter. The boat lurches and her stomach turns over and she touches the bit of hazel twig in her hair. It reminds her of the little twig of yellow flowers that Naomi kept hidden in her moccasin. Where is that now? She would like to ask if anyone knows if only she weren't so tired and sick, and if her thoughts didn't fly off randomly, landing somewhere only briefly before sailing forth again.

Once in Virginia, when Seth was a boy, an Austrian artisan came to the town wanting to cut silhouettes for a penny. He wore a badly powdered wig that sat uneasily to one side, and even when he pushed it back with his hand it fell again almost immediately, as though that side of his head had a dent.

Amos said, "We'll get a silhouette of the two boys together if he'll still charge a penny." As always, he was eager to get more for his money than anyone else.

Seth wonders now what happened to that silhouette. They probably left it in Virginia with everything else, the house that his mother and then his stepmother had filled with furniture and dishes. After his second wife died, Amos traded all he had for the supplies that would get them to the Ohio Country and, he said, to their fortune. He thought he would get rich trading with Indians. He knew their language and fancied that he knew how they thought. But Sirus Quiner got to Severne first. Amos never forgave him for that. Now Seth wonders if his father had been biding his time all these years, working iron and waiting. He would not be surprised.

They leave the skiff at the same landing where Seth and Cade sold the Quiners' team and wagon so many months ago, and walk the last ten miles to Severne. They are following the same dirt track Seth came by as a child. But this time, instead of coming by wagon with a drunkard father and a younger brother who was taller than he was even then, Seth comes upon the settlement walking alongside his beloved. He feels all the luck in this fact. He thinks of the first time he saw Susanna, how she looked at him and then looked at his brother and then looked at him again. Her hair in two red braids down her back, a dented kettle in her hands.

Ahead of them, Meera and Penelope are walking side by side talking to each other. "The Wyandots thought Naomi was a witch," Penelope is saying.

"Why?" Meera asks.

"She made the mistake of trading with a girl who fell ill, and then with an old woman who died."

Susanna plucks a small gold-yellow leaf from her sleeve. "She's otherworldly. That's what our mother used to say."

"All the farmers were in love with her," Seth tells them.

"With Naomi?" Susanna laughs. "Now we hear the truth."

She feels a breeze and looks up. The sky is clear and the same deep blue as the color of her father's eyes. No snow yet, thank goodness, but the day—it is late afternoon—holds a crisp stillness that seems on the verge of a change. In spite of a small knot in her stomach, she is happy. The air is cooler than when she left but the birds are still calling out and the frogs pipe away in their mudholes. The farmers are probably still out in their fields, Mop is still looking down the river for Indians, and Betsey T. is still telling Susanna that she's in shock, she doesn't know what she saw. A breeze brings the first smell of chimney smoke. It's a slightly uncomfortable feeling coming back home, Susanna thinks, as though you'll now need to fit your new self into the person you were here, and you don't know if that's possible. She is walking so close to Seth that she can feel the warmth of his arm. He's looking ahead, too. Any moment now they'll see it.

It might just be possible, she thinks.

The track turns, and all at once there it is: Severne. Penelope and Meera stop for a moment, and Seth takes her hand. It doesn't look exactly the same. A new building is going up near the public stable—someone starting the courthouse at last?—and its freshly cut yellow lumber stands out. The pine walkway is darker, and the pond at the end of it seems smaller. Seth squeezes her fingers lightly as if to start the blood running again. They keep walking.

Penelope says, "Betsey T. has taken care of Beatrice's bean garden, at least," when they come in sight of their cabin.

But it isn't Betsey T. who steps out to greet them, nor is it Mop, but rather a tall slender woman in a green and yellow dress. They are still too far away to make out her face. Penelope asks, who is that?

"I don't know," Susanna says. "Maybe Mop got himself a wife?" But that seems too impossible to imagine, even for her.

They come closer. The woman has red hair.

"Oh—oh," Susanna says. The pit in her stomach turns over and transforms itself into a warmer feeling of surprise and joy and disbelief and wonder. Her heart rises in her chest. And Penelope says at almost the same time: "Why, it's Lilith!"

Lilith is rubbing her hands with bear fat to keep them smooth—the day is as dry as white sand, as her Aunt Ogg used to say—when she steps out into the garden. Of course, there is no garden left at this time of year, only a few trampled tomato stalks that she pulls up in idle moments. Not that there are many idle moments. Her worry today is about who she will ask to slaughter the pig for her, and how much of its meat she'll have to offer in payment. The pig needs to last her through winter, and after that perhaps she can find a way back to Philadelphia. People are always coming and going, her sisters wrote in their letters over the years, but now that she is here she finds that that just isn't true. Severne is even more isolated than she thought. She almost, but not quite, regrets her decision to come out here. But everyone should have one adventure in their lives, her Aunt Ogg used to say.

When Lilith left Philadelphia she took with her a large trunk with her personal items and a much smaller one that contained only gloves—she and her aunt ran a glove shop just off Chestnut Street, and Lilith thought perhaps the gloves would sell in Severne. Living in Ohio Country had to be hard on a lady's hands. Her Aunt Ogg had died in late spring, and after she mourned her for a month, and without leaving off missing her, Lilith was ready for adventure. She was nearly sixteen. She'd had two marriage proposals and saw a third one coming but the men—boys, really—were not to her liking. So she sold the shop tenancy to a widow and found a ride to Severne with a little Frenchman and his wife who were moving to New Orleans. They gave her passage and agreed to cut through Severne for six minted dollars.

Bouncing along in the wagon she thought how surprised her sisters would be that she had made such a journey by herself. She was pleased with her own independence, and in the beginning she brought up the subject with the little Frenchman and his wife Marielle whenever she could, asking them didn't they think she was brave, and didn't they think her sisters would marvel. By and by, however, the couple seemed to prefer watching the scenery to her conversation, and the journey became tedious. They stayed at taverns with names like Moral Suasion and Vox Populi—brands of whiskey, she was told!—where the drinking was heavy and Lilith thought it prudent to sleep with her money belt tied to her waist. Half the time she even had to purchase and cook her own food. The tavern keepers were rough to a man but their wives and daughters were generally in need of gloves, which Lilith offered at a very good price. One of the wives wore an old-fashioned bonnet with light blue earflaps and wanted a glove color to match it. The others were just as selective, for all that they lived right in the very middle of nowhere.

By the end of the monthlong journey she'd sold twelve pairs of gloves and one shirtwaist and her aunt's cameo brooch, which she had never cared for, and so recouped what she paid for her transport and much of her food—another pleasant anecdote to relate to her sisters. She is good at bargaining. It is in her bones. Her father's people have been shopkeepers for as long as anyone can remember. But when she finally arrived in Severne and received the news about her sisters, she found herself, for the first time in her life, without a ready solution.

Still, she soon rallied. She always does. She wrote a letter to a state senator's wife back in Philadelphia, one of her old customers, asking if her husband could help. Two men had already been dispatched to Sandusky to see if information about her sisters could be found there, and she is waiting for news.

Lilith pulls up a tomato plant stalk and throws it into a pile. Later she will see if someone will cut up the pile for mulch. When she turns, she sees a small group of people walking toward her: two very unkempt white women, one man who looks Italian, and an Indian girl. The white women wear neither bonnets nor capes, and the Indian girl has a blue-and-brown blanket thrown unevenly over her shoulders with one end trailing almost to the ground. They are all of them staring at her as they walk toward her cabin—travelers hoping for food? Lilith can see that they are not ideal customers for gloves—too neglectful of their appearance—but she decides she'll try to sell them a pair anyway. As her mind turns over what she still has in stock, she sees the two white women stop for a second and then begin to run toward her, and one calls out her name in a voice like a startled bird. Lilith! Her heart clenches like a fist in her chest and she sees, with amazement, that they have red hair, that they are her sisters. Her heart lets loose and begins beating wildly. Her sisters! She's been waiting for them for so long. She begins running, too. She has so much to tell them.

CPSIA information can be obtained
at www.ICGtesting.com
Printed in the USA
FSHW021009241121
86451FS